The Secrets of Happiness

Lucy Diamond lives in Bath with her husband
and their three children. When she isn't slaving
away on a new book (ahem) you can find her on
Twitter @LDiamondAuthor or on Facebook
www.facebook.com/LucyDiamondAuthor.

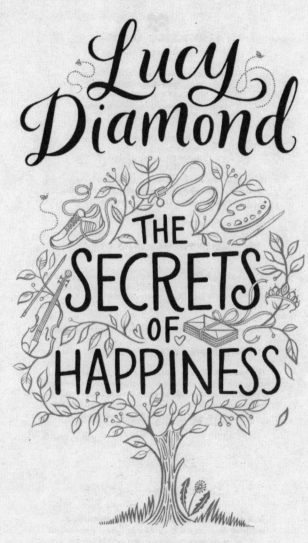

Lucy Diamond

THE SECRETS OF HAPPINESS

PAN BOOKS

First published 2016 by Macmillan

This paperback edition published 2016 by Pan Books
an imprint of Pan Macmillan
20 New Wharf Road, London N1 9RR
Associated companies throughout the world
www.panmacmillan.com

ISBN 978-1-4472-9917-2

Copyright © Lucy Diamond 2016

The right of Lucy Diamond to be identified as the
author of this work has been asserted by her in accordance
with the Copyright, Designs and Patents Act 1988.

All rights reserved. No part of this publication may be reproduced,
stored in a retrieval system, or transmitted, in any form, or by any means
(electronic, mechanical, photocopying, recording or otherwise)
without the prior written permission of the publisher.

Pan Macmillan does not have any control over, or any responsibility for,
any author or third-party websites referred to in or on this book.

1 3 5 7 9 8 6 4 2

A CIP catalogue record for this book is available from the British Library.

Printed and bound by CPI Group (UK) Ltd, Croydon, CR0 4YY

This book is sold subject to the condition that it shall not, by way of
trade or otherwise, be lent, hired out, or otherwise circulated without
the publisher's prior consent in any form of binding or cover other than
that in which it is published and without a similar condition including
this condition being imposed on the subsequent purchaser.

Visit **www.panmacmillan.com** to read more about all our books
and to buy them. You will also find features, author interviews and
news of any author events, and you can sign up for e-newsletters
so that you're always first to hear about our new releases.

This one's for Lizzy and Caroline
with love and thanks

Acknowledgements

Thanks as ever to the fantastic team at Pan Macmillan – Victoria, Anna, Natasha, Jeremy, Stuart, Wayne, Amy, Katie, all the ace sales reps (I owe you a mojito, Kate) and everyone else who has worked so hard on my books. You're all stars in my eyes. A special round of applause for Jo and Kate for another beautiful cover, and for Eloise, who didn't bat an eyelid when I brought the production schedule to a screeching halt (you can take my photo down from the office dartboard now). Plus a standing ovation for Caroline Hogg, whose editing really turned this book around. Thank you for coming to my rescue with such wisdom, tact and patience – the phrase 'Above and beyond the call of duty' springs to mind!

Three cheers to Lizzy Kremer, who, as usual, provided inspired and insightful editorial comments, brainstorming and cheerleading throughout – you are the best, I hope you realize that. Love and thanks to Harriet Moore, and everyone else at David Higham too for their enthusiasm and support.

Thanks to Christine Gibson, who answered my (many)

medical questions – obviously any mistakes are my own. Thanks also to the gorgeous Hannah Fleming for putting us in touch.

I'd like to thank Natalie Baldwin for her generosity in bidding for her mum's name to appear in the novel. Natalie was the highest bidder in a fund-raising auction for CLIC Sargent, who do such amazing work in helping children and young people with cancer. I hope you and your mum, Hayley George, enjoy the book!

Big smooch to the excellent Kate Harrison for an early read – much appreciated.

Cheers to my friend A (who had better remain anonymous) for letting me pinch the patio furniture story. Your secret's safe with me, honest.

As ever, love and thanks to Martin, Hannah, Tom and Holly for letting me talk through plot tangles over dinner, for the endless cups of tea, encouragement and title suggestions and for reminding me what's really important in life. Thanks to Mum and Dad for being so brilliant too.

Finally, thanks a million to everyone who's ever sent me a nice email or message on Facebook or Twitter. I really appreciate it whenever anyone takes the time to let me know they've enjoyed my books. I hope you enjoy this one too.

Chapter One

'We will shortly be arriving at Manchester Piccadilly station. Change here for trains to London Euston, Liverpool Lime Street and Edinburgh International. Manchester Piccadilly, your next station stop in approximately two minutes. All change, please.'

As the train nosed its way along the platform, the carriage became a bustle of activity: bags hauled down from the overhead shelf, dog-eared newspapers abandoned on seats, phones stuffed into pockets. Rachel Jackson was already one step ahead, in a line of people snaking back from the doors, jolting against the luggage rack as the train braked to a jerky halt.

'Manchester Piccadilly, this is Manchester Piccadilly. All change, please. All change.'

This was it. She had made it. Her adrenalin surged as the doors were unlocked and the hot crush of passengers began spilling out onto the platform. She followed numbly, not caring as someone's suitcase bashed against her legs. *Hello,*

Manchester, she thought, stepping down from the train. *I'm here to get some answers. Do you have any for me?*

The station felt enormous after Hereford, a cavernous space, the ceiling criss-crossed with an intricate grid of struts and girders, the tannoy echoing around them. It was early June, and the school run that morning had promised milky sunshine breaking through the clouds, but the air felt cool now and she pulled her pale-grey cardigan around her as she walked along the platform amidst a stream of other travellers. Nerves prickled through her. Now that she was here, she felt overwhelmed. The enormity of what she was doing began to pound like a drum-beat, louder and faster. Did she even want to find out the truth any more?

Yes, she reminded herself resolutely, striding forward. *Yes, I do.* After all the lies she'd been told, she needed to know, had to see this through.

There was an impatient crowd building around the ticket barriers, people muttering crossly as first a group of Japanese tourists seemed to have lost their tickets, and then an elderly couple held up another aisle by getting a tartan shopping trolley caught in the electronic gates. The agitation was infectious and Rachel felt her irritation rise. *Come on, come on. Hurry up.* If she paused like this much longer, she might change her mind about the whole thing. She had to keep moving, maintain momentum.

Finally, it was her turn to post her ticket through the

gateway with clammy fingers and be released into the main concourse, which buzzed with all human life. There were hordes of people in every direction, dragging suitcases, barking into mobile phones, hurrying towards their trains. A woman with killer heels and a briefcase barged into her without seeming to notice, barely breaking stride. The tannoy bing-bonged, mothers hauled along small children, a group of Scandi-looking teenagers with enormous backpacks and enviably tanned legs stood arguing over a map.

Rachel felt small, quiet and anonymous as she gazed around for signs to the exit and taxi rank. Miles away from the green hills and farmland of home, nobody knew her here, or had any idea that she'd even made the journey. 'A meeting,' she'd said vaguely to Sara over the road when she'd arranged for her to pick up Luke and Scarlet from school later that afternoon. 'I'll be back by five at the latest.' A flying visit, that was all. She'd phoned from the train to double check that Violet was at work that day – 'Yes, she's here, let me put you through,' a nice lady had said but Rachel had hung up instantly, heart hammering. *No.* Not on the phone. It had to be face to face, where she could look into the other woman's eyes and hear the full story.

Oh God. It was terrifying. What might Violet have to say?

Maybe she should have an espresso before she headed off, she decided, weakening as she spotted a nearby stall and breathed in cinnamon, coffee, vanilla. There was plenty of time, after all, and she could do with something to rev her up, give her that last push onwards. One sharp hit of caffeine and she would feel ready to jump in a cab, just do it, no more dithering. *Up and at 'em, kiddo*, as her dad used to say.

She joined the queue, her mind a jumble of worries, snagging once again on the incriminating newspaper report she'd discovered, the conversation at her father's funeral that had opened this whole can of worms. *Did your dad ever . . . mention me?* She wished she had never met Violet now. Even coming here seemed too reckless an idea all of a sudden. What if the whole thing was a wild goose chase?

Lost in her doubts, she jumped at the sound of a male voice behind her. 'Excuse me, love?'

She turned expectantly but as she did so, someone grabbed her handbag from the other side, catching her unawares. 'Hey!' she cried, her hands flying up to pull it back, but in the next moment she'd been shoved hard from behind, lost her balance and was falling, falling, falling . . .

There was just time to dimly register the sensation of her bag being snatched from her grasp and the sound of running footsteps, before her head smashed against the ground. Then everything went black.

'She's what? She's missing?' Becca repeated into the phone, then turned away slightly from the distracting sight of her flatmate Meredith, who was plucking a lute at the other end of the sofa. Meredith was a member of a Medieval Re-Enactment Society and spent most of her weekends in a cloak. The lute-playing was a new and unwelcome sideshoot of this hobby. 'Say that again, sorry,' Becca said, putting down her half-eaten slice of pizza in order to concentrate.

'Five o'clock, she told me,' came the woman's voice down the line, breathless and rather indignant. 'Five o'clock at the latest! And she's not answering her mobile, none of the children have a clue where she is . . . I mean – it's not like her, is it? I don't know what to think. Should I call the police? She's not with you, is she?'

Becca was finding it hard to process all this information, delivered in such a rapid-fire burst, especially with Meredith still twanging tunelessly beside her, seemingly oblivious to the phone call. 'No, she's not with me,' she said, getting up from the sofa and walking across the room to the 'kitchen area' as the landlord had optimistically termed it. She wiped a scatter of toast crumbs from the worktop with her free hand, vowing to do a proper clean-up tomorrow. 'I don't really . . .'

'Well, Mabel suggested we ring you, that's all. I didn't know who else to try! Obviously I'd have the children here a bit longer myself only we're meant to be going out, Alastair and I – oh sorry, that's my husband. We've had theatre tickets booked for ages and I'm not sure the babysitter can cope with another three as well as my two. And they can't sleep here anyway, the spare room is full of Alastair's gym equipment right now. I have *told* him to clear it all out, several times, but you know what men are like—'

Becca held the phone away from her ear a little. The woman – Sara, had she said? Sandra? – was very shrill and very loud and seemed to have developed the skill of speaking continuously without needing to take a breath. Impressive lung capacity, she thought idly, chucking out the used tea-bags at the side of the sink. Perhaps she was a deep-sea diver in her spare time. 'Right,' she said, when there was finally a pause. After all that, she wasn't sure what to say. It was sweet of her niece Mabel to have put forward her name but Becca hadn't actually spoken to Rachel for over a year. The two stepsisters weren't exactly joined at the hip.

'So what time do you think you can get here?'

Whoa. Without warning, Sara had suddenly cut to the chase. '*Get* there? What, you mean to . . .?' Shit. Was she for real? Becca was due to start her shift at the White Horse in forty minutes and hadn't even finished her tea yet, let alone started making herself look halfway decent.

'Mabel thought you were the best person to call, that's all. Seeing as you're family, and everything. She said she can look after the younger two until you get there. Our side of Birmingham, isn't it, where you live? So you could be in Hereford within . . . what, an hour or so? Hour and twenty? That should be okay.'

'Well, yes, theoretically, but . . .' But I do have a *job*, actually, a sweaty pub kitchen where I'm supposed to be working tonight, and the children barely know me, more to the point. She grimaced, wishing the woman hadn't said that bit about Mabel thinking she was the best person to call. Becca had always been a sucker for compliments. One kind word and she was anyone's.

'Thank goodness! I'll tell the children. Mabel! Your aunty's on her way, okay? Just in case Mum is much later.'

'Wait a minute,' Becca tried saying. The woman was like a steamroller. Why wasn't she running the country already?

'So should I hang fire on the police, do you think? They'd probably only tell me to wait twenty-four hours, wouldn't they? And she is a grown woman, obviously. Nobody's kidnapped her or anything. Oh dear, I shouldn't have said that, I think Luke just heard me. Don't worry, darling! Mummy's fine! Probably just . . . well, you know. Doing something else.'

Becca gazed out of the window onto the high street below, letting the monologue rush from the phone, like an unstoppable current. She'd last seen Rachel thirteen months ago at their dad's funeral when they'd made stilted chit-chat about buffet arrangements and the order of service. Becca had been late – a traffic nightmare – and had had to creep through the church hall murmuring 'Sorry, excuse me, sorry,' all the way up to the front row where Rachel had given her a look so reproachful Becca felt her toes curl just remembering. It had been longer still since she'd seen her nieces and nephew – a year and a half, she guessed; Christmas at Mum and Dad's. Luke must have been five then, dark-haired with the most enormous black-lashed violet eyes, painfully shy with everyone except his mother. Even Lawrence, Rachel's suave, confident husband, couldn't coax him into . . . Hold on a minute.

'Wait,' she said again, louder this time. Of course – she should have asked straightaway. It was ridiculous that they'd even gone this far down the conversational path. 'Where's Lawrence, then? Can't he just hold the fort until Rachel gets back?'

There was a moment's silence from Sara. A strange, wary sort of silence. '*Lawrence?*' she repeated, then gave a nervous laugh. 'Well . . . Lawrence moved out at the end of last year. They've split up. Didn't you know?'

Chapter Two

Several hours earlier

'Hello there, chick, can you hear me? I think she's coming round, Jim. Can you hear me, love?'

Rachel opened her eyes to find herself staring up at a woman in a green uniform who had long corn-coloured hair in a side plait. Christ, her head was pounding. Thumping as if it might break. She could taste blood in her mouth, metallic and warm, and her nose twitched with the tang of disinfectant. What on earth . . .?

'There we are! Hello, I'm Cathy, a paramedic, we're on our way to the hospital. Do you remember what happened?'

She was lying on a narrow bed, and could hear an engine rumbling. *Ambulance*, she thought dazedly. Her head hurt. Her jaw, too. She shut her eyes again, unable to make sense of what was going on. *Just a funny dream. Go back to sleep.* That was what she always said to the children if they woke in the night.

'You were knocked out, lovey. Flattened, by the sound of it. Couple of thugs pinched your handbag and took off at the train station, do you remember?'

The woman had a northern accent, Rachel noticed woozily. Like in *Coronation Street*. Dad's favourite. What was she on about, though – handbag? Train station? None of it made sense. Where *was* her handbag, anyway? It had her keys in. She needed them to get into the house. Key of the door. Door of the key. What was it again?

'We're just going to the hospital now because you were out cold for a few minutes and your face is rather bashed up, okay? Try to keep still, that's it. Can you tell me your name?'

Rachel blinked. Her name. Yes. She tried to open her mouth to reply but a roaring pain seized her jaw and she could only moan. Her face throbbed. Her body ached all over. There was a ringing in her ears, high and piercing, unrelenting. Was this a dream? It must be. She was safely at home in bed really, and this was all a peculiar dream. *Go back to sleep.*

'Okay, don't worry about it for the minute, we're almost there,' she heard the woman say. Her voice seemed to be coming from a long way away, as if she was down a tunnel or across a busy road. Rachel thought of the *Coronation Street* music and how her dad had always yelled up the stairs to her as it started. The mournful-sounding notes. That ginger cat in the opening credits, padding along a wall. She and Dad cuddled up on the old brown sofa in companionable silence together back in the day, her sucking fizzy cola bottles, him with a whisky mac.

Then the blackness rolled up once more, engulfing her, and everything melted away.

'So we arrived at the scene shortly after eleven-thirty, to be told that this lady had been knocked to the floor in the train station by a couple of bag-snatchers. She doesn't have any ID and we don't know her name. When we got there, she had been unresponsive for several minutes according to witnesses although she came round briefly in the ambulance and seemed confused. Suspected fracturing of the jaw and possibly cheekbone, her wrist is definitely broken . . .'

The woman was talking again. A rich, friendly voice, with that lovely accent. Rachel wondered who the poor lady was that they were discussing before realizing with a shock that it must be her. Her eyes snapped open in a panic and she stared around at her surroundings, trying to make sense of them. Doctors, nurses, the blonde woman in green, all looming above her like something from a nightmare.

'Hello there,' one of the doctors said, noticing her. He was wiry and brown-skinned with a shaved head and soft brown eyes. 'What's your name, can you tell us?'

Again, she opened her mouth in an attempt to speak but the pain ricocheted through her like an electric current, taking her breath away. 'Uh . . .' was all she could groan, tasting warm salty blood on her lips.

Rachel, she wanted to say. *I'm Rachel*. As she thought the words, the darkness that had filled her head began to recede around the edges, like smoke dispersing. Mother of Mabel and Scarlet and Luke, she remembered, pinning down each fact like pieces in a jigsaw. Thirty-nine years old, birthday November fifth. Dad's little firework baby, he used to say.

'Don't worry, we're going to give you some morphine, that'll take the pain away,' someone said and she closed her eyes, feeling defeated. She still couldn't work out what she was doing there. There was a gaping hole in her mind, blank and unfathomable, when it came to what had happened, and how she had ended up in this state. It was a mystery. Something about a train station, she vaguely recalled the blonde woman saying, but where?

Strangest of all was that everyone was speaking in northern accents except for the nurse with curly dark hair who said to her 'Sharp scratch coming up!' in broad Glaswegian. (*Sharp scratch, my foot*, Rachel thought, trying not to yelp. Dirty great stab, more like.) It was as if she'd been transplanted into another world. A confusing, painful world, where nothing made sense.

She felt the morphine spread dreamily around her body as she was X-rayed and scanned, and it was like falling slowly through water; down, down, into the depths of the ocean.

The doctors conversed in low voices just out of earshot. 'Can you feel this?' they asked, prodding and poking at her. 'How about this? Oh, she's gone again.' 'Hello? Can you hear me? I'm Geraldine the registrar, I need to ask you a few silly questions. Can you remember your name?'

Of course she could remember her name! She wasn't an idiot. She was a mother, a wife. Oh – wait. An ex-wife. Shit. It was all such a muddle. What time was it anyway? She had to get back to collect the children before three; Mabel was old enough to walk home from secondary school alone or with mates now, but Rachel still picked up Scarlet and Luke from primary every day. Their faces floated up through the dark murk of her mind; they'd be pale with anxiety if she wasn't there. *Where's Mum?*

Rachel felt panicky at the image, forcing herself to claw her way back up through the morphine haze. 'My children,' she tried to say to the woman at the bedside, but her voice didn't work properly and the sound came out slurred and wrong. This was horrible. Like a really disturbing dream. Had she suffered a stroke? Why was everything so strange? *Help me!*, she tried to telegraph with her eyes. *Help!*

'Don't try and talk for now,' the woman told her kindly. 'I'm afraid you've fractured your jaw and cheekbone rather nastily, and you've got the mother of all bumps on your head. We think you're concussed as well, so if things seem a little strange, that's why.' As Rachel stared at the woman's face, it seemed to split into three, each with the same green eyes and moving mouth. Like looking through a prism. One of those toys children had with sparkly colourful pieces at one end. Telescope – no. Periscope – no. That thing, anyway. What was it? The word had slipped out of reach. Think, Rachel. Think!

'Uhh,' she moaned in reply. It was becoming her catchphrase.

She was swung around brightly lit corridors on a trolley, lights strobing above her head. Nightclubs, she thought. Thudding music. Going home and throwing up in her stepmum Wendy's shoes. *I'm very disappointed in you, Rachel!*

Wendy, she thought disjointedly. The two of them had never got on. *You're not my mum!* she had shouted in all their arguments. And . . . *Oh*. Something clicked in her head. An image came to her of a chilly station platform, her smart shoes pinching as she stood waiting, ticket in hand. *Manchester Piccadilly*, a voice intoned. *All change, please.*

I'm here to get some answers.

Alarm swept through her as the connection was made. She was in *Manchester*, that was it. Manchester! Far from home, far from the children. Who was picking them up from school if she was in Manchester? It was like wading through treacle trying to think straight, but then came a dim memory of the car full of voices first thing; Sara's children, she thought, frowning. Yes – and Sara was collecting Scarlet and Luke in return. But how was Rachel going to get back there now? Sara would kill her if she wasn't back for five, as arranged – literally throttle her with those perfectly manicured hands.

A sob burst from her throat and she tried to haul herself into a sitting position. She had to get home. She had to tell someone to ring Sara!

The swinging movement of the trolley stopped, and a nurse appeared by her side. The Glaswegian one, she thought, recognizing the dark curls. 'All right, hen, lie down, that's it,' she soothed. 'We're just on our way up to the ward; we'll make you more comfortable there, all right? Shut your eyes for a wee while and try to rest.'

There was a clicking sound below her, and then wheels rolling, squeaking; the bed on the move again. The ceiling blurred dizzily above, the strip lighting leaving orange trails swaying in her head when she closed her eyes. 'That's it, darling, you have a snooze,' the nurse said, her voice floating in from a distance. 'Don't you worry about a thing.'

Chapter Three

Becca packed an overnight bag – or rather she threw a pair of knickers and her toothbrush into a Sainsbury's carrier bag – then phoned her boss, Jeff, at the White Horse, pretending to have come down with a disgusting stomach bug. 'I'm so . . . sorry,' she groaned down the line. She had taken the phone into the bedroom, as Meredith was still murdering the opening bars of 'Greensleeves', and perched on the edge of the bed, trying to sound ill and weak. 'I've been puking up for the last two hours,' she went on hoarsely. Just for good measure she did some fake retching. 'Can't come in for my shift tonight. Really sorry.'

Jeff, the landlord, was a broad, grizzled Wolverhampton Wanderers fan with an unerring bullshit detector, unfortunately for Becca. 'Ahh,' he said in his low growl. She pictured his baggy blue eyes narrowing with disbelief. 'That's strange, because Nick said he saw you coming out of Pizzarella about five o'clock this evening. Comes and goes, does it, this stomach bug?'

Oh bollocks. Bloody supergrass Nick! He was the spivvy little assistant manager who seemed to spend his life poking his nose into other people's business and then telling the rest of the bar about it. That was one of the problems with living in a tiny flat above a betting shop on the high street, just a few hundred metres from the pub. Everyone seemed to know every last thing she ever did.

'That . . . wasn't me,' Becca said lamely, pulling a face at herself in the mirror. Cringe.

'Tell you what,' said Jeff, not even bothering to argue. 'Take the night off, yeah? And take tomorrow off too. And the day after that, and all. Do you hear what I'm saying? I can't be doing with all these excuses, that's the thing. I need staff I can rely on, not flakes and fakers. See you around.'

Becca's mouth dropped open indignantly as he hung up and then the breath whistled out of her in a long, exasperated sigh. 'Great,' she muttered, shoving her feet into trainers. 'I've just been given the *sack*, can you believe it?' she yelled through to Meredith. Exactly what she didn't need right now. You tried to do someone a favour, and this was what happened. Plus, knowing her luck, she'd drive the whole way over to Hereford to find that – *oh, sorry* – Rachel *was* there after all, and it would all be for nothing, some silly mix-up or a flat phone battery, no doubt. Fabulous.

Meredith looked up as Becca came back into the living room. She had abandoned the lute (small mercies) and was now poring over the cryptic crossword in the newspaper. 'What? You've been sacked?'

Becca briefly explained the situation, and Meredith blinked in surprise. 'I didn't even know you had a sister,' she said. Meredith had two sisters – one older, one younger – and they met regularly to see experimental theatre, and for dinner in cheap Italian restaurants where they discussed how unreasonable their parents were.

'We're not close,' Becca mumbled, which was surely a contender for the understatement of the year. She eyed the cooling remains of the pizza longingly – the pizza that had inadvertently brought about her sacking, no less – then decided against it. *Calories*, she reminded herself, and besides, the sooner she headed off, the sooner she could be home again. Grabbing her car keys, she said goodbye and left.

If you wanted to sum up the relationship between Becca and Rachel, the phrase 'It's complicated' was a good place to start. Becca had only been a year old – pudgy and still practically bald apart from a few carroty curls (the camera never lied, unfortunately) – when her single mum Wendy met Rachel's single dad Terry. The two of them had fallen in love and married within the year. Bingo: one brand new family, like it or not.

Becca, of course, was so young as to be oblivious to the awkward beginnings of this glued-together family. For as long as she could remember she had known that Terry was not her biological father (that dubious honour fell to a charmer called Johnny, who was long off the scene), but this made no odds to her. In the true sense of the word, Terry *was* her beloved dad, and that was that. But Rachel, nine years older, seized on this as a source of great resentment. 'He's *my* dad,' she would hiss, eyes flinty, whenever Becca was wheedling to be carried or read a story or, when older, trying to cadge a tenner from him.

'There's plenty of me to go around,' Terry had always replied easily; but in hindsight, Becca could see how it must have rankled with Rachel. Becoming a stepsister might have changed diddly for Becca, but for Rachel it had meant not only having to share her precious father, but also being rudely forced from her place as adored only child into reluctant big sister; the sensible, good one who didn't make a fuss, unlike tempestuous, tantrum-throwing Becca. You could see how acrimony would start laying down foundations, how decades-long grudges could be set simmering. Even when Wendy and Terry had gone on their honeymoon, Rachel had kicked off and demanded they return after a single night, apparently.

Fast-forward almost thirty years and the two stepsisters couldn't be more different. Rachel was the beautiful swan, the success story of the family with her happy marriage (although maybe not any more), her sweet little children, her great career, big house and elegant clothes. Becca had known from an early age it was impossible to compete with such a paragon of achievement and had duly messed up her A levels, had a string of doomed relationships, travelled a bit, gone back to live at her parents' place several times when she ran out of money, and tried her hand at various careers, none of which had ever stuck. It did make you wonder how much the family dynamics had influenced the paths they'd each taken. Would Rachel still have aced at life if there hadn't been Becca to outdo? Would Becca have made such a hash of things if she hadn't been the baby of the family, the one who'd been let off the hook all along, who could get away with anything if she widened her eyes at her parents?

They were who they were, though, and unfortunately the definition of the word 'sister' had been stretched to its thinnest since Terry had died. He was the one who'd held the family together in the first place. As his funeral had drawn to its tearful close the year before, you could almost hear the split cracking right down the middle of the remaining three, with Rachel on one side, and Becca and her mum on the other. Estranged, they called it, didn't they, when family members no longer spoke. That was them. The stepsisters had let one another slip away, out of sight, out of mind, no longer needing to keep up a pretence that they'd ever liked each other or got on. Until this evening, with the phone call that had hauled Becca right back across the divide.

The car started first try – always a bonus – and she drove off, flicking the Vs at the White Horse as she went past in the hope that nosey Nick would see. Goodbye Jeff, cheerio whingeing customers, so long crappy kitchen equipment and *hasta la vista* Brian, the head chef who was in a permanent rage, generally about the low standards of his staff. Yet another bridge burned, yet another door closed to her. It wasn't that she *wanted* to be doing veg prep in a pub for the rest of her life – far from it – but at least working there had put some money in her purse and got her out of the flat five nights a week. Not any more, though.

Meanwhile, her friends were all steaming ahead of her. Stellar careers. Weddings. Babies, even, while Becca was still scrabbling about like an idiot, unable to keep down a pub job at the age of thirty. She couldn't help worrying that she would be stuck forever in this rut: broke and without any kind of life plan, still sharing a titchy flat with a woman who got her kicks from painting replica shields for medieval combat re-enactments. The worst thing was, people had started treating them as if they were a couple. 'How's Meredith?' her mum would ask fondly whenever they spoke. 'Oh, do ask your – Meredith, is it? – along too, obviously,' a friend had said last week when mentioning a forthcoming party. (It was the 'obviously' that took Becca by surprise. *Obviously*? Since when had there been any 'obviously' about her and Meredith?) There had even been a wedding invitation recently addressed to the two of them, *Becca + Meredith*, as if they came as a pair, two lonely spinsters destined to remain together for eternity. It was surely only a matter of time before someone coined the name Beredith. Please, no.

Still. The key was to stay positive. To remain hopeful of what might be round the next corner, and seize any opportunities that came her way. *Up and at 'em, kiddo!* That was what her dad had always said. How she wished he was still around to say it to her now. He would take her to the pub and give her one of his life MoTs. *You're in the prime of your life, kid! You can do anything!* he would tell her, stabbing the air with his index finger. *What are you waiting for? Get out there and have some adventures!*

'I'm trying, Dad,' she murmured aloud, slowing to a stop at traffic lights. 'I really am.'

As a man who'd worked in the motor industry most of his life (years at Longbridge as an engineer, and then later for the local Ford garage), it was ironic that he should have died under the wheels of a van – a Ford bloody Transit, no less. It had hurtled round a blind corner in a 20mph zone, mounted the pavement, knocked over a pedestrian (Dad) and smashed into a lamp post. *Darling, it's your dad, there's been an accident*: she could hear her mum sobbing down the phone even now. The driver had been drinking and lost control; given a two-year prison sentence for death by dangerous driving. But no kind of justice system could make up for the fact that Dad's life had been snatched away from them in one shocking moment; a dark pool of blood on the pavement, the hopeless wail of an ambulance siren echoing through the street, too late.

Anyway, there was no point dwelling on that. It didn't help anything.

Waiting for the lights to change, Becca raked a hand through her hair, already feeling self-conscious about seeing her stepsister again. In contrast to Rachel's obedient blonde bob, Becca had bright copper hair – yeah, all right, ginger, whatever – that was big and bushy, curls springing out dementedly in all directions. Rachel also had delicate bone structure and the figure of an athlete, whereas Becca . . . didn't. 'Aren't the girls *different*?' a particularly blunt aunt had once commented during Becca's unfortunate puppy-fat decade, her eyes flicking from Becca's doughnut hips to Rachel's collection of running trophies gleaming on the mantelpiece in a single damning second.

The difference was more apparent than ever these days. Since her dad had died, Becca had piled on the pounds, finding comfort in salty chips, iced buns, buttered toast. There was something about working in a pub kitchen, too, that meant she was constantly picking at hunks of cheese or crusty baguette. She braced herself for a look of revulsion on her stepsister's face, the insincere 'You look . . . well' remark that everyone knew was shorthand for 'You look . . . fat'. Oh, whatever. Water off a duck's back.

Traffic wasn't too bad as she followed signs for the motorway, trying to remember the children's ages. Mabel must be thirteen now because she'd been born a few months after Becca's seventeenth birthday, when babies were still a million miles off her radar. Scarlet had come along three years later and Luke . . . he must be about six or seven, she reckoned. It gave her a stab of guilt that she didn't know the numbers instantly; it showed how little she had thought of them in recent months. Rachel had made it quite clear that she wanted nothing more to do with Becca or Wendy and it had seemed easier to accept that, to allow the wall of silence to build up higher and higher.

Despite everything, though, she was curious about seeing them again, especially in light of the bombshell that Lawrence and Rachel had split up. She still couldn't quite get her head around it. *Didn't you know?* the woman on the phone had asked. No, she'd had no idea, just assumed that everything was typically rosy in Rachel's wonderful life. Mind you, Becca thought, biting her lip. When she remembered what had happened the last time she'd seen her sister's husband, perhaps she shouldn't have been quite so surprised after all.

Rachel's house was a genteel, grey-painted Victorian semi on a quiet road out of town. It was the sort of street where people kept their hedges neatly clipped and cars were washed every Sunday. As Becca parked her wheezing, rusting Ford

Fiesta outside, she felt as if she was lowering the tone of the neighbourhood simply by arriving. Then she realized that there was no other car in Rachel's driveway. Was her sister still not back?

'Hello there. Long time no see!'

Mabel answered the front door, and Becca could tell by the brief flare of hope that lit up her niece's face that she'd thought it might be Rachel come home with an apology, an explanation and the blessed relief of everything returning to normal. Her expression fell, but she pulled the door open wide anyway. 'Hi,' she said politely. 'Come in.'

Christ, she had grown up all of a sudden! Becca hardly recognized her. Still in her school uniform, although barefoot, Mabel was nearly as tall as Becca now, with grey eyes like her mum and a turquoise streak in her long fair hair, her ears pierced twice on both sides and nails bitten down to the quick. Her black pleated skirt was hitched up wonkily with an obvious bulge at the top where she'd rolled the waistband over, and there was ink on her sleeves. This was not quite the cute little hair-in-bunches poppet that Becca had been expecting.

The cream-painted hall was generously wide, with an oatmeal carpet spreading before them and up a staircase on the left. It was all very tasteful, of course: a huge gilt-edged mirror on one wall, black and white family portraits on another, shoes tumbled tidily into a wicker basket. *Look, Becca, this is how grown-ups live*, she thought, trying to banish her mean, jealous thoughts as she stepped in and hugged her niece. 'Hi, lovey. I take it she's not back then?' she asked. Hmmm. Disconcerting. Becca had been so certain that Rachel would have turned up in the time it took her to drive along the hideously slow Worcester Road, her mood had become grumpier and grumpier with the conviction that this would all be a misunderstanding, a false alarm. Now that she was here and her assumptions had been confounded, she was slightly at a loss for what else to say.

Before Mabel could reply, there came a hopeful shout from upstairs. 'Is it Mummy?'

A pyjama-clad boy appeared at the top of the stairs, thumb in mouth, clutching the banister as he stared down. Luke: all dark tousled hair, cheekbones and skinny limbs. He clearly wasn't quite as advanced as his sister in terms of social niceties because as soon as he clocked Becca, his shoulders slumped downwards and he trailed back to bed without so much as a hello. Fair enough.

'Hi, Luke,' Becca called after him as he vanished. She could hear the distant scraping of a violin being practised elsewhere in the house – that must be Scarlet, she deduced. She glanced at Mabel, who shrugged, looking awkward.

'No, she's not back yet,' the girl confirmed. 'He's a bit freaked out.' She lowered her voice. 'He's been totally obsessed with people dying ever since the lady next door pegged it. Keeps saying he thinks Mum's died too, over and over, like he's possessed or something. Which is obviously, like, really cheery and just what we want to hear right now. Yay.'

Becca smiled briefly at her niece's sarcasm but for the first time since Sara's phone call, she felt a prickle of fear crawl up her spine. It was almost eight o'clock in the evening now and it seemed very odd that there was still no word from her sister. *Should I call the police?* the woman over the road had said, before wittering on about kidnapping – and now Luke seemed to think his mum had died. Becca felt bad now for not taking the whole thing more seriously herself, for driving over grudgingly, feeling cross about her lost job and petrol money. For Rachel to have been missing this long, and with no explanatory text or phone call, seemed seriously out of character. Something must have gone wrong.

She put an arm around Mabel. 'Don't worry,' she said with fake cheer. 'I'm sure there's a perfectly reasonable explanation. I bet she's just got held up and her phone's out of charge, that sort of thing. She'll probably be back any minute.' There was a too-long pause while they both listened to the melancholic sawing of the violin, like a misery soundtrack, then Becca went on, trying to sound as upbeat as possible. 'Where's Scarlet, anyway? And has everyone had enough to eat? I can make pancakes or something if you like.'

'Pancakes?' The violin-playing stopped abruptly and another head popped out from a room along the hallway. It was

Scarlet, her hair in two neat brown plaits with rectangular glasses perched at an angle on her freckled nose. 'I bloody love pancakes. Hi, Aunty Bee.'

Becca raised an eyebrow at the 'bloody', but decided not to comment. She smiled at her instead. 'Hi, gorgeous. Lovely violin-playing there, very good.'

'I wrote that tune myself,' Scarlet replied, following Becca into the smart, taupe-painted kitchen. (Rachel had a Farrow & Ball loyalty card, at a guess.) 'It's called "Come Back Harvey, I Miss Your Silky Ears".'

Becca blinked. 'Who's Harvey? Your boyfriend?'

There was a sniggered 'Yeah, right' from Mabel, but Scarlet merely put her chin in the air. 'He's our *dog*,' she said darkly. 'Or at least he was until Dad took him away.'

'Oh,' Becca said, sorry now for her lame joke. 'That's sad.' It was getting dusky outside now, the sky a strange yellow-grey, as if it was going to rain, and darkness had begun filling in the edges of the garden; but she could see a swing out there, and a trampoline, and white roses gleaming in the shrubbery.

'Yeah,' Scarlet said, scuffing a foot against the table-leg. 'It's a bloody nightmare. He cries when we go back there, you know. He actually *cries* because he misses us so much. But Dad said it was *his* dog and it was only fair seeing as Mum got to keep us. They had a massive fight.'

Ouch. 'Poor you,' Becca said. 'And poor old Harvey.'

28

'Yeah,' Scarlet said again. 'Poor Harvey because he has to live with Welsh Grandma *and* Dad. That sucks.'

Lawrence was back at his mum's? Becca had vague memories of a stern-faced old battleaxe at the wedding, unsmiling and steely in navy blue, and felt a stab of sympathy for the dog, as well as for the children. None of this had turned out very well.

'And poor *us*, because we have to listen to Scarlet's violin-playing,' Mabel added heartlessly. 'If you're really lucky, she'll play you one of her other tunes,' she went on, dodging out of the way as her sister tried to kick her. 'My favourite's called "I Hate You, Mum and Dad". Or – what was the new one? "I Am the Darkness". It's like a musical Armageddon. Violinageddon. Ow!' she yelped as Scarlet's foot finally made contact with her shin. 'Get off me, mental-case.'

Okaaaay, thought Becca, getting out flour, eggs and milk while the girls launched into a heated quarrel. Like that, then, eh? It was obviously time to recalibrate Rachel's family from the magazine-perfect one she remembered to now include the blue-haired teenager, the shy anxious boy and the violin-playing firebrand currently trying to punch her sister – oh, and the missing husband and dog, of course. Not quite so perfect after all.

'Hey! Guys!' she pleaded, sieving flour into a mixing bowl. 'Pancakes, remember? Who wants to break the eggs?'

Eggs weren't the only things that were broken around

here, she thought as Scarlet came over to help with a last sullen glare at Mabel. Within five minutes of her arrival, the fractures within the family were already startlingly apparent. *Come home, Rachel, wherever you are*, she thought, as Mabel huffed out of the room. *Your kids need you. Come home!*

Chapter Four

Things were slowly returning to Rachel, as if a torch was shining around a dark room, illuminating details here and there. She vaguely remembered arriving at Manchester station now, being pushed from behind in the coffee queue and another person grabbing her bag; the sensation of falling hard, that split-second moment of shock and fright before everything went black. After that, though, there was nothing until she'd come round in the ambulance, however deeply she probed the shadowy fathoms of her memory. Cinnamon, coffee, vanilla, she thought woozily. And then, boom, on the floor, out.

Since being brought to the hospital, she had been patched up physically, if not quite mentally yet: the emergency doctors had put her fractured wrist in a rough cast, bandaged her injured head and dosed her up with morphine. Tomorrow they would be wiring her jaw and operating on her wrist. So that was plenty to look forward to. *Lolz*, as Mabel would say, deadpan.

By late afternoon, she had managed at last to tell them, despite the broken jaw, blood oozing from her lips and the grinding pain that left her feeling faint, that her name was Rachel. It had felt like huge progress when she haltingly made the sound and the kind Glaswegian nurse replied, 'Rachel? Rachel! Okay, great,' back at her. 'You're Rachel, that's lovely. How about your second name?'

It was the weirdest thing. She opened her mouth to reply but there was nothing there, no answer. She had stared back at the nurse in horror as her mind remained silent and stubbornly blank. 'I . . .' This was ridiculous. Her own name. It was on the tip of her tongue as well, just out of reach. Come on, Rachel! Of course you know your second name!

The nurse must have seen the panic in her eyes because she patted her soothingly. 'Don't worry, you're concussed, that's all. It'll come back. I don't suppose you can remember a contact number in the meantime, can you? People must be worrying about you.'

A contact number – yes. Absolutely. She wanted to cry with relief at the thought of a call being made, a nurse or doctor phoning home so that the children could be told what was happening. Hopefully Sara would sort something out. Rachel was not exactly pally with her but needs must when you were a single mum. She hoped the other woman would understand.

The nurse was hovering expectantly for the number, she

realized, and Rachel made a gargantuan effort to form the necessary sounds with her broken mouth. 'Oh,' she began in a strangled voice. 'Wuh-wuh-*one*.' To think that she had taken speech for granted all these years. You just opened your mouth and out it came, long chains of words to articulate whatever tiny trivial thing you might be thinking. Now, after one hard shove, one single fall, it had become a Herculean task to make herself understood.

Then it happened again. It was so strange, as if her brain had seized up, jamming midway through. She frowned, shutting her eyes in order to concentrate, but all she could see were numbers, all shapes and sizes and colours, swinging around like a carousel in her brain, making her feel nauseous all of a sudden.

'Keep going,' the nurse encouraged, and Rachel opened her eyes again, the room tilting and lurching. 'What's the next number?'

Good question. Her mind had gone completely blank now, all numbers receding into the distance. It was as if she was searching wildly through dark empty space and nothing was there. She couldn't remember. She just couldn't remember!

'Don't worry,' the nurse said again. 'I find it tricky enough remembering my PIN number at the best of times, let alone when I've had a wallop on the head, like you. Just relax, take your time. Try again in a bit.'

She *had* tried – repeatedly – but the correct sequence of

numbers stubbornly refused to reveal itself, jumbling and re-ordering in her mind whenever she tried to focus. She couldn't remember Sara's surname either, so there was no way of having someone look her up. What was it? Fitzgerald? Something fancy-sounding. Fauntleroy. Forbes. *Think, Rachel. Think!* But all that came to her mind through the shadowy depths were her children's faces – *Where's Mum?* – and she found herself spiralling into panic and angst, the numbers sliding ever further from her grasp. What would happen to the children if she couldn't get in touch by this evening? Would Sara keep them with her? Luke's lip would tremble, he would panic, Scarlet would go very quiet, bottling up her anxiety. Mabel, no doubt, would try to brazen it out. 'Social services alert!' she would say theatrically, as she did whenever she considered Rachel's parenting to be below standard (often). 'I'm phoning ChildLine!'

Wait – no. A new option struck her. Would Mabel ring *Lawrence*? A chill ran through her at the thought of him turning up and taking charge. *Oh dear*, she imagined him drawling. *Talk about an unfit mother. Wait till my lawyer hears about this.*

Tears trickled from her eyes, rolling sideways into her ears. *Think, Rachel, think.* For every minute her brain was fuzzy, that was another minute of Luke retreating into himself, Scarlet gnawing down her nails, Mabel doing her best to brazen out the situation, her resolve gradually shrinking . . .

'Hey, come on, it's all right.' The nurse was back again. Rachel had lost all track of time by now, all sense of what was happening beyond the walls around her. Was it still the same day? Was it night-time? The nurse gently dabbed her eyes with a tissue and Rachel had to try very hard not to lean against her and start bawling. 'How is your pain at the moment? I can top up your morphine again if you need it?'

Rachel nodded again. The pain was still excruciating. 'Yes. Please,' she managed to get out through her mangled lips. I'm Rachel, she repeated to herself, her mind starting to drift as the drug stole into her bloodstream. I'm Rachel and I've got to get home. I just need to remember how . . .

Chapter Five

Meanwhile, over in Rachel's kitchen, with a stack of fluffy American pancakes liberally spread with golden syrup and strawberry jam ('Mum would go *crazy* if she could see this,' Scarlet confided with a mixture of guilt and glee), Becca was trying to ascertain what might have led to her sister's out-of-character disappearance. 'So she dropped you at school as usual this morning, did she? Do you remember her saying anything about what she was doing later on? Where she was going?'

The girls exchanged a glance. 'She was in a weird mood this morning,' Mabel said, reflecting. 'Bad-tempered, sort of snappy.' She rolled her eyes with teenage world-weariness. 'Like *that's* anything new.'

'She told me off for spilling the milk,' Scarlet said, licking her sticky fingers. '*And* when I found my lunchbox from yesterday that I'd forgotten to empty.'

'She was checking something on the laptop,' Mabel remembered. 'And then I had to go, and she was like, oh my

God, is it that time already? We're going to be late!' The high-pitched breathy imitation of her mother was verging on cruel, Becca thought, wincing.

'And then she took me and Luke to school, and we had to take Henry and Elsa too, because their mum was going to pick us up later and they'd done a swap,' Scarlet said and pulled a face. 'Elsa is *so* freaking annoying. God!'

'Anything else?' Becca prompted.

Scarlet thought, head tilted on one side, small dark eyebrows angling together in a frown. 'Not really. When she dropped us all off, she said, "Remember, Sara's picking you up after school but I'll come and get you before teatime." Only she never did.' She bit into her pancake and a splodge of jam plopped out onto her white school shirt. 'Whoops.'

'Hmmm,' said Becca. 'So it just felt like . . . an ordinary day, then?'

'Yep,' both sisters chorused.

'And she took the car, I'm guessing? There's nothing outside.'

Scarlet was trying to suck the jam off her shirt but paused in order to answer. 'We usually walk to school but we went in the car this morning,' she explained, 'because Mum said she was in a rush.'

Car crash, thought Becca immediately, feeling sick at the thought of crumpled metal, squealing brakes, her sister's body flung through the windscreen like a rag doll. She shook her head, not wanting to imagine any more. But then again, no – if it had been a car crash, they would have heard from the police by now, surely? The registration plate would have been traced, someone would have been in touch, uniformed officers at the door, caps in hand, grave expressions . . .

She got up from the table and began washing up the frying pan and batter bowl, so that the girls couldn't see the twinge of panic on her face. 'Maybe she's got a flat tyre,' she said, trying to stay calm. 'Your poor mum! By the time she gets in, she'll be fed up, I bet.' Her fingers shook on the washing-up brush; she had never been a very good liar. 'In any case, I'm sure she'll be back soon. Why don't you go and get ready for bed now? I'll tell her to pop in and give you goodnight kisses just as soon as she's home, okay?'

Later on, when the house was quiet, Becca sat in her sister's tidy (and very beige) living room and watched the small slate mantelpiece clock tick its way round till nine o'clock, nine-thirty, ten. Elsewhere in the street, good little families were closing their curtains and settling down for the night. Here at the Jacksons', the phone remained silent, the front door reso-lutely shut, and no car headlights came sweeping up the road.

Becca might not be close to her sister but she knew instinc-tively that this was not how Rachel operated. Organized, in control, achieving – that was Rachel. While Becca's life tend-ed to pinball from one shambles to another, Rachel had children, responsibilities, this nice suburban detached house in a well-to-do neighbourhood: a proper, grown-up life to come home to, in other words. She gazed around the room, searching for clues, and her eyes fell on a vase of white roses standing on a side table, scent spilling from their velvety heads. People who were going to run away didn't bother cutting flowers and thinking about vases, did they? So where was she?

The sky was dark outside now; she hoped the children had managed to fall asleep despite the unusual situation. She didn't know them well enough to gauge whether they were acting out of character, if Mabel was usually so scathing about her mum's driving ('I bet she's lost. She can't even read a *map*, you know, let alone *park* without having a nervous breakdown') and whether Scarlet always needed her bedroom door to be ajar just so, the bathroom light left on, her school uniform laid out for the next morning, or if it was her way of trying to wrest back some control. Poor girls! They were toughing it out, but you could see in their eyes they were worried. So was Becca.

Mabel had hesitated before going up to bed and said, 'I hope it was all right, me giving Sara your name. Only . . . Dad's not around now and Grandma – Welsh Grandma – would only make a massive fuss and be mean about Mum.' She shrugged, looking self-conscious and suddenly much younger. 'I just remembered that time at

Grandad and Wendy's anniversary party when you were really nice to me. That's all.'

Becca's heart melted at the girl's awkwardness. 'I'm *glad* that you asked me,' she said, dimly recollecting how Mabel had confided in her on that occasion, something about a bullying classmate who was picking on her. It was nice to hear that the moment had lodged in her niece's mind; that Mabel associated her with a rescuer, someone who could help. So that made one person in the family who thought Becca was remotely competent, anyway.

A thought occurred to her. *Checking something on the laptop*, Mabel had said earlier. Might that be a clue to where Rachel had gone? She remembered seeing a laptop skew-whiff on the kitchen dresser and went to retrieve it, feeling uneasy as she switched it on. What if Rachel came back right now, walked in to her own living room to find Becca sitting there snooping at her laptop? It would be like getting caught trying on her big sister's make-up all those years ago; there would come the same shriek of horror, no doubt, the same outrage in her eyes. *What the hell do you think you are doing?! That's mine!*

But what else was she supposed to do? she thought defensively. Relax and sit back in front of the telly with her feet on the coffee table, hands behind her head? As if. And it wasn't like she was going to *snoop*, anyway, she was only going to . . .

Oh. Maybe she wasn't, after all. A screen had appeared requesting a password, and Becca's shoulders sank.

MabelScarletLuke, she tried. *Incorrect password*, the message came back.

JacksonFive, she tried next. They were the Jackson Four now, technically, with Lawrence having left, but maybe it would still . . . *Incorrect password*. Ahh.

Racheliscool, she typed, if only because her own password to lots of things was *Beccaiscool*. (Well, come on. If you couldn't big yourself up in secret digital code, then when could you?) But no. *Incorrect password*. Rachel was obviously not as tragic and insecure as her stepsister – surprise, surprise.

There was a pattering sound and she jumped before realizing it was a gust of raindrops that had been flung at the window like small pebbles. Here came the storm. She shivered to think of Rachel still out there somewhere, rain spattering a cracked windscreen maybe, drumming against the roof of her car, plastering her blonde hair wetly to her skull if she was outside . . . No. Don't think like that. She pushed the laptop away, aware that she could try different passwords all night and still not get anywhere. She'd ask Mabel about it in the morning if need be.

As the clock ticked on and the evening became later still, Becca felt increasingly unsure about what to do next. She didn't want to go to bed in her sister's room in case Rachel arrived home in the middle of the night and freaked out about her being there. Nor had she thought to ask about spare bedding and blankets so that she could camp out on the sofa. Not that she felt remotely tired yet, anyway. Her mind was turning like a hamster wheel, running through lists of what she should do tomorrow morning if Rachel still wasn't back. Look after the children, obviously, and try to keep everything feeling as normal as possible, for starters. Then she'd have to start contacting her sister's friends and colleagues to see if anyone had seen her. She would have to tell Lawrence too, she supposed, with a jolt of trepidation.

Lawrence. She couldn't help remembering that awful night in Birmingham when she'd seen him last, back in early November. She'd been waitressing, contract catering work through an agency, and working a shift at the Copthorne, some hot noisy sales conference dinner that seemed to be populated entirely by braying white men in suits. Every waitress's favourite – not. She had already had to make several sharp swerves that evening, dodging the wandering hands; matters not helped by the short black dress they'd given her as uniform that clung to her boobs and bum like a second skin. And then there he was, across the room, his eyes fastening on her with interest. She had smiled briefly, professionally, *Hi*, and went on pouring wine for a group of men who didn't seem to have learned the phrase 'thank you', but only minutes later he had come over to her, standing that little bit too close as always, a proprietorial hand on her back. 'Well, hello there,' he had murmured, low and suggestive in her ear.

She shuddered at the memory now. It felt like a betrayal

to even be thinking about it, sat here in Rachel's smart living room.

Her phone pinged and she scrabbled to open the text, but it was just a photo from her mum, who was on her first ever girls' holiday in Crete. *Mackerel for dinner, v healthy!*, the text read. *And chips. And mojitos!!!*

Wendy, the eternal dieter, thought that by 'fessing up to every calorific crime by text she was somehow atoning for her sins. Who could say what warped reasoning kept prompting her to do this, but do it she did – every day, generally. Barely registering the sun-drenched table of food in today's photo, Becca began typing a reply.

Mum, something weird has happened. Am at Rachel's. She

But she changed her mind almost immediately and deleted the message, not wanting to worry her mum. Wendy had slogged out the first year of widowhood with heartbreak in her eyes throughout; this was the first time she'd done anything nice for herself since Dad had died. ('I've bought a new cozzy and everything,' she had twittered the night before leaving. 'And three new lipsticks!') Becca could not, would not spoil her holiday and give her an excuse to come home early.

God, though. This was all too awful and strange for words. She couldn't work it out. Had Rachel maybe gone to meet a secret lover and lost track of time? Met up with Lawrence for some kind of showdown? Perhaps they were drunk and at each other's throats by now. Perhaps . . . well, who knew? Anything might be happening.

The rain was falling harder, beating against the windows, the wind swirling in the chimney. For the hundredth time Becca tried her sister's mobile, but it rang and rang. Maybe she should try to get hold of Lawrence sooner rather than later to see what he knew, she thought, uncertain of how amicable – or not – the break-up had been. She hadn't been able to bring herself to ask the girls directly, but looking round the room, she could see that there were no photos of him anywhere, not one. It was as if he'd been deleted from the family, stripped right out. What had gone wrong between the two of them, anyway?

There were no photos of her or Wendy either, Becca noticed, feeling sad, although lots of Rachel and Terry back when it was just the two of them – on beaches, in front of Big Ben, in lush green countryside with their bicycles, both pink in the cheeks as if they'd cycled a long way together. *Look how happy we were*, the photos said. *We didn't need anybody else, thank you very much! He was mine first!*

A memory swam into Becca's head, of when she was about six, and fifteen-year-old Rachel had brought back friends from school: exotic creatures to Becca, all long swishy hair, short skirts and high-pitched laughter.

'Oh my God, is this your *sister*?' cried Amanda, one of the girls, seeing Becca playing with her Sylvanian Families in the living room. 'Too cute. You never said you had a sister!'

Becca had smiled shyly up at her, dazzled by the girl's white-blonde hair and glittery fingernails, but Rachel was already pulling her friends away.

'*Step*sister,' she had said, hustling them upstairs. 'We're not related.'

There had been a lot of that. Together under duress, as Rachel was always so keen to point out. Not *my* choice.

Becca trudged upstairs to brush her teeth and wash her face, remembering how it had always hurt when Rachel said such things. Nobody liked being rejected, least of all by someone you looked up to. How she had hoped, little Becca, that her big sister would one day change her mind and love her, just a tiny bit. And how she had gone on hoping and hoping, until she had finally given up. That had hurt too.

The bathroom was gorgeous, of course – smooth pebble-grey tiles, a huge mirror lit with spotlights, and a long, deep bath. The shower was in a separate corner unit, with an enormous monsoon head, the towels were white and fluffy, and the overall effect – if you ignored the children's strawberry tangle-tackler shampoo and the Playmobil pirates standing guard around the bath – was one of sleek, stylish luxury.

All right for some, thought Becca, trying not to compare it with the cramped, mould-smelling bathroom back home, with the shower that leaked if you stayed in it for longer than three minutes. Then she brushed her teeth, frowning at her foam-mouthed reflection the whole while. Where was Rachel? Who had she gone to meet? Was she hurt or lost or stranded by the side of the road with a flat tyre . . . or had something far worse happened?

Her skin tingled all over with premonition. It was bad, she felt certain. Something really bad. And those three worried children were now depending on her, Becca the screw-up, to somehow make everything all right. Christ. She hoped she was up to the job.

Chapter Six

'Good morning! And how are we today?'

Rachel blinked out of her doze to see that a nurse had appeared by her bedside, a different one today, with high Slavic cheekbones and pale blue eyes. It took her brain a few foggy moments to catch up with everything. Pain. A hospital bed. Manchester. Oh God, yes – and the *children*. Where were they waking up this morning? Who was looking after them? She hoped Sara had helped out. She hoped even more that Mabel hadn't taken it upon herself to assume responsibility. Aged thirteen, she thought she knew everything about the world but was still such a child in reality.

The nurse's gaze was expectant, so Rachel croaked out an 'Okay', even if it wasn't true. Really, she was very far from okay – she had barely slept, she had the mother of all thumping headaches and she was dreading the operations that loomed ahead of her that day. Not to mention the fact that she had palpitations every time she thought about her kids, and how they might be managing without her. They must be completely freaked out by now. She had never done anything like this before, never dropped out of their world without warning. With the ripples from the divorce still ongoing, she had done her damnedest throughout to be the constant in their life, the linchpin who kept everything together. Until now, when a whole afternoon, evening and night had passed, and they would have woken up without her. *I'm sorry,* she thought despairingly. *I've let you all down, haven't I? I'm sorry.*

That was the scariest thing about being a single mum – that it all came down to you. Homework, arguments, bed-time, nits, dinner money, basic hygiene: she was the one who had to deliver day in, day out, to love them, feed them, keep them clean and safe. But here she was, miles away, having failed to come home and do any of those things. She could already imagine someone from social services knocking on the door, stern-faced. 'Mrs Jackson?'

Wait. There it was! Her name – Jackson, that was it. Mrs Rachel Jackson. Rachel and Lawrence Jackson. Except they weren't together any more, of course. 'Jackson,' she said, her jaw aching as she formed the word. She struggled to sit up, feeling desperate to impart this new knowledge. 'Jackson. My name. Rachel. Jackson.'

'Rachel Jackson – that's your name?' the nurse said warmly. 'Fantastic, Rachel. Great. That gives us something to go on. Has anything else come back to you? A city, or town? A tele-phone number?'

She frowned, probing around inside her mind as if searching a dark warehouse. A city or town. An image of a house swam up through the murk; a grey house – home. Yes, there was the hall with the coats hanging up, there was the living room painted a lovely soft biscuit colour. Her huge wide bed upstairs, big enough to make her feel lonely sometimes. And the name of her street was . . .

Nothing. It had gone. She mentally paced through the rooms she could remember, recounting the details: the heavy oatmeal curtains at the living-room window. The view outside onto the street. Her car. The front wall where Mabel sometimes sat with friends, getting moss on her grey school skirt. *I live in* . . . she prompted herself, but still no answer appeared.

Then a name came to her. 'Birmingham?' she said tentatively. Birmingham, she repeated in her mind. There was definitely some connection with Birmingham, she was sure. *Good old Brum!*, she could hear her dad saying. But did she live there? Oh, this was awful. Everything kept jumbling up in her mind, the details slipping out of reach.

'Birmingham, okay,' the nurse was saying, though, before Rachel could voice her doubts. 'Rachel Jackson, Birmingham. Let me pass that on to the police, see if we get anywhere. Try and rest now though, okay?'

Chapter Seven

After much tossing and turning Becca eventually drifted into a light, uncomfortable sleep on the sofa, jerking awake every time the wind howled in the chimney before her eyes finally cracked open with the sunrise around six o'clock. It took a moment to orient herself – cold, sofa, living room – and then the truth pressed down on her, heavy and unpleasant. She was in Rachel's house – without Rachel. Still without Rachel. She had slept so fitfully that she was certain the sound of a car outside or the front door opening would have woken her. So where could her sister be?

Fear slithered into the pit of her stomach as an image appeared in her mind: Rachel's eyes, glassy and still, her body mangled at the side of the road, blood and shattered glass and . . .

Stop. *Stop*, Becca. Not helping. She ran a hand through her hair and heaved herself up, feeling stiff and achey. No. She mustn't think that way. They had to hope for the best and try not to dwell on other, worse explanations. For the sake of the children, she had to stay positive.

Talking of the children . . . She became aware of light footsteps outside on the stairs and she yawned and rubbed her eyes, trying to pull herself together. Then Luke's head poked cautiously around the door. 'Mummy isn't here,' he said.

'I know, sweetheart,' Becca replied helplessly. It crossed her mind that she could make up some story to stop him worrying, but she rejected the idea almost immediately. The girls, older and smarter, would see through any fabrications in five seconds. Then they'd never trust her again.

'Come here,' she said, patting the sofa cushion beside her. 'You look like you need a cuddle. And I think your Aunty Becca does too, you know.'

He was such a solemn little thing, she thought, as he slid into the room, all big eyes and wariness. He was rigid in her arms at first, tentative, but then he leaned against her and she felt his warmth and smelled his boy smell. He was clutching a small Lego spaceship in one hand and for some reason, the sight of it gave her a lump in her throat. 'Don't worry,' she said into his soft dark hair. 'I'm going to make sure everything's all right. I promise.' She hoped he didn't clock that she was crossing her fingers behind her back.

Becca made Luke some breakfast and herself a coffee then padded upstairs to the shower, feeling skanky and ripe after sleeping in her T-shirt and jeans all night. She wished now she'd thought to bring a change of clothes, a clean bra, deodorant and a hairbrush, but she had been so convinced that she'd arrive here to find Rachel already back – and worse, annoyed with Becca for coming out at all – that she had literally only brought knickers and a toothbrush with her. In a carrier bag, because she was that classy. Well, she would just have to borrow something of her sister's for today – end of story. She was pretty sure even Rachel couldn't get too arsey about that, given her vanishing act of the night before.

Once clean, she swathed herself in towels and tiptoed into her sister's room, feeling like an intruder. Rachel had guarded her privacy zealously when they were growing up, seeming to know instantly if Becca had moved or touched any of her belongings left around the house. Twenty years later, Becca still felt the same shiftiness at being in her sister's space without written permission, as if expecting to be bawled out for it any second. But she could hardly walk the children to school in yesterday's smelly clothes like a total scuzzer. *Well, hello there, just call me Aunty Hobo* . . . No. She might be several divisions down the Glamour League from her sister, but she wasn't that much of a loser. *So tough luck, Rach. I'm here, and I'm going to take my pick of your wardrobe for one morning only. If I can find any of your clothes big enough to fit me, that is.*

The bedroom was as stylish as the rest of the house: cream walls, glossy white cupboards with opaque glass doors, everything tidied away, bedcovers smooth. It was like being in a hotel room or a display area of The White Company: clean, minimalist, chic. Becca's room back home, in comparison, was a jumble of scarves and jewellery, nail varnish pots crowding the mantelpiece, photos and postcards stuck around the big mirror, mismatched cushions heaped on the bed, various half-finished craft projects jumbled together on her desk.

An alarm clock began beeping elsewhere in the house and then a radio blared into life – the girls waking up, she presumed – so she hastily pulled open the wardrobe doors. Blouses, skirts, jackets . . . the contents were all very stylish and pretty, and so not her thing – and unfortunately she could tell from a quick rifle through that none of it was over a size 10 either. *Wardrobe Says No.*

Chest of drawers, then. The pickings were better there at least – lots of sportswear and a couple of baggy tops. Becca pulled on a soft grey T-shirt and some drawstring yoga pants, not caring how daft she might look, dried her hair and dabbed on some of Rachel's Clinique moisturizer. (Nice.) Then, with a jolt, she realized that the phone was ringing downstairs, so she turned and sprinted out of the room.

Oh my God. Here we go, news at last. Some kind of update. She almost broke her neck skidding on the bottom stair in her haste to reach the kitchen in time, adrenalin pumping. Please don't let it be bad news. Please let it be Rachel to say everything's all right.

'Hello?' She could hardly breathe as she snatched up the receiver. *Please, please, please.*

'Oh, Rachel, hello dear, it's Rita. Rita Blackwell? I'm meant to be seeing you tomorrow but I'm ever so sorry, I've got a doctor's appointment for the same time, so I won't be able to come along.'

Disappointment slammed the breath from her lungs and Becca leaned against the cool painted wall as her heart rate adjusted. 'Oh,' was all she managed to say faintly.

Mabel must have heard the ringing phone too because she had appeared in the kitchen, panda-eyed with yesterday's make-up, hair all over the place, tugging a cherry-print kimono dressing gown around herself. Her expression was urgent, impatient, a thousand questions in her eyes. *What's happening? Is it Mum? When will she be home?*

Becca shook her head dumbly. No news. Not her. I don't know.

'Hello?' The woman's voice from the receiver was that of an older lady, tremulous and hesitant, and Becca pulled herself together with an enormous effort.

'Sorry,' she managed to say. 'Rachel's not here right now. Can I give her a message?'

'Yes, dear, of course. It's Mrs Blackwell. Rita, tell her. I can't see her tomorrow, I'm afraid. Doctor's appointment. Ever so sorry.'

'Not to worry,' Becca said, grabbing an envelope and

pen from the worktop nearby and scribbling down the details. 'Okay, I'll let her know,' she said, hoping she hadn't just tempted fate in the worst sort of way. *If I hear from her, that is. If it's not already too late.* 'Thanks, then. Bye.'

Mabel seemed to have shrunk in size with the anticlimax. 'Was that one of her clients?' she asked dully. Then she glanced over at the envelope, deciphering Becca's scrawls to answer her own question. 'Oh, right, Mrs Blackwell. She's always cancelling.'

Becca couldn't get terribly excited about Mrs Blackwell and her cancellations, but it was better than dwelling on Rachel still being missing, she supposed. 'Is she someone your mum works with?' she guessed.

'Not really *with*,' Mabel replied. 'She's one of Mum's fitness clients? You know, her boot camps and that?'

Becca didn't know what she meant. The last she'd heard, Rachel was an area manager for GoActive, a large chain of leisure complexes that seemed to be springing up in every town and city. Becca had only really been hazily aware of what this entailed but she had the impression Rachel was suited and booted for the job, driving around and making sure everyone was doing what they were supposed to, rather than taking on personal clients. But Mabel had already heaved a gusty sigh and gone off back upstairs, yelling, 'False alarm. Not Mum,' to the other two.

She attached the scribbled-on envelope to the fridge with a Doctor Who magnet, hoping fervently that she would be in a position to pass on the message at some point to her sister. Today, preferably. As soon as possible.

Then she noticed the letter that the envelope had been covering. A red electricity bill, with FINAL DEMAND written across the top – the sort of bill that frequently arrived for Becca and Meredith, but one she was surprised to see here in serene suburbia. An alarm bell rang inside her head. Was Rachel having money troubles on top of everything else?

Becca bit her lip. Clearly things had been difficult for Rachel recently. She was probably still missing Dad very much too, like Becca did. And to undergo that grief on top of divorce and financial problems . . . Well, it could all get too much for a person, couldn't it? What if . . .?

She swallowed, not wanting to put the awful thought into words, to crystallize it within a sentence, but the question refused to budge. Sometimes people felt that they just couldn't go on, children or not, didn't they? Sometimes things seemed so desperate that there was only one way out . . .

'Aaargh! Oh *no!*'

A shriek had come from elsewhere and Becca, glad of the distraction, went to investigate, just as Scarlet hurtled into the room in a scraggly cerise dressing gown, panicking that she'd forgotten about her early-morning Friday violin lesson at eight-thirty and oh God, they were going to be sooo late and her teacher Mrs Brookes was like so, totally strict, she would just go bloody *mental*!

'Scarlet,' Becca said, but her niece was in seemingly un-stoppable mid-flow.

'And I'm meant to be doing my Grade 2 soon and she said if I missed any more lessons—'

'Scarlet!'

'– she would be, like, *really* cross, and—'

'Scarlet, listen!'

'What?'

'It's only twenty past seven. And it's Thursday, anyway. Your lesson must be tomorrow. We've got twenty-five whole hours before you have to be there.'

Scarlet opened her mouth and then shut it again. 'Oh! Thursday,' she said in surprise. Her face relaxed. 'Okay, cool,' she went on, sounding more cheerful. 'Can I have some breakfast?'

Looking after children was *exhausting*, Becca thought ten minutes later. Luke had had a meltdown, insisting that he didn't have any school uniform, and then Mabel went off on one too, ranting that there was no butter *and* she had the worst period pain ever, like her uterus was totally ripping itself apart – and *aargh*, why had nobody reminded her about the geography exam that was like, this *morning*, could Becca ring the school and explain that she was really traumatized about Mum and hadn't been able to revise?

It was mayhem. Carnage. Becca felt breathless with her attempts to firefight one drama after another, none of them with much success. She felt particularly thrown by Mabel's abrupt mood changes from sweetness the night before to relative civility first thing before plunging into absolute foulness now. Was that normal? 'And I'm going to Tyler's after school, all right?' she yelled as she slammed out of the house at eight o'clock.

'Bye,' Becca called, wincing as the door crashed in the frame. 'Who's Tyler?' she asked Scarlet, not entirely sure she wanted to know.

Scarlet looked gleeful. 'Her *boyfriend*. Who Mum doesn't like because she caught them *kissing*.'

Oh, great. Wonderful. 'So I take it her going to Tyler's house . . .'

'Is totally not allowed. Like, no way. Because his parents don't get back till late, Mabel says, so there are no "responsible adults" around. Last time Mum said, I'm laying the law down here, young lady, it's not happening, so you just get that into your head right this minute.'

The imitation was spot-on and Becca floundered for a moment, not least because she had the horrible feeling Rachel might not class *her* as a particularly 'responsible adult'. Now what was she supposed to do? 'Well,' she said, thinking fast, 'I'm sure your mum will be back by then anyway, so I'll leave that for her to sort out.' It was a cop-out and she wasn't sure of any such thing, frankly, but it was the best she could manage.

Scarlet smirked. 'She'll go bloody *nutzoid*,' she said with relish.

'Where *is* Mum, anyway?' Luke asked, sliding down the banister in a Darth Vader costume.

'She's gone to fight the evil Sith,' Scarlet said, grabbing his lightsabre and clonking him over the head with it.

'Ow. Has she? Really?'

'No, you moron, of course she hasn't. Because *Star Wars* isn't *real*. Derrrr!'

Deep breaths, Becca thought as she broke up the resulting scuffle, sent Luke to get changed and cobbled together some packed lunches. 'We're definitely allowed crisps, aren't we, Luke?' Scarlet had said, eyes wide with innocence. 'Only on Fr—' he had begun replying, before a surreptitious kick made him change this to an unconvincing 'Oh. Yes. We are.' 'Because you see, potatoes *are* vegetables,' Scarlet had added cunningly, like that was going to persuade anyone. Becca decided to cut them some slack, though. They were just a little on edge, that was all, and it was completely justified given the circumstances. Besides, it sounded like her step-sister was something of a stickler on the health and nutrition front. A bag of crisps and some jammy pancakes weren't about to kill anyone, were they?

As she ran around searching for hair bobbles in order to plait Scarlet's tangled brown hair – a brush would help, too – she couldn't help ruefully harking back to her usual morning routine: savouring a quiet coffee in bed with the radio on before calmly getting ready for the day, without anyone screaming down the stairs about exams and the state of their ovaries, let alone playing migraine-inducing violin tunes about beloved dogs and terrible parents so loud and frenziedly that Becca feared for the safety of every window and wine glass in the house. Violinageddon, Mabel had called it. She wasn't far wrong.

An old song, beloved of her mum, slipped into her head as she loaded up the dishwasher with cereal bowls and mugs. *Sometimes it's hard . . . to be a woman . . .*

Yeah. Especially when you had three children to get out of the house first thing in the morning. I hear you, sister.

Despite Becca's best attempts, it ended up being ten past nine before she, Scarlet and Luke actually managed to make it to their school. She had to press a buzzer and explain herself to an intercom before they were permitted to enter and do the walk of shame up to the office, where she had to enter their names in the 'Late' book. 'Whoa. We've never *ever* been late before,' Scarlet said, looking vaguely panicked at the prospect, and Becca just about managed to bite back a retort that if she'd brushed her teeth a bit faster and stopped teasing her brother, they might have been on time.

'Never mind,' she said bracingly. 'It's not the end of the world, is it?' A sniff came from the po-faced secretary, who clearly disagreed, and Becca gave her a frosty glare in response – well, as frosty a glare as she could manage when the slightly-too-tight yoga pants were going right up her bum crack. 'Have a brilliant day, both of you,' she said to the children. 'Be good! And don't worry. I'm sure everything will be completely back to normal again by hometime, all right?'

'And Mum will be back again?' Luke said anxiously.

'Probably. Almost certainly,' Becca replied, doing her best to sound reassuring. *I really hope so, anyway, kid.*

'Oh shit,' Scarlet said just then, slapping a hand to her forehead. 'Football kit. You forgot our football kit, Aunty Bee. We have a club after school on Thursdays.'

Becca counted to ten under her breath to prevent herself from arguing that *she* was not the one who had forgotten, seeing as she knew nothing about this football club. Instead she apologized for the random kit she was supposed to have known telepathically about, hugged both children tightly and sent them on their way, hoping they would be okay.

'Is everything . . . all right at home?' the secretary ventured as Becca stood there a moment longer, watching them troop into the building.

'Um . . .' Becca hesitated, unsure how to reply. Rachel had always been so proud; she would probably hate anyone knowing there was a problem at home. 'Not really,' she replied truthfully in the end. 'But I'm on the case.'

A disappearing mum was not good for anyone, she thought as she walked back through the school gate a few moments later. Her nieces and nephew might all be handling the situation in their own ways – rage, denial, fear, quite a lot of inappropriate swearing – but sooner or later there would have to come some form of resolution, some answers, otherwise the not-knowing would start to become unbearable. Today, she would begin the search and see what she could find out.

Chapter Eight

Rachel dozed in and out of consciousness. *Rachel Jackson, Birmingham*, she kept reminding herself. *Rachel Jackson, Birmingham*, as if she'd forget all over again if the facts were allowed to slip through her grasp. It didn't feel quite right, though. What was she missing? A cathedral kept coming into her mind – a handsome cathedral by the river, bells ringing. That wasn't Birmingham, was it? But the streets and buildings just slid about in her mind whenever she tried to pin them down. Oh, why couldn't she think straight? What was wrong with her brain? What if she never remembered, and was stuck like this for ever?

A nurse appeared after a while, the blonde one again. *Good cheekbones*, Rachel found herself thinking. People used to say that about her, she recalled in the next moment. *Amazing bone structure!* Someone had actually once said those words to her, admiringly; a boy who was in love with her when she was at university, she thought. Andy, was it? She could picture his donkey jacket and skinny-jeaned legs, sandy-coloured hair, a Northern accent. Andy. At university. Yes: two more facts for the jigsaw. She raised a hand to her face while the nurse took her temperature, gingerly touching the sore, swollen skin with the tips of her fingers. How did her bone structure look now? she wondered. Smashed up beyond recognition, was how it felt. Would anyone ever compliment her on her face again?

The nurse gently took her hand down and fastened the blood pressure cuff to her arm. 'So we're keeping you nil by mouth this morning because you're going into theatre later on – hopefully by ten o'clock, depending on how many other patients are ahead of you on the list, okay?' she said, pumping up the cuff so that it tightened.

Rachel gave a careful nod, her pulse thumping against the rubber.

'Ah, good, your blood pressure's fifty-eight over ninety, that's looking better,' the nurse said, jotting down the reading. 'Gosh, you must be very fit.'

Fifty-eight. Ninety. And in the next moment, something came floating up through her blurred consciousness at those numbers, an inkling that they meant something, were relevant. Fifty-eight. Ninety. She could hear herself saying them aloud, a distant memory that seemed far away, as if she was peering at it through a reverse telescope. If she could just put her finger on what they meant.

Twenty-five. Fifty-eight. Ninety. That was the sequence,

she was certain. Six numbers, in that order, she could see them in purple digits all of a sudden, printed on white card. Her heart pounded. Contact details on her business card – yes! 'Twenty-five. Fifty-eight,' she said haltingly, her jaw still agony to move, her lips feeling as if they were made of rubber. She didn't care, though; she had remembered. At last! 'Ninety.'

'What's that, love?' the nurse said, looking up from her clipboard.

Wait – there was more. The area code. Zero-one-four-three-two. That was it, just like that in her head. A camera flash of sudden, sharp memory. That was *it*! Rachel gestured for the pen and then, with some difficulty, used her left hand to write the numbers at the bottom of the nurse's observation form. As fast as she could, before they slipped away again. 'Phone,' she said, pointing at the shaky figures, triumph bursting through her like a sunrise. She smiled despite the pain. It had finally come back to her, her brain releasing this vital code that would reconnect her with home. *'Phone.'*

Exhausted by the breakthrough, she leaned against her pillows and drifted back into a shallow sleep, waking again when two new figures appeared by her bedside: the anaesthetist and consultant in charge of her operation that morning. They ran through a number of pre-op questions – did she have any fillings, piercings, was there any chance that she could be pregnant, had she had any problems while under anaesthetic in the past, that sort of thing. Rachel couldn't help thinking back to when Scarlet had had her tonsils out, three years ago, and how terrifying it had been seeing her child slip under anaesthetic, eyes rolling backwards, how Rachel had been hustled out of the operating theatre ('Come on, Mum, let's leave them to get on with it') away from that small prone body, when every maternal instinct told her to stay there and stand guard, keep a tight hold of her daughter's hand throughout. Lawrence had been waiting outside, of course, they'd still been a united front back then, and they'd sat it out together in the grim little parents' area, taking it in turns to get disgusting coffees from the machine while they tried not to think about surgeons angling knives in their younger daughter's cherry-red mouth.

This time it would be her in the operating theatre, numbed by the drug, eyes tilting back into her head, alone and vulnerable on a bed while the doctors got to work. Nobody outside in the waiting area. Nobody leaning over her while she came round, to tell her she would be all right, that they would look after her.

She answered the doctors' questions in a strangled-sounding voice, signed the consent forms shakily, not quite daring to say aloud what was uppermost in her mind: *please be careful with me. I've got three children, you know. I've got to get out of here as soon as I can, all right?*

'I think that's everything,' the consultant said with a smile. 'So we'll see you in theatre later on, okay? Try not to worry.'

Rachel stared up at the ceiling after they'd gone, attempting to dredge up some courage. Scarlet had barely complained about her operation, she remembered, even afterwards when she was groggy and confused in the recovery room, throwing up into a cardboard bowl, her forehead clammy. Rachel would just have to channel some of her daughter's determination and see this through, however unpleasant, however painful.

The consultant had moved on to the next patient, the woman in the neighbouring bed to Rachel, separated only by a faded blue curtain. Unlike Rachel, this woman had with her a man (a husband?) and a little girl, and it was impossible not to eavesdrop on their voices, confident and almost cheerful, as the three adults discussed the treatment she needed. The little girl was playing with some kind of musical toy, oblivious to her mother's predicament, because the tinny strains of 'Twinkle, Twinkle, Little Star' filtered through to Rachel.

Mabel had loved that song, she thought nostalgically, except she'd had her own version of the words. 'Tinkle Little Tinkle Sar,' she'd sung, high-pitched and sweet as a toddler. 'Sing "Tinkle Little", Daddy,' she would order, and Rachel remembered how Lawrence had gamely obeyed his miniature daughter, remembered catching his eye across the room and feeling a rush of fierce love for him as he sang along with her, his booming bass quite at odds with her small-girl cheep. Oh, she'd loved him then. They'd been happy, hadn't they, once upon a time?

Tears dripped onto the white hospital pillow, creating little wet circles. *How I wonder what you are.* Yes, she thought miserably, and how she wondered how it had all gone wrong.

Chapter Nine

Having completed the school run, albeit not particularly brilliantly, Becca let herself back into Rachel's silent house. Okay. Now what? Well, the kitchen looked as if a bomb had gone off in there, for starters. As little as she knew about her stepsister, she was pretty sure that Rachel would not want to walk back into her home to find a scene of carnage. Becca quickly put away the breakfast cereals, swept up the spilled Rice Krispies and put on a load of laundry. That was the easy bit. Now for the more important business: beginning the hunt to find her sister.

First of all, she called every hospital within the county. None of them had any record of Rachel or of a woman matching her description coming into their Accident and Emergency departments yesterday – so that was a positive start.

Next came a call to the local police station to report her missing. A helpful man took down all the details and a full description of Rachel, then went on to ask a whole host of other questions about places Rachel frequented, her health and medical condition, details of where she worked, as well as whether there had been any specific events that might have led directly to her disappearance. Becca felt stupid for not being able to answer everything fully. 'We're not exactly close,' she mumbled after yet another 'Don't know' reply. 'I'll ring you back,' she added pathetically when she couldn't even give her sister's car registration number or a work number. Hopeless.

The police officer informed her that it was a low-risk situation and that in ninety per cent of cases, the people in question returned of their own volition. 'Try not to worry,' he said. 'Chances are, she'll be home later today and there'll be a perfectly good explanation.'

'But she has kids,' Becca pointed out. 'And I *am* worried. This is really out of character.' *From what I know of her, anyway*, she thought desperately. *Which isn't an awful lot, these days.*

'I'll add the information you've given me to our database,' the officer promised, 'and I'll be in touch as soon as we hear anything.'

So that was that. Onto the database she went, along with all those other missing people. Becca hated to think of that list of names and the ripples of families around each one, all fearing the worst, all jumping every time the phone rang or there was a knock at the door.

What next? She had remembered to ask Mabel for the laptop password that morning, in between ovary updates and pre-exam meltdown, so that was another avenue to try at least. 'Masklooha,' Mabel had told her, shoving a triangle of toast into her mouth.

'Mask-loo . . . What?'

Mabel had grabbed a pen and paper and written it down. 'MaScLuHa,' she repeated. 'The first two letters of our names, and the dog's.'

MaScLuHa. Nope, she'd have been a long time trying to guess that one, Becca thought now, typing the letters in carefully. Bingo! The screen changed and she was in. Okay – browser history, that was a good place to start. A few clicks of the trackpad told her that the websites Rachel had recently visited were: Waitrose (*quelle surprise*), a Google search for 'Didsbury Library telephone' (say what?), Facebook, and National Rail Enquiries. Ahh. That last one definitely sounded like a clue. Had she taken the train somewhere yesterday? She clicked on the link, hoping to see where Rachel might have gone, but a generic screen appeared telling her that her session had timed out. Talk about frustrating.

She clicked on the Didsbury Library search page, wondering if that might be relevant. Where the hell was Didsbury anyway? Right, somewhere in Manchester, apparently. She wrinkled her nose. Strange. Why phone up a library miles away rather than use your local one? Unless it was something to do with homework for the kids, she wondered, frowning.

Her finger hovered over the Facebook link next. That really *would* be snooping, of course, if she started going through her sister's messages and posts. The two of them were technically 'friends' on Facebook, but while Becca happily splurged every detail of her life online to anyone who cared, Rachel was rather more guarded about what she posted publicly. Barely anything, actually, now she came to think of it. Perhaps Rachel had filed her stepsister in an outer circle of friends, only letting the in-crowd see photos and news. It wouldn't exactly come as a shock if so. For as long as she could remember, Rachel had never asked her opinion or advice, never shared any confidences. She had chosen friends to be her bridesmaids, rather than her own flesh and blood (step-flesh and blood. Whatever).

Just as Becca was resisting the urge to go snooping anyway (*ha! You can't hide your secrets from me any more, love*), the land-line trilled, and her hand flew away from the keyboard as if it was lava-hot, as if it was Rachel herself ringing to say, *Don't you DARE, Becca Farnham, I know what you're up to!*

Banishing her stupid guilty thoughts, she hurried to answer the phone. Was this news at last? Maybe the policeman had made a match on the database. *I'm sorry to inform you that . . .* No, she thought, picking up. Please don't let this be something horrible, *please.*

'Hello?'

'Hello there, I'm ringing about your flier?' said a man in a husky Welsh accent. 'Came through my door last week. The one that says Can I Help?'

'Er . . .' Flier? Becca's adrenalin subsided again, tension whistling out of her in a sigh. Another false alarm.

'Yes, because you see, I do need help. And especially as your name is Rachel!' His voice cracked suddenly; there was a shake in it that made him sound emotional. 'That was my wife's middle name, see. Christine Rachel Jones. We were together forty-five years and never once had an argument, can you believe. She died in February, and I still miss her so much.'

Becca bit her lip, not entirely sure why this sad-sounding Welshman was ringing her sister's number. She remembered the lady who had called earlier that morning, too. Was Rachel moonlighting as some sort of Help the Aged counsellor? 'I'm sorry to hear about your wife,' she said politely.

'I'd give anything to have another plateful of her Irish stew, you know. Anything. Not much of a cook myself, see, I don't half miss her dinners. So when your flier came through the door, Rachel, it was like a sign, a message from her. My Christine sending you along to me: *Can I help you?*' He gave a wheezy chuckle, clearly brightening at the thought. 'So that's why I'm ringing. Yes, love. Yes, you *can* help me. I just want to taste a good Irish stew again. I want to learn how to make it for myself, now that she's gone.'

'I see,' Becca said, feeling sorry for him, but still drawing a complete blank. Was Rachel giving cookery lessons on the side? Maybe it was some kind of voluntary work she had been doing. She felt a pang for this poor lonely widower; her grandad had been just as helpless when her grandma Edie died back in the day. At least he'd had Wendy fussing about him and driving over with Tupperware-packed dinners every other evening. By the sound of it, this man was quite alone. 'I'm afraid Rachel's not actually here right now – I'm her sister, Rebecca – but I can take down your details and get her to call you back, how does that sound?'

'Bless you, love, that would be smashing. It's Michael Jones, on . . . wait, what's my number again? Let me find my glasses, hold on.'

She wrote down his details and ended the call, then stared doubtfully at her own messy writing. Could this be right? Rachel had always been so brisk and – well, not *cold*, exactly towards Becca and her mum, but unfriendly anyway. Yet here she was offering help to complete strangers, by all accounts. On top of a full-time job, and being a single mother to three children! The woman was a saint. It made Becca feel positively slovenly in comparison.

Still, something was niggling at her. Something didn't quite add up. Why was Rachel giving out fliers, offering to help random people, when she was a top-ranking business exec with a flash company car and an enviable salary, according to Wendy? Was it some altruistic whim of hers, some new do-gooding resolution, maybe? You'd have thought if someone was trying to be nicer, they could have started with their own family.

(*Stepfamily*, Rachel's voice said in her head. *We're not related*.)

Yeah, yeah. So you keep saying.

Talking of Rachel's amazing career, Becca should probably let the company know that their star businesswoman had gone missing, she realized. They were surely wondering why she hadn't come in to work that day. They might even know something about the disappearance.

She would kill two birds with one stone, she decided in the next moment, looking online for the sports chain's website and contact details. The police officer had asked for specifics of Rachel's car, as well as her work number, hadn't he? Someone at her office would know the registration details. She found the number and dialled.

'GoActive, this is Lacey speaking, how can I help you?'

'Hi, could you put me through to Rachel Jackson's assistant, please?' Becca said, pen and paper ready.

There was a pause. 'Er . . . I'm afraid Rachel doesn't work here any more,' came the reply after a moment. 'Should I transfer you to someone else in the department?'

'Oh.' Becca was flummoxed. 'She doesn't work there? Since when?'

'Let me think . . . Just after Christmas, I believe. Oh yes – that's right. Definitely after Christmas, because . . .' A gossipy tone entered the receptionist's voice before she abruptly fell silent, professionalism winning out just in the nick of time. 'Well. Anyway. Should I put you through to the management team?'

Becca stared out of the window at the lush, leafy garden, trying to absorb this new information. 'No, it's okay, thanks,' she said distractedly. So as well as her marriage breaking up, Rachel also had neither job nor company car any more, it seemed. Things were not stacking up all that brilliantly for her, you had to say. And what on earth had happened at Christmas that had stuck in the receptionist's head so vividly?

Still, it perhaps explained the fliers, as well as the clients that Mabel had mentioned, at least. Hanging up the phone, Becca tried to remember the exact words her niece had used that morning. Fitness clients . . . something about boot camps? But how did that tie in with lonely old widowers wanting cookery lessons?

Two miles away, in a brightly lit reception area at the GoActive head office, Lacey Turner put down the phone, popped a mint humbug into her mouth and went back to her game of Candy Crush. Rachel Jackson, eh! She hadn't thought about her for a few months ever since she'd had to leave the company, immediate resignation. No surprises *there*, obviously. Like anyone could carry on with their job after that little performance! It had made it into the local press and everything: PR disaster or what? Samantha Tyning, the big cheese of the entire company, had gone ballistic, according to Josie, her secretary, and of course poor old Craig had ended up in hospital for two nights, as well.

The phone rang again and Lacey shifted her mint into the side of her mouth. 'GoActive, this is Lacey speaking, how may I help you?' she said on automatic pilot, clicking to switch a jelly bean with a lemon drop on her screen. Yes! She was doing well on this level, it was a really difficult one too.

'Hi, I've been given this number as Rachel Jackson's home – is that correct?'

'Er . . . no,' said Lacey, distracted as she spotted a colour bomb appearing in her game. Wait – Rachel Jackson again? What the hell . . .? 'No, this is GoActive, we're a chain of sports centres,' she went on, wondering whether or not to mention that Rachel had once worked there. *Not*, she decided after a moment. People got funny about you giving out their personal information on the phone – fair enough – and besides, after the Christmas party debacle, she doubted any of the senior management team wanted Rachel's name bringing up again to members of the public.

There was a pause. 'So this is definitely not her home number?' the woman said, sounding dismayed. 'It's just – I'm a nurse at Manchester Royal Infirmary, she's a patient here, and she gave this number as one to call.'

'It's definitely not her home number,' Lacey said, with a last triumphant click to win her game. *Congratulations!* it said on screen, and she did a little air-punch.

'Oh,' the nurse replied. 'I don't suppose . . . The thing is, she's a bit concussed and I'm trying to contact her family, so . . .'

Lacey tuned out just then because her favourite motor-bike courier had chosen that particular moment to walk into the building – sexy Rick, with melty brown eyes who always took off his helmet and shook out his lovely shoulder-length sandy-coloured hair like something from a shampoo ad as he approached the desk. She had dreamed about that head-shake numerous times, often to the soundtrack of 'Je T'Aime' in the background. Corrr. Yep. Here he was again. He must have a fit body under those leathers, she thought, trying not to lick her lips as he strode towards her.

'Hello? Did you hear me?' the woman on the phone was saying, sounding a bit impatient by now. Rude.

'Sorry, she doesn't work here,' Lacey said, smiling flirta-tiously at Rick as he put a parcel on the desk for her to sign. She leaned forward to pen her signature, jutting her boobs out, just in case he happened to be looking for a Thursday morning thrill. 'Thanks,' she mouthed, gazing up through her eyelashes as she had practised.

'Cheers, darling,' he said, turning and walking away.

Darling. Get in. Lacey gazed at his bottom and allowed herself a momentary fantasy where she vaulted over the desk and grabbed it with both hands before the woman on the phone cut into her thoughts again. 'So you don't have any contact details for her?' she asked.

'Sorry, no,' Lacey replied, feeling irritated to have been denied a proper chat with her current crush. 'Wrong number, goodbye.'

Hanging up the phone and crunching through her mint, she remembered the awful moment at last year's Christmas do when Rachel's husband had burst into the Left Bank restaurant halfway through the dessert course. Lacey had always thought he was quite handsome and sexy whenever she'd glimpsed the two of them around town together, but that night he had been red-faced, his eyes bulging as he yelled out all sorts of rude things about Rachel before going on to throw a punch at poor Craig Elliot.

Lacey wriggled gleefully in her seat, remembering the absolute uproar: the screams, the crash of crockery as a table was knocked over, the police arriving and everything. Nobody could believe it. Best. Christmas. Party. EVER!

Chapter Ten

Nice as everyone was being to Rachel, pleasant and professional as they all seemed, it was frightening being wheeled into the anaesthetic room and seeing the doctors and nurses gowned up like that, masks over their faces, ready to get stuck in. This was routine to them, she had to remind herself. This was bread and butter, what they did, day in, day out. They had worked hard through college to get here; they were trained, intelligent people whose job it was to fix bodies and make them better. They were *good*.

That said, God, she was terrified. Her heart thudded, her mouth was sandpaper-dry, her mind a choppy sea of fears. Because mistakes happened, didn't they? Things went wrong. She had never been under general anaesthetic before, and had no idea how her body would react. People died sometimes, she knew. It was a slim chance, sure, but the stats were there: people died. Ordinary, everyday people like her; their hearts stopped, the damage was done, end of story. (End of *life*.) However rationally you looked at it, there was no getting away from the fact that these masked faces might be the last ones she ever saw, this air the last she ever breathed. She pictured her children, small and black-clad, weeping at her funeral, and felt like leaping off the bed and running out of there, injuries or not. Could she really take the risk?

But she'd already signed away her decision, of course. It was too late to turn back. By this point someone was measuring the dose of anaesthetic and attaching the syringe to the cannula in her hand. And then, before she could say *stop, I've changed my mind*, a doctor was pushing down the plunger and asking her to count backwards from twenty.

'Twenty, nineteen, eighteen . . .' she began, obedient to the last, ' . . . seventeen . . .' And then it was washing through her, a huge deep blackness and the last thing she heard herself whimper was 'Mummy . . .'

Rachel couldn't remember all that much about her real mother, just a few fluttery flashes of memory that vanished if you tried to hold them too close. A sweet perfume. A low, musical laugh. A glossy sheet of chestnut hair cut with a severe fringe, and a cool, comforting hand in Rachel's. *My little Dandelion!*, she'd written on the back of a photo of Rachel as a newborn baby, no doubt because of the fluff of bright yellow hair around her infant face, but Rachel had no memory of her ever saying the words out loud.

Emily Durant, that was her name: a smiling, beautiful

woman with coltish legs and dancing green eyes. Emily Durant, who'd doted on her little dandelion and adored her handsome husband Terry, but who had been taken from them when Rachel was just two and a half. A rare and terrible form of bone cancer, apparently, although Dad hadn't liked to talk about it. Rachel always thought longingly of that hand in hers, that melodic, rippling laugh, when she saw dandelion seeds floating by on a breeze.

Glancing through the photograph album, they seemed the perfect couple, Emily and Terry. Every picture showed them smiling, holding hands, leaning against each other comfortably. Teenage sweethearts at the school disco. Getting married when they were barely in their twenties. Him posing in front of their first car, a red Datsun, with a look of intense pride. Her in bell-bottom trousers and wedge heels, a psychedelic-print scarf in her shining hair. And then baby Dandelion to complete the family a few years later, a cute pink bundle propped on Emily's hip. *Smile for the camera, Dandelion!*

Rachel had been born in the North, but she and her dad had moved to Birmingham when the tragedy struck – a brave new start, she guessed, picturing Terry driving away, the Datsun loaded with boxes, little toddler Rachel kicking her plump legs on the back seat, oblivious to the tears rolling down her father's cheeks. 'Just you and me now, kiddo,' she imagined him saying, puffing on one of his Silk Cut (although carefully blowing the smoke out of the window, she hoped). 'You and me against the world, right?'

That was the version of events she'd always been given, anyway. The ballad of Emily: the heartbreaking story that had lain in Rachel's subconscious all these years, an undertow of sadness. Her childhood had been suffused with condolences: sympathetic faces from the teachers, other mums giving her extra cuddles, clasping her to their bosoms whether she wanted to be clasped there or not. (Not, generally.) *Oh dear, you don't have a mummy, you poor little poppet, how awful.*

She remembered finding it confusing as a girl, this expectation that she was to be pitied when in fact she considered her childhood to be an extraordinarily happy one. Sure, having Mum around too would have been even better but Terry was a brilliant dad: kind, funny, practical. He was always the only bloke at ballet rehearsals, watching as she spun and jumped, his old brown shoe tapping time to the piano music in the dusty church hall, his big strong hands clapping louder than anyone else's when the pink-leotard-clad ballerinas made their curtseys at the end. The other mothers were kind to him, respectful, although sometimes she noticed one or another leaning a little too close, a friendly hand on the arm. *I don't know how you do it, Terry, I really don't.* But do it he had – and well, too. He taught her to ride a bike and make scrambled eggs and bowl a cricket ball, and they had muddled along together perfectly fine until she was nine, and Wendy came along. And that, of course, was when everything had changed.

Chapter Eleven

'Oh my goodness. She's still not *back*? I did wonder when I saw the car wasn't there this morning but I just assumed . . . Oh gosh. Come in. Come *in*!'

Sara Fortescue looked as if she'd been snipped straight out of *Perfect Wife* magazine, with her spotless white chinos, little pink T-shirt and cork-heeled wedge sandals. She even had a feather duster in her hand as she opened the door wide, ushering Becca to come in.

'What do you think has *happened*?' she went on breathlessly, leading Becca through the house to a spacious, gleaming light-filled kitchen which had a pastel blue plaque on the wall proclaiming this to be 'Mummy's Kitchen'. 'Can I make you a tea or coffee? My goodness, you must be so *worried*. Those poor children! I mean, where could she *be*?'

Becca felt scruffy and unkempt in her sister's clothes and her own smelly trainers beside the fragrant, pristine Sara in her *Ideal Home* kitchen. Every surface sparkled. There was not so much as a crumb to be spotted, even under the toaster.

'I was hoping you might shed some light on the whole thing,' she confessed. 'I don't really know much at all, to be honest.' She sat down at the table, which was covered in a pale blue polka-dot oilcloth, and propped her chin in one hand. 'Being here . . . I mean, it's made me realize that actually I'm a bit out of the loop in terms of my own sister. Stepsister. Where is she even working these days, for starters?'

Sara put the feather duster away in a cupboard and briskly made them coffee, explaining as she did so that Rachel had recently set up her own business. 'She's ever so brave, isn't she? Good for her, I say. I mean, most of the mummies around here – well, we're just mummies and we're happy to stay at home with our children. I certainly wouldn't have the first clue about business matters! But I guess after Lawrence left . . .' She gave a tragic sort of smile. 'Well, the poor thing, between you and me, he hasn't been very generous, by the sound of it. And she was such a career woman, wasn't she? So successful! Goodness, I don't know *how* she managed it, with three children to look after too. Although, well . . . I'm not saying corners were *cut*, exactly, but there were times when I did wonder if the little ones were very *happy*, you know, about going to the childminder and . . .'

Becca gazed at Sara's pink shiny face, her apple cheeks working quite vigorously as she went on and on, her criticism of Rachel thinly wrapped in fake admiration. The glee with which she spoke! Oh, this was definitely a conversation she'd had several times before with the other 'mummies', Becca could tell, picturing them all priggishly harping on about working mothers and neglected children. She felt a pang of sympathy for her sister, having to live opposite this woman and put up with this sort of shit day in, day out. 'I'm sure she's doing her best,' she interrupted pointedly, when Sara paused for breath. 'And they're great kids. They all seem perfectly fine to me.' So jog on, Sara. 'Anyway, about this business of hers. What does she actually do?'

Sara's lips parted slightly and her eyes widened at the tone in Becca's voice. 'Oh, of *course* she does her best! Absolutely! And I wouldn't want you to think for a minute I was saying otherwise. After such an acrimonious split – I mean, you could hear them arguing from *here*, sometimes –'

Yeah, I bet you could, Becca thought. With the windows wide open so you didn't miss a single word of it.

'– No woman could have worked harder than Rachel! I know *I* wouldn't fancy it – three children on my own, especially when Mabel has been so—'

Becca's face hardened and Sara dropped her gaze. 'Well. Things haven't been easy for the family,' she went on. 'But—'

'And the business you mentioned? Rachel's business?' *Can you just answer my damn question without any more of your gossipy little asides, please, you spiteful cow?*

'Yes, I was just coming to that. She's a fitness coach. A personal trainer sort of thing. Very enterprising! She dropped fliers round to all the neighbours the other week. I can show you if you like. Now where did I put it?' She bustled through a door into a utility area, her voice floating out as she searched. 'You're in luck because our recycling doesn't get picked up until tomorrow and they didn't take the paper last week. Here it is!'

She emerged with a printed A5 leaflet between finger and thumb and put it on the table in front of Becca. It showed a yellow sprinting figure against a blue background, with the words CAN I HELP YOU? in big white letters across the top.

CHALLENGE YOURSELF!
REACH YOUR FITNESS GOALS!
ACTIVATE YOUR LIFE!

Want to be fitter, healthier, stronger? Of course you do! But sometimes we all need a bit of help to push ourselves into action. That's where I come in – your new fitness coach. Call me for further details. Let's do this!

Becca thought ruefully of poor Michael Jones, who obviously hadn't read the leaflet past the opening question in his eagerness to be helped, and wondered, had Rachel been there to take the call herself that morning, how she might have responded. Somehow she doubted that Irish-stew-making had been in the forefront of her sister's mind when she'd put the flier together.

Sara's smile was somewhat patronizing as Becca finished reading. 'Of course, round here we're all members of the gym in town, so it's not really my thing,' she said, adding with a titter, 'and I know more than one woman who put it straight in the dustbin before their husbands could read it, if you know what I mean!'

Becca had had enough of this simpering snake. 'No,' she said flatly, her patience spent. 'I don't know what you mean. What *do* you mean?'

'Oh!' Sara blushed. 'Nothing bad, of course. Just that Rachel's a very attractive girl, isn't she, and . . . well, I'm sure she won't be single for long, that's all!'

Becca got to her feet. 'What, so just because she's split up with her husband, everyone thinks she's going to be after theirs? That's a bit pathetic, isn't it? What happened to female solidarity, anyway? Aren't you meant to be her friend?'

Sara's jaw dropped a fraction in surprise but then she pursed her lips. 'Well, I wouldn't exactly call us *friends*,' she said stiffly. 'And I'm not sure I like your tone.' The skin on her face seemed to tauten like a drumskin, her eyes narrowing, but Becca ignored the warning signs and ploughed right on.

'Yeah, well, I'm not sure I like yours either. My sister is *missing*, and all you can do is make snide remarks. I call that rude.' Bristling, Becca stalked through the house, resisting the urge to slap grubby handprints along the immaculate walls as she went. 'I'll let myself out,' she said, and slammed the door.

Once back in Rachel's house, Becca sank down onto the oatmeal stairs, gulping in breaths and trying to calm down. She had the horrible feeling she might just have totally over-reacted and been pretty rude herself into the bargain – to one of Rachel's neighbours, no less. Good start, Becca. Cat-fight in the suburbs klaxon! But come *on*. The woman was absolutely vile! She couldn't wait to dig her claws in and start casting gossipy aspersions. *I wouldn't exactly call us friends*, she had said – well, good, frankly. Bloody right too. Rachel was better off without a friend like that, as far as Becca could see.

She was still holding the flier, she realized, although it was now crumpled in her hand. Smoothing out the paper, she re-read it, feeling a grudging respect towards her sister – a woman who had been beaten down over the last few months, having lost both her husband and, it seemed, her job too. She must have gone through hell – and yet here she was, picking herself up and trying again with these brightly printed ad-verts. *Can I help you?* Good for you, Rach, she thought. Others might have crumbled, but not you, clearly.

In the next moment she experienced a guilty pang that she, by contrast, hadn't been quite so resilient and go-getting in career terms. Three years before, Becca had shared her flat with a friend called Debbie, and the two of them had started a jewellery business together, selling their designs at various markets around the city and at trade fairs. It had been fun and they'd even been quite successful – right until Debbie had fallen in love with a strapping Aussie hunk called Miles, and emigrated with him to Byron Bay. After Debbie had gone, Becca had taken her eye off the ball, and the burgeoning jewellery business had slid to an abrupt halt. Since then, she'd had a stab at making lampshades on commission (total number of commissions received: zero), scented candles (they served as good Christmas presents for family and friends, even if she didn't actually sell very many) and knitted socks (don't ask) until she'd finally given up on any kind of creative career, and ended up with a string of bar and restaurant jobs to show for herself instead. She supposed she'd have to start looking for another one soon.

Walking back into the kitchen, she saw that a light at the base of the telephone was flashing, and the number three was lit in the display – three messages, she thought, lunging for the phone and pressing the Play button with a clammy finger. *Oh, Rachel. Are you okay?*

Message one, a robotic voice announced, followed by a shrill *beep*. 'Hi, this is Adam Holland, it's ten-thirty and I'm wondering where you are. Your mobile seems to be switched off, so . . . Well, hopefully I'll see you in a minute but if not, could you call me, please.' *BEEP*.

Message two, said the machine. 'It's Adam Holland again.

Ten-forty now. Look, I've rearranged a conference call so that I could meet you, so . . . You know, it's not ideal for me to be hanging around here waiting. Bit of a waste of my time. Hope you're on your way.'

Becca pulled a face, still rattled by her encounter with snobby Sara. 'Calm down, love,' she muttered. 'No need to get your knickers in a twist.'

Message three, said the machine, and Becca felt almost certain she knew who it would be. 'Adam Holland again,' came the man's curt, impatient voice once more. 'I'm not very impressed with this. We agreed ten-thirty this morning and you're not here. It's not exactly confidence-inspiring, is it? So I guess I'll just go for a run myself, then. Thanks for nothing.'

'Oh boo-hoo, Adam,' Becca said sarcastically to the empty room. 'You big cry-baby.' But then she remembered that this must be connected to her sister's fledgling business, Rachel's all-new attempt to stand on her own two feet. And how many customers did she even have at the moment anyway? What if he was one of her first clients – whom she was about to lose almost at once?

Becca hesitated. She didn't like the sound of this self-important Adam Holland twerp one bit, but if her sister was receiving red utility bills, she probably needed every job she could get, idiot customers or not. Maybe Becca could smooth things over in the meantime.

She pressed in the code to find the last number received and dialled. After three rings, the man himself answered, sounding somewhat out of breath. 'Hello?'

'Hello, is that Adam? I'm Rachel Jackson's sister, Becca. I'm so sorry about the mix-up this morning, that shouldn't have happened. Unfortunately, Rachel—' She racked her brain, trying to come up with something plausible. 'Rachel is unwell right now. She asked me to ring you first thing, and I'm afraid I've only just got her message.' Crossing her fingers as she spoke, she found herself remembering how badly it had gone last time she tried telling such fibs, to her now ex-boss, Jeff at the pub. Please let Adam Holland be more gullible, she thought.

'Right,' he said, not sounding very happy. 'Well, how about tomorrow, then? Will she be better by then? I could rejig a meeting . . . let me see.' Becca could hear him clicking through something on the phone, and then he was back on the line, sounding terrifyingly authoritative. 'I could do ten o'clock tomorrow morning instead?'

Becca hesitated. What was she supposed to say? *The thing is, Adam, my sister has disappeared and nobody knows where she is. Fun times!* 'Er . . .' she mumbled, stalling while she tried to think. Surely Rachel would be back tomorrow? She had to be! In which case, Becca could take a punt on her being free for this appointment. 'Er . . . hopefully, yes,' she said uncertainly in the end.

'Hopefully yes?' Adam parroted back at her. He sounded impatient. 'Does that mean yes or no? Look, I'm really busy. I don't have time for *hopefully yes.*'

'Yes, then. *Yes*. All right?' Becca blurted out. 'Tomorrow, at ten. That's fine.' And then, because the man seemed so bossy and demanding, she found herself trying to appease him by saying impulsively, 'And if by any chance Rachel *isn't* completely fighting fit, then I'll come along to do the session myself. One of us will be there. Okay?'

Adam sounded suspicious but agreed reluctantly, and they went on to make arrangements. Afterwards, Becca put the phone down feeling as if she had made a terrible mistake. Why had she gone and said that? She knew nothing about fitness coaching. If Rachel was still missing and she had to turn up tomorrow as promised, this guy would take one look at her lardy unfit self and laugh her all the way into the nearest gym. But what else could she do? She could hardly bin off all her sister's clients, especially when he'd made a point of telling her, at the end of the call, that he had signed up for a six-week intensive programme with Rachel, and already handed over the money.

Becca gazed at the phone wretchedly, wishing someone would just ring and put her out of her misery. Rachel herself, preferably, with the good news that she was on her way home. *You'll never believe what happened!*

But there was nothing except the gentle humming of

the fridge to break the silence, and then a text from Wendy showing the full English breakfast she was presumably tucking in to. *Well, I AM on holiday*, the text read unapologetically. *Right?*

Becca could feel the beginning of a serious panic starting to grip her. She wasn't sure there were any reasonable explanations or good outcomes left as to what had happened to Rachel, and she was running out of options. Where *was* she? How much longer would they have to wait for news? The prospect of seeing the children's hopeful faces after school – *Is she back? Is she home?* – and having to shake her head regretfully made her feel sick.

She thought back to the last few times she'd seen her stepsister and realized they'd always been surrounded by lots of other people. They'd barely exchanged more than a few sentences at the funeral, and then the Christmas before in Birmingham had been noisy and busy, a frenzy of present-unwrapping, the children rushing in and out of rooms trying to snaffle as much chocolate as was possible. Rachel was annoyed with her, that was right, because Becca had given the children Nerf guns and massive German selection boxes she'd picked up for a bargain in Aldi. Okay, so even as she had been at the check-out, handing over the money for them, she'd known it would wind her sister up; but come on, the kids had fallen on their gifts like wolves. And it was Christmas!

Of course Rachel had gone on to get her back, though, by making snide dig after dig about Becca's boyfriend, who was also there. Who had she even been with that Christmas? Dazza the sexy mechanic? No, wait, maybe it was Jed, all floppy hair and doe eyes, but with very little brain. Yes, it *was* Jed, because she remembered Rachel sniggering about him in the kitchen to their dad. *Gorgeous but thick – like a Labrador*, she'd said. *Spiteful cow*, Becca had thought at the time. Just because she was smug and settled down while Becca was young and carefree and got to go around having fun with lots of lovely men. She had reacted by getting plastered on Baileys after that, and made a point of snogging Jed loudly and sloppily whenever she was in her sister's presence. *So what if he's thick? I'm getting loads here. Are you?*

Propping her chin in her hand as she gazed out of the back window, she recalled how Meredith had been surprised to discover that Becca even *had* a sister. 'I can't believe you've never even *mentioned* her,' she'd cried. 'And I've lived with you – what, nearly a year? Have you really not seen her that whole time?'

No, she really had not. It had felt bad to see Meredith's shocked face, that look in her eyes that said, *What is wrong with you?*

Guilt pierced Becca. Maybe she should have tried harder to stay in touch, to cling on to the slender thread of relationship that had been left after the funeral. Maybe the two of them could have been less gladiatorial in how they went about things; met halfway and laughed about their differences, rather than locking in endless combat. Because now, here she was on her own in Rachel's house, with all these unanswered questions and not a clue what to do next. 'I *will* try harder,' she said aloud, into the empty room. 'I promise I will, if you just come back now, all right?' Her voice cracked on the words. '*Please*, Rach. You're scaring me. What's happened?'

Chapter Twelve

Rachel came round after her operation feeling groggy and nauseous. *Still alive*, was her first woozy thought as she registered the noises of the recovery room: the quiet beeping from monitors, nurses soothing patients in low voices, the occasional *bang-swish* of doors opening, beds wheeling along nearby. *Still alive.*

Some careful probing of her tongue revealed that her mouth had been wired into a fixed position, and that there were stitches in her gums as well as in a neat line down her chin where it had split open. Her right wrist was now encased in smooth new plaster and felt heavy and sore, and there were, according to the consultant, who came to inform her that the procedure had been successful, umpteen small metal plates and screws keeping her jaw bolted together. 'Airport security are going to *love* you,' he joked, and she managed a wan smile for all of two seconds before she realized how painful it was to make any kind of facial movement.

This must have been how Frankenstein's monster felt

when first jolted into life, she thought, only with blood in the mouth and cracked swollen lips. *Hello, world. You feel . . . uncomfortable.*

The doctors had given her industrial-strength painkillers to keep the worst of the agony at bay and an ice pack to reduce the swelling, but a dull ache still throbbed through her jaw, and she was queasy from the anaesthetic. She swallowed experimentally, and winced at how raw her throat felt. 'I hope you like soup,' the blonde-haired nurse said, walking alongside her bed as a porter eventually wheeled her back to the ward. 'You'll have to stick to a liquid diet for six weeks, I'm afraid. No chewing allowed. But you can whizz up all sorts in a blender, it's not as bad as it sounds.'

Rachel thought longingly of how she'd always loved biting into a crisp apple, chowing down on a juicy steak, crunching through a baguette, and gave a little whimper. Six weeks without proper food? She didn't even like soup.

'By the way,' the nurse said when they reached the ward and the bed was finally wheeled to a stop, 'I'm sorry, love, but that phone number you gave me was the wrong one. I tried a couple of times in case I'd made a mistake but it just went through to some sports company, it wasn't a home number.'

Rachel's breath caught in her throat. Oh God. What a fool! Had she really given them the GoActive number? What did it say about her, that that had been the first number to float into her consciousness? *You've always been married to your work*, Lawrence had snapped at her more than once, when things started getting nasty. *You love that place more than your own sodding family!*

Of course I don't, she'd cried in reply – but maybe there had been some truth in his words after all. Why else would her old office number spring to mind before any others?

'Oh, and that's the other thing,' the nurse was saying, peering at her notes. 'I've got down here that you live in Birmingham, but the number you gave me was a Hereford one.'

Hereford. That was it. *Yes*. And just like that, it was all back in her head: her beautiful house, the cathedral, the river, the surrounding countryside. They had bought the house when she was pregnant with Scarlet, deciding to make the move out of London, where they'd lived for their first few married years. Hereford, that was right: because it was between Dad's place in Birmingham, and the cottage Lawrence's parents had just moved to in Wales. Another piece in the jigsaw.

'Hereford,' she repeated, her voice thick and slow-sounding. 'That's where I live.'

'Fantastic,' the nurse said. 'I'll pass that on to the police. They've been in touch again, wanting to know when you can give a statement so they can help us track down your details if need be. Unless you can remember anything else?'

Rachel thought for a moment, testing herself. Despite her grogginess, her mind seemed to have sharpened up since the operation. 'I can remember,' she said haltingly, feeling like a ventriloquist now that she could no longer move her mouth, and went on to recite what she now felt certain was her correct phone number. At last! In fact, she could remember all sorts of things, she realized: birthdays and the children's shoe sizes and the fact that she was supposed to have reminded Mabel about her geography exam. Was that today? She leaned back on her pillow, aching to be with them again.

'When can I go?' she mumbled. It was really hard trying to speak with your jaw effectively clamped in place. She was reminded of Mabel as a stubborn toddler, when Rachel had tried to coax her into eating more. 'Here's a letter for Grandad to go in the postbox!' she had cooed, pushing a forkful of mashed potato towards her daughter's lips.

'Postbox closed,' Mabel had replied doggedly without opening her mouth, eyes glittering with mutiny. 'Postbox CLOSED.'

'When can you go home, love?' the nurse repeated back at her, and pursed her lips. 'I think they'll want to keep an eye on you for a few days longer yet, I'm afraid. Just because you've had quite a nasty injury and you're concussed. Obviously when the time comes you'll need another adult to collect you and keep an eye on you for at least twenty-four hours. Is there someone at home who could do that?'

Rachel's face burned. Someone at home to look after her? Not any more, she thought. Lawrence had gone, of course, and some of her friends had reacted very oddly to the break-up, silently dropping her from their social circle as if being a single mother was the equivalent of being a leper. One mum at the school had even laughed that they would be keeping their husbands on a short leash while Rachel was single – 'Not that we don't trust *you*, it's them we're suspicious of,' she'd said when Rachel instinctively took a step back, stung.

'Um . . . Not really,' she confessed to the nurse.

'Okay, not to worry, leave it with me,' the nurse said, patting Rachel's arm. 'Let me try this number for you now, all right? I'll be back in a little while to let you know how I get on, but until then, you just close your eyes and rest. Try and sleep.'

Rachel reached up gingerly to touch the cold metal grid in her mouth as the nurse bustled away. The other mums at school needn't worry now about their philandering husbands lining up with their tongues hanging out at least, she thought miserably. Not when she must look part cyberwoman, stitched up and scarred. Lawrence, too, would probably smirk when he next saw her. Oh *dear*, she imagined him drawling. *Not so pretty are we now, eh, Princess? Not so pleased with ourselves any more, am I right?*

Rachel and Lawrence had met at a black-tie event in London when she was twenty-three. It was a cliché, yes, but their eyes really had met across a crowded room and she'd felt dizzy and all of a flutter for several long breath-held moments, until he strode confidently over and asked her to dance. Whirling around the dance floor together, his hand firm on her back, she'd had a strange sensation, as if she could see right into the future, glimpsing snatches of a possible life with him. The wedding. The honeymoon. The house . . . It was as if it was all there for the taking, if she wanted – and in that moment she was tempted. Wouldn't anyone have been? He was charming and self-assured, handsome with his broad shoulders and swept-back dark hair. He had a strong face, was a good dancer, and the way he looked at her so intently made her insides feel as if they were sweetly dissolving. The only hint of things to come was later on, when he bought her a cocktail and asked her if she had a boyfriend. 'Good,' he'd replied when she'd answered no, 'because I'd have had to kill him.'

Obviously, he was joking, but as time went by, she realized there was a deep seam of jealousy that ran through Lawrence. His jaw clenched if he thought another man was looking at her. His fist tightened if she mentioned previous boyfriends. Once he went into a cold, furious sulk for three solid days when he heard her laughing with her friends about how they all had pathetic crushes on George Clooney. Even on their wedding day – the day when she'd stood there in front of all their friends and family and made her vows of love and commitment to him – he was proprietorial, keeping one hand on her at all times, as if daring any other bloke to try anything. It was only because he loved her, she told herself each time, but all the same, she found herself learning to modify her own behaviour in the hope of pre-empting another stony-eyed meltdown.

'I think it's quite sexy when a husband goes all jealous and territorial,' another mum from school, Karen, had sighed one evening. There was a group of them out together for Karen's birthday drinks and Rachel had got tipsy and haltingly confessed to Lawrence's behaviour. 'Pete probably wouldn't even notice if I flashed my tits at the postman.'

'Nor Andrew,' agreed Diane, who was married to a stockbroker and had once admitted to loving her horses and dogs more than him. 'I'd have to be practically straddling another man on the living-room floor to drag Andrew's attention away from the Ashes.'

They'd all laughed. 'Neal, too,' Jo said, her glittery eyeshadow winking under the bright lights as she leaned forward. 'I mean – it's great to be trusting but sometimes . . .' She had lowered her voice conspiratorially. 'I kind of wish he'd be a bit more possessive, to be honest. Growl under his breath and go full caveman when I mention another bloke's name. At least it would show he *cared*.'

No, Rachel had thought, sliding into drunken gloom, it wouldn't. It would show he was insecure and unpredictable. And you'd soon get ground down by the walking on eggshells too. God knows she had.

Still, not any more, at least. Lawrence had gone now, moved on, somehow escaping a hefty fine and possibly prison after poor Craig Elliot decided not to press charges, and was now being waited on hand and foot by his old dragon of a mother in her draughty Builth Wells house, which smelled of camphor and lavender bags – and now, presumably, of Harvey their golden retriever, too. (She should never have agreed to let him take the dog. *You said WHAT?* Scarlet had shrieked, horror-struck at the announcement.)

'Good news!' The nurse was back already, a cheerful smile on her face. 'You were right second time. I called home and spoke to your sister – Rebecca, is it?'

Rachel gulped – or at least she would have done if her jaws hadn't been wired so tightly together. Had she heard that right? 'Becca?' she croaked in disbelief.

'Yes, she was really pleased to hear that you were safe, and going to be okay. She said to tell you that the children are all fine, and that she'll come and pick you up whenever you're ready to go home; I told her it would probably be after the weekend.' The nurse's nose wrinkled as she smiled again. 'So that's nice, isn't it? All's well that ends well, as they say.'

Rachel just about remembered her manners in time to say a strangled 'Thank you', but her mind was whirling. Sara must have got hold of Becca somehow, she guessed, when she hadn't made it back in time for the children yesterday. Oh God. Of all the people. No, she wasn't sure this was 'good news' at all. Her stepsister was trouble, plain and simple; not to be trusted. And after what she'd done with Lawrence, she was never to be forgiven either.

Chapter Thirteen

Becca burst into noisy tears of relief as soon as the Mancunian nurse told her that Rachel was with them, that she'd just undergone an operation but was doing well, given the circumstances, and could hopefully come home in a few days. 'Thank you,' Becca sobbed, emotion pouring from her. 'Oh my God, I've been so worried, thank you so much, that's wonderful. And of course I'll let the children know, absolutely. Yes, I can pick her up next week, no problem.'

Even after she put the phone down, the tears kept coming, the anxiety she'd felt catching up with her in a huge wave, along with the lack of sleep the night before. Thank goodness, she thought, wiping her eyes and hiccupping as she eventually calmed down. Thank goodness, she would be able to look the children in the eyes that very afternoon and say, 'It's all going to be okay. Mum's safe and coming home soon.'

She blew her nose and heaved a deep, shuddering breath. Rachel was somewhat battered about, according to the nurse, and would need a bit of TLC. Her bag had been snatched, which was why they hadn't been able to identify her immediately, and she was concussed too. Poor Rachel, it all sounded horrible. But she was alive, that was the main thing, Becca reminded herself. Alive and recovering. Soon she'd be back here, in her home, and then everything could return to normal.

Pulling herself together, she fired off a few texts, wanting to spread the good news to everyone else. First on her list was Mabel.

Just heard – your mum is ok. Up in Manchester after bad fall, broke wrist and jaw but WILL BE FINE and home in few days. ☺ xxx PS Come home straight after school btw. No snogging with boyf on my watch. Otherwise will grass you up. Got it??!

Next she called the primary school and spoke to a nice lady in the office – definitely not the arsey secretary from earlier, thank God – who promised her yes of course, she could let Scarlet and Luke know that Mum was all right, she'd do that right away. Was there anything that the school – the woman paused tactfully – should know about?

'No,' Becca assured her firmly. There would be enough gossiping about Rachel, thanks to the likes of that awful Sara over the road, no doubt. She would not fan the flames any higher. 'Everything's fine.'

Her phone buzzed with a new text as she ended the call to the school. It was from Mabel.

Manchester??? Er . . . WTF?!

Hmmm, thought Becca, frowning. Her niece had a point. Somehow, in her huge surge of relief, that particular detail had escaped her attention. Why had Rachel gone to Manchester in the first place? There was the Didsbury Library site that she'd visited online, but Becca had no clue what that could be about. And it was odd that she hadn't mentioned details of the trip to Sara, or the rest of the family, either.

Turning the matter over in her brain, she wondered if there was a mystery attached to it or not. Their dad had been from that neck of the woods, of course; maybe it was some kind of grief-inspired pilgrimage. Well, she'd find out next week anyway, she supposed.

Then she sent one more text.

Meredith! Huge dramas in the shire but think all okay now.
Prob will be here a few days though, just fyi x

A reply came back two minutes later.

Sounds alarming! Hope everyone all right. PS *selfishly* BUT WHAT ABOUT MY DIADEM?? Kidding. I'll sort something out. x

Shit. The diadem – or crown, if you were a normal person – was for a medieval banquet Meredith was attending on Saturday night, a big do out in Rutland, and she'd been planning her outfit for weeks. Having worked her way up through various lowly roles within the historical re-enactment society – serving wench, peasant, etc. – Meredith had been given the honour of dressing as one of the princesses on this occasion. Oh yes. This was a big deal, all right, and Becca had been quite chuffed when her flatmate had asked for her help with her jewellery. It would be the first time she had actually unearthed the soldering iron and silversmithing kit she had stashed in the cupboard since the heady days of her and Debbie's business empire. *And* Meredith had said she'd pay Becca's share of the gas bill in exchange. Now that she'd lost her job, she could kind of do with the financial help.

Soz – forgot. Let me see what I can do. Will come back if I can, she typed, wondering if now was the right time to tell Lawrence what was going on. She probably should have filled him in from the start, let's face it. Maybe he could look after the children for the weekend? She would check in with Mabel first, she decided, and gave a yawn. God, she was worn out after so much emotional tumult. Maybe she would just have a little snooze, she decided, before she had to pick up the children. Just for five minutes.

With that excellent idea, she stretched out on the sofa and shut her eyes.

'Is it true? Is it true?' cried Luke, barrelling straight into Becca, waiting in the busy playground amidst a sea of parents and crowds of children clutching paintings and lunchboxes and strange wonky constructions of egg-boxes and straws. He had practically exploded from the school building in his haste to get to her. 'Is Mum back? Is she okay?'

Becca hugged him. She was sweaty and unkempt from an enforced jog the entire way to school, having fallen into a deep sleep on Rachel's sofa, woken only by the sound of the local newspaper dropping through the letterbox. 'Mum's going to be absolutely fine and she'll be back next week,' she said, feeling her nephew go limp in her arms with relief, before he recovered himself and jigged about joyously. Scarlet too came out of the building smiling, and hugged Becca very tightly. 'We had to go and see Mrs Jenkins – she's the head-teacher – and she told us about Mum,' she said. 'And she let us have one of her biscuits and it was really bloody nice.'

The mention of biscuits prompted a new question from Luke. 'Did you bring a snack? Mum always brings a snack.'

'Oh,' said Becca, just as she caught sight of Sara Fortescue across the playground. Of course Sara was producing a Tupperware container with what looked like carrot sticks and grapes for her children, while all that was in Becca's bag was her phone and Rachel's spare door keys, and a ton of junk she had been meaning to clear out for the last six months. Hold on a second, though, she might have . . .

She rummaged hopefully and brought out her emergency Snickers bar, slightly squashed and battered in appearance but no doubt still perfectly delicious. 'Ta-dah!' she said triumphantly, holding it aloft.

'Chocolate!' Luke cheered, looking as if he couldn't believe his luck.

'Luke shouldn't have that,' Scarlet said primly as Becca tore open the wrapper and broke the bar in half.

'Oh, a bit of chocolate won't do any harm,' Becca replied, handing them a gooey portion each and smiling as Luke bit into his with gusto. Honestly, Rachel had really *brainwashed* Scarlet with this healthy food obsession; it was ridiculous. The quickest way to give someone an eating disorder. 'And anyway—'

'No, because he has a nut allergy,' Scarlet said, trying to snatch it from him. 'Luke! Spit it out. Now!'

Oh Christ. Oh no. *Shit!* 'Luke, I'm sorry,' Becca gulped, as he spat the wet chocolate onto the ground. A crowd was gathering. *Let's all gawp at the failure aunty, for a lesson on how not to look after small children.* 'What do I do? What do I do?' she panicked.

Luke started to cry. 'My mouth feels funny,' he said.

'We need the EpiPen. Mrs Keyes has one. This way,' Scarlet said urgently, dragging her brother along. 'Don't worry, Luke.'

'Take him to the office,' a nearby mum called.

'Should we ring for an ambulance?' asked another.

Becca rushed after Scarlet and Luke, feeling absolutely awful – frightened for her nephew's wellbeing and racked with guilt at her own casual irresponsibility. Scarlet had even said the words, *Luke shouldn't have that,* and she'd completely disregarded her. Useless, Becca. Useless! 'We need an EpiPen,' she said as they burst into the reception area. Oh great. And wouldn't you just know it, Mrs Keyes turned out to be the secretary she'd encountered earlier, the one who looked as if she had a poker up her jacksie. There was karma for you. 'Have you got an EpiPen for Luke? Please?'

Mercifully, Mrs Keyes knew exactly what to do. Within a minute she'd opened a medicine cabinet, whipped out an EpiPen and jabbed it into Luke's leg with devastating efficiency. Head bowed, an arm around Luke, who was still sobbing, Becca vowed there and then that she would never slag off school secretaries again. This one had turned out to be an utter hero.

'I am so sorry,' she said, struggling not to start sobbing herself. 'I'm such an idiot, Luke, that was all my fault. And thank you, Mrs – Mrs Keyes, was it? – for being so brilliant and coming to our rescue.' Her voice shook. 'I'm officially the worst aunty ever.'

Perhaps Mrs Keyes had got wind of the news that Rachel was in hospital, or perhaps saving a small boy's life was enough to defrost her icy demeanour. Perhaps she'd even been a crap aunty herself once upon a time. Whatever the reason, she chose to respond with benevolence rather than criticism, thank goodness. 'That's quite all right. I'm glad I was here to help. Luke, would you like one of my lollipops? You were ever so brave.'

'Should we . . . I mean, will he be all right?' Becca asked tentatively as Luke nodded, tears still clinging to his dark lashes. 'Do I need to take him to A&E or anything to get checked over, or . . .?' She pressed her lips together, shock still thudding through her. Things could have gone so dreadfully wrong.

'It's probably best to,' Mrs Keyes said, picking up her handbag and pulling out some car keys. 'I'll drive you.'

It was like a bad dream as they drove the short distance to the hospital and got out at the A&E entrance, thanking Mrs Keyes for her help, before hurrying inside. Shock and guilt tortured Becca in equal measures. How could she have been so thick? *Wake up, idiot! Pay attention! Children's lives in your hands, here!* She wasn't up to the job, simple as that. How did *anyone* manage to be up to the job of looking after kids all day, every day? It was terrifying!

Will be a bit late home with S and L, she texted Mabel faux-breezily, feeling like a hypocrite. Will be a bit late home because I nearly killed your brother was more like it, but perhaps not the best thing to say in a text. *Hope you had a good day. See you soon xxx*

The only crumb of comfort was that Luke and Scarlet seemed to have been here, done this, a number of times before. Once inside the children's waiting area they both made a beeline for a big doll's house in the corner, as if it was a familiar friend by now, and one of the nurses even greeted them by name. So there had obviously been other occasions of accidental nut ingestion before this. Other fuck-ups, hopefully by Rachel, if that wasn't too horrible a thing to think. Even so, she was dreading having to own up to her sister what had happened. *You did what? You gave him what?!* Hmm, maybe she'd save that confession for when Rachel was feeling much better. Like in six months' time, or something; preferably when Becca was a safe distance away.

'Don't beat yourself up about it,' the doctor said, when Luke was finally looked over. She was younger than Becca, tanned and hearty-looking, as if she'd never made a mistake in her life, but there was a kind sincerity about her that was reassuring. 'It happens all the time. You aren't the first person and you certainly won't be the last. The main thing is that you acted quickly, you did all the right things, and young Luke here seems absolutely fine now. Okay?'

Becca hung her head, not wanting to admit that actually it had been Scarlet and Mrs Keyes who'd done all the right things, not her. She'd take it as a lucky escape, though, and chalk it up to experience. And from now on, she would keep all Snickers bars for herself. 'Thanks,' she said shakily, giving Luke a cuddle. 'Let's go home.'

Back at the house, Becca was relieved to see Mabel had arrived home sans boyfriend – although moments later she spotted what was most definitely a livid red love bite on her niece's pale neck. Lovely. But did she have the energy to have a go at her for it? Not today. No. She looked the other way instead and pretended to be fussing around with glasses of orange squash for everyone. The younger two went out into the garden, where Luke began bouncing about on the trampoline in a satisfyingly not-dying sort of way, while Mabel perched on the kitchen table and let her school shoes drop to the floor. 'So what the hell is Mum doing in Manchester, anyway?' she asked.

God, yes. With all the drama, Becca had clean forgotten that particular mystery. 'Manchester? I was going to ask you the same,' she replied. 'Has your mum got friends there, or . . . Some business thing going on?' She hesitated, not wanting to admit she'd been snooping on the laptop. 'Has she ever mentioned Didsbury Library to you?'

Mabel looked blank. 'Nope,' she said, twisting a skull bracelet around her wrist. 'And it can't be a business thing, anyway. Didn't you hear? She lost her job last year. Well. Dad kind of fucked it all up, by the sound of things.' She gave Becca a sidelong glance, as if waiting to be told off for her bad language, then went on. 'I've been trying to think all afternoon why she would be there. A meeting, she told us yesterday, like it was no big deal. But her "business", as you call it – I mean, it's just her persuading unfit people to go jogging around the park, that sort of thing. She wouldn't be going to *Manchester* for it.'

Becca frowned, none the wiser. 'Well,' she said eventually, opening the fridge and wondering what to cook for tea, 'I guess we'll find out when she's back, won't we? And in the meantime, we really should let your dad know what's going on. Do you have a number for him?'

Mabel flipped through her phone and passed it over with the contact details on screen. 'We're going to Welsh Grandma's tomorrow anyway,' she said with a shrug. 'It's his weekend to have us, so you could always wait until then.'

But Becca had made enough mistakes with the Jacksons for one day. Tempting though it was to avoid her brother-in-law for another twenty-four hours, she decided to get it over with. 'I'll give him a call,' she said decisively, taking a deep breath.

It had been a long day to end all long days and that evening, once the children were fed, showered and finally in bed, Becca opened the cheapest-looking bottle of wine in her sister's collection, poured herself a massive glass and went to collapse in a deckchair in the garden. *And relax.* God, that felt good. The wine was cold and refreshing, the grass cool and silky beneath her bare toes, and the evening air was scented by a nearby flowering lilac and the velvety white roses in full bloom. If she had a garden like this, Becca vowed, she'd never watch a single thing on television ever again; she'd be out here every evening, breathing out the cares of the day and marvelling at the peace and quiet, watching how the colours in the sky slipped from blue to peach to gold.

She shut her eyes and leaned back, listening to the gentle pattering of a garden sprinkler nearby, a faint snatch of music through a neighbouring window, the wind whispering in the leafy trees. It seemed as if she'd been in Hereford a lot longer than a single day and night, somehow. This time tomorrow, the children would be off in the care of Lawrence and their grandma, and she'd be back in her real life for the weekend. It was so long since she'd had a Friday night without working in the pub that she wasn't sure what she would do with herself.

Lawrence had been quite curt on the phone, surprised and almost seeming suspicious to hear from her at first, before going on to bark a load of questions down the line. 'She's what? In Manchester? Well, what the hell was she doing up there?' Like it was Rachel's fault she'd ended up in hospital, like there was something fishy about the whole affair. 'Are the children all right? Should I come over?'

Ugh, no, that was the last thing she wanted. She told him she was fine to look after them tomorrow, and she gathered he was having them for the weekend anyway. She decided not to mention the fact that they too had ended up in A&E that afternoon as she said goodbye. Job done.

Tiredness spread through her as the sun finally slid below the horizon and the garden was bathed in cool shadows. She drained the rest of her glass and folded the deckchair, locked the back door and checked that all the children were asleep (yes) and then double-checked that Luke was definitely still breathing (yes). Then, with a silent promise to wash all the bed linen the next day, she curled up for the night in Rachel's huge comfortable bed and fell fast asleep within seconds.

Chapter Fourteen

Rachel lay in her hospital bed, unable to sleep with the pain still ever-present along her jaw. For some reason, she found herself thinking about how it had all started, the day they first met Wendy.

Ironically, Rachel was the one who'd caused it to happen, who brought them together in the first place. If only she hadn't been such a brat about wanting a special bakery birthday cake, like her two best friends, then everything might have been different. But no, Julia Dobbs had had a cake in the shape of a rabbit with marshmallow teeth for her recent birthday party, and Lorraine Browning a Kermit cake with amazing lurid green fondant icing – and Rachel was desperate to keep up. 'Please,' she had begged her father, putting her palms together in a little prayer. 'Please, Dad, can I?'

Terry was hopeless in the kitchen (somehow the two of them had survived on Fray Bentos meatballs and powdery Angel Delight this far), and Rachel knew he was always trying to make it up to her on the Not Having a Mum front, so he wasn't too hard to persuade once she turned the tears on. So off they went to the All You Knead bakery on the high street, breathing in the heavenly scents of cake, gingerbread and sausage rolls, neither of them suspecting that everything was about to change.

'We'd like a cake in the shape of ballet shoes, please,' Dad had said to the bakery lady. 'For next Friday. It's my daughter's tenth birthday.'

The lady behind the counter had a cloud of curly auburn hair and a smudge of flour on her cheek. Even now, Rachel could remember the way she had smiled at Terry's words. 'Your birthday? Well, fancy that,' she said. 'It's my birthday on Friday too.' Her nose gave a funny little crinkle as she directed her gaze at Rachel. 'I love the way people always set off fireworks on our birthday, don't you?'

It was as simple as that. A coincidence, a shared bonfire-night birthday, a cake order, a glint in Terry's eye. The lady had tried to talk to Rachel – 'So you're a ballet dancer, are you? Go on, give us a twirl!' – but she had felt shy, leaning her head against Terry's waist, not wanting to dance there on the bakery floor. If she had known what was to happen, of course, she'd have dragged him right out of the shop. She'd have said, *Do you know what, I'm happy with an ordinary cake after all, Dad, one from the Co-op is fine. Come on, let's go.*

Too late for that, though. Terry put down a deposit and the lady – Wendy – gave him a written receipt. 'It'll be ready to collect on Friday morning,' she had said, with a twinkly smile.

'Friday morning,' Terry replied shyly. 'Well, I'll be sure to come back then.' He had cleared his throat, sounding unusually awkward. 'Will you . . . I don't suppose you'll be working yourself that day, seeing as it's your birthday too?'

Wendy blushed, her cheeks turning as pink as her frosted lipstick. 'Oh, I'll be here,' she said. 'I'll look forward to seeing you then.'

And so the wheels were put in motion. Terry said no more about it to Rachel, but as she went up to bed that night she heard him talking to Pete, his friend, who'd dropped by. 'She was a very attractive woman,' he'd said, cracking open a can of Guinness. 'And it's been a while.'

A shiver went down Rachel's spine as she crept into bed a few minutes later, and she tucked her knees up tight inside her nightie, a sixth sense twanging a warning. *Danger, danger.* But there was no turning back. The date was set, their paths converging. *A very attractive woman.*

By dint of further eavesdropping on her dad and Pete that weekend, Rachel learned that Terry had taken a bunch of flowers along when he went to collect the cake, and suggested he and Wendy meet up for coffee sometime. The following week, Sonia, the lady next door, was roped in to babysit while Dad and Wendy went out for scampi and chips and a knickerbocker glory at the Harvester. And then, almost before Rachel knew it, the happy little Me-and-Dad twosome was no more, and she was being fitted for a bridesmaid dress in apple-green taffeta (she had hated the colour ever since). 'And guess what?' Dad had told her, beaming. 'Wendy's got a little girl too – Rebecca – so you're going to have a sister!'

'Oh,' Rachel had said uncertainly. Her friend Julia had a little sister – Tracey, who was always whingeing and telling tales and interrupting their games. She wasn't sure she wanted a new sister, *or* a stepmother. Why couldn't things just stay as they were?

Everyone made such a fuss at the wedding – a new mummy! Wasn't it exciting? What a lucky girl she was! – and to be fair, Rachel enjoyed the dancing and the buffet and being given a special silver bangle as a bridesmaid present. But then all of a sudden there was a big clamour and Dad and Wendy were setting off on their honeymoon, without her. It felt wrong to be standing in the crush of people, hardly able to see as the two of them drove away in Dad's car. Someone had tied tin cans to the back, and everyone was laughing as they rattled along the street. 'Don't worry, chick,' Sonia Next Door had said, putting an arm around her. 'You stick with me. They'll be back in no time.'

As it happened, Sonia's words turned out to be true. Dad and Wendy *were* back sooner than expected – the very next day, in fact. Unfortunately for Rachel, though, their early return was for all the wrong reasons.

'Hello there, is everything okay?' a nurse said just then, drawing back the curtains around Rachel's bed and seeing that she was still awake. Rachel hadn't even realized she'd been crying again until the nurse leaned over her and gently dabbed the tears away with a tissue. 'Can I get you anything? Some water? Are you in pain?'

This nurse was older and more matronly than the others she'd seen, with short, silver-flecked hair and kind, brown eyes. Somebody's mum, Rachel guessed as the woman carried out her checks and topped up Rachel's pain relief; somebody's grandma, even. How she wished she had a mum to lean against right now! A mum to smooth back her hair and hold a glass of water to her lips, who would promise that everything would be okay!

'Try to sleep,' the nurse said, straightening the bed covers and giving Rachel's shoulder a friendly pat. 'That's it, eyes closed. You've had a rough time of it, haven't you, love? But it'll all seem better in the morning. These things always do.'

'Thank you,' Rachel mumbled. She lay still until she heard the curtain being swished back and the nurse move on to her next patient. *It'll all seem better in the morning*, she repeated to herself. She really hoped so.

Chapter Fifteen

The following morning, Becca felt as if she knew the week-day drill a little better, even remembering that Scarlet had her early violin lesson that day. Breakfast, school uniform, packed lunches, out the door, hugs goodbye at the school gates . . . and then BREATHE. *Go, Becca,* she thought, mentally high-fiving herself for this feat of wits and stamina. *Gold star for you.* Today was going to be a better day, oh yes.

It was only on returning to the house that she remembered with a horrible lurch her rash promise of the day before to Rachel's client Adam, the grumpy man who'd left all those cross phone messages. *Oh shit.* Shit, shit, shit. She must have been insane, offering to stand in for her sister like that. Why had she said such a foolish thing? And why, she thought, cursing, couldn't she find the scrap of paper on which she'd scribbled down his sodding number, so that she could call him back and cancel? She should at least have mentioned the fact that she was in no way a qualified fitness instructor yesterday; she definitely should have offered him a refund, or a huge discount.

At the time she'd just assumed that Rachel would be back and able to take up all her appointments as usual. But no.

Ten o'clock, she'd said, and it was a quarter to nine now. It was almost laughable how ill-prepared she was to give any human being an actual fitness session. She and Debbie had once owned a Davina McCall DVD, bought by one of them in a burst of January virtuousness, to which they'd jumped around a few times before deciding that they'd rather go to the pub instead. Back further still, when she'd been in her early twenties, her mum had begged her to go along to some aerobics classes with her, and she vaguely remembered doing box steps and grapevines and sweaty star jumps in a chalk-smelling church hall. But if this Adam bloke was half as fierce as he sounded, he would laugh in her face if she started demonstrating Davina moves or box steps in front of him.

Her cheeks burned at the thought, and she wished more than ever that she hadn't blurted out her offer so stupidly. Bigmouth strikes again. When would she learn to think first, speak second?

Sod it, though: she was just going to have to go through with it, having failed to track down the elusive phone number. She couldn't have him stood up again, and then endure another tirade of moaning. He would sack Rachel and demand his money back, and that would be a client lost. Becca had already made so many mistakes as her sister's stand-in – she had to give it her best shot this time.

Firing up the laptop, she typed 'Boot camp exercises' into Google with a sigh. If she had to do this – and she didn't appear to have a choice – then she could at least be prepared.

An hour later, she had put together a rigorous warm-up routine, plotted a course for him to run, and practised a few cooldown stretches for afterwards. She had cobbled quite a lot of it from a website set up by a former Royal Marines commando, and if that wasn't good enough for Rachel's client, then she didn't know what was. *Prepare to sweat out that bad mood, Adam, mate*, she thought, scribbling down the schedule with a flourish.

Obviously there was no way she would be able to keep up with him as he ran, star-jumped and press-upped his way through the routine – she often got out of breath simply trudging up the three flights of stairs to her flat, she was so wheezily unfit – but she'd already thought that far. Her plan was to borrow Rachel's bike and cycle along next to him, calling out words of encouragement now and then, and pretending to be checking his technique the rest of the time. She had discovered a stopwatch app on her phone and everything. *Faster*, she would bark. *Keep going! Knees UP!*

Becca, she imagined him saying admiringly at the end of the session as they parted ways, him still panting, her quietly triumphant. *You've thought of everything. Amazing workout. Thank you!*

Even Rachel might be pleased when she told her what she'd done. That would be a first. *Wow, good initiative, Becca. Thanks, Becca. You're a star, Becca.*

Yeah, well, maybe that was pushing it, but you never could tell. A bang on the head might just have shaken out some of Rachel's coolness towards her. Perhaps.

Cycling into town on Rachel's slightly-too-big bike a short while later, Becca felt an unexpected sense of *joie de vivre* dazzle through her. It was ages since she'd been on a bike and although she was a bit wobbly to begin with, she soon found a natural rhythm, her legs pumping circles, the sun warm on her bare arms, and it actually made her feel quite strong and good about the world. Yes! Endorphin rush! She should do this more often. Like . . . ever, in fact. Except her bike had been nicked about four years ago, and . . . well, they were only two stops from New Street on the train, and you'd have to be some kind of maniac with a death wish to want to cycle around the Birmingham ring road for the lolz.

Never mind: she was enjoying this now, and that was enough. Her hair streamed out from under the sweaty cycle helmet as she passed the magnificent cathedral in its grounds and she smiled to herself, not even caring any more that her plump thighs were jiggling in her borrowed shorts. So what! Let them jiggle; who cared? It was a beautiful morning, the trees were in full leaf, and the air smelled of hot tarmac and blooming roses. It made a change from the smells she was used to back home: diesel and drains, and the next-door kebab shop.

They had arranged to meet in Bishop's Meadow, which her map app informed her was near the river, and she was starting to feel, if not confident, then at least less terrified than earlier. As she crossed the river on an old stone bridge, she kept her eyes peeled for the parkland she'd seen on the map. Turning left, she saw tennis courts and some kind of office building and the wide, serene river once more. There was a bloke in a baggy T-shirt and cycling shorts typing into a phone by the start of the riverside path. Ahh – might that be him? He had gleaming white trainers on, Becca spotted, marking him out as a exercise newcomer. Hey, it took one to know one, after all.

'Adam?' she asked, hoisting a leg inelegantly over the bike and walking it over to him. She unclipped the helmet and ran a hand through her hair, hoping it hadn't gone too madly fluffy. 'Hi, I'm Becca. Rachel's sister?'

She was smiling in a disarming 'Brace yourself!' sort of way, but registered only disbelief in his answering look. Disbelief and . . . well, disappointment, if she wasn't mistaken. 'You're kidding,' he said flatly, and shook his head. 'No offence, but . . .' He gave a humourless sort of laugh. 'Look, this is not what I paid for.'

Becca stopped abruptly, the hand she'd held out in a friendly manner falling to her side. In her experience, whenever people said 'No offence', they were almost certainly about to be offensive. In a big way. 'What do you mean?' Damn, that sounded a bit aggressive. 'Listen, I should have said, we can offer you a fifty per cent discount on today's session if—'

But he wasn't listening. 'I don't want to be rude,' he began awkwardly, his gaze sliding everywhere but her face, and her heart sank. Wrong! He so *was* about to be rude. 'But I signed up for a *fitness programme*? Run by an *expert*?' He paused for impact, just in case she was under any illusions that she might be an expert. Hardly. 'Her sending you along instead . . . Sorry, no. Not having that.'

Becca's face flamed at the insults implied in his words. It was because she was fatter than Rachel, she thought, stung. Fatter, and red in the face, with frizzy hair and borrowed clothes that were slightly too tight. And he'd taken one single glance, and written her off. *Sorry, no. Not having that. Not having you.* He hadn't even given her a chance!

The customer is always right, she remembered her dad saying, and tried to keep her cool. 'I've prepared a full training session,' she said through gritted teeth, pulling her exercise plan from her pocket. 'From an ex-Royal Marines commando, no less! And seeing as we're both here, we might as well give it a go, see how you get along.'

But he was shaking his head again. *I'm not taking orders from you, Fatty* – it was visible in his face. 'I don't think so,' he said. 'Look, no offence, but—'

On to the second 'no offence' already, Becca thought dismally; and once had been more than enough. He was hardly Mo Farah himself in his baggy T-shirt and box-fresh trainers, was he? 'Yeah, well, offence taken,' she blurted out in the next moment. 'Have a listen to yourself, pal, you're being bloody rude, you know. When I was only trying to help.' And before she could stop herself, she had crumpled up her exercise plan and thrown it in his face, then got back on her bike and pedalled away as fast as she could, nose in the air. It was all she could do to stop herself bellowing out 'Get stuffed!' over her shoulder, but her lungs were tightening from the hard burst of exercise, and luckily – for him – she couldn't spare the breath. How dare he, though? How *dare* he? Ignorant, charmless, bad-mannered jerk. Tosser. Knobhead!

Her heart, which had felt so joyful moments before, seemed to thump against her ribcage, a tattoo of hurt. Yes, okay, so she was kind of on the tubby side these days. Agreed, she probably didn't look a vision of good health and ass-kicking fitness at first glance either; not your standard fitness-instructor physique. But he could have given her the benefit of the doubt, couldn't he? He could have humoured her, been polite at least!

Tears smarted in her eyes as she bumped along by the river, no longer sure of where she was going. She hated the way people judged you on your size – how you could be the best and kindest person in the world and still get written off with a single look up and down, just because you were a bit of a chubster. It was so rude. So unfair!

Pedalling harder, she blinked away the tears, not wanting to dwell on it any longer. No. She wouldn't cry over mean-spirited, judgemental Adam. She wouldn't cycle to the nearest bakery and gorge herself on a chocolate eclair, as Wendy would have advised, either. (*Naughty but nice!*) Instead she would hold her head high, refuse to feel bad about herself, and get the hell back to Rachel's house as fast as possible.

And in the meantime, Adam Holland could bloody well jog on. Literally. Without her.

Chapter Sixteen

Ironically, Rachel had been quite looking forward to staying with Sonia Next Door while Dad and Wendy were on their week's honeymoon in Dorset. Sonia had white-blonde hair and wore lots of lipstick and tight jumpers like Barbara Windsor and had a naughty sort of laugh. Once she had answered the door to Terry in a black satin nightie and some fluffy pink slippers. Dad had gone bright red and looked away but Sonia had giggled behind her hand and said, 'Whoops! No peeping, Tel,' and then winked at Rachel like she didn't care one bit.

Whenever Sonia had babysat for Rachel in the past, she had brought round PopTarts and they'd watched *Coronation Street* together. But now they were in Sonia's house, the other side of the adjoining wall, and it was no longer just the two of them. There was Frank, too, Sonia's new boyfriend, who had a mean face and a sour smell about him that adult Rachel would learn to associate with men who'd drunk too much. And on the night of the wedding, while Dad and Wendy were miles away in their hotel, Rachel had woken up in

Sonia's small white-painted spare room to find Frank sitting on the end of her bed, his cigarette smell seeming to settle on her like a film of dust, catching in the back of her throat, as he leaned over in the darkness. 'Ssshh,' he whispered, sliding a hand under the covers onto her thigh as she shrank back against the pillow, bewildered and scared. 'Ssshhh.'

Almost thirty years later, the memory was still enough to make her shudder, and she forced the images violently from her head as the dread and nausea re-awoke. *No.* Don't think about it. Put that lid back down, lock it away. That was how she'd always dealt with the horror – by burying the memories so deeply they could rarely be accessed. 'It could have been worse,' she had told a counsellor once, mumbling out the story for the first time. She had suffered postnatal depression after Scarlet was born, and had come to a clinic once a week to talk to a kind, calm woman about her feelings. There was something about that quiet, lavender-painted room, the measured gaze of the counsellor, that invited confidences. 'I mean, I feel something of a fraud, even mentioning it to you now. He didn't rape me. He didn't stick his tongue down my throat – or anything in any other place, for that matter. He just came into my bedroom and put his hand under the covers on my leg. That was it. No real harm done. It's just . . .' She bowed her head. 'Somehow the shock of it was enough to make me feel really bad. Dirty. Like it was my fault.'

The counsellor was older, threads of grey through her

thick brown hair, and she spoke in a slow, gentle voice. 'It's confusing for children when adults behave in unexpected ways,' she had said. 'And the feelings it provoked have probably come up again at this time because you've got two little girls yourself now, and—'

That was it. That was the thing. 'And if anyone dared do that to my girls, I would want to kill them,' Rachel had burst out automatically, fists clenching in her lap.

The counsellor had nodded, understanding in her eyes. 'But it wasn't your fault,' she had said, leaning forward and speaking with uncharacteristic firmness. 'It was not your fault, Rachel, okay?'

As it was, the incident itself had been over in a matter of moments, thank goodness. She had refused to 'sssshh' as Frank had instructed, screaming instead at the top of her voice for Sonia, who came running in, boobs jiggling in her nightie, sending Frank packing. *It could have been worse*, Rachel had repeated to herself whenever her mind strayed back to the episode; like that made it any better. But at the time, it had been as if a fissure had cracked right through her childhood, as if a protective layer around her had been ripped away, exposing her to the horrible truth: that adults could be random and dangerous and frightening. Afterwards, there could be no turning back, no un-remembering, no mending and replacing of that protective layer; it was destroyed for good.

Rachel had sobbed and sobbed, face in her hands, refusing to look at Sonia, crying again and again that she wanted her dad. She cried all night and all the next day too, even though Frank was long off the scene by then, until Sonia, out of desperation – and guilt, in hindsight – managed to track down the newlyweds and persuade them to come home. No, she didn't explain why Rachel was so upset. And Rachel didn't, either. She kept it chained up inside herself from then on, refusing to say what had happened, turning her brutalized feelings on Wendy and blaming her completely for the whole sorry story.

Of course, Wendy, for her part, never quite forgave Rachel for it either. She didn't say as much to her face, but Rachel overheard her on the phone to a friend, moaning about how they'd cut the honeymoon short because of 'little Madam kicking up a fuss. While Becky was as good as gold at Mum's!' For Rachel, sitting on the stairs earwigging, the words had felt like hot knives stabbing into her. Even now she could remember how she'd leaned against the wall, feeling a drumbeat of injustice pounding in her blood.

A fuss, indeed. A *fuss*. The man's hard, probing fingers on her soft thigh, the terrifying weight of him on the bed, the way that Rachel was convinced she could smell cigarette smoke in her hair for weeks afterwards . . . that was not what she would term *a fuss* at all. But then, how could she try to defend herself, when she dared not get Sonia into trouble?

They probably wouldn't believe her anyway. Somehow it would end up being her fault, her overreacting. (Maybe it *was* her fault, she had thought miserably.)

After that, the damage was done. Rachel was a good girl and she tried to like Wendy, tried to jolly along for the sake of her dad; but the incident had spoiled everything, leaving a stain across the surface, so that she always felt grubby and ashamed whenever she thought about her dad's wedding. And no amount of cream cakes or buns from the bakery could ever change that.

'Good morning! And how are we doing today?' Rachel was jolted from her memories by the arrival of the doctor – a new one this time – a freckled woman with an Australian accent and brisk manner, with what looked like a posse of medical students in tow.

Rachel felt greasy-haired and haggard, bruised and tender, but she forced herself to struggle upright. *I'm a survivor*, she reminded herself. 'I'm fine,' she croaked.

Chapter Seventeen

Back at Rachel's house after the Adam debacle, Becca threw herself into the soft beige sofa and let out a scream of rage into its padding, punching the foam seat cushions a few times like a toddler for good measure. *Stupid. Horrible. Rude. Offensive. Arsehole!*

After one last punch she made herself two fried egg sandwiches with brown sauce, and a pot of brutally strong tea. It helped.

The phone rang just as she was washing the frying pan and wondering how she was going to fill the rest of the day. Wiping her hands on her cycling shorts – Rachel's cycling shorts – she picked up. 'Hello?'

'Is that Rachel? My name's Michael Jones, I've got one of your fliers and—'

Oh dear, it was the old Welsh guy from the day before. The one who wanted Rachel to teach him how to make Irish stew. Becca interrupted before he could give her the full spiel all over again. 'Hi, Michael,' she said politely. 'We spoke yesterday? I'm Becca. Rachel's sister. I'm afraid she's in hospital, so . . .'

'Oh, I am sorry,' he said. There was a pause. 'Not nice places, hospitals, I know.'

He must be thinking of his wife, she thought, remembering how he'd previously mentioned her dying. 'No,' she said, feeling sorry for him. And then, for some reason – perhaps because the mellow timbre of his voice reminded her of her dad, or because she was feeling a bit fragile herself at that moment, or perhaps simply because the rest of the day was looming emptily ahead and she had nothing better to do – she found herself saying, 'But I can make an Irish stew. I could show you.'

He sounded delighted. 'That would be very kind. And how much would you charge?'

How much would she *charge*? Becca floundered for a moment. The part of her who had been missing her dad so much wanted to brush the question aside, to tell him that there was no charge, don't worry about it. But she *had* just lost her job and was pretty skint, she remembered in the next moment. So it was the skint part of her that replied with a hesitant 'Twenty quid?'

'Splendid!' he said. 'When can you come round?'

By midday, she was knocking on Michael Jones's door. Although cooking didn't exactly fall under her sister's new business brief, Becca had worked in a pub kitchen long enough to pick up a few recipes herself, and figured that she could make a pretty decent fist of a stew. Besides, the loneliness in the old man's voice had caught at her heartstrings. So here she was, a bag of lamb, potatoes, onion and carrot swinging from one hand. She liked to think that had it been her dad in a similar situation, widowed and alone, someone else would have done the same for him.

Michael Jones was tall, although a little hunched now, with wispy white hair and friendly brown eyes twinkling through brown-framed spectacles. He was in his mid-seventies, she guessed, but sprightly and lean; not the sort of person who, on retirement, sank into an easy chair and never rose again.

The address he'd given her was of a small bungalow up near the racecourse – a bungalow that had seen better days, Becca thought, as she followed him inside. A bare light bulb dangled from a flex in the hallway, the wallpaper was brown and peeling at the edges, the carpet had worn patches and there were piles of stuff absolutely everywhere: carrier bags of old newspapers, dusty, desiccated pot plants, books stacked higgledy-piggledy in teetering towers on the floor . . . *Becca, what are you even doing here?* she thought to herself, realizing with a flash of unease that for all his friendly smiles, Michael Jones might really be some kind of psychopath with a stew fetish. But then, as she followed him through to the back of the house, she noticed a rip in the shoulder seam of his jump-er and chided herself for her overactive imagination. He was just a lonely old man, that was all, a bit shabby round the edges since his wife had died.

Besides, she thought, if he *was* a serial killer, she was still a bit fired up from her earlier encounter with Adam. He stood no chance.

'Here's the kitchen,' Michael said. Again, it was haphazard and cluttered, with crockery piled up on the work surfaces and what looked to be the parts of a trombone spread out on newspaper across the table. 'It's a bit of a mess, I'm afraid, but there's only me, see. I don't tend to bother so much now.'

'Fair enough,' Becca said, trying not to think of her mum's kitchen in comparison. Wendy was on her own now too, but she'd gone the other way if anything, taking comfort in bouts of energetic hoovering or savage scrubbing. You only had to step inside her house and she was practically spraying you with Mr Muscle. Becca spotted a Calvin and Hobbes mug on the draining board and decided she was probably safe. Nobody who liked Calvin and Hobbes could possibly be evil. 'So . . . Irish stew. I've brought the ingredients you need and printed out a good recipe. Shall we get started?'

Michael had lived quite a life, she learned, as she showed him how to cut the lamb into chunks and peel the potatoes. He had been a musician, playing the bass trombone for the Welsh National Opera Orchestra for several years as a young man, before eventually hanging up his concert tails to teach the instrument privately and in schools. He still played in a band with a few friends – 'The Old Sods, that's our name' – but other than that, seemed to lead a solitary life. There were reminders of his wife everywhere, Becca noticed with a pang, spotting framed photographs of her up on the wall, an apron hanging on a peg that read 'World's Best Nanna', a pair of floral wellingtons just visible through an open cupboard door.

'Do you have family nearby?' she asked, gesturing at the apron, as she put the potatoes, peeled and chopped, into a dish of cold water to prevent them browning.

'Australia,' he said, the light in his eyes faltering for a second. 'Our daughter Shona moved out there twelve years ago now, has two little girls.' His hands shook on the carrot he was attempting to peel, and he gave a rueful smile. 'So not exactly *near*, no, unfortunately. They come over every couple of years or so, and Danno, one of the boys in the band, showed me how to talk to them on Skype, but it's not like popping round, you know? Not the same.'

'No,' Becca agreed. 'It's not.' She thought of her mum Wendy, who lived half an hour away across town, and whom she spoke to most days. The two of them might have had their flare-ups in the past – they weren't both redheads for nothing – but they were there for each other. Solid. That was what counted.

Because of time constraints Becca mixed up stock from a cube, but she showed Michael the instructions at the start of the recipe detailing how to make it from scratch, if he felt so inclined another time. Judging by the collection of well-thumbed cookery books gathering dust on a shelf above their heads and the full utensil drawer, Michael's wife had been the sort of cook who saw through a recipe properly, stock pans and all.

'She did love to cook, my Christine,' Michael confirmed when Becca asked him. 'Oh yes. The most beautiful bread, light as a feather. And a lovely roast dinner on a Sunday.'

There was such yearning in his voice that it made Becca feel quite sad. She wondered if any man would ever talk about her so lovingly, with a tear glistening in his eye. She hadn't exactly had the best luck with boyfriends so far.

It was as if he'd read her mind then because he asked, out of the blue, 'How about you, eh? Have you got a nice boyfriend? I bet you're fighting the fellas off, aren't you? Mobbed by admirers!'

'Ha,' she said, rather awkwardly. 'Not really.' Not at all, in fact. Becca seemed to have ground to a halt on the romance front, unfortunately. There was a time when she'd considered herself a passionate sort of person, reckless and impulsive, falling in and out of love as the weather changed. But more recently it was as if she'd forgotten how to do it, as if that impetuous spark of hers had been doused. *My heart has frozen over*, she thought to herself sometimes, wondering how one went about thawing out.

'Don't give me that,' Michael teased. 'With that hair and those dimples? No way. Well, the blokes you know must be crackers, is all I can say. Crackers, I tell you!'

'That must be it,' she said, laughing.

Once the stew had gone into the oven, she asked him to play her a tune, and he went to get another trombone immediately and put on a bit of a concert for her, right there in the kitchen. Becca had always considered the trombone something of a comedy instrument, but Michael's playing was by turns so soulful and then brassily upbeat that the music gave her goosebumps.

'That was gorgeous,' she said shyly at the end.

He smiled at her and gave the trombone an affectionate pat. 'It's what keeps me going,' he told her. 'Can't beat a good old tune to lift the spirits.'

'Well, you've certainly lifted mine,' she replied. It was true as well. After the bruising start to the day with Adam, the afternoon had restored her faith in humanity a little, made her feel much better about the world. There was something about Michael that reminded her of her dad too, which was comforting. 'I'd better head off now, but I hope the stew tastes good tonight. It smells amazing.'

'I'm going to really enjoy it,' he assured her. 'You're a great teacher.' He showed her to the front door then pulled a twenty-pound note from an old brown wallet and pressed it into her hand. 'Here. Maybe you could come again another time? Show me how to make a treacle tart. That's my other favourite, see.'

'Ahh,' Becca said. 'The thing is, I live, in Birmingham. I'm just here to look after my sister's children for a few nights while she's away.' She hesitated, on the verge of saying that Rachel would be in touch about another cookery lesson, but held back. Better not. 'Sorry,' she added, feeling bad about the look of disappointment on Michael's face.

'That's a shame,' he said. He held his hand out solemnly, and they shook. 'But it was lovely to meet you, Becca. Thank you for teaching an old dog a new trick, as they say. I'm going to enjoy my stew, I'm sure. I might even ask the band round one night, and make it for all of them.'

'Good for you,' she said, smiling at him. 'Thanks very much for the money, and the concert. I enjoyed meeting you too. Take care, Michael. Goodbye.' And she walked away along the street, feeling as if she might just have done something good for a change.

Chapter Eighteen

'So what brings you to Manchester, then?' The blonde nurse was back today and changing one of the dressings on Rachel's face. Rachel could smell her perfume as she leaned close.

What had brought her to Manchester? Ahh, the big question. 'I was looking for someone who knew my mum,' Rachel replied after a moment. The wiring made her voice sound so strangled and indistinct it brought her up short every time. *Is that really me?*

'Your mum? Oh. Right.' The nurse was busily peeling away the sticking plaster keeping the dressing in place but Rachel caught the note of surprise in her voice. No doubt she'd been expecting a more light-hearted answer – *here to meet a friend; doing a bit of shopping; day out in the big city!*

'It's a long story,' Rachel mumbled, in the hope of avoiding any more questions. There was no way she was about to go into the whole thing now, put it like that. Where would she even start?

Violet Pewsey was where the story began, she supposed.

Violet Pewsey at her dad's funeral, all knobbly collarbone and elbows in her sage-green dress and matching floppy felt hat, making a beeline for Rachel, past the piled-up egg sandwiches and bowls of crisps on the buffet table. 'I knew your parents. Did your dad ever . . . mention me?'

Thirteen months on, Rachel could still remember the cloying scent of perfume and mothballs; the feel of those crepey, almost translucent fingers as the woman clutched at her arm. And oh, how Rachel's heart had leapt with foolish joy at her words. *I knew your parents* – plural. Not just her dad. Her mum, too. Terry's family had always been gruff and taciturn when it came to talking about Emily. Death was an embarrassment; emotions were best left hidden away. By the time Rachel was a teenager, bursting with questions, all of the Durant relatives were unhelpfully dead and buried themselves, unable to share their memories of her mother. Nobody had really ever told her anything.

'You knew my mum?' The room had shrunk away, the black-clad mourners seeming to recede, even the pong of egg sandwiches becoming a distant memory. Hope swelled within Rachel; she felt light-headed at this unexpected gift on such a sad day.

'Only through your dad. I was with him, you see. Terry. When it all happened. We were together until . . .' She sighed, and Rachel could see several decades of wistfulness in the single exhalation. There was something rather defeated about Violet Pewsey, despite the cheerful slick of pink lipstick on her thin lips. 'Well, you know, the trial,' she said, rather awkwardly, her eyes flicking away as she sipped her sherry. Then she asked, with barely disguised hope, 'Did he ever talk about me, your dad?'

'Er . . .' Rachel stared blankly at the woman, her mind still stuck on that unexpected word. The *trial*? There was a bead of sweat above Violet's upper lip, glinting in the light like a sequin. 'I don't remember,' she managed to reply, before blurting out, 'What do you mean, the trial?'

Violet's eyes flickered in surprise. Her pouchy little mouth fell open and she twisted the sherry glass between her fingers. Rachel's blood seemed to pound around her head. A trial. What was the woman talking about?

'I . . . I'm sorry, dear,' Violet said, after an agonizing pause. 'I shouldn't have mentioned that. Not on a day like today. Forgive me, will you? I only wanted to pay my respects. It's just . . . I always wondered what happened to your father. He was such a lovely man. And things might have been so different, if . . . Well, anyway. What's done is done.' She smiled at Rachel, but it was a nervous smile, a Did-I-just-get-away-with-that? kind of smile that did not ring with conviction. 'I'd better go, anyway,' she added hastily, knocking back the rest of her drink with an audible gulp. 'Lovely to meet you.'

'Wait,' said Rachel. She couldn't let this woman leave just like that, having opened a door so tantalizingly to secrets from the past. 'Could you . . . Could you please tell me what you remember about my mum?' she begged. 'Anything. Anything at all. I was so little when she died, you see, and nobody would ever talk about her.'

But Violet became quite agitated at this request. She took a step back, no longer looking directly at Rachel, and began fussing about the time, oh dear, she really needed to get going, she didn't want to miss her coach. An apologetic pat of the arm – *I'm sorry about your dad* – and then she was threading her way back through the busy room, the silk flowers on her hat wobbling in her haste.

Rachel watched her go, feeling thoroughly disconcerted. What was all that about? Why couldn't Violet look her in the eye? And what the hell did she mean by this *trial*? She was just about to bolt after her and plead with her to explain, when a couple of silver-haired men with moist eyes came and introduced themselves as former colleagues of Terry, back from the Longbridge days. 'He was a good fella, your dad,' they said, clasping her hands. 'A smashing bloke. They don't make 'em like that any more, more's the pity.'

The rest of the funeral had passed in a blur: Lawrence suavely solicitous, Wendy tearful, Becca blotchy-faced and drunk by the end of it, sniffling on random people's shoulders. But Rachel felt buttoned up inside, unable to think straight after Violet Pewsey had left so many unanswered questions fermenting in her head. The biggest question of all was: dare she find out more?

Well, she had, of course. Eventually. And here she was now as a result, with a bump on her head, and all sorts of broken bits in her body, having a nurse apologize for the stinging antiseptic wipe she was using to clean her stitched face. That was what curiosity did for you.

'There,' the nurse said at the end. 'All finished.' She washed her hands and gave an awkward smile. 'I hope things work out for you and your mum.'

'Thanks,' said Rachel, not bothering to correct her. *My mum's dead. Or at least that's what I always thought . . .*

Chapter Nineteen

The phone was ringing as Becca got in with the children after school, and the answerphone started up before she could reach it. 'Hello . . . Er, this is Adam Holland,' came a voice, and Becca stopped dead in the kitchen, pulling a face at the sound. Well, there was no way she was going to pick up now. 'Um . . . Look, about earlier. I shouldn't have . . .' Clearly this was a man who found apologies difficult, Becca thought, curling her lip. He could hardly string a sentence together. 'I was telling my brother about what happened, and –'

He was telling his *brother*? Laughing about it, probably. Cringe.

'– and he pointed out that maybe I'd been a bit unfair. A person doesn't have to be, er, well, skin and bone to be fit. Obviously. You could be, like, an Olympic shot putter for all I know.'

Cringe and double cringe. *Shut up, will you.* They both knew she was not an Olympic shot putter. So he was basically ringing her to point out that she was fat, again. *Thanks for that.*

'And then I looked through the exercises that you had, er, thrown at me –' Okay, so she probably shouldn't have thrown them at him. '– and . . . well, I have to say, it all looked pretty good. I wasn't sure what the "Davina Super Pump" was, but –'

'Oh,' said Scarlet, coming into the room at that moment and misunderstanding why Becca was standing there staring at the telephone. 'You can just pick it up, you know. Like this.' And pick it up she did, before Becca could lunge to stop her. 'Hello?' she said into the receiver. 'Do you want Aunty Bee? She's here.' She passed it to Becca. 'It's for you.'

Brilliant. So now she had to actually talk to the chump. 'Hi,' she said grudgingly.

'Hi.' He sounded awkward too. 'I've just left you a really rambling message. Er . . .'

'It's all right, I think I got the gist of it,' she said, before he could start banging on about Olympic shot putters again.

'Well . . . Sorry, anyway. For being rude. For upsetting you.'

Ugh. She didn't want to hear this, didn't want to talk to him full stop. 'I wasn't *upset*,' she said witheringly. Ready to punch you, maybe, she thought, rolling her eyes at Scarlet, who was eavesdropping shamelessly nearby.

'Oh, okay. Well, no hard feelings, anyway. Yeah? I think

my next appointment is for Thursday, so . . .' He hesitated. 'I guess I'll see you then.'

He guessed he'd see her again? Not in this lifetime, he wouldn't. Was he mad? 'Right,' she said non-committally. She'd be long gone by Thursday, she figured; Rachel wouldn't want her hanging around. No doubt her sister would sort the whole thing out when she was back. 'Bye.'

'Was that your boyfriend?' Scarlet said with interest as Becca hung up. The child would make an excellent spy when she was older, although she probably needed to hone her observation skills in terms of subtlety.

'No! God. No way,' Becca replied. 'He's a complete and utter . . . Anyway. Let's find you a snack. Piece of toast?' she suggested, wondering what kind of snack Rachel usually fed her children after school. Definitely not a Snickers bar, she'd established that much. 'Apple? Carrot sticks?'

'Did you know,' Scarlet said, without answering the question, 'that it takes the same amount of force to bite off the top of your thumb as it does to bite off the top of a carrot? My friend Lois told me.'

'Gross,' Becca said. 'But let's not try that one out now, yeah?' Visions of missing digits and blood-soaked dashes to A&E spun horribly round her head. If she had to return there two days on the trot . . . No. Unthinkable. She glanced at her watch – four o'clock. 'I wonder what's happened to your sister?' she said uneasily, remembering the boyfriend and yesterday's love bite. Damn it, she'd forgotten to expressly forbid any clandestine trysts, in the midst of the pre-school melee that morning. Leaving Scarlet and Luke to forage through the kitchen for food – 'Something *healthy*, all right?' – she went to find her phone. Lawrence was due to arrive in two hours, and she was already dreading him noticing what had happened to his daughter's tender neck during Becca's watch. If his daughter had gone AWOL and wasn't even *home*, he'd have far more to say, none of it nice.

Hi, she texted her niece. *Are you on way back? Dad coming to pick you up at 6, don't forget. xx*

A crash came from the kitchen and she ran back in to see that the other two were standing guiltily around a jar of strawberry jam – or rather, an ex-jar of strawberry jam, which was now decorating the stone floor, glittering shards of glass having sprayed out in all directions. 'Whoops,' said Scarlet.

By two minutes to six, Becca was feeling extremely frazzled. Mabel had eventually slunk home at nearly five – 'Sorry, Drama Club! I only just saw your text,' she had said breezily, unpopping one earphone to explain, then immediately replacing it and heading upstairs. Too many dramas in this place, Becca had thought, lacking the energy to argue. The jam and glass had been cleared up, the floor mopped, some suitable snacks eventually found and provided for all. Then the three of them had packed things for the weekend – and repacked them under Becca's supervision, so that the younger two now had toothbrushes and Mabel her home-work books. (*Nice try, love*, she thought.) To top it off, Scarlet had whipped herself up into a state of total hysteria at the prospect of being reunited with her dog for the weekend, and kept jumping off the sofa screaming 'Harvey Time!' at the top of her voice. Never had a cold beer seemed so appealing, never. Becca would have been glugging down a bottle this minute, were it not for the small fact of having to drive back to Birmingham later on. How did Rachel cope with this day in, day out? How did any parent?

'He's here!' shrieked Scarlet as a car pulled up outside. 'DADDY!' At last.

Becca opened the front door in time to see Lawrence unfold himself from the car. Tall and broad-shouldered, he had always reminded her of a menswear catalogue model, good-looking in a classic way with that slightly rumpled hair and chiselled jaw. Shame he was such a tosser. Today he was wearing jeans, but they were smart jeans, designer probably, and a grey Ralph Lauren polo shirt that he'd probably paid seventy quid for. Seventy quid for a small embroidered logo. That was how much of a tosser he was.

As Scarlet and Luke rushed out to greet him, Mabel following a cool two paces behind, Becca found herself hurtling back to that awful night in the Copthorne – how he'd grabbed her hand and scrawled his room number on the back of it. *312*, as if he was branding her, claiming her. Yuck.

'Lawrence, hi,' she said now, as he looked up and saw her there in the doorway. He'd been in a tux that night, smirking down at her, his hands big and warm through her black cotton waitress dress. Pig.

'Hello, Becca,' he replied, his gaze locking with hers. Despite her best intentions, she felt herself turn red. Please for the love of God, she thought, let's not go there now. 'It's good to see you again,' he went on. No, it wasn't. 'So I'll have these rascals back to you on Sunday evening then, shall I? You're still all right to pick up Rachel on Monday?'

'Sure,' she said. 'That's the plan.'

'Great. Let's say six on Sunday, then. Okay, rabble, let's go.' He turned back to her. 'Have a good weekend. Don't do anything I wouldn't do.'

She smiled thinly. 'I'll bear that in mind,' she said. 'Bye, then, kids.'

Mabel and Luke were already in the car and shouted goodbye, but Scarlet ran back over and flung her arms around Becca, taking her by surprise. 'Love you, Aunty Bee,' she said. 'I'll give Harvey a bloody big cuddle from you.'

'Oh. Thanks. Yes, do that,' Becca said. 'And I love you too, gorgeous nieceling. Have fun in Wales.'

Love you, Aunty Bee. And just like that, her frazzled feeling from earlier had melted away, replaced with a soft, lovely warmth spreading through her body and the feeling that it was somehow all worthwhile: the mistakes, the bodges, the spills. *Love you.* Okay. She took it back. All of a sudden, she felt quite glad to be returning on Sunday to spend another evening with her nieces and nephew. Who wouldn't?

She waved them off and went back inside, automatically reaching down to pick up the scattered school shoes and tidy them into the large wicker basket. They were good kids. In the past she'd never spent more than a few hours at a time in their company, generally at her parents' place, for Christmas or a birthday or anniversary. You couldn't really get to know a child properly on a mere handful of conversations per year, especially at big family gatherings when they were supposedly on best behaviour. Having entire days with them – having sole responsibility for them! – was a whole new thing. And while she wouldn't say she was any kind of expert in the field, and felt as if she'd been winging it most of the time, it had been fun, too. Different. Now she knew that Mabel hated noodles and loved blue nail varnish. Now she knew that Scarlet and Luke played this weird game where they tried to punch each other whenever they saw a Mini out and about. She knew what they looked like when they were asleep, or laughing, or worried. It felt . . . kind of lovely, actually.

In the meantime, though: the delicious prospect of a weekend to herself. And just ten minutes later, she was on the road too, rolling down her windows to let in the warm June air. It smelled pleasingly of hay and earth and sunshine, even on the A-road out towards Worcester; the roadside verges frothed with great drifts of cow parsley and red campion, and there were long grasses and buttercups in the meadows beyond. The forecasters had promised a barbecue weekend, and even though Becca was in possession of neither a barbecue nor an actual garden, after two days of stress and childcare she felt free as a bird – as if she had the world at her disposal.

The flat Becca shared with Meredith was in Northfield, on the west side of Birmingham. After ninety minutes of driving along the snaking, traffic-heavy roads the view from her window had changed from rolling fields and farmland to blocks of flats, double-decker buses, roadworks and tightly packed terraces of houses; a higgledy-piggledy urban sprawl. The evening sunshine was still golden, glinting off every car bonnet and wing mirror like hundreds of metallic fireflies; cats rolled languorously on dusty pavements, and the air was thick with diesel and the smell of hot chips. As she waited at traffic lights she could hear reggae blaring from an open window, and she tapped her fingers on the steering wheel in time to the beat. Hello, summer. Hello, best city in the world. I'm back.

Chapter Twenty

It was Friday evening and Rachel was gagging on a disgusting high-protein smoothie, wondering if Lawrence had arrived on time to take the kids for the weekend. Knowing him, probably not.

How she hated this, the shuttling back and forth, the passing and passing back of their children. It didn't seem a good solution for anyone. 'Do I get an actual suitcase now, like in *The Suitcase Kid*?' Scarlet had asked (she was a big Jacqueline Wilson fan) and Rachel, trying to find niceness in this worst of all situations, had bought them each special overnight bags to take for their first weekend; a pathetic attempt to soften the blow. Now she wished she hadn't. Seeing the cases lined up in the hall every other Friday afternoon, it was as if they were child evacuees in the war, leaving her indefinitely. She might as well have hung cardboard signs around their necks with their names and ages. *Please look after this child.*

Worse was the moment when Lawrence drove away with them each time, and the rooms fell empty, as if the whole house was holding its breath for their return. *Keep busy*, advised the other divorcees on the single-parent forum she had taken to frequenting. *Enjoy some me time for once – you've earned it!* But what was she supposed to do during this 'me time'? It was impossible to relax when you felt so alone. Everyone else she knew was busy with their own families; the gardens full of barbecues and laughing children and music. The sounds taunted her as she paced around the quiet house, counting down the hours until she heard his car in the drive again.

Nobody had been a winner in the divorce. Not one of them was happier for it. Whenever one of the children was upset, had a bad dream, said how much they missed Dad or the dog, or went a bit quiet after speaking to him on the phone, it was as if a hand had reached inside Rachel's stomach, grabbed her guts and wrenched. *Your fault, your fault, your fault*, her conscience kept accusing. Technically speaking, it was Lawrence's fault too, of course, but it always seemed easier to blame herself.

She wondered how the conversation would go with Becca when he picked up the children that evening. Knowing smiles, meaningful glances? Nudge-nudge, wink-wink? Ugh. Thank goodness she didn't have to witness that. She just hoped they didn't make it too obvious in front of the kids. *Mum, it was so weird, right, because when Dad picked us up, he gave Aunty Bee this really big kiss. Like, REALLY big.* Conversations you did not want to have with your child, number 3,089.

Sighing, she found herself wishing for the millionth time that she could rewind and replay things differently, prevent the split from occurring quite so messily. She wouldn't mention Craig, for starters. Would not even utter his name. She should have known not to, anyway, it was just . . . Well, he was kind of creeping her out, that was all. Calling and texting her out of work hours, standing a bit too close when they were in the office together. And she was pretty sure the silver necklace that had appeared mysteriously on her desk was from him, too. 'Oh, bore off,' she had muttered one evening, when he texted her a link to a funny news story. *Thought you might like this*, he had written jauntily. No, Craig. You thought wrong.

Lawrence had never openly said he resented Rachel's success at work, but he was always tetchy when her phone bleeped with new texts or emails in the evening. Unlike his wife, he hated his job as a middle-grade accountant and thought work should end the moment you set foot outside the office. 'Who is it?' he asked immediately.

That was when she should have said the texter who'd annoyed her was her boss Samantha or one of the cliquey mums from school, in order to close the subject down. But she wasn't thinking straight and she was stressed because she had a promotion interview hanging over her later that week, and so she blurted out, 'Just Craig, this new guy at work.'

Match to the firework, right there. BOOM. Six little

detonators falling carelessly from her lips because her mind was elsewhere. And so began the dagger-eyed grilling: Who the hell was Craig? Why was he texting her? Why hadn't she told him about this before? Keeping secrets, was she? Fancy him, did she? What else had she conveniently neglected to tell him, then? She might as well come out with it! He'd find out soon enough!

It was like the unleashing of a storm that raged and whirled and refused to be calmed. Not content with giving her the third degree at home, he turned up in the office the next morning and ostentatiously kissed her in front of the other staff members, one hand possessively clamped to her behind. One of the secretaries giggled but everyone else, including Rachel, was mortified. Craig wasn't even there to get the not-so-subtle hint.

Back at home, he kept chipping away, asking every night how Craig had been that day, had she seen him, had they worked together? Rachel was an area manager for the region and spent many days of the week in her car, but Lawrence became convinced she was sneaking off for secret rendez-vous with Craig, and would phone repeatedly to check on her whereabouts. It was like being stalked by her own hus-band; everywhere she went, she realized she was just waiting for him to surprise her with an appearance, a comment, a put-down. She found herself imagining surveillance cameras trained on her from all angles, hidden microphones picking up her every conversation, spies on each corner. Her sleep began to suffer, and she didn't get the promotion.

Things ramped up a gear one dreary, dark Saturday in November when they bumped into Craig in B&Q of all places, the children in tow. 'So this is him, is it?' Lawrence snarled over the tinny Christmas music, piped through the over-head speakers. He drew himself up to full height. 'This is the Casanova, eh? We meet at last. I'm the husband.'

'Lawrence, *please*,' Rachel begged, acutely embarrassed. They were in the bathroom aisle, in front of a display of mirrors, and every way she looked, she could see her flustered reflection, pink in the cheeks, desperate for this not to be happening.

Lawrence paid no attention. 'I've a good mind to smack you into next week,' he went on, advancing menacingly on the bewildered, blinking Craig, while Rachel hustled the children away, telling them to go and look for tree decorations in the Christmas section. *We WISH you a merry Christmas*, trilled the music, *we WISH you a merry Christmas*.

Poor Craig, who had been innocently shopping for a shower curtain, backed into a shelf full of gleaming chrome taps, dropping his wire basket with a clatter. 'I don't know what you're talking about,' he stammered, casting agonized glances at Rachel.

'Is everything all right here?' a burly shop assistant asked, glancing from Lawrence to Craig with his hands on his hips.

We WISH you a merry Christmas, and a happy new YEAR!

Christ, it had been awful. And still he wouldn't let it go. All the way home he had banged on about it, savage and cruel. 'Spineless little shit. What the hell do you see in *him*?'

'For the last time, Lawrence, I don't see *anything* in him,' she had cried, feeling like thumping her head against the car window. 'There's nothing going on. Nothing whatsoever! Now – please. Can we forget about it? I don't want to talk about this in front of the children.'

'Oh, no. Not in front of the children! We wouldn't want them thinking their mother was anything less than perfect, would we, now? We wouldn't want them knowing what a slag she was, hey?'

'Daddy, stop it,' brave Scarlet had said from the back seat, and thankfully it had been enough to silence him for the rest of the way home. But of course that wasn't the end of it. Because then, in the next week, it was her work Christmas party and Lawrence had burst in, drunk and belligerent, and had marched down the table of party-hatted staff, midway through their mince pies and chocolate fondant puddings, and swung a punch at Craig. Someone – Lacey, the receptionist, she thought – had screamed. Bruce, their accounts director, had jumped up and tried to push Lawrence away. There was grappling and shoving from the men, a table crashing over, a shrill 'Gentlemen, *please!*' from Samantha, and then along came the police, just to round the evening off nicely.

Well done, Lawrence. And a merry bloody Christmas to you, too.

Anger and shame had swirled up inside Rachel like the muddy waters of a lake, as well as a steely new determination. That was it – a line had been crossed; her limit reached. No, she thought. She would not put up with this any longer. She certainly wasn't about to condone her husband's behaviour by standing by him after *that*. 'It's over,' she had told him the next morning. 'I can't live with you any more.'

Craig hadn't pressed charges (thank God), but the story made it into the local paper and Lawrence lost his job because of the whole thing. Naturally, the likes of Sara Fortescue thought Christmas had arrived early, with all this scandal on her very own doorstep. *I couldn't believe it*, Rachel had heard her twittering to her cronies at the school gate. *I mean, he always seemed such a nice man. A bit sexy and dangerous, you know, but not* violent. *Gosh. Do you think he's been hitting her, too? And the children?*

Despite all the arguments, despite the atmosphere of constantly walking on eggshells, the children were still unanimously shocked when the news was broken to them. *Daddy's going to move out. We don't love each other any more but we do still love you three.* No words could soften such a blow, however kindly you said them. There had been that awful beat of silence as they took it in: dawning bewilderment on Luke's little face, betrayal on Scarlet's. Mabel, meanwhile, had sat there, eyes glittering, digging her fingernails into her palms before leaping to her feet and erupting. 'I should have known!' she'd yelled furiously. 'I should have known this would happen!' and then she was storming out of the house, and Rachel had to chase after her up the street and attempt to hug her, Mabel wrestling to get free, both of them streaming with tears.

Dark times. Bad times. And of course, after the Christmas party debacle, even though it was probably the worst financial move she could possibly have made, she'd felt she had no choice but to resign her job at GoActive, the job she'd loved so much and been bloody good at, too. Because how could she go back and work there alongside Craig, when Lawrence had been so appallingly abusive towards him? Samantha hadn't even argued when Rachel offered her resignation. 'Well, we're sorry to see you go, but in the circumstances . . .' she had said, leaving the sentence unfinished.

Yeah. In the circumstances, you can take that vile husband of yours and bog off, love.

Worse than all of that, though – the pinnacle of worstness – had been what he'd said to her, packing up his things on that last day, hatred radiating from his entire body. 'By the way, she was better in bed than you, you know,' he'd said casually, almost carelessly, for his parting shot. 'Way better. Your sister, I mean.'

Chapter Twenty-One

Oh, but it was good to be home, thought Becca as she walked back into her flat. The joy of nobody to look after or worry about. The smell of her own bed. A whole weekend with absolutely nothing to do. Well, okay, not strictly *nothing* – she had a medieval diadem to make for Meredith, and then it was the weekly Dad dinner with her mum on Sunday, but those were both nice, non-taxing things. Nobody needed cooking for, or soothing, or taking anywhere. Bring it on.

Meredith was in the kitchenette, and called out hello. She wearing a panda onesie, even though the temperature was still in the mid-twenties outside (and felt even hotter inside their stuffy top-floor flat), and eating a Pot Noodle. Despite being extremely clever – she worked as a research associate in the History faculty at the university – Meredith rarely attempted to cook anything more complicated than a sandwich. The Pot Noodle was actually a rare culinary achievement. 'Hey,' she said, waving a fork in the air and narrowly avoiding flinging a wet noodle at her flatmate. 'You're back. How was it?'

'We all survived to tell the tale, although Rachel's still in hospital until next week,' Becca said succinctly, retrieving two cold bottles of beer from the fridge. 'The kids are with their dad for the weekend.' She popped open the beers and passed one over. 'So, this diadem, then. What's the plan?'

Meredith beamed. 'Well, you know Galadriel?' she asked, putting the bottle to her lips. 'Cheers for this, by the way.'

'Um . . .' Becca replied, taking a cold, delicious swig. Galadriel? One of Meredith's weird mates, she guessed. Becca had once accompanied her friend to a re-enactment battle event and met so many people who called themselves things like 'Althanos' and 'Peronell' that she had tuned out after a while. Besides, they almost certainly had names like 'Steve' and 'Alison' in real life anyway. 'I'm not sure I remember her. I mean, him,' she admitted doubtfully, as Meredith looked amused. Shit. Maybe it was some famous historical queen she was supposed to have heard of.

'From *Lord of the Rings*? She's a royal Elf. Cate Blanchett played her in the film. Oh, you *do* know!' Seeing the blank expression on Becca's face, Meredith abandoned her Pot Noodle and began searching for an image on her phone. 'Whatever, anyway, she has this really cool circlet crown in the film. Like this.'

She handed over her phone and Becca peered at the image. As well as an impressive pair of elf ears, Cate Blanchett was indeed wearing a gold and silver circlet that formed a V point over her forehead, twisting into a teardrop shape at its tip. 'Nice,' she said, handing it back to Meredith, her brain already trying to work out how she could create something similar. The jewellery business she and her friend Debbie had set up had begun very simply – threading earrings and bangles – but then they'd both got really into it and taken silversmithing evening classes so that they could tackle more elaborate designs and projects. Somewhere in her bedroom, along with the rest of her kit, Becca seemed to recall there was some lovely thick silver-plated wire that shouldn't be too hard to weave into the requisite elven swirls.

'I'd like mine a bit simpler than that,' Meredith went on. (Simpler – good, thought Becca.) 'Maybe with a whopping great jewel in the middle. A midnight-blue crystal to go with my dress, if you've got one.'

'I'll have to check the colours,' Becca said, 'but essentially, yeah, I could definitely make one like that for you.'

Meredith was not a huggy type of person, but she clinked her beer bottle against Becca's and beamed. 'It's good to have you back.'

Becca spent Friday night and Saturday morning working on the circlet and – call her smug for saying so – was thoroughly proud of the result by the time she had finished. It was absolutely bloody gorgeous! She had found an oval moonstone cabochon that gleamed blue and gold for the central forehead jewel, and from there had woven three strands of silver up and out each side like wings, curling them gently so that they would lie in shining, twisting patterns around her flatmate's head. The back of the diadem was to be fastened by a black ribbon, which would lie unseen under Meredith's long brown hair.

'Oh my goodness, Becca, this is fabulous,' Meredith said, admiring herself in the bathroom mirror. 'It's really beautiful. Better than I ever thought.' She twisted her head left and right, tracking a finger along the undulating silverwork. 'Thank you so much. Consider that gas bill well and truly paid.'

Becca beamed in return, feeling a genuine glow of satisfaction. *Thank YOU*, she wanted to say. Thank you for asking me to do it in the first place. She had loved digging out her soldering equipment and getting stuck in to a new creative project; it had been so long since she'd attempted anything artistic. Since . . . Actually, it must be since before her dad had died, now that she thought about it. There had been thick dust on the top of her bead box and her tube of solder paste had dried right out (fortunately she had some unopened spares). She had forgotten how it always lifted her spirits to think creatively, to feel the unique sense of achievement that came from crafting something with her own hands. 'You're welcome,' she said happily. 'I enjoyed it.'

She decided to sort through the rest of her art supplies while Meredith went to get ready for her banquet. As well as the jewellery kit, there were all sorts of other bits and pieces – fabric and wool, some fake fur remnants from when she'd attempted to make herself a coat two winters ago, lampshade rings, paints, silver clay, even some bags of googly eyes from a short-lived stint as an after-school club volunteer. It had all been boxed up and put away for over a year now, though, as if she'd closed down that side of herself entirely. Seeing the contents again felt like reawakening something inside. There was the sketchbook she'd been halfway through when her dad had died: quick pencil sketches of a cake-themed tea cosy she'd planned to make for her mum that had never come about; ideas for stuffed toys she'd wondered about pitching to one of the posh toy shops in town; drawings of beautiful dangling earrings, silver spirals studded with gemstones. Where had it gone, that imagination of hers, that love of creating? Leafing through the pages now, it felt as if someone else had dashed off those sketches, come up with those ideas. And yet . . .

Her mind was sparking. There was a bag of small silver skulls, left over from when she and Debbie had done an Alexander McQueen-inspired grungey range of earrings (all right, a straight rip-off, same thing). Mabel would love those, she thought, picking up the bag and fingering the ghoulish contents. Then she stroked the fabric remnants and flicked back to the tea cosy designs, wondering if she should resurrect the idea for Wendy's birthday in November. If it made her feel happy, then why not?

'How do I look?' Meredith was knocking at her bedroom door, peering inside. She was wearing a velvety blue dress, floor-length, that had a low ruched front and tightly laced bodice. She had brushed out her long hair and it lay around her shoulders, with the circlet's moonstone gleaming softly on her forehead.

'Stunning,' Becca replied honestly. Meredith did not have a conventional twenty-first-century beauty. She had strong facial features and quite a broad, mannish frame that didn't suit jeans or leggings or short skirts. Somehow the old-fashioned outfit looked perfect on her, though. So right that Becca could just imagine her with a falcon on one arm, or riding side-saddle on a galloping horse, home towards her castle. 'You look *ravishing*,' she went on. 'You'll have those lords and earls vying for you. All sorts of stirrings under tunics and robes, you wait.'

She felt an unexpected twist of envy at the thought. The two of them had been flatmates for almost a year now, and in that time neither of them had had a serious relationship. A few awful blind dates, a handful of terrible flings, the occasional crush to show for themselves, but no more than that.

She turned up for these blind dates feeling uncomfortable and nervous, trying to contort herself into preconceived ideas about how she should behave, and acting out the part because she'd lost all her confidence in being her real self. She'd suck in her stomach, try not to laugh too loudly, pick at a salad in the hope that she wouldn't look greedy. In the hope that they would like her. But it never seemed to work. 'Great to meet you, Sally,' the last date had said as they parted after an evening in a French restaurant punctuated by nervous silences. She had never heard from him again.

If Meredith got herself a boyfriend, fell in love and started swooning after some bearded twerp in doublet and hose . . . there was a selfish, jealous part of Becca that would resent her flatmate for it, would be unable to respond with appropriate joy. *Great! How exciting!* she imagined herself saying, shortly before locking herself in her bedroom and crying despairingly into her pillow, alone.

'Thank you. I'd say come along, but it's ticketed, and I'm not sure there are any spares,' Meredith was saying now. 'Do you have any plans for tonight?'

Becca forced a bright smile. Plans for tonight? Her only plans were for staying in again, flicking through television channels in the hope of finding a good film and maybe nipping out for a takeaway pizza and more beer. She was so used to working at the pub most evenings that she hadn't thought to organize anything more sociable. 'No, but I've got stuff to do,' she replied, her smile becoming fixed, 'and I've got a busy one tomorrow – it's a Dad dinner at Mum's, and then I'm back over to Rachel's, so . . .' Her voice trailed off, and she was left feeling awkward.

'You're still doing those? The Dad dinners? That's nice,' Meredith said, then the intercom buzzed. 'Ahh. That'll be Leofrick. See you tomorrow!'

For some reason Becca felt vaguely depressed as her flat-mate bustled out, long skirts swishing across the floor. This felt all wrong. Mean as it might sound, she'd always felt a tiny bit superior to Meredith – humouring her rather eccentric ways while privately thinking, 'At least I'm not as weird as she is.' And yet, of the two of them, Meredith was all dressed up and off with friends about to have a really great evening, swigging goblets of mead and chomping into a roast hog or however these historical types got their kicks. While Becca was left at home with crappy summer-Saturday-night telly for company, babbling on about the Dad dinner like that was the highlight of her week. So who was the loser now?

She sighed, and put the telly on. The thing was, the Dad dinner generally *was* the highlight of her week. She would go to Mum's and they'd have steak pie, chips and peas in honour of Terry (his favourite meal), an extra place set at the table as if he was still there. They would talk about him, look through photos, sometimes have a little cry. It was lovely.

You're still doing those? Meredith had asked, seeming

surprised, and Becca couldn't help feeling defensive. Yes. They were still doing those. All right?

The next day Becca stayed in bed until ten, had a long bath and then packed up an overnight bag to take to Rachel's, this time with a hairbrush and a change of clothes. Meredith still wasn't back by the time she left, although a text had come. *Everyone LOVED the diadem!!! Amazing night xxx*

Trying not to feel too envious, Becca typed back *Fab! Back to Hereford today. Prob home again Tues xx*

Then she got into the car and set off for her mum's.

'Becky, love! How are you, sweetheart? It's good to see you!'

Wendy was tanned and beaming after her break in the sun, there on the doorstep in a loose floral-printed kaftan and bare feet. Painted toenails, no less, Becca noticed, as she was enveloped in a billowing-sleeve hug. This had been the longest they'd gone without seeing each other since Dad had died.

'I'm fine, yeah,' she said. 'How was your holiday? You look amazing.'

'It was lovely. Fun. Just what the doctor ordered. Cocktails every night and a bit of dancing . . .' Wendy's eyes sparkled, and Becca felt happy for her. Grief had knocked them both sideways for so long, it was good to see Mum with a spring in her step again.

'Come in, come in, isn't it a fabulous day? The flight back

was a bugger – landed at nine this morning and we'd hardly slept a wink the night before, so I've just been snoozing in the garden, keeping the tan topped up. Good, isn't it? I even braved it in a bikini, you know. I thought, sod it, who cares? All the girls were in them too, so it was like a mutual fatties' support group. We just went for it! And actually, after all that worrying, the men seemed to like us a *lot*.'

'You're a great colour,' Becca said. 'Good for you. Oi, and less of the "fatties" talk, by the way,' she added automatically. 'You're gorgeous just as you are.'

Wendy had had a love–hate relationship with food for as long as Becca could remember. Love, mostly. There was a sign up in her kitchen that read, 'I keep losing weight, but it keeps finding me again'. Working in the bakery for years on end had not exactly helped matters, as she constantly brought home bags of leftover cakes, pastries and bread rolls that she went on to consume almost out of obligation. 'Waste not, want not,' she'd say. 'And who in their right mind can chuck a cream puff in the bin, eh? Not me!'

Wendy set up an extra deckchair for Becca in the small, sunny garden and told her to make herself comfortable while she poured drinks. There was no sign of the usual steak pie lunch, though, which was odd; it was normally well under way for Becca's arrival, delicious smells of gravy and meat wafting through the house. Maybe Mum was on some kind of post-holiday diet, Becca thought (did *anyone* go on a post-holiday diet, though?) or maybe she was still a bit *mañana* from her time away. There was no rush. Becca didn't need to be back in Hereford until six, after all.

Unhooking her feet from her flip-flops, she leaned back in the warmth, watching a cabbage white butterfly flitting drunkenly through the air, turning slow, random loops. A few gardens away she could hear children's laughter and wondered how her nieces and nephew were getting on in Builth Wells. Happy families, she hoped.

Wendy returned with two glasses of lemonade clinking with ice cubes, and settled herself next to her daughter. 'So, listen,' she said, hitching up her kaftan to display plump brown thighs, 'I've been having a think.'

Becca glanced at her in surprise. 'What?'

Wendy reached across and took Becca's hand. 'Being away . . . Well, the thing is, it's made me realize that we've got to get on with our lives again, sweetheart. We've got to pick ourselves up and move forward. Doing this, having our Dad dinners . . . it's been lovely, but maybe the time has come to . . .' She swallowed and gripped Becca's fingers, her chin giving an anxious sort of wobble. 'To stop.'

Becca's mouth fell open for a full five seconds. It was only the sight of an approaching fly that made her snap it shut again. 'I don't . . . Why . . .? Do you really . . .? Oh,' she said, her sentences refusing to complete themselves.

Wendy went on, tanned shoulders set in determination.

'I've thought about this a lot, and although I'm convinced it was the right thing for us to do at the time, it's been over a year now. Your dad would hate to think of us two still meeting up and wallowing in our sadness.'

'We're not wallowing!' Becca felt stung by the accusation. Not in a million years had she expected the conversation to take this turn.

'We are, love,' Wendy said flatly. 'I know I have been, anyway. Deliberately or not, I used it as an excuse not to do anything for a while. *Oh, I can't come out, my husband's just died. Oh, not tonight, I'm a bit sad about Terry. Oh, I would, but you know, it's not easy being a widow.*' She grimaced. 'If it hadn't been for Jen and Pamela in my earhole about the holiday in Crete, refusing to take no for an answer, I wouldn't have gone to that either, but I did, and do you know what? I had the best time. I had fun again. Whole hours would pass where I didn't even think about him, not once.' She sipped her lemonade, her eyes trying to read Becca's expression. 'I think we've both been in ruts, ducky. We've both got a bit stuck.'

'Speak for yourself!' Becca retorted. It was all very well privately worrying that you were in a rut, as she had been this weekend; but it was another thing altogether when someone else said it. There was a moment of silence while she sieved through her brain, hoping to find some examples of how she was moving on perfectly well with her life, how she was doing absolutely great. Annoyingly, nothing came.

'What's happened to that brave, bold daughter of mine who drove all the way to Spain once because she was in love with a boy?' Wendy went on. 'Where's the sparkle that used to be in your eyes? Come on, Becky, admit it. I think you've lost your way a bit this year. I haven't even heard you laugh, properly laugh, for ages either.'

Becca was still reeling from the unexpected attack. Her mum never usually spoke to her like this. 'Well . . .' she floundered. 'The boy in Spain turned out to be a dick, didn't he, so . . .' More to the point, it had been eight years ago, when she was twenty-two, back when she thought she could conquer the world. She had grown up, that was all. Couldn't Wendy see that?

'That's not the point, and we both know it.' Wendy leaned forward. 'When was the last time you went out on the pull? Had a laugh with your mates? Did a job that you absolutely loved, got out of bed feeling great about the day?'

'Mum!' Becca protested. 'What's that got to do with – ?'

'Nor me,' Wendy said quietly.

'What?'

'I said, nor me. Until I went on my girls' holiday, I've been as miserable as sin too. Trudging through the days. Seeing out the weeks as if doing time, not really caring about anything. And you've done the same. Taking those evening jobs so you didn't have to go out with friends – don't argue! We both know it's true! Giving up on your love life. Have you had a single date, a single kiss?'

'I can't believe you're even –' She thought of the last awful date, the one who'd called her Sally, and her throat tightened. He'd left his phone on the table the whole time, seizing it whenever a message came up, as if she wasn't even there. The date before him had had BO and talked about football constantly. He hadn't called her back, either. What was she doing so wrong, that she couldn't even get an arsehole like that to want to be with her?

'I'll take that as a no. But it needs to change, kid. Do you hear what I'm saying?'

'I'm not going out on the pull with you, and that's final,' Becca said, feeling trapped. 'You've got Jen and Pamela for that kind of thing, not me.'

Wendy laughed. 'Don't you worry, I'm done with all of that. I've had the best; nobody else is ever going to compare to my Terry. But you . . . You need to promise me you'll get off your bum and see your friends again. Properly. In pubs where there might be hunky single fellas about. Do we have a deal?'

'Mum! I'm not completely clueless. For goodness' sake!'

'Do we? Was that a yes?'

Becca rolled her eyes. What had got into her mum today? 'Fine! All right? YES. Deal. Anyway,' she said quickly, before Wendy could ask about her job and she had to confess to having lost it, 'I *have* been doing stuff. I made a sort of crown for Meredith. I've been in Hereford, looking after Rachel's kids. And I'm going to . . . What?'

She'd been about to tell Wendy how she'd packed up a whole box of craft stuff to take to Hereford with her, but her mum's eyes were wide with surprise, and Becca could tell she had stopped listening a sentence ago. 'You've been at Rachel's? Oh! That's nice. Since when did you two get so friendly? I mean, don't get me wrong, I'm *delighted*, but she's been so quiet, not even a Christmas card since Terry died. I just assumed she didn't want to know.'

Somehow, with all the nagging, Becca had not actually managed to tell her mother the biggest news of all. 'Sorry, I should have said at the start. She's in hospital. She was mugged in Manchester, and—'

'In Manchester?' For some reason, Wendy seemed to latch on to this as being the key element of the story, rather than the slightly more dramatic mugging and hospital parts. 'What was she doing in Manchester?'

'I don't know, but she was knocked down and – Why? What's the big deal about Manchester?'

Wendy opened her mouth, then hesitated. She had the worst poker face ever. 'Er . . . Nothing. So how is she? Goodness! Is she going to be all right? And how are the kiddies?'

'She'll be home again tomorrow, hopefully,' Becca said, still wondering why her mum was being so weird.

Manchester? WTF? she remembered Mabel texting. There had been that thing about Didsbury Library, too, the Google search, but she'd never followed it up. 'Er . . .' she said, dragging herself back to the conversation. 'And the kids are great, actually. Really chaotic, but fun too. Luke's so sweet, and Scarlet's dead scathing and witty, and Mabel . . . Mabel's got a *boyfriend* and blue hair, can you believe? She's suddenly all grown up.'

'Blue hair, eh? Goodness. She sounds a bit of a rebel, just like her aunty.' Wendy poked Becca's leg with her bare foot and smiled. 'Hey, maybe that's what we should do, me and you, give ourselves makeovers to start our new positive outlook on life.'

'What, with blue hair? What is *in* that lemonade anyway, you nutter?' But they were laughing at least, and the tension had gone, and everything seemed a bit more normal. Just about. Now she had to keep her mum distracted from the subject of 'moving on' and 'hunky single fellas' for the rest of the afternoon. 'So, are you going to show me your holiday photos or what?' she asked. That would buy a few hours, for starters.

Chapter Twenty-Two

'Well, it's your last night here with us, hopefully,' the nurse said on Sunday evening, as she checked Rachel's stitches and blood pressure with approving noises. 'Your sister should be here about midday tomorrow, I think, so that'll be nice, won't it?

'Mmm,' Rachel said noncommittally. That was one way of putting it.

In truth, she had never particularly hit it off with her stepsister, right from when Dad married Wendy and she'd suddenly had to share him with a one-year-old. She'd hated it, actually. 'Carry me!' Rachel would cry to him when it was time for her to go up to bed, lifting her arms in the air. 'Carry me up to bed!'

She just wanted to be babied too, but her dad had laughed. 'Don't be silly! Carry a great big girl like you? Give over, Rach.' And so she had trudged up the stairs to bed every night, feeling dejected and praying that Dad would come to his senses and take the two of them away. *Please, God, I just want it to be me and Dad again, like it used to be.*

As Becca grew older, the resentment began to thicken and expand, like mutating cancer cells taking over a body. It wasn't just hearing her stepsister calling him 'Daddy' that bugged her ('He's not your daddy,' Rachel wanted to shout every time), it was the way she hogged his attention each evening when he came home from work – for bathtime, stories, the endless night-night cuddles, her chubby pale arms curled tight about his neck. *He's mine now*, her smiles and giggles seemed to say. *See how I have wound him round my little finger!* Rachel, trying to get on with her homework, would scowl and stomp off upstairs to play music in her bedroom more often than not.

Then came the wild teenage years where Becca broke every rule in the house, got cautioned by the police for shoplifting, threatened with expulsion from school for trying to set fire to the science lab, and seemed to be leaning out of her bedroom window smoking or in a clinch with some awful boyfriend or other whenever Rachel came back to visit. She had turned Terry's hair white with stress, basically. And what about the day Rachel gave birth to Mabel – one of the most important events of her life! – and she couldn't get through to her dad on the phone because he was down at the police station bailing out Becca, who'd been arrested for hunt sabbing? You just could not make it up.

She had never quite forgiven her stepsister for that alone; for the weariness in her dad's voice when she finally got through to him. *Oh, a little girl, how lovely. Well done, love!* It should have been her moment of glory, her hour in the spotlight – and yet all she could hear in the background was Becca shrieking at Wendy, and of course she felt obliged to ask what was going on. Mabel had been tucked in the crook of one arm, pink and perfect, her eyelids flickering with her first baby dream, and Rachel just felt like hanging up in defeat as her dad started detailing the latest teenage antics back home. *Actually, do you know what? I don't care,* she wanted to say. *Can we go back to talking about me now, and my baby?*

If Rachel had found it hard to forgive, her dad and step-mum were a different case altogether. Oh, they let Becca off every single time, however awfully she behaved: babying her, rescuing her from this plight and that, letting her get away with murder, basically, while Rachel was slogging away, the diligent first-born, quietly acing a degree in Newcastle, getting married, becoming a mother. She had done all the right things and yet it was her unruly stepsister that commanded the limelight. There was justice for you – not.

As for what Becca had done more recently, what she'd been up to with Lawrence, their double betrayal . . . Well. Rachel should not have been surprised, frankly. She might even have predicted it, if she'd had her wits about her. It wasn't the first time her stepsister had behaved inappropriately around men, after all – there was that cringeworthy scene at Mabel's christening, where Becca had been drunk and flirted atrociously with Lawrence's friend Sam, and that Christmas Eve at Dad's a few years ago when she'd snogged the barman in their local pub. 'There was mistletoe! And it's Christmas!' she'd said when she saw Rachel's disapproving expression, like that made it any better. *Grow up, Becca*, she'd thought, pursing her lips.

Obviously being a bit wild was one thing. But to go after your own brother-in-law like that . . . To be so shameless, so don't-give-a-shit . . . It took your breath away, it really did. Especially as she'd now shown up in Rachel's house, apparently, as if butter wouldn't melt in her mouth. Talk about a cheek.

Rachel realized she was gripping the bed covers, knuckles white and pointy as the nurse went away, checks completed. This time tomorrow, she'd be home and in her own bed, she reminded herself, letting go. And even if she had to put up with her stepsister for a few hours, it would all be worth it eventually. Wouldn't it?

Becca drove back to Hereford that evening, her mind churning. There was a lot to digest and not just the enormous roast she'd put away, courtesy of the local pub. The way her mum had spoken to her . . . it had never happened before. Not since she was nagging on about GCSE revision and life choices and the fuss she'd made discovering a packet of fags in Becca's jacket pocket once, anyway. But as an adult, Mum had always seemed proud of her. She and Dad had helped Becca move into the flat, they'd bought a bottle of fizzy wine and a pot plant, saying how pleased they were that she was standing on her own two feet and making a go of things. (The subtext being, of course, thank God you're not sponging off us any more and have finally given us an extra spare bedroom, but you know, the main thing was they supported her.) She'd gone along when Becca and Debbie did their first trade fair at the NEC, even though it was a bridal fair and she was not exactly the ideal customer. Becca had always felt so loved by her parents, so adored, that to have Wendy now telling her she had to buck up her ideas – it was like being slapped round the face. In the kindest possible way.

Her mum thought she was a loser. *You've lost your way.* (What even *was* her way, anyway? How was she supposed to know how to find it?) Her flatmate clearly agreed with her mum. *Oh, are you still doing that?* Her brother-in-law viewed her as a slut. *Well, hello there.* Her nieces and nephew now knew better than to trust her with their lives after Snickersgate. And her sister – sorry, *stepsister* – had been all too quick to cut any slim ties and walk away. It felt, in short, as if she had nobody left who thought she was any good. Maybe just a sweet, elderly Welshman in his lonely bungalow, although even he might have forgotten by now that she had ever been there.

The worst thing was, she knew her mum was right. She had stopped in her tracks since losing her dad. Her heart had calcified, the laughter had died away, the light had vanished from her life. She'd had a boyfriend at the time, Ben; they'd been living together for six months when the accident had happened, but he'd dumped her pretty quickly and moved out, unable to cope with the emotional deluge that poured from her incessantly, embarrassed and awkward when she kept bursting into tears on his shoulder. Her world had shrunk down to a pub job and the safety of her flat. Meredith had answered her Room to Let advert and moved in, head-in-the-clouds Meredith, who was kind, and thankfully didn't seem to mind if her flatmate started crying for no apparent reason. Becca had become like a bad queen in a fairy story, banishing joy and letting brambles grow up around her in a thorny tangle, too dense for anyone to break through.

We've got to move on, Mum had urged, earnestness shining from her eyes. Becca found herself sighing as she drove.

Why, though? Why did they have to? The thought of throwing herself back into the world, of dancing at parties, putting on lipstick, flirting – it all seemed disrespectful to her dad's memory. Inappropriate for a bereaved daughter. But then Wendy had come out with that killer line – he wouldn't want us to go moping around forever, or however she'd phrased it – and the words had sunk right into Becca's skin, sharp with pertinence. It was true. Dad would have hated them to stay sunk in gloom for ever. He had been a cheerful, busy man, never happier than when solving a problem or fixing something mechanical. Maybe he'd been gazing down at them all this time, aghast at their mournful 'Dad dinners'. *Come on, girls! Turn those frowns upside down, for goodness' sake. Hopers, not mopers!*

She smiled to herself ruefully. Hopers, not mopers, indeed. It had been his catchphrase when she did her exams and she could hear him saying it now, his voice ringing with optimism. 'All right, all right,' she muttered under her breath as she approached the turn-off for Rachel's street. 'I'll give it a whirl.' Tomorrow her sister would be home again, and Becca could return soon after to Birmingham and get stuck into Life, Part Two. She would do some serious thinking, draw up a plan, decide where she went from here, rather than rushing straight into the first menial job that came her way. Maybe she could go back to college, retrain, feel excited about work again. She would make an effort to reconnect with the friends she'd neglected, perhaps organize some kind of night out for her birthday at the end of the month. And just to get her mum off her back, she might even ask Meredith if Baldrick, or whatever his name was, had any sexy mates. Positive thinking from here on in, she told herself. No looking back.

Chapter Twenty-Three

It was Monday and Rachel had been deemed well enough to go home. Boxes had been ticked, papers signed, medication prescribed; she had almost made it, the end in sight. In a matter of hours she would be back with her children again, she would hug them and mother them, sink into her own sofa, sleep in her own bed. She had never been one for gushing or kissing random strangers, but it took every last scrap of self-control she possessed not to fling her arms around the registrar's neck as the news was confirmed.

'We'll send your notes on to Hereford and get them to contact you with your first follow-up appointment at the fracture clinic,' he said. He was a tall, balding man with a wonky tie. 'In the meantime, rest up, and don't push it in terms of exertion. No exercise for six weeks, obviously no driving until your arm's out of plaster, and I'll get one of the nurses to give you some leaflets on various things – looking after the cast, eating, keeping your teeth clean, all that sort of stuff.'

'No exercise for six *weeks*?' she repeated dumbly. He was already walking away and she felt like grabbing that wonky tie to stop him. Hold on a minute, sunshine. She hadn't actually thought beyond getting home and seeing her kids again, but of course there were all of her new clients to consider – Adam, Hayley, Elaine et al. – people who had paid in advance for fitness sessions. If she wasn't allowed to exercise for six weeks then her fledgling career was in danger of falling from the sky, wings clipped, before it had even had a chance to really take off.

'Definitely not. Lots of rest while the fractures heal. Gentle walks are fine when you feel up to it, but nothing high-impact for the time being.' He gave her a smile, not seeming to notice how devastated she was by this news. 'Think of it as a chance to put your feet up for a change, let everyone else look after you, okay? All the best.'

Rachel tried to smile as she thanked him, but inside she felt nothing but dismay. Let everyone else look after her? What, her three children? There *was* nobody else to look after her, no loving husband, no doting mother on hand; had he not considered that? Sure, she had friends nearby, but . . . A sigh whistled from between her lips. Well, she had her pride, didn't she? Nice as her friends were, she had never been one to accept charity – not six weeks' worth, anyway.

If only her dad was still there! He would drop everything to help, she knew it – rolling up his sleeves at once, mucking in with his Fray Bentos pies and tinned potatoes for tea every evening, just as it had been when she was young. God, how she missed him still; a full year after his death. Back in the spring she had marked his birthday by lighting a candle for him at the dinner table, and Luke had asked, 'Will we ever see Grandad again?'

'No, darling,' she'd had to reply. 'We won't ever see Grandad again, I'm afraid.' It was one of the saddest sentences in the history of the world.

Her heart sank as the registrar went away, and panic began to balloon inside her about how she would cope. Even a mundane chore like dropping the children at school every morning seemed beyond her right now. The thought of leaving the house, so battered and disfigured, the bruises still purple and black around her jaw, made her break out into a sweat of anxiety.

A tear rolled down her cheek. What was she going to do?

'Jesus Christ. Oh my God. Rachel, it's me. Are you all right?'

Rachel had drifted into a light doze, but was woken by the incredulous-sounding voice of her stepsister some hours later. She opened her eyes, trying to keep her composure as a complicated mix of feelings swirled up inside: relief and anger and hurt. Surprise, too, at how much weight Becca had put on, how puffy her face seemed. 'Hi,' she said, through clamped lips. *Go on, then, say it*, she thought. *Tell me how horrendous I look, let's get it over with.*

Becca was staring, aghast. 'Bloody *Nora*,' she gulped. 'Shit, man. This is worse than I thought. They said you were a bit bashed up, but I never expected . . .' She put a hand hastily to her mouth. 'Sorry. Me and my big gob. I'm not helping, am I?'

'No. Not really.' Not at all, in fact. Rachel had never exactly considered herself a raving beauty, but when she had glimpsed herself in the mirror after the operation and seen for the first time the bandaged, swollen new version of herself gazing back in horror, she'd had a similar reaction. She had stared and stared, trying to reconcile the bruised, stitched face in the mirror with the fact that this was actually her. 'A face like a bag of spanners,' her dad would have teased. One cheek was so grotesquely swollen, you could probably have fitted an entire socket set in there.

'Do I need to sign anything, by the way? Do you have anything else with you?' Becca was asking, and Rachel snapped back to the here and now.

'No,' she said dully. 'They took my bag.'

'Of course they did.' There was a new ferocity in Becca's eyes and she reached out a hand as if she wanted to hug Rachel, then seemed to change her mind about it. 'The bastards. The bloody sods. Have the police said anything? Was there CCTV at the station, or – ?'

'No,' Rachel replied. A couple of police officers had appeared by her bedside on the Thursday – or was it Friday? – but she hadn't been able to give them a shred of detail, other than to say, *two men, average height, one possibly wearing a black T-shirt*. She could see in their faces that it was a hopeless cause. They had urged her to cancel her bank cards as soon as possible and left her to it, probably filing the whole interview in the bin upon leaving the ward.

'Oh, God. I'm so sorry. What a horrible experience,' Becca said, and Rachel shut her eyes for a moment. *Don't start being nice now*, she thought. *Not after what you did.*

'But let's get you home, yeah?' Becca went on. 'The kids are all desperate to see you. They've been brilliant,' she added quickly, as Rachel's eyes jerked open and tears started to swell again. 'Absolute troupers. And I'm sure everything will seem much better once you're back. Here, I brought you some clothes to change into, I hope these are okay. Shall I help you?'

'No, thanks.' Slowly and awkwardly, Rachel fumbled to undo the ties of her hospital gown and attempted to dress herself. My God, doing up a bra strap with only one working hand was seriously difficult. Infuriatingly difficult, in fact. Hating her own helplessness, she eventually muttered, 'Could you just . . .?' and turned her back so that Becca could do it for her.

'There. Shall I help you with the top as well?'

'No.' It was bad enough that she would have to accept favours from anyone while she was recovering, but from Becca . . . It was like the universe was rubbing her nose in it. *So, tell me*, she imagined herself saying, *did you rate my husband in the sack as highly as he rated you? You nasty little back-stabber. Couldn't resist, could you? First you muscle in on my dad and ruin his life. Then you set your sights on my husband. Fuck. Off.*

Finally she was clothed and decent again, and got gingerly to her feet, the world swinging and swaying around her as she made her first tentative steps. 'You take care of yourself,' said the nurse on duty, swooshing the curtains back, then starting to strip the bed. 'No bungee-jumping for a while, eh?'

Off they went, Rachel clutching some heavy-duty pain-killers in a paper bag along with several leaflets on how to care for her recovering body parts. It was a relief to be vertical again after five days of doing little else but lying flat, drifting in and out of morphine dreams and pain; but it felt odd, too. She had always been a strider, Rachel, couldn't bear dawdling along at a snail's pace, but she was now reduced to a shuffler, feeling vulnerable and broken with her wrist in a sling, frightened all the metalwork in her head would start rattling if she went any faster.

Becca offered her arm and Rachel said she was fine, she was not a cripple, in perhaps too snappy a voice because Becca flinched and backed off. But once they were outside and Rachel felt fresh air on her face for the first time in what seemed like weeks, the rest of the world came crowding in – vehicles, people, the distant wail of a siren – and she felt an unexpected panic seize her. It came back in a flash: the fear, the shock, the pain of impact on that cold hard floor – and she felt herself shivering and breathing hard, as if braced for the same thing to happen all over again.

'We're parked just over – are you okay?' Becca asked uncertainly. Probably thought she was about to get her head bitten off again for daring to ask another question.

Rachel's shoulders were tight and hunched, her body rushing with adrenalin. Goosebumps prickled up her arms and her head began to pound, sweat wetting her armpits and back. 'I'm fine,' she managed to say, gulping in air. She was not about to confess her sudden alarm to Becca, that was for sure.

'Right. 'Cos you really look it,' Becca said dubiously, but didn't comment any further. Thankfully they reached the car and she opened the passenger door so that Rachel could cautiously swing herself inside, lungs heaving with the effort. *Breathe*, she told herself. *It's all right. Don't get hysterical now, for goodness' sake.*

Becca's car smelled of cheese and onion crisps mingled with cheap perfume. A psychedelic My Little Pony figure swung from the rear-view mirror, and there was an empty Diet Coke can in the passenger footwell. As Rachel tried to get comfortable, something rustled beneath her – a sweet packet, she discovered, reaching around with her good arm to investigate. Lovely.

'Sorry about the state of this shit-heap,' Becca said as she hopped into the driver's seat and clipped on her seatbelt. 'Ready to go? Wagons roll!'

Chapter Twenty-Four

The journey back from Manchester felt rather uncomfortable. Becca had imagined herself bursting into the ward and hugging her sister, tears of emotion pouring down their faces perhaps, but somehow even in a hospital bed, having recently been mugged, Rachel was still able to give off distinct Don't You Dare Pity Me vibes and so Becca's arms had flapped uselessly by her side. No hugs allowed, that was clear. Take your sympathy and shove it.

Becca had never been one to stick too closely to any rules, though – and besides, it was impossible *not* to pity her sister right then. Not with those purple and black bruises around her eye sockets and her face so swollen. As for when she talked in that strange, can't-open-my-mouth way, so different from her usual assertive tone . . . it was enough to break your heart. She was thin, too. Rachel had always been slender and sporty, lucky thing, but in a healthy, athletic sort of way. Now she looked positively scrawny.

Not that Becca dared say any of this out loud, obviously

after her initial shocked outburst. She might have a big gob on her, but she wasn't a complete moron.

'So I hear you're a fitness instructor!' she said breezily as she pulled out of the car park and headed back towards the ring road. 'That sounds good. I've been getting lots of phone calls from your clients.'

'Who?' Rachel asked, although it sounded as if she didn't care all that much. With a broken wrist, cheekbone and jaw, she was banned from pretty much everything bar sitting still for the next few weeks, and certainly wouldn't be able to do any fitness instructing for a while. Whoops. Maybe this had been the wrong conversational topic after all.

'Let me think. A lady called Rita was the first one – ringing to cancel,' she replied. 'Mabel said she's done that before.'

'Mmmm.'

'And a lovely old man called Michael rang, and then this guy Adam, who was moaning about a missed appointment –' She broke off, not wanting to talk about Adam. Ever since their acrimonious parting, she had bristled at the thought of him. 'What a great idea, anyway, setting up your own business,' she prattled on quickly. 'Being your own woman – very impressive.'

'Thanks,' Rachel said. With her wrist encased in plaster, held uselessly on her lap, she reminded Becca of a bird with a broken wing. Quite a fierce bird with a broken wing, mind.

An eagle in a bad mood. A really mardy vulture who'd peck your eyes out, given half a chance.

'This guy, Michael, he must have read your advert wrong, because he rang up wanting to know how to make Irish stew!' she went on with a little laugh. Becca couldn't bear a lengthy silence between two people, it made her nervous. 'Bless him, he must have got as far as the bit on your flier that said "Can I Help You?" – and dialled without reading the rest.'

Rachel snorted. 'I've had a few nutters,' she said.

Becca felt compelled to defend Michael. 'Oh, he wasn't a nutter,' she said. 'He was ever so sweet. Just lonely – his wife had died and he was all on his own, not looking after himself very well. So I went round and showed him how to make a stew—'

'You did *what*?'

'Well . . .' Becca felt wrong-footed all of a sudden. It was hard to tell with the wiring around Rachel's jaw, but her last word had had a distinct ring of disdain. 'I went round there,' she said, wishing she'd never started on this subject, 'because I felt sorry for him, that's all.'

Rachel looked exasperated. 'I'm not running some kind of Meals on Wheels affair,' she said. It was the longest sentence she'd come out with so far, and unfortunately not a pleased-sounding one.

'I know you're not! And I obviously explained that to him,'

Becca said hastily. 'I just went off my own bat, while the children were at school, that's all. In between running around to your neighbours and phoning the police and trying to find out what had happened to you.' Her voice rose with a sudden burst of defensiveness, and she pressed her lips hard together before she said anything else. Come *on*, though, Rachel. Honestly! When she'd only been trying to help as well.

'Anyway, no harm done,' she said. Time to change the subject. 'So. Do you want to . . . talk about what happened in Manchester?'

'No,' said Rachel, turning her head to stare out of the window.

'Or even –' Becca forced herself to go on, even though everything about her sister's body language was screaming SHUT UP! – 'what you were doing there in the first place?'

'No,' Rachel repeated, more forcefully. Then she shut her eyes.

Becca glanced over at her, wondering if there was any point trying to say anything else. Probably not. She found herself thinking of friends she had with sisters – Lorna, who went on spa days with her sister, sitting around in waffle robes together, putting the world to rights; Michelle, who was so close to her sisters that they'd both been at the birth of her baby recently; Aimee, who went on holiday with her sister still, and told her every last thing about her life.

Much as Becca had always wished she could have that

kind of sisterly relationship with Rachel – even *liking* each other would be a start – she knew, too, that you could only help someone if they let you. Even though they hadn't seen each other in ages, even though they'd shared a childhood and lived under the same roof for years, she had the distinct feeling that she was wasting her time. Injured or not, Rachel still somehow managed to make Becca feel as if she was in the wrong.

The next hour and forty minutes passed in silence and Becca was just parking in the driveway when Rachel's eyes flew open as if she was remembering something. 'Oh,' she said. 'My car.'

'Yeah, I was going to ask you about that. Where is it?'

'Shit. I left it at the train station,' she said and made a small noise in her throat that might have been an attempt at a laugh, but could possibly have been a sob. 'Probably been towed away by now. The ticket was only valid for twelve hours.'

Becca switched off the engine, silently relieved that she'd actually made it to Manchester and back without needing to top up with petrol or breaking down on the hard shoulder. Thank you, Goddess of Decrepit Old Bangers. 'Right,' she replied. 'Well, I can get on to the station if you want, see if I can track it down for you. Not that you'll be able to drive for a while, I guess, with your wrist.'

She had a sudden flash of memory to when Rachel had first passed her driving test. Dad had bought her this knackered baby-blue Mini Metro, which she had blinged up with purple furry seats and stickers stuck all over the dashboard, and Becca – who must have been about eight or nine – thought it was the coolest, most awesomely grown-up thing ever. For a time Rachel had just wanted to drive everywhere – to college, to the corner shop, to her friends' houses, with her windows rolled down, music blaring. She had even offered to drive Becca to and from Brownies every week that first summer she'd had the car; a rare experience of sisterly bonding. Becca could remember the feeling of the purple furry seat beneath her bare legs even now, the orange-scented air freshener dangling from the mirror; the two of them singing along to Kiss FM at the tops of their voices. She had always been secretly sorry that the journey had to end so quickly.

Rachel's face had fallen. 'No, I won't be able to drive,' she said.

'How about your stuff that got nicked?' Becca asked. 'Has anyone cancelled your credit cards or done anything about your phone?'

'No.' Rachel sighed. 'Bollocks. Next month's bills are going to be fun.'

'Okay, well, not to worry, I can get all of that sorted out before the kids come home,' Becca said, trying to sound positive. 'You've got me for another day, remember, the nurse said I had to keep an eye on you, so you might as well put me to good use.'

Thank you, she mouthed sarcastically to herself when no such response came. She got out of the car so that Rachel couldn't see the expression on her face. *That's really thoughtful of you, Becca. Wow, yet another kind thing you've suggested on my behalf. I'm soooo grateful.*

She got the door keys out of her bag, then hesitated, momentarily self-conscious. 'This feels wrong, me letting you in to your own house,' she said, holding them out to Rachel as her sister emerged slowly from the car. Her shoulders were drawn and her head lowered as if she didn't want to be seen, although – too late – Becca was pretty sure there had been a sharp twitch of Sara Fortescue's curtains over the road just then.

Her right wrist cradled in a sling, Rachel took the keys in her left hand and tried shakily to open the front door. Oh God, it was pitiful, it really was. Of course, if Becca had been permitted to display any outward signs of sympathy, she would have taken the keys from her sister and done the deed herself; they'd be inside within two seconds. Instead, she had to pretend she was taking her time locking the car in order to avoid watching the ordeal.

Eventually the key turned, the door opened and they were in. 'Welcome back,' said Becca apprehensively, hoping Rachel couldn't smell the faint odour of burned toast that lingered from earlier that morning. She was just about to close the front door and suggest a late lunch when she noticed a familiar figure bustling across the road, blonde ponytail swinging, immaculate white sandals gleaming with each step. Oh, great. Her brand new friend. She couldn't even wait five minutes to get her beak in.

'Was that Rachel I saw coming back?' Sara asked, her plummy tone carrying on the still air. Her face was alight with expectation. 'How *is* she? What *happened*?'

Chapter Twenty-Five

Rachel stiffened at the voice and ducked into the living room, out of sight. What had she done to deserve living opposite Sara Fortescue, with her sharp little nose and all-seeing beady eyes? She tried not to groan aloud as she heard the woman calling to Becca in honeyed tones of fake sympathy, barely disguising her breathy eagerness to know the gossip. It was a miracle she'd waited this long, frankly.

To Rachel's relief, Becca wasn't having any of it. 'She's fine,' she replied coolly. 'Anyway, must get on, so—'

'But she's all right?' Oh, Sara wasn't going to be fobbed off so easily, no way. Rachel could picture her, hands clasped together earnestly, scandal antennae twitching. 'Everyone's been so *worried*!'

Rachel rolled her eyes. Bollocks, had they. Nosey, more like. *Please, Becca*, she thought, feeling tired and sore and vulnerable. *Don't let her in.* The last thing Rachel wanted was to be gawped at by the Breaking News queen.

'No need to worry,' Becca said. 'As I said, everything's fine. I'll pass on your best wishes. Bye now.'

Then came the blessed sound of the door being shut. Thank goodness. Rachel leaned back against the chair, a headache tight around her temples. Through the window she could see Sara retreating to her own house, shoulders stiff, mouth no doubt pursed in a knot of annoyance.

Becca sidled into the living room again, looking shifty. 'Er . . . That was the woman over the road,' she said. 'I hope I wasn't too brusque with her, but . . .' She pulled a face. 'Well, I wasn't sure about her, that's all. Is she really your mate, or just a one-woman neighbourhood watch scheme?'

'She's not my mate,' Rachel replied. She paused, and added, 'Thanks for getting rid of her.'

'No problem,' Becca said, with a guilty glance out of the window. 'Anyway, we should have some lunch. I'm famished, and you must be too. I'll make us something.'

Rachel felt her spirits sink even further. Eating was usually something she enjoyed enormously, but it had lost all appeal for her since the operation. All food had to be soft and liquid while her jaw was wired: soup, smoothies, runny porridge, apple sauce . . . nothing that required chewing, basically. Baby food. She had a flashback to all the purees she'd made her own children when she was weaning them – the sweet potato mush and stewed pear, poured into ice-cube trays and frozen for convenience. Bags of them in the freezer, carefully labelled and dated. Those were the days when she thought she had motherhood down pat. Ha!

'I'm not very hungry,' she lied. 'I might just go to bed.'

'Have something first,' Becca insisted. 'You stay there, I'll whiz up some soup. Won't be long.'

Before Rachel could argue, Becca was in the kitchen peeling and chopping carrots, rifling through the spice jars to find cumin and coriander, and hauling Rachel's biggest pan onto the hob. Kind as she knew her sister was being, Rachel just found it irritating, having her waltz into her kitchen like that, clanging pots around as if she owned the place. It was only when she remembered that Becca had been here several days minding the fort, looking after her children, that she was able to swallow back her disgruntlement. 'I'm making enough to keep you going for a few meals,' Becca commented, as Rachel limped in and lowered herself to a seat at the table.

'Thanks,' Rachel said, without much enthusiasm. Soup reminded her of Wendy and her ridiculous diets. She'd had them all eating cabbage soup for days on end one January when she was on a new year's self-improvement bender. The house had smelled so disgusting that Rachel had joined the school athletics club, preferring to be outside every dark rainy evening, running laps on a floodlit track, than at home, being slowly gassed to death by the stench of cabbage and farts.

'I was sorry to hear about you and Lawrence,' Becca ventured after a while. Her hair was sticking damply to her face with the heat from the soup pan, and she pushed it away. 'You don't have to tell me about it if you don't want, but . . . Well, what happened?'

The fingers on Rachel's good hand clenched into a fist under the table, as Becca began crumbling stock cubes into a jug. *Don't you dare*, she thought. *Don't you dare even mention his name to me.* She looked pointedly away, willing her sister to shut up, and Becca, for once, got the message.

'Sorry. None of my business,' she said, sounding awkward. 'Forget I asked.' She prodded a piece of carrot with a knife, then drained the pan and whizzed the cooked carrots in the blender, adding pinches of spice and several turns of ground black pepper, before returning the mixture to the hob and stirring through the vegetable stock. Meanwhile, Rachel leaned back on her chair, sapped by tiredness, looking ahead to the moment when school would be out in an hour or so and her babies would be home.

Of course, Becca couldn't stay quiet for long. 'Well, it sounds like you've totally been through the wringer,' she said eventually. 'But do you know what? You've kept going and held things together, and even started your own business when most women would be on their knees crying. Can I show you my admiration with a bowl of spiced carrot soup?'

Rachel forced a smile. The soup looked and smelled

revolting, but she feared she had little choice. 'Yes, please,' she lied.

'MUM!' cried Scarlet later that afternoon, bounding through the front door and into the living room. Wiped out after the journey home, Rachel had retreated to the sofa while Becca did the school run, and must have dozed off. She struggled to sit upright as she heard the door, but Scarlet had stopped dead at the sight of her. 'Whoa,' she said, eyes round behind her glasses. 'Shit a brick, Mum. Luke, come and see.'

'Scarlet!' Rachel remonstrated feebly. There was no mother alive who actively wanted her ten-year-old daughter to say things like 'Shit a brick', but she knew this wasn't the moment to start carping. 'Come here and give me a hug. Oh, I've really missed you,' she cried as Scarlet ventured closer and then all the way over for an embrace. Rachel put her chin on her daughter's head and breathed in the smell of her, feeling her own body relax in response. Now she felt properly at home. This was what she needed – forget soup, forget morphine: the best cure was to have your own child back in your arms, safe and close. 'How are you? How's school? Has everything been all right?'

'Your voice sounds so weird,' Scarlet said, her own voice muffled from being hugged so tightly. 'Like you're gritting your teeth the whole time.'

Rachel released her a fraction and stroked her daughter's

freckled cheek. Precious girl. Precious, funny, tell-it-like-it-is girl, she thought. 'That's why I didn't phone you. I know it's a bit hard to understand what I'm saying, but you'll get used to it, I promise. Hey, Luke,' she added, seeing her son sidle into the room. 'Hello, lovely. Are you all right? It's still me, under the bruises, don't worry.'

He was staring saucer-eyed, hanging back in the doorway as if he was scared of her, as if he didn't quite trust that it really *was* her.

'Come and look, Luke, you can see all the stitches and bits of metal where they fixed Mum,' said Scarlet, who was far less squeamish about such things.

'Did you have a fight with someone?' Luke asked, coming a few brave steps closer. 'Does it really really hurt?'

Rachel tried to make her eyes smile, because she knew her mouth wasn't up to moving in the proper directions just now. 'It does hurt a bit,' she admitted, 'but I'll be all right. That's the main thing, okay? I'll be fine. And how are you? How was school? Tell me all about your day.'

It took a minute or two for them to get over their shock at seeing her so wounded and unlike her usual self, but eventually she had both of them nestled against her on the sofa, telling her stories about their day at school, catching her up on all the important news she'd missed – that Scarlet had nearly taught Harvey how to roll over at the weekend, that Luke had been invited to a swimming party next week, that Scarlet had got a new best friend, this girl who'd just joined the class, called Lois. 'Oh yeah,' said Scarlet, as if tacking on an after-thought, the least important thing to have happened, 'and Luke went to hospital on Thursday.'

'Yeah, Mrs Keyes took us in her *car*,' he said, 'and had to jab me in the *leg*, but she did give me a lolly and said I was really brave.'

Rachel couldn't speak for a moment. *WHAT?*, she wanted to screech.

Becca came in just then, catching the tail end of the con-versation, and her creamy freckled skin flushed pink. 'Ahem, yes, I was going to tell you about that,' she said guiltily, set-ting down a tray of orange squash and a plate of cut-up apple pieces. 'I'm so, so sorry, Rach. It was all my fault. I didn't know he had a nut allergy and I gave him some of a Snickers bar. But he's fine, it was dealt with really quickly and there was no harm done.'

'Apart from the jab in my leg,' Luke pointed out.

'Apart from that, yes,' Becca said, chastised.

Oh my God. Rachel felt dizzy with horror. She stared at her sister, wondering if this was some kind of joke. Judging by the pleading light in her eyes and the way she was clasping her hands together so nervously, it wasn't.

'I helped,' Scarlet said importantly. 'I took him to the office.'

'You did,' Becca said. 'Scarlet was very cool in a crisis.'

'And I was brave,' Luke prompted, determined to hang onto the spotlight.

'You were brave.' Becca bit her lip, gazing at Rachel. 'And I'm really sorry. He's absolutely fine now, obviously. I just . . . didn't know.' *How was I supposed to know?* begged those blue eyes.

'Right,' Rachel said, lost for anything else to say. Thankfully, the front door opened again then and in came Mabel, with a ton of make-up on (banned at school), her wrists jangling with bracelets (banned at school) and her skirt hitched up to mid-thigh level (banned at school). 'Hi, love,' Rachel said, wondering whether or not she had the stamina to take her daughter up on any of these crimes. 'Did you have a good day?'

Mabel stared at her. 'Oh my God, Mum, you sound like Stephen Hawking,' she said, reaching for her phone. 'Hey, can I take a photo of you to put on Instagram?'

Rachel was not used to being an invalid. All her life she'd been healthy and strong, sleeping well, eating well, loving to run, swim and dance. Growing up without a mum for years had taught her to be independent, to look after herself and others. She'd been so terrified of the same fate befalling her children that she'd done her utmost to stay fit for their sakes as much as her own. It was only really when she'd gone through childbirth and the immediate aftermath that she'd had the experience of being looked after, and even then, she'd insisted on getting up and carrying on as soon as possible. No need for any assistance, thank you very much.

Back in the hospital, she'd felt similarly keen to escape. Of course she'd be fine, of course she would manage, did they not realize who they were talking to? But it only took a few hours of being at home for her to reconsider that actually, much as she hated to admit it, things were going to be pretty difficult for some time. Taking a shower, for instance, when you had one arm in plaster that you had to keep completely dry. Trying to help your kid with homework when your brain was so fogged by the mega-strength painkillers, it was all you could do to keep your eyes open. Buying food from the supermarket when your car had been towed away (Becca was on the case), you'd had to cancel all your credit cards (ditto) and couldn't actually face going out in public . . . Not to mention the fact that she had client appointments to keep, and bills to pay. The next six weeks of enforced inaction were already looming in a scarily daunting way. What was she going to do? Oh, how she wished none of this had happened, that she'd never met Violet Pewsey and never boarded the train to Manchester in search of the truth!

She was just having a little moment of panic in her bedroom that evening, having said goodnight to Luke, when Becca knocked on the door, the phone in her hand. 'For you,' she said. 'Someone called Hayley George, about tomorrow?'

God, yes, lovely Hayley, one of her new clients. Her smiling face swung into Rachel's mind and she hesitated, at a loss for what to do. 'Can I ring her back in five minutes?' she asked in a low voice, and Becca nodded and withdrew again.

This was the downside of not working for a big company, of course. No sick pay, no team of staff to pick up the slack when necessary, no-one available to stand in for her. She was going to have to cancel her clients, one by one, because none of them would want to wait six weeks until she was fit enough for another appointment. It seemed such a shame, though, when she'd managed to build up a decent list, when she was just starting to feel that she might be getting somewhere. If only there was some way around it!

There came another gentle knock at the door. Becca again. 'I've written down her number – or I can phone her back and pass on a message, if that's easier,' she said. 'And . . . Look, tell me to bugger off if you want, but . . . are you sure you'll be all right if I go tomorrow? I know they said to hang around just for twenty-four hours, but . . .' She shrugged. 'The thing is, I lost my job last week, so if you want me to stay here another few days, that's fine. I can take the kids to school for you, do the cooking, basically step into your shoes as best I can.' She gave an awkward smile. 'I promise I've learned my lesson on the peanut front, too.'

Rachel considered the offer. As angry as she'd felt with Becca over the last seven months, there was no getting away from the fact that her stepsister had been pretty heroic in recent days, stepping in at the drop of a hat, keeping the home fires burning in Rachel's absence. 'How come you lost your job?' she asked while she tried to decide.

'Um . . . Well, to be honest, I was meant to be working the night I came over here,' Becca confessed, scuffing a foot around on the carpet as if she was a child. 'I made an excuse to my boss, but he saw through me and gave me the boot.'

'Oh God. Sorry.' Rachel hadn't even thought about the consequences of Becca having to uproot herself following Sara's phone call, putting her own life on hold.

'It's all right. It was a shit job, anyway. But I don't have to rush back, that's what I'm trying to say. And I've spoken to quite a few of your clients already, so if you want me to ring around the others for you, or . . . or whatever, then just say.' She paused. 'It's been nice spending time with the kids, they're really brilliant. And maybe you and I could . . .' Another awkward shrug. 'Could get to know each other again?'

Hmm. Rachel wasn't so sure about that – *Like you got to know my husband, you mean? I don't think so* – but one of Becca's earlier comments had come back to her, about how she could step into Rachel's shoes. It was a long shot, but maybe, just maybe, it was worth a try. There was only one way to find out. She took a deep breath. 'Can I ask you a favour?'

Chapter Twenty-Six

Rachel had been very un-Rachel-like since she'd come home, Becca thought: quiet and subdued, not making much eye contact. This was Rachel the reboot, without the can-do briskness, the go-getting energy that had always left Becca feeling sluggish and slobbish in comparison. The only time she remotely came to life was when she was talking to the children and her face softened with love for them. Poor Rachel. It made Becca feel uneasy to see her so lacklustre, as if the world had shifted off its axis, as if the zombie apocalypse might be nigh.

Still, they had struck a kind of deal, born out of necessity. Becca was going to stay there for the week, to look after them all while Rachel caught up on her rest. Mabel had grudgingly allowed Scarlet to move into her bedroom for the duration, so that Becca could sleep in Scarlet's bed (surrounded by about a hundred pictures of Harvey the golden retriever, all pink lolling tongue and adoring eyes). Becca was also – and this was the bit that terrified her the most –

going to look after Rachel's clients. Yep. Not joking. Rachel was going to work out a detailed programme for each of them while Becca guided the clients through each session, exercise by exercise.

'I must be mad,' she whispered on the phone to her mum that evening, from the safety of Scarlet's bed. 'I mean, *me*. Supposedly giving them a proper hard workout. They'll all laugh at me like that horrible Adam bloke did. It's going to be awful.'

'You'll be great!' Wendy assured her. 'They'll love you. And think how thrilled your dad would be if he knew what you were doing for your sister. Think how happy it would have made him to see you two under the same roof, getting on so well!'

Becca pulled a face. She wasn't sure they *were* getting on all that well, to be fair. Rachel still seemed quite cold towards her; stand-offish, as if she was only putting up with Becca because she absolutely had to. She'd probably be even un-friendlier, cross even, when Becca made a hash of things with her clients too, she thought glumly; but she had promised to try. 'I was just so surprised that she even *asked* me, Mum,' she confessed. 'It caught me off guard. I don't think she's ever asked me for a favour before. I know it sounds a bit pathetic, but I felt sort of . . . flattered.'

'That all sounds really positive to me,' Wendy replied. 'Maybe this will be the start of a new friendship between you two, you never know. Good luck, anyway. Up and at 'em, as your dad would have said.'

'Thanks, Mum,' Becca replied. Then her phone pinged with a new text as she hung up: Meredith.

Hey! Long time no see. How are you? Banquet was DIVINE. Everyone loved the diadem! My friend Alianor wants one too – can I give her your no.? xxx PS Am rather smitten with Leofrick.

Leofrick, that was it – not Baldrick, as she'd called him the other night. Becca read the message again and smiled at how Meredith-ish it was.

YES! she replied. *Please pass on number. Tell her she can pay the elec bill! (JOKE.) Am here for another week. I miss you! What happened with Hot L then? Tell all. xxx*

She was about to press Send, but Wendy's words from the Sunday chat of doom rang around her head as if her mother was right there in front of her, finger wagging again. Oh, all right then, she thought. If I must.

PS Has L got any sexy mates, btw??

She pulled a face, but pressed Send. What the hell. At least she could tell her mum she was trying.

★

Once the children were safely dropped at school on Tuesday morning, Becca girded her loins for the next job on her list: the ten o'clock appointment with Hayley. After the disastrous experience with Adam Holland the week before, the last thing she felt like doing was undergoing any more ritual humiliation at the hands of sporty people, but when she had phoned Hayley back the night before and explained the situation to her, offering her a cut-price discount, Hayley had sounded about a million times nicer than Adam.

'Just promise to say the magic words "Wedding Dress" to me whenever I look like I'm about to give up, that's all you need to know,' she'd said to Becca, a hint of scouse accent in her voice. 'And give Rachel my best wishes.'

Being nice on the phone was one thing, but Becca still had butterflies in her tummy as she cycled across town to meet her client. She hoped Hayley would still be so easy-going about the situation when she opened her door to find Becca standing nervously there with her pale, wobbling thighs and her decidedly non-six-pack belly. *Oh*, she imagined the other woman saying in polite dismay – an improvement on grumpy Adam's *You're kidding me* response, admittedly, but still enough to make her feel terrible. What if she, Becca, was the sole cause of all Rachel's clients dropping out, one by one, because she literally wasn't fit for the job? Heat surged into her face at the idea. The shame she would generate would be enough to power the Birmingham Christmas lights.

Hayley's house was a nice old Victorian semi with an olive-green front door, just off Holmer Road. Becca's faint hopes that Hayley would be the same sort of size as her, and that the two of them could compare notes about their favourite crisp flavours and the injustice of a slow metabolism, died an instant death when the front door was opened to reveal a slim, smiling woman with long chestnut hair in a ponytail. Oh God. Hayley was gorgeous *and* skinny. Why the hell did *she* need a personal trainer? With big brown eyes and dimples, plus great legs, she was the sort of woman who could look amazing in a sack, let alone a beautiful wedding dress with flowers in her hair.

'Hi,' Becca said apprehensively, positioning her cycling helmet faux-casually so that it hid her stomach and trying to swallow back the nauseating rush of nerves. 'I'm Becca. Obviously. Hi there.'

'Hello. Gosh, you don't look like Rachel! I'm Hayley, pleased to meet you. And this is Wilf,' she added as a whippet appeared behind her in the hallway, tilting its elegant head to stare up at Becca. 'You don't mind if he joins us, do you? Only I've got so much work and wedding stress and –' she threw her hands up – 'general *stuff* going on, that I thought I could combine today's workout with his too. Get us both out of the house together.'

'That's fine,' Becca said. She was so desperate for approval – and keen not to antagonize another client – that she probably would have agreed to anything. She cleared her throat and took a last quick look at the sheet of paper, printed with the list of exercises that Rachel had drawn up. 'So . . . Shall we get started?'

Becca talked Hayley through a series of warm-up stretches, then they set off for a jog along a lane and into nearby woodland, Wilf trotting alongside them. Well – she said 'jog', but Becca was pedalling away on her bike, for the simple reason that her face was sure to puff up into a red tomato if she tried to run as well, and she'd barely be able to breathe, let alone call out instructions. Rachel, naturally, would have jogged along with her client, offering tips about technique and setting the pace, but never mind. Now if only Becca could think of something fitness-instructor-y to say, other than admiring Hayley's cool neon-blue trainers.

'Ahh, fresh air,' Hayley said before Becca could blurt out any other inane remarks. 'That's better. Kind of defeats the point of living near the countryside if you stay in all day slaving over a hot laptop, right? This feels good.'

'I know what you mean. Makes a change from the Birmingham ring road, too,' Becca agreed. The fresh air *was* kind of nice, she thought to her surprise. She had never been much of an outdoorsy person, unless there was a pub garden involved, but she was glad not to be working in some sweaty pub kitchen or cafe with limited daylight right now. It was still early enough to feel fresh rather than sticky, and now that they were into the woodland, the sun was casting dappled light on the path. Somewhere in the distance she could hear a tractor's slow chug, and closer by was the sound of birdsong. Much as she'd always prided herself on being Brummie, there was definitely something to be said for country living too.

'That's where you're from, is it? Ahh, I love Birmingham. My dad's a Villa fan. The rest of the family are from Liverpool, so you can imagine all the earache we give him.'

'Poor guy,' Becca said with a polite laugh, even though she knew nothing about football. 'So when's the big day, then?' she asked, changing the subject. 'Are you wildly excited?' Her front wheel wobbled slightly as she turned towards Hayley, and she panicked for a moment she was about to swerve into the dog. There must be a way to hold a conversation and keep your bike pointing straight ahead, but if there was, she didn't seem to have cracked it yet.

'First Saturday in October,' Hayley replied, jogging steadily along. 'And I *am* excited – well, at least I will be, once I've stopped being so stressed. Aarrgh. The mother of the groom is slightly doing my head in, put it like that. Imagine Genghis Khan in a pastel polyester frock, that's her.'

'Sounds tricky.'

'She's just . . .' Hayley made a noise that sounded as if she was being strangled and the dog looked up at her in alarm.

'It's like she thinks it's *her* wedding, do you know what I mean? Like, just because her son is getting married, it some-how means she gets to call all the shots, make all the deci-sions.' She gave a hollow laugh. 'Well, take it from me – that is not going to happen. Even if we end up literally coming to blows across a wedding cake. *My* cake, by the way, which has gorgeous colourful macarons all around the top, not the break-your-teeth granny fruit cake she wanted us to have.'

Becca laughed. 'Oh dear.'

'Yes. Totally "Oh dear". That's partly what I like about coming out for a run. No phone calls, no texts, no emails with her telling me about Dorothy, some godawful friend of hers who can fold serviettes into the shape of swans, and do we want her to do ours at the wedding breakfast?' Hayley punched the air as she ran, and Becca couldn't help but giggle. 'No, Dorothy, we sodding well do not, but . . . Sorry,' she said, breaking off. 'I'm ranting, aren't I? Ranting when I don't even know you. I promise I'm not always like this. That woman brings out the worst in me.'

'Hey, rant away,' Becca told her. 'Get it off your chest. Do some primal screaming if it won't frighten the dog.'

'Oh, he's used to it,' Hayley said. 'Anyway, I'm supposed to be enjoying being out of her reach. Let's not talk about her. How about you, are you married? I could do with some tips if you've got any.'

'Nah,' Becca replied. 'I'm hopelessly single. In fact, things have been so dire, I've just had my mum, of all people, telling me I need to go out on the pull.' She raised an eyebrow and Hayley laughed breathlessly. 'She even made me promise I was going to "get out there" again and find myself a "hunky fella". Like it's that easy!'

They chatted away for several minutes, Hayley jogging, Becca cycling, and Becca felt the tight knot of tension she'd carried all morning slowly begin to unwind. Hayley was *lovely*, really friendly and bubbly, and easy to talk to. By now the path had petered out and they were going along the forest floor, which was muddy in patches from the overnight rain but smelled gloriously fresh – of damp earth and pine needles. This was good, Becca thought in surprise, bumping in the saddle as she rode over a tree root. She was actually, weirdly, enjoying herself, even if her bum was going to be black and blue by the end of it. She'd be able to give Rachel a run for her money in the bruising stakes. Oh, but talking of Rachel . . .

'Shit!' she gulped, suddenly remembering what she was supposed to be doing. Working, not just gossiping and idly cycling along. 'Sorry. I think we were meant to have started something called interval training now. I was so enjoying chatting, I forgot about it. Do you mind if we stop a minute so that I can check?'

Hayley thudded to a halt, hands on her hips and panting while Becca consulted the creased piece of paper that she'd extracted from her back pocket. 'Right, yes. Interval train-ing,' she said, scanning the instructions. 'God, this sounds grim. You have to run a bit faster now for a minute – more of a challenging pace, Rachel said. Then you walk for two minutes so that you catch your breath. Run, walk, run, walk, repeat to collapse.' She pulled a face. 'Rather you than me, girl.'

Hayley let out a groan.

'And she said to be really strict. I've got a stopwatch thing on my phone and she said I've got to make sure you're run-ning till the last second of each minute.' She frowned, trying to envisage how this would work. 'I'm not *quite* sure how I'm going to cycle and look at the timer, so I'll set an alarm, is that okay? Right, here we go. Ready? Thinking about wedding dresses? Thinking about gasps of wonder as you step foot on that aisle?'

'Always thinking about wedding dresses,' Hayley con-firmed. 'Let's get this over with, then.'

The interval training looked pretty gruelling, it had to be said. Becca tried to liven things up with wild cheers of encour-agement for her client, which led to an even more haphazard pedalling style. Then a squirrel made a kamikaze dive in front of them, proving irresistible to Wilf, who leapt joyfully after it, right in front of Becca's bike, causing her to swerve straight into a tree. Both she and Hayley ended up laughing helplessly, despite the fact that Hayley could hardly breathe.

'Sorry,' Becca gurgled. 'I'm shit at this, aren't I? I'm a bloody awful personal trainer, I know. But I promise I'm trying to do my best. Don't tell Rachel how crap I am, will you?'

'No, of course not,' Hayley said, trying to recover herself. 'And you're not crap. This is actually really good fun. Are you all right, by the way? Your face, honestly . . . Brilliant. Wilf, you'll be banned from coming next time, you lunatic. Come here!'

Becca heaved her bike back onto the track. One of the pedals had scraped the top layer of skin off her shin where she'd lost control, and she'd somehow whacked her funny bone on the handlebars, hard enough to know she'd be feeling the knock for the rest of the day. 'This week on *You've Been Framed* . . .' she said ruefully, rubbing her elbow.

'Ahh, no, you're very professional,' Hayley spluttered, still laughing. 'I feel like I'm training with . . . Kelly Holmes or someone. Jess Ennis.'

Becca grinned, pushing an escapee tendril of hair back up in her cycling helmet. 'People are always mixing me up with those two,' she said, and consulted her phone, trying to gather together the last shreds of her dignity. 'Okay – just five seconds before another sprint. Get ready – go!'

Towards the end of the hour, it was hard to say which of them looked more exhausted as they went through a series of cool-down stretches in the back garden – Hayley or her trainer. Both of them were red in the face and sweaty, and weak from all the laughter too. 'That was fab,' Hayley said, undoing her ponytail and shaking out her hair. 'Really good. Nice one!'

Becca was delighted. 'Do you mean it?' she asked.

'Yeah! I've never laughed so much during an exercise routine – *and* it was a bloody good workout too. Thanks.'

Becca could feel herself beaming. 'Well, thank *you*. Thanks for being so nice and not . . . well, not judging me on sight, basically. Giving me a chance. One of Rachel's other clients last week actually took one look at me and told me not to bother, so—'

'You're joking! How rude.'

'I know.' Becca sighed. 'The worst thing is, he's only gone and apologized, so Rachel's insisting that I carry on with his sessions, starting Thursday.' She made a sick face. 'Looking forward to *that* one, like a hole in the head. Anyway! Enough moaning, I'd better go. Great to meet you. Same time next week?'

'Definitely,' Hayley said. 'I'll look forward to it. See you then.'

Chapter Twenty-Seven

Dear Violet,

Forgive me for writing out of the blue. We met at my father, Terry Farnham's funeral last year, and ever since then I've been mulling over some of the things you said at the time, particularly about my mother, Emily. When you mentioned 'the trial', I was confused and didn't know what you meant, but I have since done a bit of research and found a clipping from the Evening Post, *from 1978, with reference to a charge of child cruelty and negligence. Obviously this came as something of a shock . . .*

The children were at school, Becca had gone to meet Hayley, and Rachel was typing one-handed at the laptop. Her mission to speak to Violet in person might have failed but the unanswered questions about her mother were still buzzing around her head. She had to get some answers, dig deeper to uncover the truth, if only to distract her from her injuries.

After they'd had that peculiar conversation at the funeral,

Rachel had decided to put the whole thing out of her mind. She just didn't want to know, she told herself; sometimes you were better off remaining ignorant. Besides, she had a lot of other things on her plate in the coming months: grief, her marriage breaking down, unemployment, all that fun stuff to be getting on with. But the other woman's words would come back to her every now and then like whispers in a dream, tantalizing her with what had been left unsaid. *I was with your dad, you see, when it all happened. Did he really not mention me?*

The temptation to find out eventually wore her down and so, almost a year after she'd spoken to Violet, Rachel eventually cracked. After one too many glasses of wine one night, she had turned to Google and typed in her mother's name. A second later, up had come the damning report from the newspaper archive, as if it had been waiting quietly there for her all this time. 'Mother Abandons Tot on 24-Hour Binge', read the headline. And in that moment of discovery, Pandora's box was cracked wide open. No going back now.

The article referred to beautiful, doting Emily as drunk, aggressive and thoughtless; it detailed how, one particular December Friday night, she had left two-year-old Rachel all alone in the small flat where they lived while she went out dancing. The police had been called by a neighbour when they heard the baby crying the next morning – 'Pitiful, it was,' the neighbour, a Mrs Ruth Farraday, had said, 'like she knew she'd been abandoned' – and the police had ended up breaking the door down to rescue the little girl. Her.

Seeing those words, that story, in black and white newsprint had devastated Rachel. It was as if someone had picked up everything she thought she knew about her past and tipped it upside down. She told herself at first that it must be a mistake – a coincidence, maybe, a second Emily Farnham. It couldn't possibly be true. Her mother had loved her! *My little Dandelion*, she'd called her; written the words herself on the back of the photograph, in that distinctive sloping handwriting.

But Violet had mentioned a trial, hadn't she? And deep down, Rachel knew in her heart that the story must be true. She had pored over that short news report again and again until she knew it backwards. Then she'd combed later online issues of the newspaper for stories about the court case. Emily was up for child neglect and abandonment, but Rachel could find no further information about it. Had the court pronounced Emily an unfit mother and ordered that her daughter be taken away? Had Emily been punished with a prison sentence, even? What had happened next?

Questions swirled around her head: all the many gaps in the newspaper story, the missing details she wanted to know. What else had Dad not told her? And where had he been, anyway, when the family home was falling into chaos, his wailing daughter abandoned in some scuzzy third-floor flat?

Off snogging Violet Pewsey, by the sound of things. He must have taken the decision to gloss over the unpalatable truth of why they'd left Manchester in the first place, airbrushing over it with his confection of lies.

Amidst all the uncertainty, there was one question that beat louder and more insistently than any others. What if Emily hadn't really died of bone cancer, as Terry had always said? What if she was still alive?

It hadn't been hard to track Violet down, a year on. Wendy had set up a memorial page for Terry on Facebook and Rachel had ploughed through the archived posts, searching for clues. Before his death, her dad had been quite a fan of social media and as a result, there were many messages of condolences: former colleagues, as well as mates from the cricket team and pub, neighbours, a load of Manchester United fans he'd become friendly with on various forums. Her heart almost thudded into arrest every time she saw that someone called Emily had left a comment, but further investigation ruled them quickly out of contention. Then came the message from Violet.

Violet Pewsey: Such sad news. Terry u were a good man. I'll never forget the giggles we had that weekend in Blackpool. A star has gone out in the sky. Miss u. xxx

Weekend in Blackpool, eh? Was that what Violet meant about them being together 'when it all happened'? Had Dad done the dirty on Emily, and she'd reacted by going on a sod-you bender herself, throwing caution to the wind by leaving Rachel alone? Maybe she'd only meant to slip out for a drink. Maybe she was struggling on her own, upset about Terry – *just a quick one*, she might have thought, quietly shutting the front door of the flat so as not to disturb the baby before sneaking down to the nearest pub. But then somehow it had all gone wrong . . .

Rachel knew herself how tough it was being a single parent – it was the hardest job in the world. She hated to think of her mother cold and heartbroken in the depths of winter, tired and unhappy, with only a toddler for company. Everyone made mistakes, didn't they? And okay, so if Emily had intended to leave Rachel alone that night for an hour or so just while she had a quick, morale-boosting drink with a friend, then it wouldn't have been the absolute worst thing in the world, would it? She must have been waylaid, that was all. Maybe even kidnapped! Assaulted in an alley on her way home – it could have happened!

Maybe, though – and this was the darkest thought of all, the one that refused to go away – maybe it had been Rachel's fault. Maybe she had played up that day, whingeing and whining, winding up her mother until Emily had reached the limit of her patience. Maybe Emily plain old hadn't liked her, wished she didn't have a daughter at all, tying her down. Had Rachel been the real one to blame for her mother's actions?

She leaned back against the hard kitchen chair, feeling miserable. Once she'd discovered Violet on Facebook a fortnight ago, it had only taken a few quick clicks to find out more about the woman. She didn't seem to have any security or privacy settings on her account, and Rachel had thus discovered Violet still lived in Manchester, worked as a librarian, and was single although, as she said in her own words, 'Still hoping to meet Mr Right!!!' She was a vegetarian, a wildlife lover and active within the local Woodcraft Folk group. Within minutes, Rachel had made a few calls around the Manchester libraries to pin her down to the one in Didsbury. Bingo.

Her plan last Wednesday had been to travel to Didsbury and just turn up at the library, persuade Violet to have coffee or lunch and provide some answers, face to face; lay the ghosts – or not – to rest. Of course, one bang on the head and a close encounter with the concrete floor of the train station had put paid to that notion. She wasn't exactly in a fit state to repeat the journey any time soon, either. But she could send her a message instead, word by word, question by question.

She resumed typing, determined to seek out the truth once and for all.

Chapter Twenty-Eight

Becca's second client that day was the elusive Rita Blackwell. In her seventies and now in a retirement home, she had been bought a series of fitness sessions by her daughter, who had rung Rachel, concerned that her mother had become inactive and put on weight as a result. Yet after only one appointment, Mrs Blackwell had phoned with an excuse every single time afterwards. 'I try to rearrange the sessions, telling her that they're all paid for,' Rachel explained, 'but she's obviously very busy because she can't seem to fit me in at any other time, apparently.'

Becca knocked back the rest of her coffee. She was still feeling pleasantly glow-y from the success of that morning's session with Hayley, although perhaps that was the caffeine. Rachel had actually thanked her for it, though, and said the magic words 'Well done', which felt rather like being awarded the Nobel Prize for sisterly achievement. 'So what do you want me to do? Try to find out why she's not keen?' she asked now. Just listen to her, the expert! The sports psychiatrist! But oh, it felt nice to be discussing this with her sister, as if they were a team after all these years. Are you watching this, Dad? she thought, her gaze flicking up to the ceiling. See what a good sister I can be, too!

'If you can. She rang while you were out to say she couldn't make the 1.45 appointment as planned because of . . . I can't remember what it was now, there's been so many reasons. The dentist this time, maybe. But if you go along there early – say for one – then you might be able to catch her for a chat.'

'Roger that.' Becca rather liked the thought of an exercise-resistant client. At least she'd have something in common with this one. It was nice, too, the way that Rachel was speaking to her – almost like an equal, like a colleague. Ever since Rachel had got married and had children, she'd been somewhat haughty and patronizing, as if her life was worth more than Becca's, as if she was better, full stop. If nothing else, the accident seemed to have made her humbler; more civil. Almost human, in fact.

The retirement home was out on the Ledbury Road, and easy enough to find on the bike. Becca was feeling more confident in the saddle already, and enjoyed being able to whiz past stationary cars at the traffic lights. Forget the clients getting fit, she thought in amusement, navigating her way through town. By the end of her stay with Rachel, she was going to have thighs like Victoria Pendleton and a tiny little bottom. Bring it ruddy well *on*.

Willow Lodge smelled of cooked fish and ammonia, with a top note of rose air freshener. The light, bright June morning seemed a distant memory to Becca as she was shown through to an overheated lounge where a group of residents sat dully in a semicircle in front of *Bargain Hunt*. One was knitting, her needles clicking together like the rattle of a typewriter, but the others were slumped in stupefied silence, eyes on the screen.

'Rita? You've got a visitor, love,' the receptionist said.

It was the knitting lady who glanced up. Becca was rather hoping it would be. She had a round, jolly sort of face with lots of laughter lines, framed by silver-grey curls, and was wearing a white cotton blouse with a rosebud print and navy blue slacks. 'Ooh dear,' she said, seeing Becca standing there. There was a mischievous glint in her eye. 'You're not from the council, are you? Have I done something wrong?'

'I'm not from the council,' Becca said, just as the lone man of the group let out a cackle.

'They've come to take Rita away!' he cried gleefully. 'About time, and all.'

'No-one's taking anyone away,' Becca said. 'I was wondering if I could have a quick word, that's all. Maybe outside?'

Rita put down her knitting. 'A word outside! The plot thickens!' she announced to the group, none of whom responded in any way – apart from the man, who gave another wheezy laugh and slapped his bony corduroy-clad thigh.

'Here, this way, darling,' Rita said, gesturing towards a door. 'We can sit in the courtyard away from all these nosey parkers. We don't want the likes of Malcolm earwigging on my great lottery win, or whatever it is you've come to tell me about.'

Outside, they settled themselves on a bench in the sunshine. The courtyard was small and rectangular, surrounded on three sides by the home, and Becca could hear the sounds of someone washing up through an open window nearby as well as the faint rumble of traffic from the road. The fourth side of the rectangle consisted of an ornamental wooden barrow, planted up with purple geraniums, and a path leading out onto the main garden. A fat wood pigeon strutted around the lawn beyond, chest puffed, as if it owned the property.

Becca explained who she was and why she was there, and Rita's cheerful expression immediately faded to one of guilt. 'Oh no! I'm sorry,' she said, with an embarrassed laugh. 'You caught me out. I don't really have a dentist appointment later,' she confessed, looking up through her lashes. 'Just like I didn't have a doctor's appointment the week before. I'm a terrible woman, aren't I? I'm an ungrateful old baggage, I know.'

'No!' Becca cried. 'Absolutely not. And I'm certainly not here to tell you off or make you feel bad. We just want to know why.'

Eyes down, Rita appeared every inch the penitent. 'You see, the thing with Carol – my daughter – is that she means well but she doesn't always take the time to think things through properly. I'm sorry, but I'm just not sure this exercise lark is for me. There. Now I've said it.'

'You didn't enjoy the session you had with Rachel before?' Becca asked. 'Not your cup of tea?'

'No! Not at all.' She glanced unhappily at Becca. 'No offence to your sister, I'm sure she's doing her best, but . . . Well, she had me doing star jumps and jogging on the spot, out here in the gardens. Where all and sundry could see me! It was ever so embarrassing. Malcolm – that's the old goat you just saw in there – kept calling me Jane Fonda. For weeks afterwards! He's only recently stopped, and I'm hoping he's forgotten about it now. Alzheimer's, he's got. Forgets our names, half the time. Typical, that was the one thing he *did* remember – and boy, didn't he enjoy teasing me about it, as well!'

Rita was quite pink in the cheeks by now, and Becca felt sorry for her. If *she'd* been forced into huffing and puffing through public star jumps and jogging, in front of all the people she lived with, then she'd have hated it too. 'Okay, point taken,' she said. 'Tell me how you kept fit in the past, then. Is there something else that we could try instead? Swimming, maybe, or cycling? I'm not the fittest person in the world either, as you can probably tell, but I've quite enjoyed getting back on a bike recently. We could have a go at that if you wanted, find a nice flat cycle path without any cars . . .'

A look of relief had passed over Rita's face as she realized Becca was not about to bully her into a round of press-ups, right there and then, in her slacks. But now she was shaking her head. 'Cycling? I haven't been on a bicycle for twenty years, love,' she said. 'I'd be a bit scared to take it up now as well, after my fall. That's how I ended up in here, see – because I fell over on my own kitchen floor like an idiot, and broke my hip. Carol and her husband decided I was too old and feeble to live by myself any more. Too old! I'm only seventy-seven, thank you, that's practically a teenager compared to most of them in here.'

Becca felt a bit sorry for her. 'You don't seem very feeble to me,' she commented.

Rita's chin jutted. 'You're telling me, kid! I'm not! I can't bear being stuck in here,' she said. 'When I think about the new people in my house now, letting my garden get overgrown – oh yes, I went back and had a look to see what they'd done. And they've cut down my pear tree, the savages, and concreted the front right over. How could anyone do such a thing?'

Becca didn't know what to say. 'Sorry to hear that,' she ventured. 'You liked gardening then, I take it?'

'Oh yes. I'd be out every day, I loved it. I shared an allotment with friends too, so I'd be busy there as well. Nothing like being outside, seeing something grow, feeling the seasons change.' Her eyes misted over. 'I miss it.'

Becca looked around. The courtyard had a few large pots – one with lilies in, another couple with olive trees – but down the path and beyond the building there was the garden itself, with herbaceous borders and mature trees. 'Can't you do some weeding and digging in this place?' she asked. 'I'd have thought they'd love you to help. And I keep reading what good exercise gardening is, all that bending and stretching.'

'It *is* good exercise,' Rita agreed. 'And makes you feel great too! But me, help? Well, I tried that. Health and safety issues, apparently.' She gave a snort that made it quite clear what she thought of the home's health and safety issues. 'I'm not sure what they're worried I'll do. Cut off my toes with a spade or trip over a daisy, goodness knows. Scared I'll sue them, probably. Me!'

'How daft,' Becca said. 'How about we go for a walk today, then?' she suggested. 'Stretch our legs. Maybe drop in for a coffee somewhere nice, have a bit of a chat. Nobody could call you Jane Fonda for that, could they?'

Rita hesitated, then nodded. 'Go on, then,' she said. 'Seeing as you're here and all. A walk would be all right.'

'You can tell me about your knitting too,' Becca said as they got up and began ambling slowly away. 'I'm a knitter myself – well, I used to be, anyway. Was that a windmill stitch I saw you doing back there?'

Rita smiled. 'Very good,' she said. 'Very good!' She tucked an arm into Becca's in a companionable sort of way. 'Do you know, I've got a feeling you and I are going to get on just fine.'

Chapter Twenty-Nine

It was Wednesday morning and the phone was ringing, but Rachel didn't move from her chair. Her friend Jo had left a few messages by now – friendly, are-you-okay sorts of messages – but she had ignored them all, just as she had ignored another friend, Diane, who had knocked unexpectedly on the door the day before. Rachel had stayed silent and hidden in the kitchen while the other woman called through the letterbox ('Rach? Are you in there? It's Di'), only emerging when she was quite sure her friend had gone. Since the accident, she had left all phone calls and knocks on the door for Becca or the children to deal with – it was easier that way. Unfortunately for today's caller, Becca had just gone to put a bin bag in the dustbin, so they were out of luck.

The answerphone message started up. *Please leave your name and number after the beep.* Then came a voice.

'Rachel? It's Wendy here.' Her stepmother sounded unusually timid. 'Becky told me what happened, and I just wanted to say how sorry I was to hear you'd been hurt. Let me know if you want me to come and help at any time, won't you? Or if you want to . . . Well, chat. About anything. Just let me know. Lots of love to you all. Okay, bye, then.'

Rachel hobbled over and deleted the message. If she wanted to *chat* about anything – what did Wendy mean by that?

Becca came in, wiping her hands on her jeans. She had a turquoise scarf in her hair and was wearing a bright pink top with a parrot print; quite an eye-popping combination against her flame-red curls. 'All done. Shall we head off to the fracture clinic? Might take a while to find a parking space at the hospital, if it's anything like the one in Birmingham.'

'Sure,' Rachel said. 'Thanks.'

'By the way,' Becca said, grabbing her car keys, 'was that the phone I heard ringing?'

'Yeah,' Rachel replied, turning her face away as she put on her shoes, 'but it was nothing, just some sales thing. No-one important.'

The fracture clinic was heaving with broken people, limbs in plaster, some patients swinging in carefully on crutches or in wheelchairs, children in school uniform with arms in slings, leaning against their mums, looking fed up. It was the first time Rachel had actually left the house since returning from Manchester two days ago, and as soon as she had stepped outside her front door she'd experienced the horrible panicky sensation again, her heartbeat speeding up, her breath short.

Oh no, oh no, oh no. People would see her. People might hurt her again. There would be questions and stares and double-takes. Could she do it? Could she actually do this?

Before dread could completely overwhelm her, though, Becca took a firm hold of her left arm and steered her into the car, and then somehow or other they were off and driving down the street. Her sister the rescuer, Rachel thought, dizzy with relief. It felt strange to have their roles reversed like this. She'd always seen Becca as a flake, someone inept and babied, used to having their dad rushing around fixing her car or mending the washing machine for her. Rachel had always felt secretly contemptuous of women who couldn't change their own fuses – she'd never needed rescuing before now. Yet here they were: her meekly in the passenger seat, while Becca took the lead and drove confidently down the road. Maybe leopards did change their spots now and then. Or maybe her sister had finally grown up a bit after all this time; who knew?

WAITING TIME TODAY: APPROXIMATELY 50 MINUTES, it said on a big whiteboard in the waiting area of the clinic, and Rachel groaned in frustration as she sank into one of the green vinyl seats. 'Balls to that,' Becca said. 'Shall we grab a coffee somewhere and come back later?'

Rachel, who had never been a risk-taker (she wouldn't dream of going over the speed limit when driving, even on the emptiest of country roads), shook her head. Knowing her luck, they would have just walked out of earshot and her name would be called, the queue miraculously contracting by some quirk of fate. 'I'll stay here,' she said. 'Just in case.'

Becca strode off to find the nearest coffee place while Rachel tried to get comfortable, her thoughts returning to the message she'd sent to Violet the day before on Facebook. Had Violet read it yet? What would she say in reply? And how would Rachel feel when the truth finally crashed into her inbox?

Searching online for answers had proved fruitless. Dad had taken her away from Manchester, that much was clear, and they'd come down to Birmingham together – presumably to make a new start in life, to forget all about police and social services and court cases. But what of Emily, left behind? A person wouldn't get sent to prison for neglecting their daughter one single time, would they? Surely it was always in the best interests of the child to stay with their mother? Unless the mother in question was really, really dreadful or didn't even want the child in the first place . . .

The thought pained her. That couldn't be right, could it? Surely Rachel would have had some deep-seated memories of fear, of unhappiness, if Emily had been anything but a loving mother. The brief flashes of memory she did have were happy ones – the hand in hers, her mother's laugh. *My little Dandelion . . .*

Her head spun as she tried to make sense of the situation. What if those memories were false ones, though? It did happen sometimes, your mind playing tricks on you. Maybe the cool, reassuring hand she remembered was some other woman: her reception teacher Mrs Carlton, maybe, or a kind neighbour. Oh, who knew? Who could say, after all these years? She hated doubting herself, though. She hated muddling around in the dark for information; guessing, speculating.

'Rachel Jackson?'

She jolted from her thoughts at the sound of her name, and said 'Here' like a child in school, to the male nurse standing at the edge of the waiting area.

'If you could just take this along to X-ray,' he started saying as she approached him, but then a loud, shrill voice from behind drowned him out.

'Rachel? Is that you? Rachel Jackson? Dear Christ. What the hell happened?'

Oh no, thought Rachel, a rush of alarm rising in her like a spring tide, and then the panic was back, flooding her system as if it had never been away. Of all the people to bump into here today, it had to be Melanie Cripps, head of the PTA and Queen Bee of the playground. Melanie Cripps, Sara's croney-in-chief, who never took no for an answer, who kept on at you until you bought a raffle ticket or volunteered to help with the cheese and wine evening. There was no Becca to rescue her now, either. 'I—' she floundered, reeling backwards a step, the words catching in her throat.

Melanie's meaty face loomed, her frank gaze pinning Rachel to the spot. She was large and busty, with a big mouth and an even bigger voice. 'Let's have a look – WHOA. Face-ache. My God! Did you go three rounds with a lamp-post or something?'

Everyone was staring. The whole waiting area had fallen silent; all eyes and ears tuning in to the drama. Rachel felt her knees buckle. *Don't fall again*, she thought in fright. *Don't fall!* 'I—' she tried a second time, her voice little more than a whimper.

'Just kidding!' Melanie said, but her wide blue eyes were darting here and there, taking in all the details of Rachel's injured face. She'd have her camera out any minute. *Selfie time!* 'Jesus, though, love. What did you *do*? Makes a sprained ankle look like nothing, right, Jode?' This was to her daughter, small, thin Jodie Cripps, who currently had one finger rammed up her nostril. Poor Jodie, doomed to a lifetime spent bowing her head in deference to the Force Ten gale that was her mother.

'If you'll excuse us,' the nurse beside Rachel said just then, as Melanie drew breath for further questioning. His voice was polite but firm, and he took a step forward so that he was between the women, his body shielding Rachel's. 'We're on our way to X-ray. Take a seat and someone will see you shortly.'

'Oh. Right. Sure.' Melanie didn't look too thrilled at being interrupted in full flow, but the nurse was already ushering Rachel away. 'Call me!' Rachel heard her yell as the nurse took her around a corner and out of sight.

The danger over, she felt limp, her adrenalin retreating like a tide sucked back into the sea. She could feel herself shaking, her vision clouding, and she fought hard to control herself. 'Sorry about that,' she mumbled. She was gripping onto his arm with her good hand, she realized in the next moment, and let go hurriedly. Now he would think she was a right sap.

'God! No need to say sorry,' he replied. He was about her age, his brown hair just greying a little at the temples, a calm sense of authority about him. There was a crease in his sleeve where she'd been clinging onto it, she noticed, and she looked away, ashamed of her own weakness. She never used to be so helpless. 'I hope you didn't mind me interrupting,' the nurse went on as they walked down the corridor. 'Is she a . . . friend?'

Rachel gave a mirthless laugh. 'No. Absolutely not. She's just one of those mums at school who . . .' Oh, why was she going on about mums at school to this nice man who probably couldn't care less? 'She's just a bit . . . in your face,' she amended, her cheeks burning. *No shit, Sherlock.*

'Yeah. I kind of got that impression,' he said drily. 'Here we are, anyway.' They had arrived at another waiting area, and he put a printed sheet of paper in the receptionist's tray. 'Take a seat; you shouldn't have to wait too long to be seen. Once the X-ray's over they'll give you a form. Bring it back with you to the clinic waiting room and either give it directly to me, or there's a box on the wall where you can leave it, okay?'

'Okay,' Rachel echoed, although she'd hardly taken any of this in. He had such kind eyes, she was thinking: mocha brown with flecks of amber, the sort of eyes you could trust. She blinked and looked away, worried that she'd been staring, then gave a nod. 'Absolutely.'

'Great. See you in a bit, then,' he said, and disappeared down the corridor.

Once the X-rays had been taken she made her way back towards the waiting area, but as she got nearer she could feel her breath tighten once more, dread liquefying in her stomach at the thought of bumping into Melanie again. The woman had the volume of a public address system, and all the tact and sensitivity of an ironing board. At least with an ironing board, you could put it away in a cupboard and shut the door. Alas, not with Melanie. Rachel could already imagine the chit-chat in the playground: *Just like Frankenstein's monster, I'm not joking. Stitches all over her face and wires in her mouth . . .*

I heard it was the husband. The ex-husband, I mean. Remember last year when he beat up one of her colleagues? . . .

You can't trust the handsome ones, can you? You just can't.

She shuddered, drawing to an abrupt stop in the corridor, her feet suddenly refusing to go any further. In the past, she'd have been able to deflect Melanie's over-loud, personal questions with a gracious smile and a throwaway line, before swiftly changing the subject to the woman's favourite topic of conversation: herself. But now she felt too raw, too vulnerable. She hadn't realized until the accident just how much confidence she had always taken from her appearance – and how different this new patched-up face of hers made her feel. People had noticed her in the past, especially men; but she had known, without wanting to sound vain, that it was because she looked a particular way. Tall and slim, with blonde hair and good cheekbones . . . rightly or wrongly, the combination had lent her a certain cachet.

The stares and second looks she was receiving now were of a different sort, though. The bruises on her face were gradually turning from dark purple to blue and green, and her cheeks remained swollen. Even in a hospital waiting room, where everyone else was injured, she could feel other people's gazes rest on her a shade too long. It was horrible, like being a caged animal, viewed as a freak.

And still her stupid feet wouldn't carry her forward. Still her heart was pounding too fast. She leaned against the wall, imagining herself becoming trapped in this corridor forever because she was too scared to go out and face Melanie Cripps and her foghorn mouth.

'There you are!' Oh, thank goodness for Becca, appearing around the corner just then, coffees in hand, flip-flops slapping along the floor in her haste. 'I thought you'd done a bunk on me. Is everything okay?'

Rachel gave a shaky laugh. 'Just . . . having a moment,' she replied, feeling like an idiot. 'I don't suppose . . .'

'What? Are you all right?' Becca's eyes searched her face. 'You've gone really pale.'

'Is there . . .? Did you notice . . .?' Rachel made a valiant effort to pull herself together. Deep breaths. 'A woman. Big, tall woman with a little girl, in a school dress like Scarlet's . . .'

'Bouffey sort of hair? Loud voice?' Becca launched into an impersonation. 'Jodie, don't scratch. Jodie, sit nicely on your bottom. Jodie, start saving up for therapy, darling, because you're gonna need it by the time you're a teenager.' She cocked an eyebrow. 'Her?'

Rachel nodded. 'Yes. Her.'

'They've just left. Telling everyone what a disgrace the car park fees were in this place, or something, I'd tuned out by then.' Becca's face changed. 'Ahh – of *course*. Yes, I've seen her at Scarlet and Luke's school, blah-ing on at top volume. She's gone, anyway. Coast is clear. And by the way –' She leaned in closer. 'You've been missing some hot male nurse action in there. This dude on duty, he's absolutely bloody gorgeous. Come back and let's do some shameless ogling together while we wait.'

Shameless ogling indeed. Only Becca would suggest such a thing at the fracture clinic. All the same, though . . . 'I think I know who you mean,' Rachel confessed. 'Six-foot-ish, brown hair, nice eyes?'

'Nice arse, you mean. Corrr!' Becca's eyes were bright with enthusiasm. 'Don't pretend you haven't noticed, because I won't believe you.'

They were stood there whispering together like – well, like *sisters*, Rachel thought, the word taking her by surprise. Like proper sisters, like friends, confiding and confessing. 'I don't know *what* you're talking about,' she tried to say primly but Becca gave her such a look, she found herself feeling giggly. Sharing a joke with Becca! And then of course, who should come down the corridor but the man himself, he of the kind eyes and pert bum (yes, all right, so she *had* noticed), this time wheeling an elderly lady along.

'Everything all right?' he asked. 'You're not lost, are you?'

Becca elbowed Rachel in a completely unsubtle way. 'We're fine, cheers. In fact –' she caught Rachel's eye, and her lips twitched wickedly – 'you could say we're better than fine. Right, Rach?'

Rachel turned bright red with embarrassment. 'Yes,' she squeaked.

The nurse gave them both a doubtful look, but didn't comment. *Patrick*, Rachel read on his name badge as he drew level. 'Okay, great,' he replied. 'I'm just taking Mrs Amos here through to X-ray, then I'll be back. I think it's nearly your turn.'

'Thank you,' Rachel managed to say, not daring to look at Becca again. Honestly! She was acting like a teenager.

'*Phwooarrr*,' Becca whispered under her breath as they walked back along the corridor. Her wired jaw prevented Rachel from laughing but she could feel a rising hysteria, the awkwardness of the moment reducing her to a schoolgirl.

'You're a bad influence,' she hissed to Becca, as they made it back into the waiting room and collapsed into a couple of chairs in the corner. Rachel could tell she'd gone bright red, and tried to pull herself together. 'You're a nightmare!'

Becca was grinning, her eyes dancing. 'Don't give me that,' she replied. 'You loved it.' She elbowed her again, making kissy noises. 'Mmm, Patrick. Mmmm.'

'Shuddup,' Rachel said, elbowing back, but unable to help a snort of mirth, especially as Becca went on to entertain her with various awful photos and descriptions of men that her flatmate Meredith had been texting her recently.

'That'll teach me to go round asking if her new crush has got any sexy mates,' Becca moaned after one particularly awful photo of a potato-headed man with full beard and cloak who apparently called himself Ulric the Wolf.

Careful, a voice warned in Rachel's head as she found herself experiencing an unexpected rush of affection for her naughty younger sister. *Don't start getting too close to her, remember. Not after what she did.*

'Rachel Jackson?' a nurse called just then, and she got to her feet.

'Want me to come with you?' Becca offered but Rachel shook her head. She had to keep Becca at arm's length, she reminded herself. Forgiveness had to be earned. But all the same, she felt disconcerted as she walked over to the consultant's room. Every now and then she forgot about being angry and found herself actually *liking* her sister. It was all very confusing.

Chapter Thirty

Becca woke up the next day with a sense of impending doom. Oh joy, she had an appointment with her least favourite person that morning: Arsey Adam Holland himself. She knew already that the hour's session he had booked would drag by like an entire week.

'He seemed all right when I met him,' Rachel had said, surprised to hear of Becca's misgivings. That didn't cut any mustard with Becca, though. Yeah, she thought sourly, pulling on some leggings that just about passed for sportswear. Of course it had gone all right for *Rachel* and Adam – because Rachel was a proper fitness instructor, respected by other adults, due to her impressive athleticism and natural air of competence. Becca, on the other hand, with her bouncing bosoms and lardy behind . . . well, she didn't need to dwell on it. They all knew what had happened last time, and her skin still tingled with mortification whenever she replayed the scene. By now, she had built up this second appointment so much in her mind that she was half-afraid she'd give Adam a shove straight into the river as soon as she clapped eyes on him.

'Please don't,' Rachel said wearily when Becca voiced her concern. She had been a bit tetchy ever since she'd spotted another red love bite on Mabel's neck that morning, and the two of them had had a bust-up over breakfast. (Scarlet had immediately begun composing a song on her violin about the incident, entitled 'Vampire Boyfriend, You Are Gross'.)

Having assured her sister there would be no river-shoving or client deaths, Becca cycled off to meet the dreaded Adam in the same place as last time, not daring to be a minute late. Rachel had laboriously typed up a programme that Becca would supposedly oversee, starting with a five-minute warm-up (including jumping jacks and skipping – ha!) then a three-mile run, some torturous-sounding lunges, sit-ups and press-ups, and another shorter but faster run, followed by a cool-down. As little as she looked forward to seeing this client again, Becca had the feeling she might kind of enjoy watching him suffer his way through that lot. She would be *really* strict, too, and blow her whistle at him any time he appeared to be flagging. That might teach him to watch his manners in future. Yeah!

Back through the city centre she cycled, winding her way down past the majestic cathedral and Bishop's Palace and round the bend till she reached the river front. It had rained in the night, and the Wye looked full and fast-flowing as she cycled over the old stone bridge. Nearly there. *Keep your cool*, she reminded herself. Sixty minutes and it would be over. Plus, if she kept him running and leaping about fast enough, he wouldn't have any breath left to insult her.

'Hello again,' came Adam's voice as she wheeled the bike across the grass and onto the riverside path. He was striding along towards her in his running kit, his expression inscrutable. He wasn't scowling and sneering this time at least, but all the same, it was kind of awkward meeting him again when their last encounter had involved her throwing balled-up paper in his face.

'Hello,' she said coolly. Professional and chilly, that was her motto today. Nothing he could say would get to her: fact. She pulled out Rachel's exercise plan and pretended to study it, glad he didn't know how clammy her hands suddenly were. 'So! Let's get on with it, then.'

'Ahh,' he said, as if he found something amusing. 'Have you still got the hump? I thought we were over all that now.' His sorry-but-not-all-that-sorry expression reminded Becca of the similar face Scarlet had shown that morning, when Rachel had told her off about ringing the RSPCA and reporting Lawrence's mother for not looking after Harvey properly. ('Well, it's true!' she had replied, unrepentant. 'She doesn't give him enough hugs. And she *never* brushes him properly like I used to.')

'I have not got the hump,' Becca assured him. 'So . . .'

'I did say sorry,' he reminded her. 'I *am* sorry. This is all a bit of a novelty to me, you see.'

'What, doing exercises?' Becca retorted. 'Or being civil to people who are trying to help you?'

Whoops. So much for professional composure. Now he was back to glowering, his jaw ominously taut.

'Joke, obviously,' she said, hastily. 'And apology accepted. Now – shall we get on with it?'

He ignored her, fiddling with some app or other on his phone; one of those fitness trackers, she guessed, and her earlier resolve seemed to buckle. She wasn't very good at this, she thought to herself pessimistically – well, not with him, anyway. Fifty-eight minutes to go.

'So! Without further ado,' she went on, 'let's warm up. Marching on the spot first, arms by your sides. Let's do this!'

It wasn't long before Becca was rather enjoying herself. Quite frankly, the power of making a grown man do all sorts of stupid things in public was awesome. Especially when she took it into her own hands to improvise a little and embroider some of Rachel's (quite boring) instructions. Oh, she had him skipping up and down, she had him clapping his hands overhead as he marched, she got him doing the grapevine move she remembered from her own aerobics classes all those years ago. 'And *clap*, that's it,' she called out, trying not to laugh, as he grapevined his way along the river path, in front of dog-walkers and pram-pushers, looking ungainly and uncoordinated and basically ridiculous. Revenge was *sweet*.

'What the hell *is* this warm-up?' he grumbled eventually. 'I feel like flaming Beyoncé.'

Perhaps it was time to stop making a spectacle of the man. They did tend to hate it, blokes, if they thought a woman was laughing at them, didn't they? And the last thing she wanted was him complaining about her to her sister. Becca shrugged innocently. *Nothing to do with me, mate. Just following orders.* 'Rachel swears by it,' she said, trying to keep a straight face. 'And do you feel warm?'

'Yes,' he had to concede.

'Excellent! Warm-up completed,' she said, pretending to do a big tick in mid-air. 'Now for the really tough stuff. We're off for a nice three-mile run. Well – *you* are. I'm going to cycle alongside you, cheering you on.'

He raised an eyebrow. 'Cheering me on?' he echoed.

'Yeah! Woo! Go! And again! Lovely running! Super running! Woo! You can *do* this! Yeah! Feel the burn!' she yelled, forgetting momentarily that she was supposed to be playing it cool and professional. She had never been much of a natural at either. 'Not really,' she added meekly, seeing him look appalled. 'Just another joke. Right – come on, then. Off we go.'

By now he was positively scowling – maybe she'd over-egged the pudding there – but he did start running, at least, and she quickly hopped onto her bike and pedalled hard to catch up. She just had to hope that there wouldn't be any rogue squirrels or overexcited dogs causing her to fall off the ruddy thing today. He would love that, wouldn't he? Might even actually crack a smile for once.

'So,' she said, once she was level, 'why did you decide to get a personal trainer, then? What's your story?'

He glanced sidelong at her without breaking his stride. 'My story? Does there have to be a story?'

She considered the question, then reflected on Hayley, the stressed fiancée; Rita, the overeating lady who missed her friends and allotment; and the two women she was booked in to see later on, Jackie and Elaine, both of whom were determined to lose a few stone having become concerned, apparently, that their husbands didn't fancy them any more. 'Oh yes,' she said. 'There's always a story.'

'Well . . .' He fell silent all of a sudden, his face inscrutable. Aha. So there *was* a story – one that he didn't want to tell her. But before he could answer, his phone rang and he stopped to take the call. 'Hello, Adam Holland speaking? Yes. Yes, I did. I've asked Polly to check over the figures, but if the merger is to go ahead, then . . .'

Having screeched to a halt, Becca frowned at him, but he didn't seem to notice. Er . . . hello? In the middle of a session here? Warm muscles rapidly turning chilly, three-mile run kind of meaningless if you stop for a phone call? He didn't seem to pick up on her *WTF?* vibes, though, and carried on as if she wasn't even there.

'Right, on we go,' he said a few minutes later, shoving his phone back in his pocket and resuming jogging.

Just like that. Okay. *You're the boss.* Becca pulled a face as she cycled after him. 'So, about your story,' she prompted. 'You were just about to tell me when we got interrupted.' Damn it, she wanted to hear the wretched story now, to know what had turned him into such a grumpy bastard.

'Was I?' he replied infuriatingly.

Becca had to fall in behind him as they passed an old footbridge where a group of tourists had stopped to take photographs and were spilling onto the path. 'Yes,' she called after his retreating body. 'You were. But don't worry. If it's really boring or embarrassing, I won't judge you too harshly.'

'I could ask you the same thing,' he said as she caught him up. 'How come you're here, filling in for your sister when – no offence, I swear – I get the impression that it's not your thing?'

Ahh, the old *no offence* again. That hadn't taken long, had it? And he 'got the impression' that this was not her thing – right. So basically he was saying, dressed up in fake politeness, that he thought she was shit at it. (He had a point, you know, but all the same: manners.) 'Well . . .' she began, but then his phone beeped, and he immediately pulled it out of his pocket.

'Just a sec,' he said, slowing to a walk as he peered at the screen. Then he stopped altogether again, and began typing a quick message. *You're kidding me*, thought Becca. Was he for real?

She clamped her lips together very tightly while she waited. The customer is always right, she told herself. Even when they've paid out good money for an hour's fitness training and seem more bothered with their own personal telecommunications, the customer is still always right. What a load of cobblers *that* was.

'There.' Phone back in pocket, off they went for a third time. He glanced across at her. Was that a *smile* on his face? she thought, disconcerted and not a little wary. Maybe he'd just had some good news. Maybe it was a sex text from his girlfriend. Hey – or boyfriend, of course. Both, perhaps. She was cool with that.

'So. Your story, then,' he said, and she realized too late that the smile she thought she'd seen on his face was more of a smirk. 'Don't worry if it's boring or embarrassing,' he went on. 'I won't judge you.'

Touché. Too-bloody-shay. It was all Becca could do not to steer her bike right over his stupid foot, to be honest. That might wipe the smug look off his chops. 'We're not here to talk about me,' she replied primly. ('Hoity-toity!' Wendy said in her head.) 'We're here for your fitness training. So—'

Wouldn't you know it, his phone rang *again* then, and, as

before, he stopped to take the call. 'Well, just deal with it, can't you?' he said impatiently to the person on the end of the line, turning his back on Becca.

Becca felt very much like cycling straight on, flicking the Vs as she went. This was getting ridiculous. With Rachel's other clients, she'd been able to have a laugh and a joke, there had been some easy camaraderie; but with him, it felt like unrelenting hard work – combative, point-scoring. Was that his pathetic way of making sure she knew her place? He didn't seem to want to be there; she certainly didn't. And they still had forty whole minutes to go, according to her watch. Maybe he'd have a full-on conference call next and she could sit down and have a break while she waited. Twiddle her thumbs. Make some plans for world domination.

She lengthened her neck as a cool breeze rustled through the trees, and wished she'd been brave enough to wear shorts rather than leggings today. It was only mid-morning, but the air already felt sticky.

He was taking his time on this call, getting very aerated with someone on the other end of the line. Becca rolled her eyes, remembering Hayley a few days earlier, who couldn't wait to get away from her phone and emails, to leave everything else behind while she cleared her head and ran. She had given her full attention to the hour's training and really got something out of it. Adam, meanwhile, didn't seem able to switch off for longer than five minutes.

'Sorry about that,' he said, once the call had ended.

'Why don't you just ignore it next time?' she couldn't help asking as they set off again. 'Other clients have said to me –' Oh, get her, the pro! – 'that they really enjoy stepping away from work things, and just being in the moment while they exercise.'

'Do they,' he replied tightly. 'That's nice. Unfortunately, in my job, business doesn't stop simply because I feel like "being in the moment".' He made speech marks with his fingers, just in case she hadn't noticed he was mocking her.

'It would stop if you let it,' Becca pointed out. She was done with being polite now. After today's session, she would go back and tell Rachel that actually, she didn't want to see Adam again. Give the man a refund, for heaven's sake, it just wasn't working out for either of them. 'Looks to me like your phone has taken over your life,' she went on. 'How can you concentrate on anything when you leap to attention every time it makes a sound?'

A muscle twitched in his jaw. 'And you're a business expert, are you? The next Karren Brady? Remind me what it is you do again . . .?'

She flushed. *Bore off, Adam, you patronizing bellend.* 'Time for a sprint,' she announced, changing the schedule on the spot. 'When I shout for you to go, you have to run as fast as you can for a minute. *Go!*'

What the hell, it was time to wheel out Plan B: get him

out of breath so he couldn't actually speak any more. She watched him sprint away, and cycled serenely after him. With a bit of luck, he'd have a heart attack and collapse by the end of the hour, she thought callously. And then she'd never have to put up with him again.

Chapter Thirty-One

It was dinner time, and everyone was at the table – apart from Luke, who was standing on his head on the kitchen floor, his face rapidly turning red. 'What would happen if I stayed here for, like, hours and hours?' he mused.

'Your head would explode,' Scarlet said, making a series of squelching sounds.

'No, it wouldn't,' Luke said, but there was a flicker of doubt in his eyes nonetheless.

'What would happen is you'd miss out on your tea,' Rachel said, dishing broccoli spears and garden peas onto the children's plates and trying not to look at her own boring bowl of soup and yet another disgusting protein shake. Christ, she'd had enough of invalid food now. 'Get down, please, and sit at the table.'

'You'd better not spray blood or brain juice on me when your head explodes,' Mabel grumbled. She had come home late from school again, her hair smelling suspiciously smoky, and had merely shrugged, muttering something about hanging out by the river with friends when Rachel tried to interrogate her any further. ('What? Am I not allowed to have *friends* now?' she had huffed, before putting an imaginary gun to her head and pretending to shoot.) Rachel was going to have a little talk with her after dinner, she vowed. Lay down a few ground rules. If she had the energy, that was. If she could get through this mealtime without losing her patience.

'Squish, squash, splatter,' Scarlet sang ghoulishly, grinning at her brother. His legs wobbled and then down he crashed, just missing Becca, who was carrying a dish of pasta bake to the table.

'Oi, careful,' she said. 'Right, grub's up. How was everyone's day?'

'Luke got told off for fighting,' Scarlet said immediately. 'He had to see Mrs Jenkins and everything. Hashtag *in the shit!*'

'Less of that language, thank you,' Rachel said, Lawrence's latest tirade still ringing in her ears. He had left a number of voicemail messages recently, telling her how disgraceful the girls' language was as well as detailing the RSPCA debacle with grim fury. 'And Luke, I don't want to hear stories about you fighting, understand? Punching someone is never the right answer.'

'It is if they punch you first,' Scarlet said.

'Or if you're actually a professional boxer,' Mabel added smartly.

'Or if they say please-please-please punch me, I'll give you a hundred million pounds if you punch me,' Luke said with an angelic smile.

Rachel gave him a look. 'That seems unlikely,' she pointed out. 'But the thing is—'

'To be honest, I felt like punching someone too today,' Becca put in just then, dishing the pasta onto plates.

Brilliant, thought Rachel, with a little sigh. *Wrong message. Not helping.*

'Only I didn't punch him,' Becca went on, oblivious. 'I gritted my teeth and rose above. Teeth – gritted.' She put down the serving spoon to demonstrate. 'Fists – ever so slightly clenched but not actually punching.' She raised an eyebrow at Luke as she gave him his plate of food. 'If you go around punching people when you're a grown-up, you get arrested, you know.'

'I didn't *punch* her anyway, I just kicked her. And pulled her stupid hair,' said Luke, unperturbed.

'Luke!' Rachel cried, spluttering on a mouthful of soup. 'You mustn't kick people *or* pull hair. Do you understand?'

'Who did *you* want to punch, Aunty Bee?' Scarlet wanted to know. (Of course she did.)

'Was it a robber?' Luke asked.

'Why don't we change the subject?' Rachel asked, but nobody took any notice.

'It was this jerk called Adam,' Becca said, pulling a face.

'Who is a total and utter –' She broke off, perhaps remembering Rachel's earlier rebuke about language.

'PooHead?' Luke supplied helpfully.

'Thank you, Luke. Yes – that. Adam PooHead,' Becca said.

The children all burst out laughing, and Rachel felt herself bristle. 'Can we please not insult my clients in silly, puerile ways?' she snapped, but the children were already talking over her.

'Does he have, like, a big fat poo instead of a head?' Scarlet giggled.

'Wobbling around when he walks!' Luke sniggered.

'Why did you want to punch him, anyway?' Mabel wanted to know.

'Oh, just . . .' Becca had been laughing too, but caught Rachel's eye and sobered up quickly. 'Um. He was getting on my nerves. But obviously violence is absolutely *not* the answer, so I was very professional and polite. Honest. Anyway! Scarlet, was that Lois I saw coming out of school with you today?'

'Yes, she is so cool,' Scarlet said happily, and then was off chatting about this new friend of hers, to whom she seemed to have taken a massive, adoring shine.

And relax, Rachel thought, relieved, spooning up more soup, right until Scarlet said, beamingly, 'And guess what, Lois doesn't have a mum, so we thought it would be really cool, Mum, if you could marry her *dad*, and then we'd be sisters *and* best friends!'

Rachel spluttered on her soup. Stepsisters, you mean, she nearly said. Be careful what you wish for . . .

Chapter Thirty-Two

That evening, while Rachel and Mabel had their little chat in the living room, Becca retreated to the kitchen and opened up the slightly random box of arts and crafts supplies she'd brought from home. Spying her younger niece drifting past the doorway, she hauled out the length of fake fur fabric and called her in. 'Scarlet? I've had an idea,' she said. 'I saw this and thought of you – well, I thought of your dog, really. I know you miss him and nothing can replace him but I was wondering, maybe, if we cover an old cushion with this lovely brown furry fabric, it might be the next best thing to cuddle.'

She thought for a moment Scarlet was going to curl her lip at her – the girl was not one to fake a smile or give a person any bullshit – but after a moment's stern consideration, her niece rewarded her with an approving nod. 'Yes!' she said. 'And we could put some floppy ears on too, and a tail, and I can cuddle it in bed.'

Phew. 'Exactly!' Becca unfolded the fur. There was about two metres left of it, caramel-brown and shaggy, far better suited to a dog cushion than her disastrous coat endeavour. 'So we just need an old cushion – or even a pillow . . .'

'I'll get my pillow,' Scarlet said, bolting from the room at once and thumping up the stairs.

Luke had wandered into the kitchen too by now. 'Can I make one?' he asked.

'I don't have enough fur for two doggy pillow covers, I'm afraid,' Becca replied, 'but . . .' She cast about for an idea, and her eye fell on the utensil jar on the worktop. 'We could make some wooden spoon people?' she suggested, remembering a similar activity at the after-school club where she'd briefly worked. 'With hair and eyes and clothes. That might be fun.'

He nodded. 'Yes, please,' he said, sitting at the table and rummaging through her box of stuff. 'Hey, googly eyes,' he exclaimed, holding up the packet. 'Can I make a wooden spoon ME?'

'Absolutely,' Becca said, examining the spoon collection in the jar. Hmm – a fancy olive-wood ladle . . . she should probably leave that one free of googly eyes or wool hair. But in the drawer below there were four or five wooden spoons that looked perfectly ordinary. She could pick up some replacements the next day, they only cost fifty pence or so each. Rachel wouldn't mind, would she?

She plucked out two spoons, hoping it would be all right. 'Here – one can be "you", and one somebody else,' she said. 'Let me track down some glue and we'll get started.'

*

The three of them settled down to a cosy session of cutting, stitching, gluing and colouring. This was how Becca had always imagined motherhood: arts and crafts on the kitchen table, home-made Christmas cards, potato prints, glitter everywhere. It was heavenly – and both Scarlet and Luke seemed to be enjoying themselves enormously, too. A feeling of luxurious tranquillity unrolled across the three of them. Scarlet hummed as she sewed running stitch along the second side of her pillow. Luke kept up a detailed commentary as he stuck eyes and hair to his first spoon, then drew on the nose and mouth with felt-tip pens. He made arms out of pipe cleaners, winding around the stem of the spoon, and Becca showed him how to cut two T-shirt shapes out of red fabric and glue them back to back onto his figure.

Just as Becca was starting to think she'd got this childcare business licked – for once! – she heard thunderous footsteps down the stairs and then Mabel stormed into the room, her face angry enough to curdle a milk pudding, as Wendy would say. 'I hate Mum!' she yelled to the room at large, before slamming out of the back door and marching down the garden.

'Oh dear,' Becca murmured.

'I don't hate Mum,' Luke said loyally.

'Do you think I should go after her?' Becca wondered, as Mabel yanked open the shed door and vanished inside. Then came a muffled scream.

Okay, so that decided things. Becca jumped up and ran down the garden, fearing the worst – a lawnmower falling on her niece, a garden fork stabbing her foot . . . 'Mabel?' she called. 'Mabel, are you all right, love?'

The shed was cobwebby and cramped inside when Becca arrived, and Mabel was sitting on a bag of garden compost, sobbing her heart out. She'd clearly been a visitor here before because there was a collection of dog-eared paperbacks on one shelf, along with a biscuit tin. The scream, Becca now realized, had been one of rage and frustration rather than actual bodily harm.

Perching on a splintery wooden crate, Becca listened while her niece wept into her shoulder, railing against her mother's 'stupid rules', and pouring out how she loved Tyler with a wild passion and felt like running away with him.

'I know,' Becca said wretchedly, remembering the anguish of teenage love all too well. Those were the days. 'I know, darling. It's only because she cares about you, though. She was worried about you coming back late, that's all. You've got to start letting us know where you are, what you're doing after school. Because of course she's going to worry when you don't come home. Fuck!' she cried as a huge spider scuttled across her foot, and she jumped up, banging her head on a shelf and knocking over a tin of varnish. At least it made Mabel laugh, though, the unsympathetic wretch.

'Come on,' Becca said, putting her arm around her. 'And

listen, I was thinking of you earlier. I've got some really cool silver skulls. I thought you might want to use them to make earrings or a necklace, or something. What do you reckon? Fancy joining my arts and crafts gang? Only the coolest kids in town are invited, you know.'

Mabel raised an eyebrow sarcastically – *Seriously?* – but then nodded. Who could resist some personalized skull jewellery, after all? 'Okay,' she mumbled.

'Brilliant,' Becca said. 'Right, I'm getting out of here before an even bigger spider comes along for me. Let's do it.'

The next day, it was Friday and Becca was driving home for the weekend. Golden sunshine drenched the landscape and she felt very chipper as she sang along at top volume to a cheesy ballad on the radio, slapping the steering wheel for emphasis. Earlier that day she'd had a fantastic session with Rita, the reluctant, exercise-hating lady from the retirement home, and although Rachel had provided her with a full list of gentle exercises they could do, Becca had made the executive decision to secretly disregard them all. Instead she had sneaked a garden spade, fork and trowel from the Jacksons' shed into the back of her car, plus a couple of pairs of gardening gloves, and then she and Rita had driven across town to the allotments.

'I won't tell if you don't,' she said to Rita when her client stared at her in surprise. 'And my dad always used to say that gardening was good for the soul, as well as the muscles. So . . . where shall we start?'

The patch of allotment Rita had previously worked on was shared with a couple of friends and she wasn't technically responsible for it these days, but nevertheless got stuck in with such zeal that she was stripping off her cardigan after just ten minutes' vigorous hoeing. 'Hasn't the rhubarb shot up? Look at the runner beans! Haven't they done a great job with these strawberry plants?' she kept marvelling. She seemed to know everyone else there, and almost all the other gardeners present came over to say hello. By the end of the hour, Rita might not have done a single sit-up or toe-touch as Rachel had prescribed, but she was pink in the cheeks from fresh air and sunshine, had weeded her entire salad bed, dug up lots of carrots and generally seemed like a new woman, laughing and chatting, and full of life. *And* she presented Becca with a bag of rhubarb, some sweet young peas and two heads of lettuce for her efforts. What Rachel didn't know wouldn't hurt her, Becca had thought back at the house as she surreptitiously scrubbed the dirt from under her fingernails. And in the meantime, she had one happy client who wouldn't be phoning in any more excuses for the foreseeable future.

It had been a good week, all in all. She liked nearly all of Rachel's clients, was convinced her thighs were already seeing the benefit of so much cycling (result!) and what was more, was really coming to love the Jackson children in all their bolshie, funny glory. They were maddening, loud and not ones to hold back on the personal remarks ('Aunty Bec, your bum takes up the *whole* chair!' Luke had remarked in astonishment just that morning over breakfast – charming) but she loved the rough and tumble of family life, the manic energy that pulsed around the house.

Despite all of that, Becca had decided to take off for the weekend. This was partly to give the four of them their own space again, but also because there was still a strange undercurrent between her and her sister now and then. She couldn't quite put her finger on what it was. Sometimes it felt as if they were getting on okay, actually having a laugh together, but at other times she would catch Rachel looking at her, a frown in her eyes, and feel quite disconcerted by it. *Come on, Rach*, she felt like saying, more than once. *I thought we were moving on from the past. I thought we were being friends now?* She wanted to be friends, anyway. She thought Rachel was amazing. But something was stopping her sister from letting Becca in, from fully accepting her. And so she had crossed her fingers behind her back and breezily invented a blind date for the weekend that she couldn't possibly miss.

'You don't mind, do you, if I go home today? I mean, I can come back again on Sunday if you want me to. Or not, obviously.' Becca bit her lip as she waited for her sister's response. Leaving now was a calculated risk, but she was fairly confident the Jacksons would manage without her. Still one-handed and weak, Rachel was limited in what she could do around the place, but Mabel was a pretty competent thirteen-year-old and able to help out. The fridge was full, the laundry was just about under control, and Becca had made up a new vat of spicy sweet potato soup for her sister that morning. She had even found a whiteboard in the garage and hung it in the kitchen. TODAY WE ARE . . . she had written at the top, followed by everyone's names, in an attempt to keep track of the family's whereabouts and stave off any future humdinger rows between Rachel and Mabel. ('This way, nobody will be on your case if you just fill in what you're up to each day,' she'd explained to her elder niece.)

Rachel actually looked quite relieved to be getting shot of her, all told. 'We'll be fine,' she kept saying. She had even fished a purse out of the kitchen drawer and laboriously plucked out a handful of notes. 'Here – take this. I'm sorry it's not more, but it's a start at least.'

Becca had stared down at the notes in surprise: fifty pounds. 'Oh!' she said. 'You don't have to.' Were sisters supposed to *pay* each other for helping out? she wondered uncertainly. Surely the idea was that sisters dropped everything for one another out of the goodness of their hearts, rather than reducing the transaction to being one of hard cash? But then again, she *was* skint. Even as she was saying the words, she was thinking, rent. Takeaway curry. Beers . . .

'I really do,' Rachel said. 'And next week . . . if you're sure it's okay then, yes, it would be great if you could come back and do the same again. Maybe even for a couple of weeks if that's not too much to ask. Please.'

'No problem,' Becca said. Her heart swelled. Rachel wanted her back! Maybe she'd been imagining the frosty looks and the barrier between them, after all – getting paranoid in her old age. And the money was surely because Rachel knew she had lost her job to come here. It was *kindness*, that was all. Gratitude.

'Thanks,' said Rachel. 'Have a lovely weekend and enjoy your date. It's not Ulric the Wolf, is it, by the way?'

'No way!' Becca spluttered. She'd had to tell Meredith that she had changed her mind on the 'sexy mates' issue, because every last one of her flatmate's suggestions had made her feel like becoming a lesbian. Or a nun. Possibly both.

Then something weird happened. Rachel's face went a bit hard and pinched-looking and she blurted out, 'Oh no, I forgot, that's right. You prefer to go for the married ones, don't you?'

The *married* ones? Becca had stared at her, nonplussed. The nice moment where her sister had given her fifty quid, and asked – quite humbly! – if Becca would be back the following week, seemed as if it had never happened all of a sudden. 'What do you . . .?' she started saying, but before she could finish Scarlet was in the room, her finished dog pillow tucked under one arm as she ran over.

'Oh! Are you going? You *are* coming back, aren't you?' she cried, hugging her aunt, the furry pillow soft and ticklish between them.

Becca glanced across at Rachel, who had turned away, pretending to tidy up Mabel's school books on the coffee table. 'Um. Yes,' she said doubtfully. 'I think so, anyway.'

She remembered the oddness of the moment again as she chugged along towards Birmingham. After that, there hadn't been a chance to ask Rachel what she had meant by the remark, because the children had been swarming around her, hanging off her and saying goodbye.

You prefer to go for the married ones, don't you? Er, no. No, thanks. She wasn't that desperate that she had started getting off with people's husbands. In fact, as Wendy had been so keen to point out, she had barely got off with anyone in the last year. So what had Rachel meant?

It came to her like a crack over the head as she neared the city and saw the first few tourist signs for hotels. *Lawrence*. She was talking about Lawrence.

Chapter Thirty-Three

As Becca left for the weekend, Rachel was also replaying that exchange. God, her stepsister had brazened it out well, she thought; you almost had to admire her shamelessness. She was obviously a bloody good actress, too, to have wrinkled her forehead and widened those blue eyes so convincingly. *Who, me? Innocent little me? I don't know what you can possibly mean.*

Oh, really. Pull the other one. Rachel knew the full sordid story: the November sales conference in Birmingham, Becca in a short black waitress's dress with tinsel round her neck, sitting on Lawrence's knee during the dessert course as she teasingly fed him the raspberry sorbet . . . It was enough to make you sick.

The night her husband moved out, his parting shot having blasted a whole new crater in the already smoking ruins of their relationship, Rachel had made the dumb mistake of glancing at Becca's Facebook page only to have it all confirmed. A selfie with some grinning mate in the empty dining room at the Copthorne, each balancing a fork on their top lips like pewter moustaches. *Working hard!!* read the caption. There was the black waitress dress as described by Lawrence, there was the gold tinsel looped on the walls in the background, just waiting for bad, bold Becca to tear it down as her own personal adornment. Then came a photo from the morning after: Becca with bed hair, and a crazed hangover, by the looks of things. Caption: *Was v v bad girl last night. Don't ask cos I'm not telling. SSSHHH.*

And there you had it: all the evidence Rachel needed. It wasn't as if she had ever held her stepsister in great regard or been close to her, but even so. You didn't do *that*. You certainly didn't make boastful remarks on Facebook about it, either, for the delectation of your mates. (Sixty-seven 'likes', she noted sourly, wishing there was a Do Not Like button, or even one that simply said BITCH.)

Despite everything, she had actually found herself warming to Becca over the past week, though. Sure, she was annoying at times, loud and thoughtless, and a bit haphazard when it came to things like housework; but the bottom line was, she was *doing* that housework, unasked, unpaid, because Rachel couldn't. She was taking the children to and from school every day because Rachel kept having minor panic attacks every time she thought about going outside. And she was kind, too, doing arts and crafts with the kids, listening to them witter on, smoothing over arguments with an easy grace. That dog pillowcase she'd helped Scarlet make! It had barely left her daughter's arms since its creation. When Rachel had looked in on her last thing the night before, Scarlet had been deeply asleep embracing it, her face pressed into the fur, a smile on her rosebud lips.

But. BUT. A million doggy pillowcases and skull earrings and drawn-on wooden spoons and shared jokes in the fracture clinic could not make up for what Becca had done. Sorry, but no. How could it? Nothing could erase the moment when Lawrence had looked her full in the face and sneered that Becca had been a better lay than her, his wife. It showed remarkable self-restraint, frankly, that Rachel had only snarled out the single dig so far at her sister, as Becca had left for the weekend. The rest of the time it had been like a game of chess, neither letting on to the other what they knew. *Are you going to say it first, or shall I? Or shall we both keep on pretending that nothing happened that night?*

Saturday was a warm, muggy sort of day. Before the accident, Rachel had always thrown herself wholeheartedly into active, all-involved family weekends – swimming or cycling, sometimes driving out to the nearest stables for an afternoon's slow, bumpy pony-trekking, or packing up a picnic and going for a hike. Obviously, none of that would happen today. Becca might have got her car back for her from the pound (after an eye-watering fine – ouch), but Rachel wasn't able to drive yet, and she still felt nervous about facing the outside world anyway. So instead she dug the paddling pool out from the shed, brushed off the dust and cobwebs, and filled it with water for the younger two to shriek about in. Mabel, who was apparently far too grown-up for this sort of childish thing, vanished to 'do homework with friends' (hmmm), and Rachel got on with a few jobs around the house – laborious as they all were, with only one hand in use.

The hours passed, everyone got along without major injury or World War Three breaking out and it ended up being a pleasant enough day all in all – an easy sort of day. What was more, she had coped single-handed, which gave her a huge swell of triumph. *Well done, Rachel. You did it.*

By nine o'clock the children had gone up to bed, the water of the paddling pool was silently floating with leaves and dead flowers and the dishwasher rumbling politely through that day's crockery. She mixed herself an exceedingly pokey gin and tonic – sod it, she'd earned a drink – and switched on her laptop for the now nightly ritual of checking whether Violet had replied to her Facebook message. It had been four days since she'd sent her own tentative enquiry, but so far it had been met with a deafening silence.

Clicking through to the site, she saw at once that a reply had finally come in and her breath stopped for a moment. Moment of truth, as they said on TV. So what did Violet have to tell her?

Dear Rachel,

Thank you for getting in touch. I must say, I had been rather expecting to hear from you after our conversation at your father's funeral. I am very sorry if I unwittingly spoke out of turn.

From what I know of your mother, she was an unhappy lady. She and Terry split up when you were about six months old, I think. He was too polite a man to speak ill of anyone, Terry, but I know they had terrible arguments and he ended up feeling as if Emily (and you) would be happier without him, and all the shouting. He felt quite low about it when we first became friendly – ashamed of himself. What kind of father am I, walking out on my own daughter, he said, more than once. But he honestly felt it was the best solution for you. He didn't want you growing up with parents at each other's throats all the time.

Terrible arguments? Parents at each other's throats? The words on screen seemed to cut straight through Rachel's heart. This was not the idyllic babyhood she had always fondly imagined. This was not Terry and Emily, love's young dream! She shut her eyes for a second, wanting to delete the message, pretend it had never arrived. But of course, having read this far, there was no way she could turn away now.

Me and Terry started seeing each other around the time of your first birthday. We were at a bonfire party, and I remember him being sad that he hadn't been allowed to celebrate the day with you. He lived in a little flat off Hyde Road and sometimes got to take you to the park in your pram. You were such a sweet little chick, with that cloud of yellow hair.

The first we heard of the trouble was on a Sunday, the following year. We'd been to Blackpool for the weekend, our first proper trip away together and it had been a really happy time. When we got back, we dropped into the pub and everyone was talking about it, how Emily had been arrested and the little girl – you – taken into care. Well, I thought your dad was going to keel over, he was that upset. He just ran from the pub – ran full-tilt – to the nearest police station, me chasing after him.

You probably know what happened next. Your dad decided that the two of you should make a fresh start, away from Manchester and all the talk. He was so hurt and angry with your mum for putting you in a vulnerable position that he was determined to get away. Sadly (for me), that meant that we split up. 'I've got to focus on Rachel,' I remember him saying, clear as day. 'I can't let her down again.' Broke my heart, that did, but I knew it was just him stepping up as a good father. I couldn't hold it against him.

Oh God. So it was all true, then. She really had been left alone all night, crying, wet, hungry, frightened. Tears pricked her eyes for the sad little girl – her! – and for her mum, too, arrested and put in a cell. It seemed so dramatic, so serious, and yet she couldn't remember any of it. She imagined the police breaking down the door of the flat, an officer lifting her crying from her damp cot, and it seemed unreal, like something you might see on television. Yet, according to Violet, it had all happened. To Rachel.

A tear rolled down her face and plopped into her lap. She had not wanted to believe the words of the newspaper article, preferring instead to cling to the things her father had always told her. She'd gone on to have a happy childhood, after all; she hadn't been traumatized. Why should any of this matter now? she reasoned fiercely. What difference did it make? But it did matter. It had changed everything.

> *As for your mum . . . I'm sorry to have to tell you that she died some time afterwards. She had always been a bit of a drinker, and after the trial, where she was charged with neglect and ordered to pay a fine, she slid downhill and could only find comfort in the bottom of a bottle. She must have been in her early thirties when she died. Liver disease, I heard.*
>
> *My apologies for what must be a very difficult message to read, Rachel. It has not been an easy one to write either, but you did ask me for the truth. Families have a way of surprising you when you least expect it, and I can see that this must have been a terrible shock. But I'm glad that you went on to have*

such a lovely stepmother at least, and that Terry found such
happiness again.

My very best wishes

Violet

Now the tears were really falling. So Emily had plunged headlong into alcoholism, by the sound of things – Rachel glanced guiltily at her own gin and tonic – and died a lonely death, unmarked by either her daughter or ex-husband. Oh God. How pitiful, to sink so low. How desperately sad, especially that she had never got to make amends in the years afterwards. She and Rachel could have got to know each other, formed some kind of relationship, leaving her with something more than just a few faint flashes of memory. But Dad had taken the decision to freeze Mum out, and none of that had happened.

What a mess it was. A mess of secrets and lies. She supposed she could understand why her dad hadn't told her the truth back when she was growing up; the story of her mother being beautiful and good and kind was way more palatable to a young, impressionable girl than the bald facts of neglect. Fair enough. She probably would have done the same. Just look how she kept gilding the situation with Lawrence in her own marriage break-up, never stooping to slagging him off to the children, however much she felt like it. Of course Terry had glossed over Emily's real character, back in the early days; it was the kind thing to do.

But for the lies to go on and on, for him never to have sat her down and said, *Listen, I think you're old enough for me to explain things now . . .* Well, that was different. That was a total cop-out, frankly – lame and cowardly. And now she had lost out on those years while Emily was still alive, forfeited any chance of getting to know her. It felt like a terrible double blow.

Finishing her gin, she got up without a second thought and went into the kitchen to make another. *She could only find comfort in the bottom of a bottle*, Violet had said. Well, guess what, Mum? Me too! Like mother, like daughter, eh? I'm just thrilled that we're so alike, after all my worrying that I could never live up to you!

It was ironic, when you thought about it. Parents at each other's throats – tick. Father moving out – another tick. Mother drinking too much – yep, here I am. Next on the list was clearly liver disease, and early death to look forward to. Whoop-de-doo.

She felt a momentary pang of guilt then, remembering Violet's last comment about Wendy. *I'm glad you went on to have such a lovely stepmother at least.* And there she had been all along, despising Wendy for not being Emily, constantly measuring them up and finding Wendy a failure in comparison. *You're not my mother!* she had yelled hundreds of times, usually before a slam of the door. It gave her a creeping sense of shame now, on discovering that Wendy had actually made a better job of it than her real mum ever had.

Had Dad told Wendy about Emily? she wondered. Had Wendy spent those years biting her tongue and thinking, *You don't know the half of it, love?*

She stood there silently in the half-lit kitchen, as the darkness thickened outside. TODAY WE ARE . . . proclaimed the writing on Becca's whiteboard, and it was all Rachel could do not to snatch the pen and write IN DANGER OF SELF-DESTRUCTING underneath. She poured herself another drink instead and drained it in two gulps, not wanting to think any more.

Chapter Thirty-Four

It wasn't the most scintillating weekend of Becca's life, all said and done. Wendy had gone off on some spa weekend for a friend's sixtieth and Meredith was in Devon for her brother's wedding, so the flat was empty and quiet, bar an elusive bluebottle that spent the entire time buzzing neurotically from room to room and ignoring all the open windows like a total thicko. Becca couldn't help reflecting on how small and poky the flat seemed compared to Rachel's elegant house and garden, how the walls seemed to contract ever smaller the longer she stayed in a room. Bored and restless, with nothing planned, she felt like a fraud whenever she thought about how she'd lied about going on her amazing date. Her amazing, *unmarried* date, obviously, she corrected herself, remembering her sister's words.

If the remark *had* been about Lawrence, as she was coming to suspect, then what exactly had he *said*? Had he been shit-stirring? she wondered uneasily. The whole night seemed like a surreal dream now: the overheated dining hall at the hotel, fat boas of golden tinsel swaying overhead, the huge artificial Christmas tree in one corner with ribboned presents artfully scattered about its base. By the end of the night some braying idiot in a suit would have fallen over into it, landing on his back like a tux-clad beetle as his mates all cheered. And then there had been Lawrence, catching her eye across the room and closing in for the kill.

It had been him, all him, she insisted to herself afterwards whenever she replayed the evening in her head. Him grabbing her waist, him trying to pull her onto his lap despite her awkwardly twisting away, him writing his room number in black marker on her hand like that, laying claim. It wasn't just rude, it was arrogant. Presumptuous. Insulting. 'Lawrence, I'm working,' she'd protested, feeling embarrassed, as all the yobs on his dinner table started whooping and clapping. *Get in there, my son.*

He'd played to the crowd, of course, tipping them the wink. He always had been a show-off. 'Got to love a working girl,' he'd said, loud enough for everyone to hear, and the laughter rose even higher, Becca's face turning crimson in response. Was he trying to insinuate she was a prostitute? She had wriggled from his grasp and walked away, ears burning at the sound of the jeering mob behind her.

'What a wanker,' her friend Niall had said indignantly, seeing her trying to scrub the black numbers from the back of her hand. 'Want me to swap tables with you?'

'Yes, please,' she'd muttered, fanning her hot cheeks and trying to regain her composure. She needed the money, otherwise she'd have ripped off her apron and gone home there and then, stuff the morons and their sales conference dinner. As it was, with rent to pay and Christmas looming, she would just have to suck it up as best she could. *Not* literally.

Thanks to Niall, she'd managed to avoid her brother-in-law for the rest of the evening. Then the two of them had marked the end of their shift by going and getting completely hammered in a cocktail bar down the road, singing along with the cheesy piped Christmas hits as they became more and more drunk. 'Idea,' Niall declared after a while, raising a finger in the air. They were onto their fourth or fifth round of mojitos by then, and the room had started to spin. 'Naughty idea,' he added.

'Oh good,' said Becca. 'My favourite.' She leaned forward, her elbow slipping off the table. 'Whoops. Go on. What's your idea?'

'That prick who wrote his room number on your hand. We should totally get him back. Can you still see the number?'

Becca squinted at her hand, where the figures were still smudgily marked despite her attempts to erase them. 'Yeah. Three-one-two,' she sighed. 'Why? What are you thinking?'

'I'm thinking, let's order him up some little room service

surprises,' Niall said wickedly. 'Maybe a nice pizza delivery at four in the morning. Or a wake-up call heinously early. Or a stripper . . .'

'You are a *genius*,' Becca said, saluting him with her cocktail glass. 'Hell, yes.'

The flat Niall shared with his boyfriend Marc was the closest, so they staggered back there to put the plan into action. It wasn't long before they had ordered not only an American Hot pizza to be delivered to Lawrence's hotel room at three in the morning, but also a room service breakfast at four ('A large bowl of porridge and some figs, please'), followed by a wake-up call request at six. 'Just in case the figs aren't enough to get me going, if you know what I mean,' Niall had said on the phone, his eyes boggling with the strain of trying not to burst out laughing. 'Yes, I realize I'm not calling from the room right now, is that a problem? Do I need to speak to your *manager*?'

No, it had not been a problem, thankfully. No, the terrified-sounding minion did not want to get the manager involved. After Niall hung up, he and Becca had a moment where they felt bad for the poor innocent hotel worker who'd had the misfortune to take their call, before they fell about laughing at the thought of Lawrence's increasingly furious face as he was woken again and again.

Served him right, Becca thought as she clambered into Niall's spare bed later on, the room spinning about her in a worryingly vomit-inducing manner. Even if it had just wiped out most of what she'd earned that evening, revenge felt *good*.

The next morning, waking up with a shocking hangover and the feeling that she had behaved quite badly, Becca had been braced for a frosty response from her brother-in-law – a terse phone call telling her that she was immature, perhaps, or even – you never knew! – an apology for having been out of order. Dream on. Nothing came from either him or her sister, and so she concluded that Lawrence had decided to stay quiet about the whole thing. She figured he wouldn't exactly be in a tearing hurry to explain to his wife why her sister had gone after him seeking vengeance, funnily enough.

But maybe he *had* said something about that night after all. Maybe he'd complained to Rachel about her in some way, and Rachel was still cross with her about it, she thought now, remembering the hardness of her sister's eyes as she'd made that strange comment.

Or maybe, of course, Becca was just madly overthinking all of this and getting stupidly paranoid. Either way, she certainly wasn't going to raise the subject of What Happened at the Copthorne with her sister to find out, no chance. Tell a woman that her husband had tried it on with you, drunkenly manhandled and pawed at you . . . how did you even start to go there?

The weekend limped by in a rather pathetic fashion. She had a new diadem to make, this time for Meredith's friend

Alianor, which she enjoyed; but otherwise, time seemed to drag. Her mum's words about getting out there on the pull and setting her life back on track kept nagging at her, and it made her feel even more of a loser. Asking Meredith's help on the man front hadn't exactly turned out well, either.

Something had to change, though. Because here she was, on her own again, with nothing to do on Friday or Saturday night for the second week on the trot. That wasn't right, was it? That wasn't how things were supposed to go when you were thirty. Much as it killed her to admit it, maybe her mum had a point.

Perhaps it was Becca's guilty conscience still at work over the room service revenge, but when she arrived back at the Jacksons' house on Sunday evening, Rachel's first words to her weren't quite the welcome she might have hoped for. To be fair, her sister did manage to say, 'Hi Becca, come in,' but then almost immediately plunged straight into, 'Listen, I'm not being funny, but why do I keep getting phone calls from old ladies asking me to take them gardening? Is this anything to do with you?'

Becca's shoulders slumped. *Seriously, Rachel? Do we have to do this right now?* she thought. 'Hi,' she replied, stepping into the hall. She was half-inclined to step right out again. 'Did you have a nice weekend? Yes, my journey was great, thank you. No problem.'

Rachel's look of exasperation became tempered with sheepishness. 'Sorry,' she muttered. 'Fair enough. Did you have a nice weekend?'

'Not really,' Becca said, abandoning her bag and the new box of arts and crafts things she'd brought in the hall. She'd ended up bringing quite a lot more with her, including her silversmith equipment – Mabel had been a keen earring-maker the week before and might want to try something more complex next, she figured – as well as a nearly-finished lampshade she thought she would crack on with. She had remembered the bare light bulb swinging so dejectedly in Michael Jones's hall, and wondered if it would be cheeky of her to present him with the completed effort. Probably. 'Can I make a cup of tea?'

'Yes. Look, I'm sorry to have a go the moment you walk in,' Rachel said. *Clearly not that sorry*, Becca thought, sighing to herself as she went past her towards the kitchen. 'It's just that the phone has been ringing all afternoon. If it's not the old ladies wanting gardening lessons, it's that bloke Michael, wondering if you'll go round and help him make ginger biscuits. I mean . . .' She threw up her one good hand in annoyance as she followed Becca into the room. 'I'm trying to run a personal trainer service here. That's the business – fitness and health! It's not gardening or painting or cooking or whatever else you've been doing. It's got to stop, Becca, all right?'

'All right,' Becca said through gritted teeth, filling the kettle. She noticed that the whiteboard had some new additions. Under the TODAY WE ARE . . . heading, Mabel had written HATING BOYS, Luke had drawn what looked like R2D2 and Scarlet had put 'Missing Harvey' with a sad face. It looked as if she'd missed out on a fun weekend in Hereford.

Rachel was still talking. 'I mean, it just muddies the waters if you—'

'I said *all right*. Point taken. Loud and clear.' Becca banged the kettle down onto its base. 'Jesus, keep your hair on. Rita loves gardening, that's all. And it's good exercise! I just used my initiative, I don't see what the problem is.'

'The problem is, I'm being paid by her daughter, who's going to be annoyed if Rita tells her she's been fannying about on an allotment rather than having proper exercise sessions.' Rachel folded her arms crossly. 'Did you have her do *any* of the exercises I wrote up for you?'

'No. But listen—'

'No, *you* listen. You've got to stop interfering like this, thinking you know best. Stop meddling with everything.'

'Okay! Got it! You don't have to keep repeating yourself!' Becca was right on the edge of losing her temper by this point. 'Just shut up, all right? I'm not in the mood.'

No longer caring about tea, she marched out into the back garden before her sister could say another word. God! Where had all that come from? And why was Rachel being so vile today? Interfering in people's lives indeed – meddling! – how dare she? It was called *helping*. Being kind. Doing favours. If Rachel had such a problem with her so-called 'interfering', then why had she asked Becca to come back for another week and keep the house running while she was out of action? Her 'interfering' had suited Rachel just fine then, hadn't it? Talk about two-faced!

The Jacksons' back garden was long and narrow and there was a hammock conveniently strung between the cherry tree and the maple, down at the far end. She strode past the rampant lilac, which was humming pleasantly with bees, and breathed in the sweet delicate fragrance, the too-long grass tickling her ankles. (Another thing that would need doing around here, she thought grumpily. Lawn-mowing: add it to the never-ending list of chores for 'interfering' Becca!)

She was about to fling herself full-huff into the hammock when she realized that Luke was already in there, playing some sort of game with his wooden-spoon people. 'Oh! Sorry,' she said, stepping back at the last second. 'I nearly sat on you. Are you all right? Hey!' she added, spotting several additions to the second wooden spoon that must have been made over the weekend. 'You finished the other one too. Can I see?'

Luke gave a toothy smile and squinched up his pale bony knees so that she could lower herself in beside him. He handed Becca the second spoon: a figure with wild brown woollen hair, eyebrows that sloped down towards the centre and a big wide open mouth. A pipe cleaner had been wound around the stem to form arms, and he'd bent one halfway so that it pointed up at a right angle. Ahh, waving, that was nice. Two paper triangles, scribblingly coloured with grey felt-tip and stuck together around the base, formed a skirt. 'Who's this, then?' Becca said. 'Is she the other spoon's friend?' She gave Luke a little nudge. 'Is it his *girlfriend*?'

Luke shook his head, and she noticed that his sooty lashes were lowered. 'That's Mean Girl,' he replied.

Oh. Perhaps not girlfriend material, then. 'Mean Girl,' she repeated, peering at the spoon face again. 'Her mouth looks a bit . . . shouty.'

'Yes, and she's got a punching arm, too,' he said, pointing at it.

So much for the friendly waving arm Becca had imagined. 'I'm not too sure I like the sound of Mean Girl,' she said.

'No, she's really horrible. She says mean things to the boy.'

'The boy?'

Luke held up his other spoon, the one that had originally been 'him', and Becca felt disconcerted. How much of this was in his imagination? she wondered. Or was he trying to tell her something? 'Oh dear,' she said, wiggling an arm around him so that he leaned against her, his soft dark hair flopping forward. 'What sort of things does she say?'

Luke was silent for a moment and she thought he wasn't going to reply but then he held up the Mean Girl spoon so that it towered over the Luke spoon, and said in a high voice, 'Your mum looks weird!'

Becca's jaw dropped. 'What a nasty thing to say,' she replied indignantly. She could see the nape of his neck, white and vulnerable, as he leaned forward, and for some reason it gave her a pain in her chest. Who had said that to Luke?

'She looks like a science experiment gone wrong!' came Mean Girl's high voice as she whacked the boy spoon with her own demented-looking head.

A science experiment gone wrong . . . Ugh. Those were spiteful adult words, put in a child's mouth by someone cruel and unthinking. But who? And how? Rachel had barely left the house since she'd come home from Manchester. Who had even seen her since the accident? Unless . . . Her mind spun. Unless this was something that had happened over the weekend. Something that had put Rachel in such a foul mood, perhaps?

'Mean Girl is being very unkind to the boy,' Becca said firmly. 'Nobody should say things like that. They just shouldn't.'

Luke heaved a world-weary sigh and leaned against her. 'But they do,' he said quietly.

'I think the boy should tell somebody, then. Tell his mum or his kind aunty, who both think he is the awesomest. They might be able to help make her stop.'

He was silent, considering. Becca tried again. 'Is Mean Girl . . . someone at school?' she guessed. 'Or someone who lives nearby?' If it was Sara Fortescue's daughter, she found herself thinking furiously, she would be over there in a shot and bawl them out, mother *and* child, just see if she didn't.

'Someone at school,' Luke mumbled eventually.

Becca pushed against the ground with her bare foot so that the hammock rocked gently between the trees, the rope creaking with the movement. A breeze set the leaves whispering above them. 'Does Mean Girl have a name?' she said. 'I bet she has a really horrible name, doesn't she, like Witchy McWartbottom. Or Smellyface Weeweebreath?'

To her relief, a tiny smile quirked his mouth. Good old toilet humour. It never let you down. 'Am I right?' Becca pressed. Come on, Luke. Tell me.

He shook his head, and she decided to wait it out. Sometimes silence was the best way to get a person talking. She rocked the hammock again and gazed up at the dappled canopy of leaves above their heads, just able to detect the faint smell of the pastel-pink sweet peas scrambling up a beanpole wigwam in a nearby flower bed. Luke remained silent, his thin shoulders tense. Tell me, Becca thought again, as the seconds ticked by. Just give me a name.

'It's Jodie,' he said after a minute or so, his voice so low and mumbly she could hardly make out the words.

'Jodie?'

'Yeah. Jodie Cripps, she's in my class.'

Cripps . . . that rang a bell. Someone in the playground? There were so many of them, the super-mummies, vying with their competitive talk and displays of superior parenting, like peacocks jostling to peck one another's eyes out. Wait, though. Not in the playground. She remembered now: the overbearing woman who'd freaked Rachel out in the fracture clinic the other day. Gotcha. 'I don't think I like this Jodie Cripps very much,' she said, wondering how much Rachel knew about this.

'Nor do I,' he said, head lowered. Then he haltingly confessed, 'I kicked her.'

'Ahh,' said Becca, vaguely remembering a dinnertime story about him fighting. 'Oh dear.'

'And then I got into trouble with Mrs Jenkins. And Jodie said on Friday she's going to get her big brother on me, so at school tomorrow he'll . . .' He drew a line across his throat, then gazed up worriedly at her, his freckles standing out on his pale skin.

Not if she had anything to do with it, Becca thought fiercely. 'Maybe me and your mum should have a little word with Mrs Jenkins ourselves,' she suggested. 'Or even a chat with Mrs Cripps.'

'No!' cried Luke, appalled. Obviously the Don't Snitch laws of the playground were still a thing.

'Well, we can't have Mean Girl's big brother duffing you

up, can we?' Becca replied. She felt like snapping the Jodie wooden spoon over her knee and throwing the pieces against the nearest tree. Take that, you . . . you wooden spoon, you. Better not. Rachel had already given her the evils that time over dinner for saying she wanted to punch Adam. Violence was not the answer, et cetera. Blah. But what was?

'How about if I just talk to your teacher tomorrow morning, ask her to keep an eye on you?' she said in the end. 'I don't have to mention Jodie's name' – she so *was* going to mention Jodie's name, and her hooligan brother's – 'so it's not like you're telling tales or anything. But at least then someone will be there if you *do* feel like talking to her.' She ruffled his hair. 'It's either that, or I dress up as your bodyguard for the day, big dark sunglasses on my big stern face, ready to do some business.' She punched a fist menacingly into the palm of her other hand before remembering she wasn't supposed to be advocating violent solutions. Whoops.

But there was another small smile on her nephew's face at least, which was something. 'Okay,' he said reluctantly. 'I suppose so.'

'What, me dress up as your bodyguard? Okay, no prob—'

'No! You tell Miss Ellis. But not say Jodie's name.'

'Got it. I'll tell Miss Ellis. And she'll make sure you're safe.'

He nestled against her, his body soft and relaxed once more. There was just something about having a child lean on you that she found inexplicably lovely. Like they completely trusted you. Accepted you. 'Thanks, Aunty Bec,' he said after a moment.

'Any time, Captain.'

He scrambled out of the hammock and went to bounce on the trampoline and Becca watched him, chewing her lip and hoping she'd said the right things. When she'd agreed to step in and help Rachel look after the children, she had never expected to feel quite like this – so fierce about them, so protective. Being here at Rachel's had caused all sorts of new emotions to unfold in her brain, in her heart; flashes of joy, pain, pride, love. Tiny real moments that made her remember what it was to be a human, rather than a grief-zombie trudging from week to week.

She lay in the hammock, watching the leaves dreamily swaying in the breeze above her head, listening to their soft whispers. Since her dad had died, it had been as if there was a block of ice lodged in her chest the whole time, the feeling that she could never quite be warm again. Maybe, just maybe, the ice was finally starting to melt.

Chapter Thirty-Five

Becca wanted to have a word with Rachel about Luke that evening, but her sister seemed to be avoiding her, claiming a splitting headache and sloping off to bed early. This left Becca to supervise Scarlet's violin practice, assist Mabel with researching the 'fascist–communist horseshoe' for her history homework and help Luke draw an entire comic strip, featuring SuperLuke and his Bad-Ass Aunty B who went flying around the world together, sorting out all the bullies and botherers. She didn't mind doing any of this, of course. She had come to absolutely love spending time with her nieces and nephew and enjoyed their company, especially when she was rewarded by three separate bedtime hugs for her efforts later on. Nonetheless, as she put on her pyjamas and snuggled down in Scarlet's bed that night, pictures of the tongue-lolling Harvey beaming dementedly from the wall, a flatness descended upon her. It was all very well stepping into her sister's shoes for the duration of her injuries, but this was not her place, her home, these were not her children. She was here on borrowed time, and before long she would have to return to Birmingham and start over, with the rest of her life looming uncertainly ahead. And what, exactly, would she do with it?

Good weekend? Wendy had texted earlier that evening, freshly home from her face-packs and salt scrubs. *What did you get up to?*

They both knew what that meant. How is the New Life plan coming along? Any snogging to report? Are you leaping out of bed with a smile on your face yet?

Becca had deliberated over her reply. *Home for the weekend, catching up with friends*, she eventually wrote with faux cheer, but felt horrible for lying to her own mother. *Back with R now, here for at least another week. All good!*

All good! No, it wasn't. Her nephew was having a tough time at school, her sister thought she was a meddler (and possibly worse), plus she had just spent the quietest weekend of her life back home. Pressing Send on her deceitful text made her feel hollow inside, especially when Wendy replied with a single *FAB!* and a row of smiling emoji. Still, silver linings, she thought the next day: at least being here gave her precious little time to dwell on such failings. Barely had her eyes closed on Sunday night than it was Monday morning, alarms trilling around the house, Scarlet screeching 'SHIT!' at the sight of a huge spider in the bathroom, and off they went all over again.

Monday's weather matched her mood – drizzly and damp, more like October than mid-June. It was the kind of low-spirited day that might have seen her staying in bed ordinarily, making excuses to whoever was employing her at the time. Not today, though. She had the children to badger into their uniforms, packed lunches to make, the usual last-minute sprint up to school and then a quick word with Luke's teacher begging her to save him from any potential fisticuffs with Mean Girl's Mean Big Brother. All that, and she had a session booked in with Hayley at ten o'clock, too. *Go, go, go.*

Rachel had provided her with a new list of exercises for Hayley, including a whole range of 'bingo-wings banishers' that she insisted Becca perform in front of her before setting off so that she could check her stand-in was up to the job. 'I'm not wasting my time here, am I?' she asked. 'You will do all these exercises with her, won't you?'

'Yes!' said Becca indignantly. 'Of course I will. You don't have to keep going on at me.'

Rachel provided her with two pairs of dumb-bells ('One each, so you can demonstrate'), and a skipping rope for Hayley to use in the aerobic part of the routine. She looked kind of sad as Becca packed it all up ready to go, and there were dark circles under her eyes. 'I miss skipping,' she said wistfully. 'I miss all of it, to be honest. I can't bear sitting around the house feeling sorry for myself day after day like this.'

Here's an idea, then, Becca felt like retorting. Don't. Get out of your pyjamas, brush your hair and try re-engaging with the rest of the world again, maybe starting with your own son, who's unhappy at school, by the way.

But despite the scratchy sort of tension that still crackled between them, Becca knew better. She couldn't be quite so brutal when Rachel was pale and drawn and still on pain-killers round the clock. She looked exhausted, too, following her weekend alone with the children. And there wasn't time to get into the whole story of Luke now – she was already on the verge of being late. 'Yeah, I know,' she replied instead, wanting to make things better between them. 'Just another month or so, though, eh? You can do it. I know it must be hellish watching me galumphing off in your place, but one day you'll look back and this will all seem like a weird dream.'

Rachel gave a small, crooked smile, which was something, Becca supposed.

Over at Hayley's, once they had warmed up, Becca got stuck into the upper-arm exercises that her client had requested for wedding-dress purposes. 'I normally wouldn't be seen dead without sleeves,' Hayley shuddered, a dumb-bell in each hand as Becca demonstrated lateral raises. 'But the dress I've chosen is strapless, so it's all going to be on show. I need to tone these wobblers right up, basically.'

'Wobblers? Don't give me that. There is nothing wobbling

on you, girl,' Becca told her, conscious of her own jiggling upper arms as she lowered them again. 'But I'll humour you, okay, because Rachel keeps telling me how the client is always right. So give me two sets of ten, on the lateral raises. That's it, shoulder height. Don't pull faces, think of how amazing you'll look in those wedding photos. Gorgeous, darling, gorgeous. You are *working* that dumb-bell!'

After a whole series of arm exercises, they went out into the back garden with a skipping rope and Wilf trotted after them like a lean grey shadow, cocking his head in a hopeful way. 'Sorry, pal, we'll go out properly later,' Hayley told him. 'I'll try and time it for my daily phone call from the old bag – I mean, my beloved, delightful mother-in-law-to-be,' she added to Becca.

Becca laughed at the comic look of disdain on her face. 'Still giving you grief, is she?'

'And the rest! She's started taking matters into her own hands now, can you believe. Actually turned up here the other day with the most hideous tiara she'd bought me. I mean . . . it's *horrible*, properly vile. Naff plastic flowers – I'm not even joking.' She rolled her eyes. 'The day that thing goes anywhere near my head is the day I've officially lost the plot, believe me.'

'Yikes.' Becca might only ever have seen Hayley in her joggers, but you could tell from her elegant house that plastic flowers were very far from her idea of good taste. 'Maybe there could be some terribly unfortunate accident involving the dog chewing off the plastic flowers, or burying the whole thing in a flower bed?' she suggested, reaching down to scratch Wilf behind his ears. 'You'd do that for your mistress, wouldn't you, eh?'

Hayley smiled as he made a low, loyal *woof* in his throat. 'I'm just going to have to nip out and buy one myself this week and pretend I had it all along. I wasn't here when she dropped it off the other day, so at least if I act fast, I might be able to get away with it. Oh *sorry*, Brenda. So kind of you. You know how much I adore plastic flowery headgear, but . . .'

'Or you could make one,' suggested Becca, thinking of all the bridal tiaras and other pieces of jewellery she and Debbie had made to flog at the National Wedding Show at the NEC back in the day.

'Make a *tiara*? I wouldn't know where to start.'

'Yeah, but I would,' Becca said, handing her the skipping rope. 'Five minutes, please. Single steps to begin with, then we'll go for some evil double-footed jumps.' She stood well back out of rope-lashing range. 'I've got some kit here at Rachel's with me, actually. Some gorgeous pearly beads, and proper Swarovski crystals, too. Honestly, I could help you make a really lovely one, and then your mother-in-law would have to shove her stupid flowery thing up her . . . Well, you know.'

Hayley began skipping as Becca clicked the stopwatch. 'That's what you do, is it? Make jewellery?'

'Yeah, I used to,' Becca replied. 'My friend and I had a little business a while ago, I've just been getting back into it. I made a couple of headpieces for my flatmate and her friend the other day, I can show you pictures on my phone.' She hesitated, not wanting to give one of Rachel's clients the hard sell; it was hardly her place to do so, plus Rachel would probably bollock her for it. 'It's just an idea, though. I totally understand if you'd rather go out and buy your own tiara, obviously . . .'

'It's a great idea!' Hayley said. She was turning pink in the cheeks from the skipping, the rope hitting the patio slabs with a steady swishing rhythm. 'I've not seen anything I love in the shops but if you could help me design my own style . . .'

'Absolutely! You're on. Let's sort out a date for you to come over once we're finished here.'

Hayley was soon breathless with her skipping, so Becca let her gaze roam around the garden as she waited for the last few minutes to tick by. In contrast to Rachel's outdoor space with its trampoline, hammock and paddling pool, Hayley's garden was a more sophisticated affair, with a rattan patio table and matching chairs in one corner, and oriental-looking metal lanterns hanging from the walls containing half-melted candles. Becca thought of her airless flat in

Birmingham, without so much as a balcony, and couldn't help a twist of envy.

Her stopwatch beeped, making her blink. 'Okay, now for the gruelling bit,' she warned. 'Feet-together jumping for a minute. Come on! Imagine you're stamping on the flowery tiara. Jump! Jump! Jump!'

Chapter Thirty-Six

Rachel spent Monday feeling rather sorry for herself at home. The pain was still ongoing, and she was fed up with not being able to yawn or laugh or eat anything without it being uncomfortable. And then there was Violet's damning email, which had added a whole new layer of misery since the weekend. She knew she had been unfair in taking her bad mood out on Becca a couple of times, but hadn't been able to stop herself. Besides, it was hard to stand by and say nothing when her sister seemed intent on running Rachel's business her own sweet way; the wrong way, in Rachel's opinion.

There was still the unresolved matter of Lawrence between them, too, with neither sister having dared broach the subject yet. Should she say something, just get it out there? Rachel wondered uncertainly. At least they'd know where they both stood and could have it out, once and for all. But what if they ended up having an enormous row? Becca might storm off, denying everything, and leave Rachel alone, unable to cope. On a purely practical note, that would spell disaster for the Jackson family. Like it or not, they needed her here, Rachel realized. They all did.

Sighing, she gazed out of the window, drizzle falling softly against the glass. She was just going to have to bite her tongue a while longer, it seemed.

That evening, once the children had gone to bed, Rachel was in the living room flicking through the television guide in the hope of something cheerful and distracting, when Becca walked in with two of her eye-watering vodka tonics and plonked them down on the coffee table.

'I've not had a chance to talk to you about it before,' she said without preamble, 'but Luke's had a bit of bother at school. He was upset last night because this kid has been mean to him. Did you know about that?'

Rachel felt as if she'd just failed a basic parenting test and been doused with a bucket of cold water. 'No,' she admitted in alarm. 'Which kid? Who's been mean to him?'

'It's that girl we saw with her monstrous wildebeest of a mother in A&E the other day,' Becca replied. 'Jodie something or other.'

'Cripps,' Rachel supplied, her face flaming as she remembered the incident. 'What's she been saying?'

Becca hesitated, looking awkward. 'Um . . . Well. I think the gist of it is, vile things about you, I'm afraid. Sorry. And Luke kicked her, and then Jodie was threatening to get her big brother on him, and he was really worried.' Becca sipped her drink. 'I wanted to tell you yesterday, but . . .'

The sentence didn't need finishing. But Rachel hadn't given her the chance, because she'd had a go at her the minute she walked in and then sulked off to bed early in a foul temper. And in the meantime, Luke had needed her and she hadn't been there. She hadn't even noticed! 'Oh God,' she said, racked with guilt. 'Thanks for looking after him. I feel awful. Is he all right?'

'He seems better today,' Becca assured her. 'I spoke to his teacher, who was brilliant about it, and he came back happy as Larry this afternoon, hasn't mentioned it since. Hopefully it was just one of those flash-in-the-pan things.'

'Yes, but . . .' Rachel still felt bad. 'I'm his *mum*, it should have been me helping him solve the problem.' She raked a hand through her hair. 'Shit. I need to up my game here. I need to sort myself out.'

'Don't beat yourself up about it,' Becca said. There was a delicate pause, and then she went on, 'You have seemed a bit . . . fed up, though, since the weekend. Is everything all right?'

Now was the moment, of course, for Rachel to confront her. *Well, you know, there is the small matter of you having slept with my husband. It's kind of been bugging me.* It might even be the right time to talk through the confusing feelings she'd had since Violet's email. *Actually, I found out two days ago that my mum was done for child neglect and died a lonely alcoholic. I know, right? Didn't see that one coming!*

Neither option was exactly an easy conversation, though. Did she really have it in her to go through with either one right now? But then Becca was speaking again and the moment had gone, her chance missed.

'Look, I know things have been really shit for you, I know you're still recuperating,' her sister began, 'but maybe we could pull together a bit of a plan, to make you feel better. I was thinking a walk, for starters – stretch those legs, take in a bit of nature . . . we can be back in time for school pick-up, no problem. And before you start quibbling about not wanting anyone to see you, then don't, because we can drive out into the countryside and go for a walk where we won't see another person for miles and miles.' She wagged a finger. 'See – one step ahead of you, Rach.'

Rachel felt a faint flicker of warmth inside. The very fact that Becca had been thinking about this – 'How to help my big sister' – was sweet. Cheering, in fact. And there was something about a hike far from civilization and gossiping locals that was actually tempting. The last time she'd gone walking in the Black Mountains, one soft spring Sunday, they'd seen red kites and lapwings, and taken a picnic to share at the top, with all the world spread out below them. It seemed so long since she'd felt her muscles ache from exertion, since she'd felt the wind in her hair. 'Yes,' she said after a moment. 'I'd like that.'

'You can start getting dressed again too, you manky old slacker.' Becca poked her pyjama-clad thigh with her toe. 'At least before this new friend of Scarlet's comes round, as she keeps begging us to arrange, or you'll never hear the end of it.'

Rachel smiled weakly, picturing the scandalized expression on her daughter's face.

'*And*,' Becca went on, 'you should really start answering your friends' phone calls. Or at least let them in the house next time one of them knocks for you. The few I've met – Diane, Karen and Jo – seem lovely, and they're all worried about you. Why don't you swallow that stupid pride of yours and go out for an evening with them? I'll babysit, obviously. Your face is definitely less swollen and bruised now, and it would make you feel tons better, I'm sure.'

Tears pricked Rachel's eyes. It was true, she had completely cut herself off from her friends, dreading their pity, however well-meaning they might seem. She *had* been stupidly proud, agreed. And yet they'd stuck by her in their own way; they hadn't given up on her. Nor had Becca, for that matter. Even Wendy had made a tentative phone call of support. Rachel wasn't sure she deserved to have anyone on her side any more.

'Hey, come on, don't cry, they're not that bad,' Becca said, and Rachel gave a snotty sort of laugh. 'Oh, and by the way, Hayley's coming round on Thursday evening, I'm going to help her make a tiara for her wedding. So that's another sociable thing you can do, too.'

Rachel felt somewhat apprehensive at the prospect of a guest in the house – gawping! Pitying! – but managed to nod all the same. 'Okay,' she said shakily. 'Thank you.' She scrubbed at her eyes with her fist. 'I'm sorry I've been a bit off lately,' she found herself mumbling. 'I'm not exactly the best sister in the world, am I?'

Becca looked uncomfortable and took a few moments to respond. 'Well, neither am I,' she said eventually, and Rachel held her breath. Was this it? The big confession? Were they going to get to the nitty-gritty, after so long looking the other way?

'But . . . Well,' Becca went on, haltingly. 'Me being here . . . it's a chance for us to start again, isn't it?' She bit her lip. 'I just keep thinking about how pleased Dad would be to see us here together, if that doesn't sound too sappy.'

So they weren't going to talk about Lawrence. And actually, Rachel felt relieved. It had almost got to the point where she didn't want to discuss him anyway. Why put herself through more pain? 'No,' she replied, 'it doesn't sound sappy to me.' She got to her feet. 'I'll get the vodka,' she said. 'Then we can work out where we're going to go on our sisterly hike. Deal?'

Becca smiled at her. 'Deal,' she said.

Chapter Thirty-Seven

Tuesday brought about Becca's least favourite hour of the week: her next appointment with Adam. He had phoned the night before and she'd felt quite excited for a moment, thinking he might be ringing to cancel on her. No such luck. Instead, he actually wanted to bring their session forward two days as he now had a very important meeting on Thursday morning. Of course he did, Becca had thought, rolling her eyes at Rachel as she made the arrangements. Just like he'd had all those very important calls and emails to attend to last time. Well, if the miserable git dared to answer his mobile every five minutes this week too, then his precious smartphone was in danger of being hurled into the River Wye, she vowed. 'Just you try me,' she muttered, cycling off to meet him with a heavy heart.

The day felt fresh with a brisk wind bustling around the city, although the sun was doing its hazy best to poke a ray or two out from between the clouds. Down on the river, a swan led a line of fluffy cygnets in stately procession towards the bridge, and a graceful weeping willow tree reached out to dangle its leaf-tips in the eddying water.

'Morning! Lovely day for it!' he called when she saw him by the river's edge. He was actually jogging on the spot while he waited for her, in spotless white T-shirt and black jersey shorts, seemingly full of the joys of summer. *Oka-a-ay*, Becca thought, clambering off her bike. *So today we're happy, are we? Has Grumpy Adam been put back in his box for a change?*

'Morning,' she said, giving him a quick, polite smile. One measly hour of her life. She could do this. 'Right, so, this morning, Rachel wants us to focus in on a couple of different areas . . .'

'Are you all right?' he asked, stopping jogging momentarily to peer at her. 'I know I pissed you off with the phone business last week, but look – empty pockets.' He turned them inside-out to show her. 'I left it at home this week. Corporations could be crumbling this minute, clients falling to their knees, pressing Redial in despair, but . . .' He shrugged. 'Well, I'll find out about that in an hour, I guess.'

She eyed him suspiciously. Was he taking the mick? 'Great,' she said, deadpan. 'Cheers. So if we could . . .'

'I've never been very good at taking time off, you see,' he said in a rush, as if she hadn't spoken. 'Not used to it.' Then he stopped, looking self-conscious. 'But you're waiting to start and I'm still talking. Right. Go on, then. What's the warm-up? I really hope it's more of those ridiculous dance moves because that wasn't embarrassing at all last week.'

Despite her earlier froideur, she found herself giving the tiniest of smirks at the memory of him gyrating like a clubber on the river path. Embarrassing? He knew nothing. She could do much worse if she felt like it. 'Don't give me that,' she scoffed. 'Looked to me like you were loving it last time, especially when you twirled around and nearly headbutted that tree.'

He grinned, a dimple flashing in one cheek. He actually looked quite nice when he wasn't growling and grumbling. Dirty-blonde hair, a bit on the shaggy side, brown eyes, good teeth. She wondered what had cheered him up so much today. Sex, probably. Men were nothing if not predictable, in her limited experience.

'Tell you what,' he said. 'I'll do whatever stupid warm-up moves you like, if you do them too. Fair's fair.'

She considered the proposition. They were in their usual meeting spot by the river and the breeze seemed hell-bent on directing itself straight for her, whipping around her goose-pimpling arms and legs. She was actually kind of chilly, now he mentioned it. 'Go on, then,' she said, propping her bike against a tree. In for a penny, in for a pound. 'So let's kick off with a few grapevines,' she said, channelling Davina as best she could. 'Remember that from last time? Well, just mirror what I'm doing, and imagine some great music in your head, like we're at the best party ever. And! One, two, three, clap. One, two, three and clap . . .'

'Can I just point out,' Adam said, as they began the sideways grapevine move, 'that I would not be doing this at the best party ever, however many drinks I'd had?'

'We can have a go at the Macarena, if that's more your cup of tea,' she teased. 'Or "YMCA". Oi! Don't forget to clap, by the way.' She sniggered as he hammed up his next clap for her benefit. 'That's better. Okay, now for the box step. Forward, forward, back, back . . .'

The warm-up got under way, from grapevines to box steps to a kick-and-punch move, lunges, squats (accompanied by some Seventies-style hand jives for added interest) and finishing with a funky scoop-and-clap dance move that she invented on the spot. By the end of it, not only did she feel warmed up, but she felt quite chipper herself too. There was something spirit-lifting and vaguely comedic about performing a series of energetic dance moves in public to no music, especially with an uncoordinated bloke facing you and trying to keep up. True to his word, he matched her step for embarrassing step, clapping and skipping with abandon. They even high-fived at the end, in an unexpected burst of laughter, much to the bemusement of a couple of mums walking by with their prams.

Well, well. So there was a turn-up for the books, at least. 'Now for the aerobic part of the workout,' she said, trying to remember her businesslike manner. She was starting to get the hang of this fitness-instructor lark now. Warm-up, aerobics, core or strengthening exercises, cool-down – that was the general routine. Everyone moaned about the strengthening exercises as a rule – the sit-ups, push-ups and lunges – but they tended to love the cool-down stretches, beatific smiles on their sweaty faces with the bliss that it was almost all over.

Today, Adam was down for a twenty-minute run, according to Rachel's notes, stopping every five minutes or so to jump with both feet onto a suitable park bench and off again six times. (Rather you than me, Becca thought, shuddering at the prospect.) Without his phone pinging and ringing every two minutes, the actual running bit turned out to be a far more civilized affair this time. They spoke to each other like human beings and everything.

'How's Rachel doing, then?' he asked. Shock! Grumpiest client makes conversational opener. It was enough to make an unfit woman fall off her bike in surprise.

'Getting there,' she replied. (Not falling off her bike, obviously. Like she would ever be so uncool.) 'It's going to take another month until she's fully recovered, but we're back at the fracture clinic in a couple of days, so we'll know a bit more then.'

'And in the meantime, you're Being Rachel, are you?' He paused, swerving to avoid some tourists who'd stopped to take photographs of a strange wooden statue of a pug. 'Womanning the helm?'

She wrinkled her nose. 'Doing my best to. Although . . .' She glanced across at him and decided to risk a confidence. 'She's one of those people who are so bloody good at everything, it's not been easy to follow in her footsteps. There have been a few mistakes, shall we say, although I'm enjoying looking after her kids. Have you got kids, by the way?'

'No,' he replied. 'Much to my parents' dismay and never-ending hinting.'

'Oh, same,' she confessed. 'Being an aunty is pretty cool, although I am kind of struggling with the discipline. Just this morning I overheard the youngest two discussing tactics for getting their dog back from their grandma's house, one of which involved trying to make the poor woman so angry with the dog that she was desperate to get rid of it.'

Adam snorted. 'Go on. Enlighten me.'

'Their idea was – and I kid you not – that whenever the dog crapped in the garden, they would scoop it up and leave it in the house. In her *bed*, my nephew suggested.' She glanced across at him, suddenly worried that it wasn't exactly professional to discuss such things with a client but to her relief, he was looking amused.

'Christ almighty.' He guffawed. 'They sound a right pair.'

'Exactly. On her *pillow*, my niece said next! I mean, can you imagine? So I had to tell them off and be really really stern, but inside I was just about howling with laughter imagining this poker-faced old Welsh grandma discovering what they'd done.' Her mouth twitched at the memory. 'Naughty little so-and-sos. Oh, and then – ' She suddenly realized she was talking a lot, and felt awkward. It wasn't as if she even knew him very well. 'Sorry. Am I going on?'

'No, not at all. Tell me more. This is way better than the tedious sort of conversation I usually have on a Tuesday morning. You don't get many stories about dog-shit subterfuge in business calls, more's the pity.'

Becca laughed, and checked her watch. Another minute before they had to stop so that he could try the awful-sounding bench-jumping exercises. She was determined to do everything properly today. 'The other thing I've found tricky is knowing what to say when they're upset,' she went on. 'I had my nephew telling me he was getting a hard time at school the other day, and I had to try and come up with a proper, adult response, rather than saying, "Punch the little shitbag in the face."'

'So what is the proper adult response? "Kick the little shit-bag in the nuts"?'

She laughed again. 'No, it's more like, "Let Aunty Becca punch the little shitbag in the . . ." Joking. No, I sensibly told the teacher instead, and she's keeping an eye on him. Them. But . . .' She glanced over at him. 'I don't know. Boys. What would you have said to him, just out of interest?'

He thought about it for a moment. 'Well, I always did karate as a kid, and made sure everyone in my class knew about it,' he replied. 'I might have overplayed the black belt situation *slightly* – make that flat-out lied about it – but nobody ever started trying to punch me or anything. Maybe I'd have suggested to your nephew taking up some kind of self-defence? Even if he never has to use it, it'll make the lad feel more confident. Give him a bit of swagger in the playground, too.'

Becca gave an appraising nod. 'Do you know what, that's a bloody good idea,' she said thoughtfully. She could already picture Luke gleefully attempting karate chops, especially on his sisters. 'I'll run it past Rach, see what she –' *Bollocks*. Her sister's name brought her back to what she was supposed to be doing. Not going for a pleasant cycle ride and chat, but cracking the whip in a tough boot-camp fitness session. 'Bench!' she yelled, seeing one ahead and braking to an abrupt stop. 'Sorry, Adam. I'm about to make you cry.'

Jumping two-footed up onto the bench and down again was obviously as hardcore as it looked because after just four jumps, Adam looked pained. 'I'm sorry,' Becca said sympathetically as he puffed and panted through another two.

'You'd be . . . a shit . . . dominatrix,' he managed, finishing the set with a groan.

'Sorry, yeah. Wait, why am I apologizing again? You're the

one paying to undergo this kind of hell. Weirdo. Now stop talking and START RUNNING!' she yelled, and he gave a sighing sort of laugh but duly set off. She allowed a minute or two to go by in silence and then, when she was sure that he'd be able to breathe *and* talk, said, 'Tell me something about you now. Are you from Hereford?'

'No, Bedfordshire originally,' he replied. 'My grandparents lived around here though, and we used to stay in the summer holidays, go walking with my grandad in the Black Mountains. When things went belly-up in London, it felt like a good idea to come back and make a new start.'

Ahh, so there *was* a story after all. She knew it. 'What happened in London?' she asked when he paused. 'If that's not too nosey a question, of course.'

'Well, to cut a long story short, I kind of . . . burned out,' he said after a moment. 'I had a really successful business, I was working all the hours under the sun. Basically pushed myself too hard and paid the price. Ended up having a heart attack—'

Her bike wheels wobbled, she was so shocked. 'A heart attack? Shit, Adam. Are you even supposed to be doing exercises like the last one?' Worse, she remembered her very own thoughts the week before: how she'd been so angry, she'd punished him by harder exercises than she was supposed to give him in the hope – *yes, Becca, you awful person* – that it would give him a heart attack. She'd actually thought those exact words, to her shame. Christ, she must never tell Rachel that she had been so cavalier with the routines her sister had painstakingly worked out.

Thank goodness telepathy was beyond Adam. 'I'm fine now,' he said, unaware of her evil thoughts. 'It was nearly two years ago, anyway. I was thirty-five, not looking after myself. Drinking and smoking too much, not eating properly, never exercising . . . I barely left my desk. Slept there sometimes.'

'Bloody hell,' she said. 'Sorry, but that sounds completely joyless. Apart from maybe the drinking bit.'

'Yeah,' he said simply. 'That was what my wife said, too. Then I ended up in hospital, our marriage imploded, and then my doctor sat down and basically said I was going to be dead by the time I was forty if I didn't make a few big changes to my life.'

'Jesus,' Becca said, trying to imagine being told such a thing. She thought of all the wine and vodka she'd been putting away recently, how she'd never really done much exercise herself until she came to Hereford and ended up cycling everywhere. She had taken her health – and her heart – completely for granted, as he presumably had too, in that I-am-invincible thirty-something way. 'So coming here, trying to lead a slower life . . . those are your changes.'

'Yeah,' he said, 'although it's not been that easy, to be honest. I've been here six months, and I've filled up the hours with work, basically, set myself up as a freelance consultant, trying to build up a new business from scratch. It's not exactly been a stress-free way of life.'

'Ahh. Things haven't changed all *that* much, then.'

He pulled a face. 'Not at first. But I'm trying. It was when I went to see the doctor to get some sleeping pills and she took one look at my record and said no, do some exercise instead. Factor in proper breaks. Find a training partner, she said, book some sessions at a gym so that you have to go. And then of course I got home to find a flier from your sister on the doormat – problem solved, I thought.'

'Until I turned up, and you regretted shelling out for so many sessions in advance,' Becca couldn't help reminding him.

He had the grace to look sheepish. 'Yes. Sorry about that. Look, I'm not trying to excuse my behaviour but I'd had a difficult week of it. Ex-wife announced she was going to marry my old boss, the very same bloke she always used to slag off for being the most repulsive man alive.' His expression became scathing. 'Funny how becoming a millionaire makes even the most repulsive man alive oddly attractive, right?'

'Oh, that is pants,' Becca agreed, feeling sorry for him. 'What an absolute cow. Sorry. I mean . . .'

He waved a hand. 'No need to apologize. They're welcome to each other. I happen to know he prefers men, so it's not exactly what you'd call a love match anyway.'

'Ugh,' Becca said. 'Isn't it just the most special thing in the world when someone reveals their hidden shallows?'

'Absolutely.' His expression was stern for a moment, but then he gestured at their surroundings and his features relaxed. 'This is good, though, don't you think? Trees. Fresh air. Getting away from a laptop screen . . . It puts everything into perspective somehow. Makes me feel better.'

'This *is* good,' Becca agreed. 'And actually doing this for the last couple of weeks, I can really see the difference it makes to people's lives. Time away from the day-to-day routine, putting on a pair of trainers and leaving your problems behind . . . it's almost like therapy. Makes me feel better too.' She checked her watch: almost bang on five minutes again. 'Okay, time's nearly up, I'm afraid – prepare yourself for more torture.' She grinned. 'You might change your mind and be desperate to get back to that laptop by the time I've finished with you today.'

Chapter Thirty-Eight

Sometimes it took a pokey vodka tonic and a metaphorical kick up the bum to shake a person from their torpor, Rachel thought the next day. Because look at her now, out in the depths of the Herefordshire countryside, miles from the comfort zone of her own four walls. This would have been unthinkable a few days ago, but Becca's plain speaking had resonated. And after all her agonizing, being out in the fresh air felt plain glorious. The bracken was springing into life, there were larks carolling high above, and the air smelled of hot, sweet earth. They'd taken it easy, only tramping along for a mile or so before stopping for a cold drink and a chance to admire the view, but that was enough to leave Rachel feeling like a new woman as she gazed out at the lush green countryside around them: dense, leafy woodland, a snaking silver stream, golden fields of rapeseed and wheat. *This makes me happy*, she thought, almost surprised by the sudden surge of joy that rushed up inside her. *I feel happy again.* There was something about getting away from it all, being amidst the unchanging hills and valleys, standing under the big old sky, that put a person's worries into perspective. The world was still turning, the sun would go on rising and falling, and the hills and rocks and trees had seen it all before. For the first time in weeks, her mind felt completely at peace. The secret of happiness: climb a mountain, she thought.

'Thank you,' she said to Becca. 'This is exactly what I needed – to climb high and look out at the world again. It's perfect.'

Becca was glugging back a bottle of water and wiped her mouth on her hand. 'I agree. And I say that as someone who always assumed the countryside was for people with nothing better to do.'

Rachel smiled. The boulder she was perching on was warm beneath her bare legs as she turned her face to the sun and shut her eyes, the sun painting colours on the insides of her eyelids. 'Lawrence and I first came up here years ago, before the kids were born,' she said. 'His mum lives about forty-five minutes away. It's a lovely part of the world.'

Becca said nothing immediately. 'How . . . how do you feel about him these days?' she asked tentatively after a few moments.

'About Lawrence? Sad, mostly,' she replied. She opened her eyes but looked away over the valley, not wanting to see her sister's face. It felt strange to be discussing her ex-husband with her when they'd both been avoiding his name.

'Sad that it didn't work out. We were good together for a long time. Everyone said, so it must be true,' she added, mocking herself.

'So what went wrong? If it's okay to ask.'

'He was . . .' She swallowed, her mouth dry. 'He was quite a jealous person,' she said carefully. 'And insecure. Things got . . . out of hand.'

There was silence again, Becca seemingly waiting for her to go on. But what else could Rachel say, without getting into the whole grim story? The day felt too golden, too hopeful, to start digging up the details of Craig, and the B&Q show-down, and the Christmas works do punch-up. Squirming, she was just about to change the subject to one more inane, less awkward, when Becca spoke first. 'Rach, I've been wonder-ing whether or not I should have said something earlier,' she began nervously, and Rachel's heart seemed to constrict in response.

Oh no. Here it came, the conversation nobody wanted, the elephant that stubbornly refused to leave the room. 'It's all right,' Rachel said quickly, trying to head her sister off. *Not today. Let's not do this today.* 'You don't have to—'

'There was this night last year,' Becca went on doggedly. *No. No. Don't say it. Don't tell me.* 'And Lawrence . . . tried it on with me.'

Rachel flinched as the words fell like grenades around her. But they weren't quite the words she had been expecting.

'Lawrence tried it on with you?' she echoed, eyes narrowed. That wasn't how he had described it, of course.

'I am so sorry. I didn't want to tell you, but . . .' Becca wrung her hands. 'He was drunk at this conference. I was—'

'You were waitressing, yeah, I know.' Oh, she knew. The raspberry sorbet spooned into her husband's mouth, the black dress, the tinsel. *Was v v bad girl last night.*

Becca stared at her. 'He . . . he told you? What I did?'

'That you slept with him? Yeah.' There. The accusation was out, stabbing into the air like a thrown knife. Over to you, Becca. Wriggle out of that one.

'That I *slept* with him?' Becca's eyes were as wide and blue as the sky. 'Wait, no. But I didn't. I didn't sleep with him, Rach. He tried to. I mean, he was groping me and writing his room number on my hand . . .' Becca's mouth twisted awkwardly, she flapped a hand as if trying to fly away from the situation. 'But I never . . .' She shook her head, the sentences trailing to a halt. 'I didn't *sleep* with him.'

Rachel turned away, her mind in tumult. 'He told me you were all over him,' she said quietly. 'Sitting on his lap. Feeding him dessert. He said you were way better than me in bed, too, by the way.' She gave a hard, painful laugh. 'So there you go.'

'Well, he's lying.' Becca's voice was loud with indignation. 'I promise you, Rach, I swear on my life, he's lying.'

They stared at each other. There was complete silence

save for a bird calling in the distance; they were alone together, miles from anywhere, and push had just come to
shove. 'Just a minute ago, you said, and I quote, *He told you?
What I did?*' Rachel pointed out, eyeballing her. 'If he's lying,
why did you say that?'

'Because . . .' Becca hung her head and Rachel stared at
her sister's coppery curls, glowing around her head in the
sunlight as if she'd been plugged into the mains. *Tell me the
truth. Just tell me.* 'Because me and my friend, we sort of took
our revenge on him,' Becca mumbled. 'Because he'd been so
horrible to me.'

Rachel's expression was steely as the story came out.
Room service. Pizzas. Disgusting breakfast and a wake-up
call. Childish and silly, but with just enough details to give
it the ring of truth, perhaps. Becca might be creative, but
Rachel wasn't sure even she could make up that lot on the
spur of the moment. Her head swam uncertainly as she tried
to make sense of the conflicting versions of events. Who
should she believe? Who did she *want* to believe? She hated
the thought of either of them lying to her face, but one of
them obviously had. 'I guess there's only one way to find
out,' she said eventually, jerking her thumb approximately
westwards. 'We'll pay Lawrence a visit and ask him what he's
got to say about it.'

Becca looked panicked. 'What – now?'

'Yes, now,' Rachel said. She was done with not knowing

who she could trust, she realized. She'd had it. They might as well clear this up, once and for all, then put the thing to bed. So to speak. 'Let's go.'

Lawrence had grown up in Hampshire, but on retirement his Welsh-born parents had sold up and moved back to Builth Wells to live out the rest of their years in rural peace, surrounded by rolling hills, greenery and tea-shops. Lawrence's dad had died several years ago but his mother, Janice, was very much alive (frighteningly so, in fact). As the two sisters trudged back down the hill towards the car in an uneasy silence, Rachel found herself hoping that Janice would be out when they arrived. Plain-spoken and matronly, if Janice thought for a minute that her daughter-in-law was waging an attack on her precious son, she would leap to his defence, probably brandishing a floury rolling pin.

Once in the car, Rachel gave stilted directions and they headed off, Becca staring intently at the road rather than chattering away in her usual style. Rachel could tell she felt awkward and embarrassed about the forthcoming confrontation, after revealing her juvenile behaviour on the night in question. (*If* she was telling the truth, of course.) Rachel, meanwhile, was already regretting her impulsive decision to go at all. This was not what anyone would call a win–win situation.

A long, uncomfortable hour later, Rachel uttered the

words, 'And it's just down there on the left, the one with the big hedge,' and Becca heaved on the handbrake.

'So here we are,' Rachel said needlessly as Becca switched off the engine. Janice's street was a tranquil, pretty one, full of stone cottages and well-kept front gardens. Caravans stood in repose. A cat lay on the dusty pavement in a patch of sunshine and licked its front paw in quiet contentment. This was not the sort of neighbourhood where squabbling sisters arrived to settle an argument, hell-bent on a screaming match with an ex-husband. Oh, what were they even *doing* here? The whole thing felt like a wild goose chase now, their lovely sisterly walk turned on its head, tarnished by the ugliness of suspicion. And she was the one who'd forced the issue, who'd insisted that they come at all.

'Here we are,' Becca repeated dully. 'We'd better get on with it, if I'm to be back to pick up the kids at three-fifteen.'

'Yes,' Rachel agreed. It was one o'clock already, she noticed; they'd have to leave again in an hour. 'Right. Let's see if he's in.'

She felt a peculiar sort of bravado as she marched up the front path, Becca hanging back in her wake. Janice's car was not in the driveway, thank goodness, but Lawrence's silver Beamer sat there, a relic from his old job that he'd been able to buy at a cut price when he was given the push. (He would have to sell it if he didn't find himself some new form of employment soon, she reckoned. He was a proud man,

Lawrence, he wouldn't want to be out here sponging off his mum for eternity, however good her Welsh cakes and bara brith.)

Knocking on the white-painted door, heart in her mouth, she was cheered to hear the sound of an answering bark from inside: Harvey. Oh, Harvey! Somehow she had forgotten he would be here too. He had always been such a loyal companion, such a lovely, funny, cheerful dog. At least she was guaranteed a rapturous welcome from him, if not from her ex.

The door opened, and there was Lawrence; unshaven and not a little paunchy in a faded FatFace T-shirt, jeans and bare feet. Harvey immediately barrelled out from behind him and greeted Rachel with a volley of delighted barking, his feathery tail beating the air in joy. She crouched over him, hugging him, accepting his slobbery welcome, glad of the excuse not to look at Lawrence immediately. 'Hello, my darling. Hello, lovely boy. Yes, it's me. Yes, it's me!'

'Hello,' said Lawrence, sounding mistrustful. 'What's all this about, then?'

Rachel stood up again and he jerked in horror at the sight of her altered appearance, his eyes boggling as they took in first the yellow and green patterns of bruising around her jaw and then her plaster-encased wrist. 'Shit, Rach. Are you all right? I heard you were . . . Fuck. Excuse me. Get down, Harvey, you idiot. Is everything okay?'

'Can we come in?' Rachel heard herself say in an artificially bright sort of voice. 'We won't stop long.'

Looking uncertain, Lawrence acquiesced and then led them down the hall. The house smelled of Pledge and Janice's lavender perfume, as it always did, with an added whiff of burned toast (Lawrence's contribution, she suspected). His hair needed cutting, she thought, following behind, and the left pocket was starting to come away from the back of his jeans. Not her problem any more, though. Nothing to do with her.

Once in the living room, with its sludge-green paint and the huge red-brick fireplace that took up far too much wall, the three of them formed a strained sort of tableau: Rachel perched on the edge of one of Janice's mustard-coloured armchairs, with Harvey shoving his face in her lap, tail still pumping like a metronome set to *allegro*; Lawrence posed by the fireplace like something from a cheesy 1960s catalogue; and Becca leaning against the radiator near the door, as if planning a quick escape.

Lawrence looked from one sister to the other. 'So,' he said gruffly. 'What's all this about, then?'

Rachel folded her hands in her lap. 'We're here to clear up a little misunderstanding,' she said demurely. 'It won't take a minute. Basically: did you, or did you not sleep with Becca?'

Whatever he'd been expecting, it was definitely not that question. 'What on *earth* . . .?' He swung round to glare at

Becca before turning back to his ex-wife. 'Is this some kind of joke?'

'No,' Rachel replied. 'It is not. It's a very simple question, in fact, Lawrence. Did you, or did you not—?'

'I heard you the first time,' he interrupted, one hand tightening into a fist. His eyes were stormy, but he had been caught off guard, Rachel knew it. You could almost hear his brain whirring as he chose his next words. 'And . . . Look, what's the point of going over this sort of thing? The past is in the past. You've got to move on, Rach.'

'How can she move on?' Becca put in, her voice clear and cutting. 'When you told her such a lie?'

'I –' His lip curled, and he gave an exasperated snort. 'Oh, I get it. Best friends, you two, all of a sudden, are you? Ganging up on the ex-husband, is that the idea?'

'Nobody is ganging up,' Rachel replied evenly. 'But you still haven't answered the question. You told me you had slept with Becca. She says you didn't. I'm asking you now what's really the truth.'

He smacked the flat of his hand against the hearth. 'Why does this even matter?' he blustered. 'Look, I get it. You're angry. You're trying to score a point. Let's kick Lawrence while he's down. Girl power. Whatever.'

Rachel stared at him, incredulous. 'Lawrence, this is not about girl power or scoring points,' she said. 'It's a simple yes–no question. Why won't you answer it?'

'Answer the bloody question!' said Becca, hands on her hips. 'Tell her the truth, for goodness' sake, and then we can all get on with our lives again.'

'What's going on?' came a sharp voice, and Rachel quailed inside. Oh shit. Janice was back, and now they were in for it.

Harvey gave a low *woof* of greeting as she entered the room: a tall, forbidding woman in a navy padded gilet, tweed skirt and polished brown walking shoes, hair set in pewter-grey curls. 'Hello, Rachel,' she said. A flicker of surprise passed over her face as she took in her daughter-in-law's injuries, but she was not a touchy-feely sort of woman, nor one who went in for personal remarks. 'I'm Janice,' she said to Becca, holding out a hand.

'Becca,' said Becca, shaking it somewhat apprehensively. 'Rachel's sister. Um. I think we met at the wedding.'

Rachel smiled politely at her mother-in-law, hoping that nobody could hear the rapid thump of her heart. Hoping that there wasn't a rolling pin within grabbing distance, either. 'We're just trying to settle an argument,' she said, shooting a sideways glance at Lawrence.

'So I heard,' said Janice severely. Something about her tone of voice made Rachel wonder exactly how much she *had* heard. Then to everyone's surprise, the older woman steepled her fingers together and turned her gaze on her son. 'Go on, then, Lawrence, you'd better answer the question,' she said. 'Even I want to know what you've got to say now.'

'I . . .' he began, a genuine look of fear flashing across his face. Nobody messed with Janice. 'Look, there's been a bit of a mix-up, that's all,' he said, floundering under her direct stare. 'Of course I haven't slept with Becca. That's ridic—'

'But you told me you had,' Rachel cut in. *No, Lawrence. You're not getting away with this 'mix-up' line*, she thought, cold anger creeping through her. 'Why would you tell me you had done such a thing if it wasn't true?'

There was a moment's silence, save for the ticking of the gold carriage clock on the mantel. 'Yes, Lawrence,' Janice said coldly. Her gaze flicked from her son to a framed photograph beside the clock. 'Why would you do that?'

Rachel had never expected to think the words, 'I love you, Janice,' but there they were in her head, as her mother-in-law went on to unravel the whole messy situation and then – in a wholly unexpected turn of events – plant herself firmly on the side of the women. 'How could you?' she exploded, as the story emerged. 'To do that to your *wife*, and to her *sister*. What were you thinking, for heaven's sake? I'm very disappointed in you!'

Lawrence hung his head. 'I'm sorry,' he mumbled, spots of colour in his cheeks.

But Janice wasn't done yet. 'I should think you *are*!' she thundered. 'You should apologize to poor Rebecca too, this minute, for besmirching her reputation. For shame,

Lawrence. For shame! This is not the way your father and I brought you up. To lie to women. To cause trouble like this, between sisters!'

Another flicked glance to the photograph, Rachel noticed – and then the penny dropped. Of course. Janice was one of three sisters herself, and very close to them both. There they were in the photograph, flanking her, the three of them faintly terrifying even when smiling into a camera.

She sat there, fussing Harvey's gorgeous silky ears and quietly enjoying the spectacle of her former husband making slavish apologies while his mother berated him. She would have to make her own apology later, to Becca, of course, for ever doubting her word. But weirdly, she realized how glad she was that it had been Lawrence that lied, not Becca. The deceit hurt less that way around, somehow.

She reached down to pat Harvey's side and he turned his head to gaze up at her adoringly. *I wonder . . .* she thought, an idea suddenly occurring to her. Could she somehow turn this situation to her own advantage?

She cleared her throat. *Do it, Mum*, urged Scarlet in her head.

'Before we go,' she said, one hand still resting on Harvey's warm flank, 'there's just one more thing. The dog?' They all looked at the dog, who wagged his tail, *swish-swish*, across the porridge-grey carpet. 'Perhaps it's our turn to have him, in Hereford,' she went on, heart hammering at her own daring. 'The children would all love him to come home and –' She shrugged innocently. 'Perhaps this could be your way of making amends, Lawrence.'

Lawrence looked as if he was about to argue, but Janice got there first. 'That sounds like a very good idea to me,' she said firmly. 'Besides,' she added, narrowing her eyes, 'it's shedding everywhere at the moment, that creature, and it's ruining my upholstery. I'm having to hoover twice a day.'

'Nightmare,' clucked Becca sympathetically.

Knowing there could be zero argument to be made against dog hair and twice-daily hoovering, Lawrence seemed to deflate by the fireplace. Game over. 'Fine,' he muttered with a shrug.

'Great,' Rachel said, just about controlling her urge to punch the air and cheer. Now to leave while the going was good. The going – in fact – could not be bettered. 'Shall we make a move?' she said to Becca, and rose smoothly to her feet. 'Come on, then, Harvey, you too. It's time we went home.'

Chapter Thirty-Nine

Rachel and Becca managed to keep straight faces while they made their goodbyes, accepted from Janice the bag containing Harvey's food and water bowls plus his favourite tartan blanket, and then accepted from Lawrence yet another gritted-teeth apology.

Then they were in the car, Harvey ensconced in the back seat, and just as soon as they drove round the corner Becca pulled over again so that the two of them could cheer and high-five each other in semi-hysterical disbelief, Harvey barking too as he sensed their excitement. 'Oh my GOD,' Rachel gasped, leaning back to pat him. 'Did that really just happen? Oh Harvey, mate. We've got you. We've got you!'

'Scarlet is going to *combust* with happiness,' Becca said. 'She's just going to bounce off the walls. Hey, and she's actually quite a dude, old Janice, isn't she? I loved her back there – she was awesome. Solidarity with the sisters!'

'She was amazing,' Rachel agreed, then felt herself sobering up. 'But Becca, oh gosh, I owe you such a huge apology.

For believing him. For putting you in that situation at all just then. For wasting half a tank of petrol on a whim today – I promise I'll give you the money for it. And I'm sorry. Really bloody sorry.'

'Shucks.' Becca waved the apology away. 'You believed your own husband. That's what you're supposed to do, right? I understand. Obviously I am deeply wounded that you could *think* such a thing of me . . .'

She was joking but sort of not-joking too, Rachel realized. 'Sorry,' she repeated, hoping it would be enough.

'It's all right. We're cool,' said Becca. A moment passed, and then her eyes sparkled with another smile. 'I'm just glad he didn't mention the room-service revenge, to be honest. I was convinced he was going to throw that one in my face and have a go at me about it. But instead – we won!' They high-fived again, and she started up the engine. 'Now we'd better head home. We've got some children to make very, very happy. Right, Harv?'

They set off down the road and Rachel let her shoulders fall back, feeling as if a weight had been lifted from them. Becca *hadn't* betrayed her, she thought dazedly. Quite the opposite, in fact: Becca had turned *down* her lecherous brother-in-law and then tried to protect Rachel from the whole grisly story. She'd even driven them out to Builth Wells to help Rachel face Lawrence down. That was good, wasn't it? That was proper sisterly behaviour, the real thing. And with this cheering thought, the final barrier between them seemed to come down at last, crumbling to dust. A second chance had been issued, and they could start again.

As for Lawrence . . . Well, she probably should have guessed that he had made the whole thing up to hurt her. Competitive to the last, he had resented being pushed out of the house, and if she'd been able to think straight she could have seen how entirely predictable he was in being unable to resist a last cheap pot-shot. Much as the taunt had hurt her then, it now made her feel steely towards him. Their marriage really was over. She owed him nothing. And after that little episode, she had the feeling he would think twice before trying to pull any future stunts, too. Especially with Janice up in arms about the sisterhood.

'You all right there, smiling away to yourself like a mad-woman?' Becca asked, glancing over just then.

Rachel nodded. 'I'm good,' she replied. 'Listen, thank you. For all of it – dragging me out today, and going along with my mad impulse to drive out to Builth Wells, and—'

'And for not sleeping with your husband—'

'Yeah, that too. Everything. For being a bloody good sister. Thanks, Becca.'

Becca glanced back at her again, and she was smiling too. 'You're welcome.'

★

Rachel's new-found happiness stayed with her for an entire twenty-four hours: through children screaming with sheer unconfined joy over the return of their canine companion, a really positive return trip to the fracture clinic the next day (especially the bit where they glimpsed the gorgeous male nurse again, even if Becca did keep teasing her and saying '*Swit-swoo*' under her breath in a stupid voice) and definitely through the lovely hour she spent in the garden with the dog, feeling the sun on her face as she threw ball after ball for him to chase. Becca had mentioned her idea – Adam's idea – about karate lessons, and she went online and found a club nearby that Luke was keen to join – so that was great, too.

For a whole glorious day and night, it was as if her troubles were temporarily suspended and she was able to forget them all: the anguish she'd felt on discovering the truth about her mother, the debilitating physical pain she'd experienced in the last fortnight, the doubts still plaguing her about her long-term future as a single parent and whether she was seriously up to the job.

But everybody knew that happiness was only ever a split-second away from turning into something else; that problems had the annoying habit of creeping right back in. And sure enough, that very next evening, along came trouble in the form of her elder daughter.

If she'd told her once, she'd told her a thousand times: Mabel was supposed to be home by four o'clock every afternoon, unless she'd expressly let either Rachel or Becca know otherwise in advance. There was even the whiteboard up in the kitchen now, supposedly charting everybody's whereabouts so that no-one could be in any doubt. And so when four o'clock came and went that day, swiftly followed by five o'clock, Rachel felt her stress levels begin to rise.

There had been a few texts, for what they were worth – *At homework club, revising* first of all, followed by *Going back to Zoe's for a bit* – whoever the hell Zoe was. Rachel hadn't been allowed to meet very many of Mabel's new friends, let alone have any contact details of their parents ('God, Mum, no way! That would be, like, so completely embarrassing and weird'). Instead she had to contend with these vagaries of her daughter's whereabouts, the lateness home, the unthinking, unapologetic attitude. ('I was *fine*! What's the big deal? Nobody else's parents go on at them for hanging out with mates after school.')

Be back for seven, please, she texted back, but no further word came in reply, and then they were eating dinner with an empty place at the table, with Becca setting all her jewellery kit out afterwards in readiness for Hayley's arrival that evening.

By now, Rachel was feeling sick. She had tried ringing Mabel's number but the calls went unanswered. It had got to the point where she felt more anxious with every minute that passed on the clock. *Where are you?* she texted at seven-

fifteen. *Come back NOW or you will be grounded for a week.
I mean it!*

Still no reply. Maybe Mabel's phone had run out of battery
– it had a convenient habit of doing this when Rachel was
trying to get hold of her. But maybe, also, it had been stolen
from her as she walked home alone, a vulnerable thirteen-
year-old in the badlands of Hereford. Well, all right, not the
badlands as such, but still . . . *Oh, Mabel. Just come home*, she
willed her. Don't do this to me. She tried to summon up the
calm she'd felt up in the hills the day before, but the feeling
had deserted her. At what point did you give in and start ringing round people in the hope of locating your child? At what
point did you panic and call the police?

The doorbell rang and her heart jumped in relief – but it
turned out to be Hayley, looking very pretty with her long
brown hair falling in waves around her shoulders, wearing a
crisp white shirt and cut-off jeans.

'Look at you, in your nice clothes and lovely hair,' Becca
said, welcoming her with a hug on the doorstep. 'I hardly
recognize you without your ponytail and trackie bottoms.'

'I could say the same,' Hayley laughed. Then she caught
sight of Rachel hovering further down the hall, and her eyes
widened. 'Rachel! Good to see you! How are you?'

Rachel shrank back, unable to help feeling self-conscious,
knowing that the other woman had last seen her at full fitness, demonstrating sit-ups and press-ups, jogging with her

through the woods. 'I'm on the mend, thanks,' she said shyly. 'Nice to see you too.'

'I have silver, I have jewels, I have wine,' Becca was saying. 'Shall we get stuck in? I've set everything out through here.'

They went off to the kitchen, and Rachel was about to follow – she would be brave! She would be sociable! – when the doorbell rang again. Oh, thank goodness. It *must* be Mabel this time, having forgotten her keys. She yanked open the front door, the scolding ready to trip off her tongue, but words failed her at the sight of the man in dark uniform by Mabel's side.

'Evening. Mrs Jackson? I'm PC Foster from Hereford police. Is this your daughter?'

It turned out that Mabel had not been at Homework Club, revising like a good student, after all. She hadn't been at the mysterious Zoe's house either. Instead, she and a group of mates had been mucking about down by the river and generally annoying the people whose gardens backed onto the water, according to the policeman. 'Do you want to tell your mum what happened next, or shall I?' he said grimly.

Mabel was tearful and shaken up as they sat there in the living room, door closed, so that Hayley's lovely tiara-making session wouldn't be tarnished by sordid tales of youthful wrongdoing. Her face was puffy, her mascara in black trails down her cheeks, and she looked about ten all of a sudden, any last traces of cockiness and bravado snuffed out by the presence of an actual police officer sitting heavily in the opposite armchair. Not so grown-up now.

'We weren't doing anything wrong,' she began, twisting a lock of hair between her fingers. The turquoise streak she'd added had almost washed out by now, leaving a ghostly blue residue only visible in certain lights. One of her school socks sagged below the knee and the nearest cuff of her blouse looked as if it had been nibbled. She was such a child, still. Rachel could look at her and see that little blonde imp still visible, the tot who'd wanted to be a Disney princess not so very long ago. 'We were just having a bit of a laugh,' Mabel muttered. 'But this old bloke—'

'I presume you're referring to Mr Davidson, a retired local magistrate who is now the full-time carer for his ill wife,' PC Foster put in severely. His face was unsmiling, his eyes as hard and grey as granite. Rachel felt terrified of him herself, and she was approaching forty. Goodness knows how her daughter must have felt when he'd arrived on the scene.

Mabel wrung her hands in her lap, looking anguished. 'Yes,' she said, her voice barely louder than a whisper and the dog, sensing her distress, went over and put his head on her knee.

'Perhaps you'd like to tell your mother what happened with Mr Davidson,' PC Foster said.

Mabel swallowed, and Rachel braced herself for the worst.

A bit of teenage mucking about, she had been prepared to overlook. Trying a puff on a cigarette, or maybe a swig of alcohol . . . well, she'd been a teenager herself, she knew these things went on. But she didn't like the sound of what might have happened by the riverside one little bit. What on earth had they done?

'Mabel?' she prompted, dread sloshing through her. She thought of the whiteboard in the kitchen. *TODAY WE ARE . . .*

MABEL: IN TROUBLE WITH THE RUDDY POLICE!

RACHEL: OFFICIALLY THE WORST MOTHER EVER!

Mabel's lip curled. 'He kept having a go at us,' she muttered. 'We weren't doing anything wrong. I swear, Mum! We weren't in his garden, we were just on the river path. Just hanging out.'

PC Foster raised an eyebrow. 'We did confiscate a bottle of Thunderbird and some alcopops,' he said, dobbing Mabel right in it. 'And there was evidence of cigarette-smoking too, when all the children present were under age.'

Rachel gave her daughter a stern look. 'What do you think your dad's going to say about this?' she asked, for the benefit of the policeman as much as anything else. *Two parents involved in her upbringing, all right? No need to make any judgements about me as a single mum*, she was saying in not so many words, even though she kind of hated herself for doing so.

Mabel coloured all the way up to her blonde hairline. '*I* didn't drink anything,' she said, turning her face to Rachel.

'I didn't, Mum, I swear. Are you really going to tell Dad?'

Not if I can help it, Rachel thought. 'Let's hear the rest of the story,' was all she said. 'Go on. You might as well finish telling me.'

Mabel stroked the dog's head, her fingers trembling. 'Well, some of the boys . . . got a bit fed up with him telling us off,' she mumbled, and PC Foster gave a sarcastic sort of snort.

'Yes?' Rachel prompted.

'And they . . . They threw some of his garden furniture in the river.' Mabel put her head in her hands so that her final words were muffled. 'And it all sank.'

Garden furniture in the *river*? Rachel had a vision of a patio table and chairs sailing through the air and splashing into the Wye, before sinking to murky oblivion. She almost wanted to laugh in hysterical relief. Was that it? Was that all?

Not that she was about to let on to her daughter how she felt, though. 'Oh, Mabel,' she said severely. 'What a stupid thing to do. Those poor people – imagine if someone had done that to Grandad when he was around. That's really horrible.'

Mabel was crying now, perhaps at the invocation of her grandfather, who she'd absolutely adored. 'I'm sorry,' she wept. 'I didn't join in, though, Mum. I promise. I wouldn't do that.'

PC Foster cleared his throat. 'As you can imagine, the Davidsons are extremely distressed at the theft and vandalism of their property. I am, however, led to believe that your daughter was not directly involved in this, so I won't be taking it any further with her personally.' A sob burst out of Mabel, her face still buried in her hands. 'However, I would advise her – and you – that she appears to have fallen in with a bad crowd. We've seen it all before, Mrs Jackson, and let me tell you, the slippery slope cannot be exaggerated. I am sure you understand what I'm saying.'

'Yes,' Rachel replied. 'And I appreciate you bringing Mabel back home and talking to us about this. Mabel, have you got anything to say to PC Foster?'

Mabel scrubbed at her wet eyes and took a gulping breath. 'I'm s-s-sorry,' she stuttered.

'All right,' he said gruffly, getting to his feet. 'Consider this a warning, okay? Your mates aren't getting off quite so lightly as you. Mr Davidson wants to take the matter further and press criminal charges, so I strongly recommend that you steer clear of these so-called friends in future. If the two of us cross paths again, I might not be so willing to let things go another time. Do you hear what I'm saying?'

'Yes,' Mabel whispered, shame-faced, pleating her school skirt with inky fingers.

'Okay. Good. Well, I'll leave you to get on with your evening, then.'

As PC Foster went back out to his car, Rachel noticed a familiar curtain twitching across the street. Of course, Sara

Fortescue *would* pick that moment to beak out of her window and spot their unexpected visitor, wouldn't she? She was probably already dialling her cronies to pass on the latest bit of gossip. *You'll never guess who's just been in our street. The police! Dropped back Rachel's eldest, you know, that sulky one with the blue hair. I dread to think what's happened now. She'll be on drugs next, you wait. That's divorce for you.*

Rachel waited until the officer had driven away, and then, giving the house opposite her very best Paddington Bear hard stare, she stuck up two fingers and went back inside.

Chapter Forty

Meanwhile, Becca had absolutely no idea what was going on in the front room as she and Hayley unpacked her bead box in the kitchen and started sorting through the contents. Becca put some music on and poured them a glass of Sauvignon Blanc each, and then they leafed through pictures of various designs Becca had printed off the internet to try and pinpoint the kind of look Hayley was going for.

Hayley eventually chose a fairly simple style with a pattern of beads and crystals, and picked out the freshwater pearls and Swarovski crystals she liked best. Then Becca showed her how to twist silver wire around the base of the tiara and create dainty wire stalks, each topped by a bead, along the rim. It was pleasantly fiddly work, and the wine slipped down easily as they chatted. It was a shame Rachel hadn't felt brave enough to join them, Becca thought, wondering what her sister was up to; but never mind. One step at a time.

Every now and then, Hayley paused in what she was doing and took a photo of the tiara in progress. 'For my blog,' she explained, when Becca shot her a look. 'You don't mind, do you?'

'Of course not,' Becca said, and was just about to ask what blog this was, when they heard raised voices – Rachel and Mabel – through the wall and then the familiar thud of Mabel storming up the stairs. 'Oh dear. That'll be the teenager off in a strop. Never a dull moment around here.'

Hayley had nimble fingers, and it took her less than an hour to complete the bead-topped stalks and then add a row of sparkling crystals along the front, all wound in tightly with the silver wire. 'There,' Becca said, showing her how to fold in the last end of wire. Once finished, she positioned the tiara in Hayley's hair and instructed her to go and admire her reflection in the downstairs loo mirror.

Hayley came back wreathed in smiles. 'I can't believe I *made* this,' she gushed, eyes shining. 'I absolutely love it – it's exactly what I wanted.' She raised a hand gently to her head, beaming as she ran her fingers along the gleaming crystals. 'Wow, Becca. I'm so cack-handed usually, I never expected anything home-made to look quite so stylish. I'm going to wear this all evening now. Princess Hayley, that's me. And you – well, you're just Queen of Awesomeness.'

'Now, come on,' Becca said, laughing. 'Queen of Threading a Few Beads Together, maybe, but . . .'

'No. No modesty! If you can teach an amateur bodger like me how to make this sort of thing, then you've got some serious skills there, believe me.' She held up her phone and took a selfie. 'Sorry to be vain. I'm just really chuffed,' she laughed.

'Well, I'm chuffed too,' Becca said. 'It's lovely being able to make something for your own wedding. Whether it's the cake, or dress, or presents for your bridesmaids – even a pair of gorgeous wedding-day knickers – it puts your own stamp on it, don't you think? Makes it much more personal.' The happy glow was back, she realized: the glow inside that came from flexing her creative muscles. This must be how people like Rachel felt after doing sport, she thought to herself as Hayley texted the pictures to her best friend. It was the craft-worker's equivalent endorphin rush of joy, although without a sweaty bra to show for it.

'She loves it,' Hayley said, as a reply text pinged swiftly back. 'Ahh, thanks, Becca. Do you know, we've shelled out so much money to big companies for this whole do – hotel, caterers, jewellers for the ring . . . even the dress came from a shop and was probably made in China. It's so nice to have one little part of it – this! – that was made right here in Hereford. By me!' She finished her wine with a gulp, and then looked thoughtful. 'Wait . . . did you say wedding-day knickers? Don't tell me you can make those as well?'

Becca laughed. 'Yeah, I can make wedding-day knickers. I did a load for a friend's hen party a year or so ago, had everyone making their own knickers and garters. It's not as hard as you think.'

'You are seriously clever,' Hayley said, so admiringly that Becca felt herself blushing. 'I wouldn't have a clue. Now, before I head off, how much do I owe you for my bling?'

'Oh!' Becca hadn't thought that far ahead. 'Don't be daft. I had the beads anyway, so . . . No, honestly. Purse away,' she said, as Hayley began digging in her handbag. 'Call it an early wedding present.'

'Are you kidding me? Absolutely not. Those crystals alone must be worth a fortune. And actually, thinking about it, I'd love to commission you to make a few more for my bridesmaids. Would that be all right? Do you have time, even, with everything else you've got on?'

'Well, yes,' Becca said, feeling delighted at this turn of events. More lovely artistic work to get stuck into. Paid work, no less! 'Tiara-making is way more my thing than fitness training,' she confessed. 'I'd love to make some for your bridesmaids. Absolutely!'

Hayley pulled out her purse and withdrew a handful of notes. 'There you are, then,' she said, pressing them into Becca's palm. 'Call that a down payment for the time being. I'm having six bridesmaids, so let me know how much it'll cost once you've worked out the figures, yeah?'

Becca felt thrilled to bits as she hugged Hayley goodbye a few minutes later. She had work again! Proper, interesting, artistic work; a job that she would really enjoy. Brilliant! Once Hayley had left, she headed straight for the living room to tell Rachel the good news.

'Hey, you'll never guess what,' she said, bursting in. Then she stopped in alarm. 'Are you all right? What's up?'

'It was a policeman at the door,' Rachel said, her eyes red as if she'd been crying. She was sitting there with her arm around the dog for comfort, drooping against his hairy body. 'Came to drop Mabel back home.'

'A *policeman*? Shit, why? What's happened?' Her niece must have been attacked, Becca thought at once in alarm. 'Is she all right?'

Rachel went off into a story about patio furniture being thrown into a river and warnings from a dour-faced policeman. 'Well, that doesn't sound *too* heinous a crime,' Becca said tentatively. 'I know it's not great, but . . .'

'The thing is, though,' Rachel interrupted, voice shaking, 'it's bad genes. That's what scares me. I've got them. She's got them. We're going to be a family of delinquents, I know we are.'

'What do you mean? Hey!' Becca put an arm around her. 'Come on. You don't have bad genes. Why are you saying that?'

'My mum . . .' And then she broke down, tears spurting from her eyes. Becca bit her lip, feeling nonplussed. Rachel's mum? Emily, the tragically beautiful one beyond compare?

'I . . . I didn't tell you before, but I found out some stuff about her,' Rachel went on, eyes down. 'And it's not good.'

Becca listened in amazement as out came a terrible tale of infant neglect, and how Rachel had only been given the first inkling at their dad's funeral. 'That's why I was going to Manchester,' she said shakily. 'Because I didn't believe it could be true. But it is true. It did happen. And now I'm just paranoid that I might turn into her – and that my children might, too. Mabel's going off the rails at thirteen, and I don't seem to be able to stop her. I just . . .' Her face, already so pale and thin, was despairing. 'I'm scared that I take after Emily. Alcoholic, couldn't-give-a-shit Emily. That I'm a waste of space too.'

'Oh, Rachel, no.' Becca couldn't take all of this in. She remembered from childhood the way that Rachel had idolized her dead mother, invoking her memory at the drop of a hat, particularly when Wendy was trying to get her to tidy her room or wear less make-up. *My mother would never have said anything so bourgeois*, she would yell condescendingly before storming out of the house. (Becca remembered that one in particular because she'd asked Wendy later on what it meant. *She means I'm boring and old-fashioned*, Wendy had replied wearily. *But better that than . . . Well, never mind.*)

'Just because your mum behaved the way she did, it's no reflection on you,' Becca went on. 'Look at your three – none of them are mini clones of you or Lawrence, are they? We're not always miniature versions of our parents.'

'No, but . . .'

'And throwing a bit of furniture in the river . . . I mean, it's bad behaviour and yeah, Mabel shouldn't have done it, but nobody got hurt, did they? It sounds like that copper really shook her up, anyway. I don't think she'll be going round terrorizing other pensioners any time soon, do you?'

Rachel dabbed her eyes. 'No,' she admitted.

'Honestly, I don't think she's going off the rails. She's just an ordinary teenager, working through various things – first love, exams, you and Lawrence splitting up . . . It would be more worrying if she *wasn't* reacting, you know. At least slamming a few doors and yelling at us means she's getting her feelings off her chest.' She reached over and squeezed Rachel's hand. 'I'm sorry to hear about your mum. But it doesn't have to change anything about you or your family. You're still the same person, aren't you?'

Rachel nodded, and there was silence for a moment. The light was just starting to dim outside, and Becca could see lamps being turned on in houses across the street.

'You know . . . Something I feel really awful about is the way I treated Wendy,' Rachel confessed eventually. 'Who *was* a good mum – or rather who would have been to me, if only I'd let her. I need to talk to her. Apologize.'

Becca thought back to the last time she'd seen her

mum, out in her small neat garden when they'd not had their Dad dinner. Then something occurred to her. 'Actually,' she said slowly, 'I've got a feeling that Mum might have known about your mum anyway. I mentioned that you'd been up to Manchester, and she went all funny. You know what a crap liar she is; I knew something was up, but I couldn't work out what.'

'I wondered the same,' Rachel admitted. 'She left a cryptic message on the answerphone the other day, sort of hesitant, as if she couldn't quite bring herself to ask anything outright.' She sighed, both arms around the dog, who licked her face sympathetically. 'I wish I'd never found out, to be honest. It's changed everything I thought I knew.'

Becca patted her arm. 'Not necessarily,' she said. 'Dad was your number one parent and role model, not Emily. And anyway,' she said firmly. 'It's never too late. If you rang Mum and talked all of this through with her, then do you know what? I reckon she would understand.'

'Maybe,' Rachel said. There was a moment's doubtful silence before she added, 'Do you really think so?'

'Yes,' said Becca, looking her squarely in the eye. 'I really think so.'

Chapter Forty-One

Becca was still pondering the conversation the next morning, thoughts of both her sister and elder niece turning circles in her mind. What Rachel needed was to get her head around these maternal revelations, then make things right with Wendy. Mabel, on the other hand, was an altogether more complicated prospect . . . what did *she* need? Stability, love, confidence, boundaries – but freedom, too. Rachel had grounded her for a week, plumping for Route One parenting and coming down on her like a ton of bricks. Once Mabel had seen out the punishment, though, would anything have changed? There had to be a new way for them both to get along, thought Becca, frowning at her reflection as she brushed her teeth.

There was no time to work out the nuances of every scenario this morning, though, as she had her next appointment with Rita, the garden-loving lady from the care home, who'd caused Rachel's phone to ring off the hook last weekend with hordes of other gardening wannabes, apparently. Busted.

'Please don't invite any more geriatric plant-botherers to ring me up,' Rachel groaned when Becca announced that she was off to see Rita. She had slept badly, by the look of her crumpled face. 'And maybe try to actually follow the exercise plan this week, rather than buggering off to an allotment with her the whole time?'

'You've got it,' Becca replied, hands up. 'Lots of stretches and a brisk walk, no problem.' She wasn't even lying. She would park the car half a mile away from the allotment – perfect for the brisk walk – and then ensure Rita got stuck into the weeding – lots of bending and stretching. And what Rachel didn't know wouldn't hurt her, Becca thought, setting off.

This week at the allotment there was a crop of new potatoes to harvest, clumped like golden pebbles; buried treasure on the end of the gardening fork. There were scarlet radishes, more beans than they could pick and the first ripe strawberries, so sweet they made Becca's eyes pop. The flower bed that Rita's friends used as a cutting garden was a riot of dazzling summer colour too, with bright orange poppies on feathery fronds, jewel-toned dahlias and rich blue cornflowers turning their heads to the sun.

'So, er . . . Rachel said she had a few calls over the weekend,' Becca said, as the two of them weeded companionably together. 'Some of your friends wanting to come out gardening too.'

'Ahh yes. I did pass on the number to a few of them. They

were jealous, you see, that I'd got to do something fun. Bored silly, most of the time in there. Oh, the staff are kind enough, but they're so busy that nobody ever *does* things with us.' Rita rocked back on her heels. 'They just park us in front of the television and bring us stewed tea on the hour. It's not what I would call fun, to be honest.'

'That's a shame,' Becca said. It wasn't what she would call fun either. 'The problem is, it's my sister's business, really,' she went on, wishing there was more she could do. 'I'm just care-taking while she's out of action. And she's all for press-ups, and feeling the burn – well, you met her, didn't you? She's old-school about exercise, so I'm not really sure what she can do to help. But let me talk to her, all right? Maybe we can come up with a plan between us.'

'Thanks, darling,' Rita said. 'In the meantime, I'm going to make the most of you while you're around. It's heavenly being back here. I can't tell you how much I'm enjoying myself.'

'I can see why you like it,' Becca replied, gazing around. Hours of work had gone into the allotment, you could tell. The rude good health of the plants, the rich brown soil that crumbled beneath her fingers, even the homely feel of the little shed with its kettle and folding chairs . . . it was enough to gladden anyone's spirits. Everyone had their secret short-cuts to happiness, she had come to realize. For her, it was making something, using her hands, being creative. For her sister, it was exercise and the big outdoors. For Rita, it was clearly gardening that worked the magic: getting stuck into a vegetable plot or flower bed with a trowel, the sun on her face, tending her beloved plants.

Becca thought back to the unkempt back garden she'd glimpsed at Michael's bungalow when she'd been round to help him cook, and how it could do with even a tenth of the love and care that had been shown to this particular patch of ground. His shortcut to happiness had been through music, she remembered. A good old song to lift the spirits.

'Have you got a nice garden at home?' Rita asked just then. 'I'll take some cuttings for you, if you want.'

'Well, I . . .' Becca was about to decline regretfully, not having so much as a windowbox to call her own, when an idea struck her. 'Actually,' she said. 'I don't have a garden myself, but I know someone who could do with a splash or two of colour in theirs.'

'No problem,' Rita said. 'Let's see. What do you think they would like? Some lavender? These marigolds here? A nice little cosmos?'

Becca wasn't much of an expert, but felt pretty confident that just about any plant would make Michael's garden look better. Maybe that would give him a boost too, as well as his trombone-playing. 'Yes please – to anything,' she said. 'Thanks so much, Rita.' Then another thought occurred to her. 'Actually . . . He doesn't live that far from here. If you're not in a hurry to go straight back to the home, we could always drop in and see him when we're done here. That way you could advise him on how to look after the plants, if that's okay?' *Meddling again?* she heard Rachel groan in her head, but shooed the voice away. Yeah, so she was meddling again. What of it?

Rita smiled back at her. 'I'm never in a hurry to go back to Willow Lodge,' she replied. 'Right, where did I leave that trowel? I'll put a few pots together for him.'

Becca hoped that Michael wouldn't mind them popping by with a few flowers to get his garden going. He might not even be in, for all she knew. But as they walked up to his front door later on, a tray of small potted plants in her arms, she heard the mournful notes of a trombone, which answered her second concern at least. 'Sounds like he's at home,' she said.

'Yes,' replied Rita, looking thoughtful.

Nothing could have prepared Becca for what happened next. When Michael opened the door, he said, 'Hello again, love! This is a nice sur –' but then his eyes fell on Rita, and he stopped dead. 'Rita. Rita Blackwell. It's not, is it?'

'Michael *Jones*?' Rita's hand flew up to her chest. 'Well, I never. Is it really you?'

'You two know each other?' Becca cried. Oh, but this was perfect!

'Well, we used to,' Michael said. He couldn't take his eyes

off Rita. 'My goodness me. It must be thirty years or so. Our daughters were best friends for a while, weren't they?'

'Heavens, yes, they were thick as thieves! All the way through school. It was like having another daughter, the number of times your Shona would be at our tea table, and vice versa.' She chuckled fondly. 'Do you know, as soon as I heard that trombone through the open window there, it made me think of you. I nearly said, I used to know a trombonist – and then you opened the door . . .'

'And then I opened the door,' he echoed. His face split in an enormous smile, and his voice had gone extra-Welsh with the excitement. 'Come in, anyway. How do you two know each other? Has Becca been teaching you to cook as well?' He stopped himself. 'What am I saying? You were always a smashing cook. I remember those birthday cakes you used to bake for Carol . . . Wait till I tell Shona I've seen you!'

They had stepped into the narrow, dingy hall with its dismal bare bulb – Becca really must finish that lampshade and bring it round, she thought – and maybe Rita could detect the lack of womanly presence in the dusty air, because she asked uncertainly, 'And . . . Christine, was it, your wife? How is she?'

'She died,' Michael said simply, as he led them through to the living room. 'So there's just me now, knocking about on my own. Take a seat, both of you, that's it. How about . . .' He scratched his head. 'Sorry, I can't remember his name. George, was he called?'

'He died too,' Rita said, lowering herself to the faded red velour sofa and sitting with her hands in her lap. 'Seven years ago. Pneumonia, God rest his soul.'

Becca was starting to feel like something of a gooseberry, perched awkwardly on the arm of the sofa, still holding the tray of plants. 'It's a small world,' she said, when she could get a word in. 'So Michael, you're probably wondering what we're doing here . . . I was just up at Rita's allotment with her and she offered me some cuttings and I thought of you, and wondered if you might want them for your garden. I can give you a hand sometime, if you like, or . . .'

'Or I will,' Rita said at once. 'I'm in a care home now, Michael, can you believe – Willow Lodge, on the other side of town – and I'm bored out of my tiny mind there. I'd love to help with your garden, if you can put up with having me bossing you around.'

Michael looked positively delighted at the suggestion. 'That would be wonderful,' he declared.

This had been a good idea, Becca thought with a smile. Two lovely people, both rather lonely in their own way, with their daughters and a few pot plants in common. Whether it was just as companions or something else, there was the potential for this meeting to blossom into a beautiful new friendship.

'Tell you what,' she said, 'I'll put the kettle on and make everyone a cup of tea. Michael, why don't you show Rita the garden, and then we can get stuck in?'

Chapter Forty-Two

It was Lawrence's turn to have the children that weekend and Rachel was rather amused to see that he was every inch the polite, courteous ex-husband as he arrived on time and whisked them away, Harvey bounding into the car boot to accompany them. (After weeks of enforced separation it would have taken a harder heart and a deadlier threat than some extra hoovering at Builth Wells for anyone to try and argue with Scarlet about *that*.) Becca headed for Birmingham soon afterwards, the two sisters surprising each other with a goodbye hug on the doorstep.

Rachel had felt somewhat apprehensive about being left to her own devices for the whole weekend, but was determined to manage alone. She had an early night on Friday, then busied herself with housework on Saturday morning: laboriously and slowly stripping all the beds and putting the linen to wash, tidying Luke's bedroom, and tackling the ironing. Then she sat down with all the bills that needed paying, a frown pinching her forehead as she totted up the 'incoming' figures on her spreadsheet. Despite Becca's best attempts to keep the business ticking over, it was all looking pretty desperate, unfortunately. And then, once she was fully fit again at the end of July, it would be the summer holidays, and both time and money would be stretched even tighter. She was going to have to ask Lawrence to step up his game, she decided. Pay her more maintenance, for starters, and take the children for a whole week in August so that she could really go for it on the work front, maybe run some kind of holiday boot camp . . . She rubbed her eyes, feeling uncertain and not a little despairing. It was at times like this that she missed having a husband by her side – or anyone! – to say, *We could try this*, or *Maybe this might work*, or even a simple *Don't worry. We'll be all right*.

The doorbell rang just then and she stiffened in her chair. It was two in the afternoon, too late for the postman, too soon for any returning members of her family. Jehovah's Witnesses? One of her friends trying to ambush her with a surprise visit?

She hesitated, wondering what to do. She still felt so awkward and self-conscious around other people, she was tempted to ignore whoever it was. Then the letterbox rattled. 'It's me!' came a familiar voice. 'Open up!'

Becca? Rachel went to the door feeling confused, certain her sister had said she'd be back on Sunday. And yet there she was on the doorstep, looking shifty, rushing to get in an explanation before Rachel could speak. 'Don't be mad,' she said. 'But I thought we should all have a chat. I wasn't sure you would ever get round to organizing it so . . . I did.'

'What?' Rachel asked, not following, but then the passenger door of Becca's decrepit car opened and it all became clear. Because there was Wendy clambering out, a vision in a lime-green top and denim skirt, sunglasses pushed up in her hennaed hair. There was just the very faintest flash of nerves in her eyes as she tottered up the drive with a bunch of yellow roses.

'Oh,' said Rachel faintly. Becca, you *didn't*, she wanted to say in exasperation at her meddling sister. But of course she had. 'Hello.'

'Hello, love,' Wendy said, and the two of them hesitated for a moment, then leaned forward to give each other a brief, polite peck on the cheek. 'I hope you don't mind us turning up like this. Becky assured me it would be fine, but we all know how some of her other impulsive ideas have turned out. That bubble perm three years ago, for starters. So . . . *is* this okay? We'll bugger off again if you've got plans, obviously. Oh – and these are for you.'

The roses dumped in her arms, expectant gazes mirrored in Becca's and Wendy's faces, it was impossible to refuse. 'Of course,' Rachel said, forcing a sickly smile. 'Come on in.'

'Ooh, I'd forgotten what a lovely house this is,' Wendy said, taking off her sandals in the hall. 'We've brought refreshments, by the way,' she added, delving into the voluminous gold shoulder bag she was toting. 'Vanilla ice cream and bananas.' She passed a Tesco bag to Rachel. 'I would have brought cake but Becky told me that eating was a bit tricky, so I thought I could whizz us all up some naughty smoothies instead.' She pulled one last item from the bag – a bottle of rum – and winked. 'What do you say?'

Rachel had been about to offer tea, coffee, elderflower cordial, but she knew when she was beaten. 'Lovely,' she said instead, shooting Becca a look that said *We'll talk about this later.* If she survived the afternoon, that was.

It was a mild late-June day – white cloud and soft warm air – so once the first batch of naughty smoothies had been created, the three of them settled themselves around the patio table outside, Britishly making the most of the fact that it wasn't actually raining. 'What a smashing garden,' Wendy said, sipping appreciatively, her blue eyes widening a fraction as the zing of rum hit her. 'Cor, that's got a kick. Shall we toss a coin for who drives home later on, Becky? I'm going to be plastered by the bottom of this glass if I'm not careful.'

Becca started scoffing at her mum, calling her a lightweight ('You've only had one sip, for goodness' sake!'), but Rachel felt on edge with nerves. Wendy had never been one for pulling any punches or holding back, especially after a drink. She pushed her glass fractionally away, determined to keep her head clear for whatever turn this conversation might take.

'Is that a hammock down there?' Wendy was saying, squinting down the garden. 'I've always wanted one of those. You've got it looking ever so nice here, Rachel.' She elbowed her daughter. 'See? This is how grown-ups live, Becky. Not in tiny shoebox flats with sex-pest neighbours and a bookie's downstairs. Proper nice houses and gardens, with *hammocks* and shrub roses. When are you going to get on and live like that, eh?'

'Oh Mum, don't start,' Becca said. 'The sex pest moved out a year ago anyway, there's a nice old lady there now. A nice old lady, by the way, who doesn't go around making pointed remarks and trying to guilt-trip her own daughter about her so-called shortcomings. Just saying.'

'She sounds like she's kidding herself to me,' Wendy sniffed, hitching up her skirt a little as the sun threatened to make an appearance. Then she turned to Rachel. 'Tell me now, Rachel. I've been trying to get this one to sort her life out recently. Has she done anything about finding herself a nice man?'

Becca groaned loudly, the look of indignation on her face so comical that Rachel couldn't help a snigger. 'Well, there is this one guy she seems quite keen on,' she replied.

'What? Who?' said both Becca and Wendy at almost exactly the same time.

'He's Welsh, he plays the trombone and he's learning to cook,' Rachel said, unable to resist it.

'Oh, shut up, you, I thought you were on my side,' Becca said, sticking out her tongue.

'Go on. Sounds good,' Wendy urged. 'I do like a Welshman, I have to say.'

'Don't listen to her, Mum, she's winding me up. He's in his seventies, I've just been helping him cook a few things,' Becca said. 'And before you say it, no, it's not some creepy dad substitute, so don't even bother going there, all right? Anyway, I've actually fixed him up with a new lady friend.'

'You didn't tell me this. When?' Rachel asked. 'And who's the lucky lady?' Honestly, her sister, what was she like? She just could not stop herself.

Becca looked sheepish all of a sudden, though. 'Er . . . Well, don't get mad, but . . .'

Oh no. Now what had she done? 'What?'

'It's Rita. Rita Blackwell.'

'Rita Blackwell, my client?' Rachel shook her head in disbelief. 'And how did this come about? Tell me not during her exercise session. Becca?'

'Well . . .'

'After you promised me and everything?' Her sister's expression was so rueful and you-got-me that Rachel needed to hear no more. She put her head in her hands and shook with mirth, just at the sheer badness of her.

'I'm sorry,' Becca mumbled, shame-faced. 'But they were so sweet together, Rach. So happy. I think it's actually going to be a really cool summer romance for them, you know.'

'I apologize for my daughter,' Wendy said, although she was laughing too. 'She is a dreadful one for poking her nose in. I can't think where she gets it from.'

Becca and Wendy looked at each other then, and it was such a teasing, affectionate sort of look that Rachel found herself experiencing a sudden twist of envy, a pang of longing. She wished she had somebody to be like that with, so easy and good-humoured. She sipped her smoothie and then found herself blurting out, 'I hope when my girls are grown up, I get on with them like you two do.' Her cheeks flamed as they both turned to her in surprise. God! How much rum was *in* that drink?

'What a lovely thing to say,' Wendy replied, putting a hand to her plump brown cleavage.

'You do get on with them. You're great with your kids,' Becca told her.

Rachel pulled a face. 'Not all the time. And especially not with Mabel right now. Most days I feel like I'm getting it completely wrong.'

'Oh, sweetheart, take it from me, every mum feels like that,' Wendy said at once. 'And you've got a teenager now as well – a teenage daughter.' She gave Becca a meaningful look. 'We all know how hellish they can be. The things your dad and I had to put up with, with Miss Lady here. You just have to grit your teeth and hope that they come out the other side and turn back into half-decent human beings. And she will.' She patted Rachel's hand, a look of understanding in her eyes. 'In the meantime, there's always a boozy smoothie to get you through.'

'I'll drink to that.' Rachel smiled at her stepmother as if seeing her for the first time. Maybe it *was* just the alcohol, but she felt almost as if the ice field between them was splintering, breaking apart after years of permafrost. 'Wendy, I need to tell you something,' she heard herself saying in the next moment and then rushed straight on before she could change her mind. 'I found out the truth about Emily – my mum. A woman at the funeral said something weird, and I went digging. I . . .' Her voice cracked. 'She wasn't exactly the mother I thought she was.'

Wendy nodded, not seeming terribly surprised. 'Becky mentioned you'd been up to Manchester when –' she gestured at Rachel's face. 'When that happened. I wondered if you'd found something out.' Reaching forward, she took Rachel's hand in hers. 'I'm sorry. That must have been a shock.'

So she *had* known. 'Yeah.' And the rest. She risked a glance up at Wendy's face, dreading seeing pity in the other woman's eyes, but found only compassion. 'I wish Dad had said something, you know. Told me himself. Why did he let me go on believing a lie?'

Wendy sighed. 'He should have told you, I agree. I did badger him about it. I even wondered if I should mention something myself, but it wasn't my place. You'd never have believed me, anyway.'

'No.'

'Besides, you know what he was like. Typical man: no good at big emotional dramas. And he loved you, too, of course. He didn't want to be the one who shattered your heart with the truth.'

Rachel nodded. It all sounded plausible. 'Oh well,' she said, trying to shrug it off. Having Wendy being so sympathetic and nice was making her feel uncomfortably vulnerable. 'I know it's not the end of the world, or anything.'

Wendy was silent for a moment. 'She did love you, you know, I'm sure of it. Terry didn't talk about her very much, but every now and then he would let slip something so sweet.'

Rachel's eyes felt hot and gritty, as if the tears were just waiting for an excuse to come. 'Like what?'

'Oh gosh, let me think. Well, back when Becky was little, your dad was really surprised that I didn't know the Happy Nappy Song.'

'The happy *nappy* song? What's that?'

'Exactly. I asked the same. Turns out it was this song that Emily always used to sing as she changed your nappy – I don't remember the words now – but obviously she'd made it up, invented this whole little routine with you, to make you laugh. Terry assumed that every mother knew it, that it was just this thing we all did, but no.'

Rachel didn't trust herself to speak for a moment. That *was* sweet. Personally she'd always been in a tearing hurry to get nappy changes over and done with as quickly as possible, rather than make a song and dance of the occasion.

'And she made lots of your clothes, did you know that? I think Terry was a bit taken aback when I kept buying baby clothes for Becky, rather than making them myself.' Wendy sipped her smoothie and looked down at the table for a moment. 'You know, reading between the lines, I think nowadays she'd have been treated for postnatal depression,' she said slowly, cautiously, 'but obviously back then, it just didn't have a name. You got on with it and coped – or you didn't. And for Emily, coming as she did from a family of big drinkers, the booze was her way out. Sadly.'

'Yes.' There was silence for a moment. Postnatal depression. It did make sense. Rachel knew herself that you could love a baby, and have wanted that baby, and yet feel unable to cope, as if a fog was around you. She'd been lucky enough to have counselling to help her through, but that hadn't been an option for her mum. Her eyes prickled again at the thought of the happy nappy song, and the home-made clothes. She *had* been loved, though. She had been looked after, until things went wrong.

'I'm just sorry that . . .' Now it was Wendy's turn to falter.

'Sorry that you and I never really hit it off when you were growing up. I wanted to be a mum to you, but obviously you can't simply walk in and take someone's place, I get that now.' Her mouth twisted, her eyes sad. 'I just fell in love with your dad, though, that's all. I never wanted to make anyone unhappy.'

She had such an open face, Wendy. Behind all the teasing and the banter, there was something so genuine about her, so sincere, Rachel thought. 'It was my fault, too,' she admitted quietly. 'I never gave you a proper chance. The thing is, the night you went away on honeymoon –' But the next words stuck in her throat, jammed there, hard and painful. Oh God. Could she really do this? Tell them what had happened, after nearly three decades of silence?

'Yes?' Wendy prompted.

Rachel took a deep breath and then choked out the story, sentence by horrible sentence. Sonia's spare room. Frank's warm hand on her little-girl thigh. The cigarette smoke in her nostrils, a smell she'd never been able to stand since. Her shrill scream of fear . . .

Wendy burst into shocked sobs as the words came out, her shoulders shaking. Becca too had tears running down her cheeks. Rachel, by contrast, felt numb, dispassionate even; the only one of the three not to show any outward emotion. 'It kind of changed everything for me,' she finished by mumbling.

'Oh my darling, of course it did. Of course it did,' Wendy cried, hugging her, tears dripping onto Rachel's back. 'That bastard, Frank! That bastard! I could kill him. I could punch his lights out. What were you, ten? The same age as your Scarlet? The dirty old pervert. I swear, if I ever see him again, I'll wring his bloody neck. I'll put cigarettes out in his *eyes*.'

There was something oddly comforting about having someone so furious on your behalf, even when their threats of violence were worryingly graphic. 'It's all right,' Rachel managed to say eventually. 'It was a long time ago. I was just frightened, that was all, and freaked out. And I blamed you, even though it wasn't your fault.'

'Oh, Rachel,' said Wendy, her face wet against Rachel's. 'I understand. Of course you did. Because I'd taken your daddy away just when you needed him most. I'm sorry. I'm so sorry that happened.'

Becca, who'd remained quiet for perhaps the longest period of her waking life until then, came over and hugged them both. And as if it had been planned, as if it heralded some official celestial benediction, the sun chose that moment to slide out from its cloud cover and shine down on them, a small interlocking triangle of women in a suburban garden. It was more than that, though. It was the sound of a slate being scrubbed clean, a new page turned, a unifying pact being made without anyone needing to say another word. And boy, did it feel good.

Chapter Forty-Three

After such a momentous conversation everyone needed a coffee, and Wendy blew her nose three times and passed around some tissues. Then, once they'd recovered and all eyes had been wiped, the talk turned to easier subjects. 'I was going to suggest you join us for the "Dad dinners" from now on,' Wendy said, explaining what these were, 'but we're moving on – aren't we, Becky? – so perhaps we should think of something else we can all do together. Girly weekend lunches, maybe, when the kiddies are with Lawrence. Or cocktails in fancy bars in Birmingham – you get some good deals on Groupon now and then.'

'I would really like that,' Rachel said. To her surprise, she genuinely meant it. She felt lighter suddenly; an old hurt soothed, an old enmity wiped out. 'Yes, we must, that would be great.'

Wendy went on to ask about the children and Rachel gave updates on them all, finishing with Mabel. 'Like I said before, I'm slightly at my wits' end with her,' she confessed. 'We used to be so close. Thick as thieves. She'd tell me everything not so long ago, unpack her entire day for me after school each time and we'd chat through whatever had happened. But now . . .' She pulled a face. 'Well, you've seen her, Bec. She's so prickly and angry all the time, so secretive and private. I'm just not sure how to get through to her.' She hesitated, conscious of the fact that she'd never deigned to ask for help before from either of these women at her patio table, dismissing their opinions without even hearing them. *You arse, Rachel. Since when did you know it all?* 'I was wondering . . . do you two have any ideas?'

If Becca was surprised at being consulted, she didn't let on. 'I've been thinking about her too,' she said, draining her coffee cup. 'And I know since I've been staying, I've deprived her of her own room, now that Scarlet's in with her. Maybe part of the problem is that Mabel needs her own space, some-where she can go with her mates rather than hanging around by the river getting into trouble.'

'A room of her own where she can shut the door on the world and have some privacy,' Wendy agreed.

Rachel nodded. 'Maybe I should put Scarlet in with Luke instead,' she suggested, mentally measuring up Luke's tiny bedroom for space. They could just about squeeze a mattress on the floor, she supposed, although it wouldn't give either of them much elbow room.

Becca was gazing out across the garden. 'I've had a better idea . . .' she said.

Twenty-four hours later, it was almost time for the children to come home and Rachel stood in the middle of the shed, gazing around it with an air of exhilaration. *Everyone needs an art project*, Becca was fond of saying – and Rachel was starting to agree. Between them, they had got stuck in on Saturday afternoon, clearing it of all its clutter – toddler bikes that could go to the charity shop; ancient lilos hissing with punctures, fit only for the bin; a cracked old slide that should have gone to the dump years ago – and then sweeping away the dirt and cobwebs.

Becca had had to drive Wendy back to Birmingham at six on the Saturday – 'I know you're both going to mock me but I've joined the local W.I., and it's *brilliant*,' she had announced, 'and we've got this handsome beekeeper coming to talk to us tonight, I can't miss it' – but had returned the following day, with some paint charts and fabric for curtains from which Mabel could choose.

Becca then had to get on with her bridesmaid tiaras for Hayley but Rachel carried on with Project Shed, scrubbing the windows and putting a beanbag and a rug inside to make it look more homely. Now she just had to cross her fingers and hope that her daughter approved of the whole thing.

True to form, Mabel appeared suspicious when she and

her siblings arrived home later on and Rachel said she wanted a word with her in private. 'What have I done now?' she muttered, glowering.

'Nothing,' Rachel assured her. 'Don't look like that.' She led her into the garden. 'It's just that I've been doing a lot of thinking this weekend, about mums and children, you and me. And while I'm not about to condone what your friends did last week, I do know that it's tough being a teenager.'

Mabel made a non-committal noise as they walked across the lawn. 'Aunty Bec and I were talking,' Rachel went on, feeling nervous as they approached the shed, 'and she had the brilliant idea of . . . Well, of *this*.'

She flung open the shed door, her heart pounding a staccato beat, hoping and hoping that Mabel wouldn't scoff contemptuously or give her a blank *so what?* kind of stare, as she so often did these days.

'It's an . . . empty shed?' Mabel said warily.

'Yeah. And we thought it could be *your* empty shed. Your not-so-secret hideout. We can get some paint and decorate it. Aunty Bec said she would help make curtains if you choose the fabric. We can wire up some fairy lights, and you could put posters up . . . whatever you want. Then we can get you a padlock for the door, so it's just your private place, and you can invite friends round and . . .'

The corners of Mabel's mouth turned up a fraction and Rachel held her breath in the hope of a positive response.

'Does that mean I'm not grounded any more?' her daughter asked hopefully.

Rachel met her gaze. 'You are still grounded,' she replied, 'but you can have friends round here. Girl friends,' she amended, as her mind flashed up an alarming image of Mabel and Tyler locking themselves in the shed for after-school passion. She wanted this to be a nice, safe place for her daughter, not some kind of teen knocking shop. 'Although . . . Well . . . I suppose Tyler can come to the house too, as long as bedroom doors stay open and . . .'

Mabel gave her what could only be described as a re-proachful look. 'Me and Tyler broke up ages ago,' she said, before adding something that might very well have been 'Not that you'd care anyway.'

Oh God. Another mothering fail. 'I'm sorry,' Rachel said, feeling wretched. How had she missed this? By slumping on the sofa feeling sorry for herself, probably. You took your eye off the ball, you disengaged, and this is what happened. There had even been something on the whiteboard about Mabel hating boys, she remembered too late – and she hadn't even joined the dots. 'Really, I am,' she said, putting a hand on her daughter's back. 'I know you liked him. Are you all right?'

Mabel pushed her lower lip out. 'Yeah. Whatever,' she said, which quite clearly meant 'No.'

First love, first heartbreak – ouch. 'I'm sorry I've not been the best mum lately,' Rachel said after a moment. 'I think life just knocked me down for a while, and it's taken me this long to get back up on my feet. But another time, I will be there, okay? I'm your biggest fan and I'll always listen if you want to talk to me. I promise.'

Mabel shrugged. ''S'all right,' she said. 'He's an idiot anyway.'

Tempted though Rachel was to agree, she knew she mustn't. Rule number one: don't slag off the ex. Instead she put her arm around her daughter and gave her a hug. 'Well, it's his loss,' she said staunchly. 'You should do what your Aunty Bec keeps telling me to do, and paint yourself better. Have a think about what colours you'd like for this shed, and we can pick some up for you.'

Mabel was stiff in her arms initially, but then she hugged her back. For the first time in weeks it was a proper, affection-ate hug, one that felt genuine, as if they might just be head-ing back to a good place together. They stood there in the shed for a moment, mother and daughter, side by side, and Rachel felt peace descend.

'Thanks, Mum,' said Mabel, leaning her head against Rachel's shoulder. 'That would be really cool.'

Chapter Forty-Four

'Happy birthday to you, happy birthday to you – happy birthday, dear Becca, happy birthday to you!'

'Surprise!' cheered Luke, as Becca blinked blearily at the vision before her. It was the following Thursday and there at the bedside were the four Jacksons – Scarlet with her violin in hand, having accompanied the birthday chorus, and Mabel, who was bearing a tray laden with a fry-up, mug of coffee and a posy of garden flowers. Rachel was already dressed and smiling rather bashfully, while Luke capered around the bed as if he had the proverbial ants not only in his pants but all the way down his pyjama bottoms and between his bare toes. Even Harvey, who wasn't usually allowed upstairs, was present, his nose twitching enthusiastically at the scents of bacon and sausage.

'Wowzers,' Becca said, just about recovering her senses in time to have the breakfast tray plonked in her lap. 'Thank you! What a lovely surprise.'

'And there's going to be another surprise later,' Luke said, bouncing up and down alarmingly close to the coffee. 'A surprise *cake*, but it's a secret 'cos—'

'LUKE!' howled his sisters, before he could say any more. 'Do you even *know* what the word "secret" *means*?' Mabel added, raising her eyes to heaven.

'Luckily I was so busy admiring the flowers I didn't quite catch all of that,' Becca said tactfully, hoping to avoid full-blown fisticuffs over her scrambled eggs. 'What did you say, Luke? Something about a surprise?'

'Nothing,' he said, turning red in the face as Scarlet elbowed him. Then his eyes slid to his aunt's breakfast plate and he gave her his best hopeful-puppy face, head tilted, eyes wide. 'Can I have your hash brown, please?'

'Luke!' Rachel remonstrated, laughing. 'No, you can't. Tell you what, you kids go and get dressed for school while Aunty Bec has her birthday breakfast in peace. Then you can give her your cards and presents, okay? Shoo!'

Becca felt quite touched by all of this fuss. There was an actual lump in her throat, and it wasn't from the mouthful of too-hot coffee she'd just gulped down, either. 'Thank you,' she said, as Rachel perched at the end of the bed. 'This is amazing.' It was only then that Becca noticed her sister seemed to be wearing make-up for the first time in weeks. And had she actually blow-dried her hair? Surely this honour wasn't all for Becca's birthday, was it?

'I'll take the kids to school today, by the way,' Rachel said breezily, as if this was a perfectly normal occurrence.

'You'll—' Becca almost choked on her food. 'What? Seriously?' Her sister still hadn't managed a single school run, more than three weeks since the accident. The bruising and swelling had finally left her face, but Becca knew she was cripplingly self-conscious about her altered looks, and had been dreading the initial mob of gossips flocking around her like flies after meat – led, no doubt, by that nosey old horror over the road, and Melanie Cripps.

'Yeah. Today's the day.' Rachel gave a nervous laugh. 'So you can stay in bed as long as you want this morning. Enjoy your breakfast. I promise I made Luke scrub his nails before I let him anywhere near it, by the way, so you're quite safe to dig in without fear of terrible gastroenteritis later.'

Becca didn't quite know what to say. Today was the day, all right. This was a major breakthrough, right here in one suburban bedroom. This was big, big news. One ten-minute walk outside with the children was the equivalent of one giant leap for womankind in Rachel's case. Step by step, day by day, her sister was venturing her way back to normality. Brushed hair, make-up, determination . . . it was all starting to reappear, and Becca felt inordinately proud of her. 'Good for you.' She saluted her with the coffee mug. 'And thanks for this,' she said again. 'It's bloody fab. Not just the breakfast but the kids, the singing, the flowers . . .' She could feel herself getting emotional. When was the last time anyone had sung

'Happy Birthday' to her? Such a silly little thing, but oh, it was lovely. It reminded her of how birthdays used to be – waking up with a proper thrill in your stomach, ribboned presents and cards through the post, feeling special all day at school, candles flickering on a cake . . . 'I feel like I'm part of the family now,' she confessed.

'You *are* part of the family,' Rachel said at once. 'God, Bec, you are most definitely part of this family now – you've been the heart of this family lately.' Their eyes met, and then Rachel looked a bit embarrassed and got to her feet. 'Listen to us, we sound like a pair of cheesy fridge magnets. Kids!' she yelled, turning and heading for the door. 'Are you nearly ready?'

It felt such a luxury staying in bed while she heard first Mabel leaving for school, and then Rachel with the younger two children. Becca stretched her arms above her head, patted her full tummy and then wandered through to the bathroom for a leisurely shower in glorious peace and quiet.

Wiping condensation from the mirror, she leaned forward and examined her face. Ever since she'd been a child she'd always expected to see that year's difference suddenly apparent in her reflection the very moment she had a new age. How can it be, she'd wondered, aged seven, eight, nine, that I'm a whole year older and yet look exactly the same as I did yesterday?

Maybe it was the clouds of steam lending her a misty out-line but the funny thing was, today she actually looked a bit younger, if anything, than she had done six months earlier. It must have been all the fresh air and cycling, she guessed, because her skin seemed clearer, her eyes a little brighter, and she knew without having to squidge them that her thighs and bum were definitely more toned than they had been for years. Country living clearly suited her. Country living, and the fact that she wasn't just eating pizza and takeaways these days either, she was cooking family meals from scratch. God, she was becoming sickeningly virtuous, she thought, raising an eyebrow at her reflection. Maybe her birthday meant that it was time to stuff her face and drink lots of calorific wine to counteract so much goody-goody behaviour.

She'd just finished drying her hair when she heard Rachel come back. 'I'm upstairs,' she yelled, pulling on some cycling shorts and her favourite mint-green T-shirt in preparation for her first appointment of the day. 'Everything all right?'

Rachel did look rather pale, it had to be said, but there was a set to her shoulders that was reminiscent of the tough, uncrushable Rachel of old. 'Well, I survived the mum mafia,' she replied drily, coming into the bedroom and sinking onto Scarlet's bed. 'I had six people stopping me and saying they'd heard about the accident. Another three asking if Mabel was all right because they'd been told she'd been escorted home by the police – no guessing how *that* little story got around.'

She rolled her eyes. 'And then I had old Neighbourhood Watch herself, Sara, trying to get me to sign some awful petition or other, to get Luke and Elsa's teacher disciplined.'

'Oh Lord, what a welcome back,' Becca said. 'I heard some of the other mums talking about that stupid petition yesterday. Apparently Miss Ellis was spotted at some nightclub or other in a skimpy dress, going for it on the dance floor. How dare she have fun out of school hours, etc. etc., because that clearly makes her a terrible example to the children. None of whom, obviously, were actually *in* the nightclub at the time, of course. Honestly!'

'She is just the limit, that woman,' Rachel agreed. 'Anyway, I refused to sign, so now she'll hold that against me too. Oh well. The better news is that I saw Jo and Karen and . . .' She looked shy, all of a sudden. 'Well, Jo's having a girls' night in on Saturday, she asked if I would go along.'

Excellent. Jo and Karen were two of Rachel's nice mates who'd always been friendly to Becca, without ever being nosey or pushing themselves on the family. 'I hope you said yes,' she replied.

Rachel nodded. 'I did. I said yes. If you don't mind holding the fort here, that is, otherwise I could ring my usual babysitter and—'

'Of course I don't mind. It's about time I had the telly to myself without having to watch all your shit programmes every night . . . Joking! No, that'll be brilliant. Good on you.'

She glanced at her watch. 'I'd better push on, actually, I'm meant to be meeting Adam in fifteen minutes.' She squirted her wrists and neck with some of her new perfume – Jo Malone, a present from Rachel, who had perhaps noticed her own bottle mysteriously running low – and then, just for the birthday hell of it, added a quick slick of coral lipgloss and some mascara. Hey. It wasn't every day you turned thirty-one, was it?

Watching, Rachel gave a meaningful quirk of her eyebrow. 'This for Adam's benefit, is it?' she asked teasingly.

'Certainly not! For my benefit,' Becca said, sticking out her tongue. Then she ran down the stairs singing 'I Feel Pretty' at the top of her voice, hopped on her bike and pedalled away, grinning to herself like a lunatic.

She'd had a good few days, all in all. Hayley had been thrilled by the delivery of tiaras at the start of the week and had promptly booked Becca in for a knicker-making slot too as part of her hen night celebrations. 'Oh, and you'd better give me your email address,' she'd said as they parted ways at the end of the session. 'If that's all right? I'll pop it on the end of my blog, in case anyone's interested in getting in touch.'

'Cool, thanks,' Becca had said, scribbling it down. She was about to ask more about the blog, but Hayley's mobile rang at that moment and she made an apologetic face, taking the call. Becca had waved and mouthed, 'See you next week,' before leaving her to it.

Still, a knicker-making event was always a laugh, especially with a bunch of rowdy hens where the prosecco flowed freely. The only danger was making sure nobody got so drunk they sewed their own finger to the fabric, but she'd be there, keeping an eye on health and safety at least. The hen night wasn't until August and it felt good, having one nice little job there on the calendar already. *The future starts here*, she kept telling herself, determined to stay positive about the no-job situation. Tomorrow, she promised, cycling over the river and taking her feet off the pedals to freewheel down the hill. She'd get on the case tomorrow.

It would be a wrench to leave Hereford, she found herself thinking. She might only have been staying here a few weeks, but that had been enough time for her to start feeling part of a community, thanks to all the different people she'd met around the city. Part of a family as well, she thought, remembering her lovely birthday breakfast. God, she was going to miss Rachel and the children most of all. More than she'd thought possible, if she was honest.

She locked her bike up in the usual place, trying not to think about that. She had agreed to stay for another fortnight or so, until Rachel was back to full working order (*Will I ever see you again? I miss you!* Meredith had texted plaintively), and then after that . . . Well, not to put too fine a point on it, she had been wondering if her old flat in Birmingham was really the right place for her any more. Coming here, making a change, trying a different lifestyle on for size – she had enjoyed it. Maybe she was ready to move on at last. She was even thinking she might . . .

'Morning!' came Adam's voice, and she jumped. Miles away.

'Hi,' she said. He was smiling again, she saw as he approached. Good. She'd quite enjoyed the last session with him, much to her surprise; he was actually a laugh once you got beneath the gruff exterior. 'How are you today? I take it your business empire didn't collapse last week while you were away from your desk for that single hour, then?'

He grinned. He had very nice teeth, she noticed, and his eyes went kind of sparkly whenever he smiled. 'Astonishingly, no. The empire is intact. I've even been going out running independently a few times this week, phone left deliberately at home, and am still somehow in business. It's all good. So how are you and how's that nephew of yours?'

She loved that he remembered the conversation about Luke. All these high-powered clients of his, and he was asking about a six-year-old boy. 'He's fine, thanks – LOVED your idea of taking up some kind of martial art. Rach has got him down for some karate holiday club already, so cheers for that.'

'You're welcome. How about you? You look chipper this morning. I hope that doesn't mean you've lined up an absolutely heinous hour of fitness punishment for me.'

She laughed. 'I *am* ludicrously cheerful, thank you, despite being another year older today,' she told him. 'And as for this morning—'

'It's your birthday? Happy birthday!'

'Thanks. But don't think this means you're getting away with an easy workout. Especially now I know you've been sneaking in extra training sessions. Let's crack on.'

She joined in with an energetic warm-up once more – why not? She was entitled to make a prat of herself on her birthday, after all – then gave him his instructions for that morning's training run. It was strange to think she'd only be doing a few more of these sessions, she thought, as they set off in their usual running–bike configuration. Rachel would be deemed fit enough to pick up the reins of her business once six weeks was up, and she'd already been making noises about wanting to come along to certain sessions next week, to advise from the sidelines and check in with her clients personally. Becca wasn't altogether sure how she felt about that. She'd got to like the clients after weeks of seeing them and building up relationships; they felt like *her* clients now – mates, even, some of them. Besides, she knew Rachel wouldn't exactly approve of some of her more unorthodox fitness-training methods, once she got to hear about them. Perhaps she'd better print up a bunch of confidentiality agreements before then.

'So,' Adam said, as he jogged along, 'it's your turn this week. I bored you with my story last time, now the spotlight's on you. Spill, Birthday Girl. Let's hear the details. My

Wonderful Life, by Becca, aged . . . what? Twenty-five?'

She pulled a *Seriously?* face at him (Mabel would have been proud). 'Thirty-one, actually, although nice try with the flattery. As for the gory details of my life . . .' She hesitated, not quite sure what to say. 'Well, what do you want to know? My career hasn't been quite as resounding a success story as yours, let's put it like that. Er . . . I make a bit of jewellery here and there. Used to have a little business with a mate, until she emigrated. I can make lampshades and knit things and cook and . . . Oh, I've been asked to do a hen party and make a load of frilly knickers too.' She could hear her own voice sounding lamer by the second. 'You know. Stuff. Anyway, we should probably stop so I can make you do some press-ups in a minute.'

'So this is all on a sort of ad hoc basis, is it?' he asked, ignoring the bit about press-ups. 'You're self-employed?'

'Yeah,' she said, then wrinkled her nose. Self-employed made it sound like a much bigger deal than it really was. 'To be honest, I've been working in a pub kitchen all year,' she admitted. 'I didn't feel like being creative for a while. But then my flatmate Meredith asked me to make her this medieval diadem – well, more like Galadriel's one, actually, you know, from *Lord of the Rings* – and then the other week I helped someone make a tiara for her wedding, and . . .'

He looked thoroughly confused by now. Obviously he had never come across anyone quite so haphazardly crap in his long history of business consultancy. She blustered on, trying to make her point. 'And I really enjoyed it, that's what I'm trying to get across – I loved doing it, in fact, it made me feel so happy again! – and I'm going to try and do more of that sort of thing, I want to "find my way" again, as my mum would say, and . . .' *Oh God, Becca, just shut up*, her brain started screaming. *SHUT UP!* 'Yeah,' she muttered eventually, as if that was any kind of way to end an explanation. 'Right, anyway. Press-ups!' She stopped cycling, and pretended to consult her list of exercises.

'I think that sounds good,' he said quietly. 'For what it's worth.'

'So Rachel said to –' She broke off again, feeling like a dork. 'Oh.'

'Doing your own thing, I mean. Doing something that makes you feel happy.' He shrugged. 'I reckon you should go for it. Why not?'

She'd been so sure he would laugh at her or mock her shambles of a 'career' that she stood there dumbly for a moment or two, waiting for the 'KIDDING!' It didn't come. 'Anyway, it's all a bit up in the air, so it's academic right now,' she said. 'Just bits and bobs to be getting on with, you know. But it's a start.'

He nodded, his dark eyebrows bunching together in a thoughtful frown. 'Right. So how are you going to turn these "bits and bobs" into something more concrete? What are you doing to grow the business?'

'Grow the business?' Stupidly, she found herself thinking of Rita, her careful watering and mulching up at the allotment. 'Um . . . Well, to be honest, I've been really busy,' she said by way of an excuse. 'Running around after Rachel's clients – a couple of mums, and this lady at the care home across town, and there's this sweet old man I've been teaching to cook, so . . .'

'So there you are. Captive audience – your first potential customers. You should start being a bit more proactive with them all, put yourself out there. Go for it!' He was standing leaning against a tree now, the fitness session forgotten, she registered dimly, but her brain was taken up with trying to come up with a reply.

'Well . . .' she said again, doubtfully. It wasn't exactly as easy as he was making out. 'The knicker-making job did actually come from one of Rachel's clients,' she told him.

'You presented the customer with the idea, did you? You gave a pitch, won the business?'

'No,' Becca admitted. 'She just asked me, so . . .' Her voice trailed off.

'That's what I'm saying. You need to take control. Get onto those school mums and organize a knicker-making party with them, too. Go back to that care home and start . . .

I don't know, a knitting club with the residents. See if your tiara friend has got any good contacts—'

'She's putting me on her blog, actually,' Becca felt compelled to say, just about managing to resist adding, *so there!* She felt uncomfortable, though, on the back foot. How had their training session turned into a business meeting? *'Anyway.'*

He didn't look quite as impressed as she had hoped. 'No offence –' oh, here we go – 'but everyone and his dog has got a blog,' he went on. 'She probably only has about twenty readers too, if the average is anything to go by. Look, have you thought about—'

'Have *you* thought about the fact that it's my birthday and you're making me feel a bit shit about my career prospects?' Becca interrupted huffily, before he could go any further. 'Right – press-ups now. Definitely.'

Adam obediently got down on his hands and knees – that was more like it – with a somewhat sheepish expression on his face. 'Sorry,' he said. 'Force of habit, that's all, from work. I didn't mean to piss you off. That's just what I do, poke my nose into people's businesses, ask annoying questions.'

Becca's flash of temper subsided. She was a fine one to criticize someone else for poking their nose in, after all. 'It's okay. You're probably right anyway, I need to get my act together over the next few weeks, make some decisions, sort my life out.' She pulled a comical face. 'Okay. Drop and give me twenty, as they say. And no more talking.'

He did what he was told – it gave her a bit of a thrill, actually, saying 'Drop and give me twenty' like that – and then rose up afterwards, dusting his hands off on his shorts. 'I am sorry, though,' he said again. 'I forgot it was your birthday, I shouldn't have lectured you like some kind of patronizing old twat.' He held out a hand. 'Friends?'

She laughed. 'You're not a patronizing old twat. Don't worry, I'm going to plunder your knowledge shamelessly once I actually get started on any kind of business plan. Anyway, you've given me some good ideas.' She took his hand and shook it firmly. 'Friends,' she declared. He had nice hands, she thought. Large, strong, tanned . . . Then she realized she was still shaking it like some kind of a weirdo, and let go hurriedly. 'So anyway . . .' She consulted her sheet. 'Calf drives! That's what we're doing next. And it's not some strange rodeo experience, it's for your Achilles tendons and calf muscles, according to Rach. Allow me to demonstrate.'

'What are you doing later, then? For your birthday, I mean?' he asked, not seeming to pay any attention as she took off into a jump.

'What? Oh,' she said, taken aback. 'Er . . . I think my nieces and nephew are planning some sort of revolting birthday cake surprise later on,' she replied, 'but other than that . . .' She shrugged. 'All my mates are back in Birmingham, so not a lot, I shouldn't think. Right, so the aim of the calf drive is to—'

'Maybe I could take you out for a birthday drink, then,' he said, apparently uninterested in the new exercise. 'After the revolting birthday cake surprise, I mean,' he added. He was smiling but the air around them seemed to change with his words. She could almost feel it sizzling with a strange new tension.

'A . . . a drink? Oh!' Was this a *date*? Was he asking her on a *date*? Oh my God. Wait till she told her mum! (Ugh. She could not *believe* that was the first thought that had occurred to her.) 'That would be lovely,' she said politely. 'Sure. Thank you.' And then, because she felt weird all of a sudden as well as a tiny bit excited and jittery too, she changed the subject. 'Anyway. Where were we?' she said firmly. 'Calf drives. Let's do this.'

Chapter Forty-Five

That afternoon after school, Rachel gathered the children in the kitchen and shut the door. 'You're not allowed in here,' Luke bellowed through to his aunt, just in case she had failed to notice. 'We're going to do some secret things now, and you can't come in!'

'How exciting,' they heard Becca reply, a laugh in her voice. 'Are you sure I can't just peep?'

'No!'

'Or sit here on the other side and listen?'

'No, Aunty Bec, you can't!' Luke was delighted at this opportunity to order her around. 'You have to stay in the living room, otherwise . . .' He paused for inspiration. 'Otherwise we'll eat the whole cake ourselves!'

'Oh, LUKE!' his sisters groaned while he clapped a hand guiltily to his mouth. Rachel found herself laughing. He had never been the best at keeping secrets, her boy.

There was a good atmosphere between the four of them

as they mixed and whisked and just about managed to break all the eggs without showering pieces of shell into the bowl or gooey albumen on the floor. They were making a two-tier chocolate sponge, with whipped cream and raspberries; reportedly Becca's favourite, according to Scarlet, who'd undertaken some discreet quizzing earlier in the week.

Everyone seemed happy, Rachel thought with a small sigh of contentment as she watched them taking it in turns to stir the mixture, dipping their fingers in the spilled cocoa powder when they thought she wasn't looking. The storm seemed to have passed. Ever since the weekend, Mabel had been spending every spare minute out at the shed, painting the outside electric blue (you could probably see it from space now) and the inside walls gleaming silver. Becca had helped her run up some curtains for the window, and she'd rigged up an extension cable from the house so that she could plug in a lamp and a string of fairy lights, hung artfully from corner to corner like glittery bunting. Her own place, six square feet of private space, and it had made such a difference to her daughter's mood. She'd already invited a few friends over this coming weekend, so eager was she to show off her new hangout.

'Everyone needs a little art project,' Becca had said, and Rachel was starting to think she might just be right. She hadn't told her sister yet – imagine the crowing! – but she had actually picked up a few tester pots of paint herself the other day. A soft rose pink. A dusty mauve. A light, bright aquamarine that reminded her of swimming in the sea. Becca was always taking the mick out of her and her 'middle-class beige home', and Rachel was prepared to concede that she had a point. Maybe the time had come to leave the dull neutrals behind and cheer the place up with some colour.

Meanwhile, Scarlet, too, was an infinitely happier child now that the dog was home. Her violin playing had changed from frenetic, angry sawing to softer, more mellow lullaby-type tunes. She had taken her Grade 2 exam that week and seemed quite confident that it had all gone okay. She had also put herself forward for the end-of-term school talent show, and she could be heard laughing again, her face no longer quite so pinched and pale. It was so good to have that infectious laugh ringing through the house once more.

As for Luke, she had seen a change in him as well. He had apparently told Lawrence about the forthcoming karate lessons and to Rachel's surprise (and delight), Lawrence had found some short karate move videos on YouTube and downloaded them onto his iPad so that he and Luke could both have a try. Parenting teamwork, she thought, sending Lawrence a mental high-five of gratitude. Just learning a few simple moves seemed to have boosted her son's fragile confidence already, even if it did mean endless 'Haiiii-YAH!' screams as he went around karate-chopping cushions, his bed, the sofa. She could live with it, though, if it meant he was happy.

Maybe, just maybe, she thought, the Jackson family were collectively on the mend at last.

The doorbell rang as Becca was blowing out the candles on her birthday cake. The birthday cake, by the way, that had been a complete triumph, right until Scarlet had dropped it on the (less than spotless) kitchen floor, and Rachel had bit back a scream of frustration, somehow managing to say, very calmly, that they would have to throw this one away and bake another. That was why it was now seven-thirty in the evening, and really, Luke should have been in bed.

'Who's that at the door?' Mabel asked as Becca scurried off to answer it.

Good question. Who, indeed? Why, it was Adam, the previously detested client, who was now apparently taking her sister out for a drink. Talk about a change of heart – this was a tyre-screeching U-turn if ever Rachel had seen one. Laid-back Becca had actually become quite flustered earlier, panicking about what to wear, how dressy she should go, was it a bit much if she wore earrings *and* a necklace? Could she borrow Rachel's black sandals? For someone who had always bitched and moaned about Adam, she was certainly making an unheard-of effort for this one single drink.

'It's someone for Aunty Bec,' Rachel replied to her children's inquiring faces, before plunging the knife into the cake and cutting the first slice. 'Let's see if he wants to stay for some birthday cake, or if he wants to whisk her away.'

'Is it a *boy*? Is it her *boyfriend*?' Scarlet and Luke asked in loud voices, just as Becca came back into the kitchen followed by Adam.

Becca was wearing her nicest jeans and a teal-coloured floaty chiffon top with jingling gold bangles on her wrist. Her pale freckled skin surged with colour as she heard her niece and nephew's questions and she shot them a fierce sort of look. 'Guys, this is Adam. Adam, you know Rachel, of course, and these rapscallions are Mabel, Scarlet and Luke.'

'Wait,' Scarlet said in confusion, 'I thought you didn't like Adam?'

'Well –' Becca stuttered, shooting her niece an even more ferocious 'shut *up*' look.

'Adam the PooHead?' Luke echoed. 'I don't like him either.'

Oh God. Out of the mouths of babes, and all that. Loyal, protective babes who had memories like elephants, no less. 'Different Adam,' Rachel said quickly, because Becca seemed to have temporarily lost the power of speech. 'This is nice Adam, not Adam the, um, PooHead. All right? And he's going to have a piece of cake – well, I hope he is, if you lot haven't just frightened him away – so can we all remember our manners, please.'

Adam's mouth was twitching as if he found the whole thing hilarious. 'This Adam PooHead guy sounds a bit of a douche,' he commented, as Rachel went back to cutting slices.

'Yeah. Aunty Bee *hates* him,' Scarlet said. 'She said she wanted to *punch* him but—'

'Scarlet, that's enough,' Rachel warned in her most severe voice, easing out the first slice of cake on a plate for her sister. 'Here you are, Bec,' she said, passing it over.

Becca was still squirming. First lesson of living with children, Rachel thought: be careful what you say when small ears are flapping. They remembered *everything*, and you could never tell when it might be used against you for future humiliation. 'Thanks,' she said in rather a strangled voice.

'Where are you two going, then?' Rachel asked, before Scarlet could pipe up with some new tactless comment or other. Thankfully the children all had their eyes glued to what was happening with the cake, monitoring with forensic precision how big each slice was and which they were hoping for.

'I thought we'd drop in at Leo's,' Adam said, accepting the plate she handed him. 'Do you know it? Little wine bar on a side street near the cathedral. It does really great tapas.'

'Oh, good idea,' she said, and smiled at her sister, whose high flush of colour was only just starting to ebb away.

'There's a lovely courtyard garden, it'll be perfect on an evening like this.' She turned back to the children and started doling out cake to them all, feeling a disconcerting twist of emotion inside. Envy? Was that really envy she was feeling? Not because Becca was out with *Adam*, per se, just that she was about to head out on a date with this man who was smiling so attentively at her, laughing at the crumb of chocolate cake that appeared to be welded to her top lip, his eyes soft with affection as he brushed it away. It was the romance that she envied, she thought, turning so as to hide her face. The romance of putting on lipstick, your heart beating a little bit faster, wondering what might happen at the end of the night. Hoping that an evening together and a bottle of wine might just lead to something else . . . And Leo's Bar *was* gorgeous. The garden would be festooned with little lanterns, and the climbing roses would be in full bloom and smelling heavenly, and the night sky would darken around them, from a gauzy shade of peach to an inky midnight blue . . .

When had she last sat in a warm, scented pub garden and held hands with a man across a weathered wooden table? It had been years. Too many summers had somehow slipped by while she and Lawrence were too busy, too tired, too whatever to make romantic gestures for one another.

'Thank you so much, everyone, that was delicious,' Becca said, putting down her empty plate and licking her lips appreciatively.

'It was excellent,' Adam agreed. 'Very good. Which bakery did you say it was from again?'

Aww. The kids' faces. '*We* made it!' Luke cried.

'It wasn't from a *bakery*,' Scarlet added gleefully.

Even Mabel, who was wise to the fact that he was clearly flattering them, looked chuffed and then promptly tried to take advantage. 'We take commissions, by the way,' she said, batting her eyelashes. 'Only twenty pounds for a cake.'

'Twenty-five,' Scarlet said immediately.

'Fifty,' Luke said in the next breath.

Adam laughed. 'I think you three could teach your Aunty Becca here a few entrepreneurial skills,' he said, then dodged out of the way as she pretended to swipe at him. 'It was a spectacular cake. My compliments to the bakers.' He tilted his head towards the front door and smiled at Becca. 'Shall we?'

'Let's,' she said. 'Thanks, everyone, I've had a fab birthday so far. See you all in the morning. Don't wait up!' And then with a kiss blown for each of them, she winked at Rachel and left. Rachel could hear their laughter floating down the hallway as the front door closed behind them.

'So who *is* Adam PooHead?' Scarlet wanted to know, wiping a wet finger around her plate in the vain hope of catching any last molecules of cake she might previously have overlooked. 'I'm completely confused.'

'That *was* him, imbecile,' Mabel told her. 'Which wasn't

embarrassing at *all* for Aunty Bec, having you two slagging him off right there. God!'

Scarlet's jaw dropped for a full five seconds. 'But I thought . . . I thought she hated him? Why is she going out with him if she hates him?'

'Well, I like him,' Luke pronounced. 'Especially if he gives us fifty pounds.'

'He's not going to give us –' Scarlet said, exasperated. She still looked baffled by the whole sudden turnaround, though.

She'd learn, thought Rachel, stacking plates. 'That's just one of the mysteries of love,' she told her. 'Love and hate can be closer than you think.'

'Eww,' Scarlet said with a shudder. 'Well, I hate Josh Rawlins and I'm telling you now, there's no way I'm ever going to love *him*. So there!'

Rachel gave a wry smile as her daughter put her nose in the air and stalked off. Love and hate . . . she had experienced both of them during her marriage, but felt as if she might just have come out the other side now. Her love, then hatred, for Lawrence had given way to a sort of grudging acceptance these days. Civility. Not that *that* was anything a romantic young dreamer would aspire to, of course, but it was way better than previous hostilities.

She loaded up the dishwasher, wondering how Becca and Adam would get on together, if they were still laughing, if they would manage to nab one of the tables outside at Leo's. Was this the start of something exciting for her sister? She really hoped so. Becca deserved the best, and Adam seemed a good bloke. Just as long as his PooHead ways were behind him now, of course. Because if not, he'd have big sister Rachel and her three gobby children to contend with – and then he'd *really* have something to be sorry about.

Rita Blackwell had come to consider her daughter in a new light recently. After all, if it hadn't been for Carol's arranging for Rita to have a series of exercise sessions, she would never have met the delightful Rebecca and been able to return to her allotment this summer, just in time for the soft fruit season. *And* of course, she wouldn't have been re-introduced to Michael Jones either. That alone was almost worth the indignity of having to do jumping jacks in the car park of Willow Lodge that one and only time, with Malcolm Banks sniggering out of the window.

But now there was Michael, back in her life. Lovely-as-a-Welsh-cake Michael Jones! To say she'd been surprised to see him was an understatement. She'd actually gone a bit fluttery with the shock, thought for a moment it was her angina plaguing her again, before she realized that it was in fact sheer delight causing her to feel so giddy. Goodness, she hadn't felt this way since her beloved George took her dancing at the Hillside Ballroom back when she was a teenager! It was funny how circular life could be, it really was. By the time you were into your seventies, you became better at predicting a course of events, you'd seen life's recurring patterns all before. But nobody could have predicted that she would be helping Michael Jones out in his overgrown garden, and that the two of them would be chatting away about their respective daughters as if Shona and Carol were both still in knee socks with their hair in bunches.

'Goodbye,' they had said rather awkwardly at the end of that initial reunion last week, when Becca had looked down at her watch and said they had to go because the staff at Willow Lodge would be wondering where they had got to. It had been such a pleasant afternoon, Rita had found herself dragging her feet, not wanting it to be over. 'Well, ta-ta, then. Lovely to see you,' they said on the doorstep, eyes on each other; a whole other silent conversation unfolding.

A second passed, then two. There was the chime of an ice-cream van in the distance somewhere, an old familiar tune – *Oh where, oh where, has my little dog gone?* – and the sound made Rita feel nostalgic for her youth, all those years gone by. How many ice-cream summers did they have left? she wondered. She'd never been one to waste time if she could help it.

'Maybe we could—' she began, just as he said, 'How about we—'

Becca had moved a discreet distance away to her car, and was checking something on her phone.

'Ladies first,' said Michael, gallant as ever. Tall and spry, still with that twinkle in his eye and that lovely Welsh lilt to his voice. She had always liked that voice of his.

'Well, I was thinking,' she began, nervous all of a sudden. (Nervous! Her!) 'It's been so nice seeing you again, maybe we could catch up some other time too? Perhaps we—'

'Yes,' he said shyly, just as she was wondering if she was about to make a fool of herself. 'I would like that.' The years seemed to melt away as his gaze remained on hers, steady and sure. 'Same time next week? I could make us some biscuits, I'm a dab hand at this baking now, you know.'

'And I could give that vegetable patch of yours a proper dig-over, get some beans going there for you.' She could feel her smile stretching, a gladness filling her up inside. 'Same time next week, then,' she said.

And so here they were again the following Friday, she and Becca, having been made to swear she wouldn't tell Carol or Rachel that they weren't actually doing any proper exercises today. As Becca knocked on the door of Michael's bungalow, Rita felt positively girlish at the prospect of seeing him again. Girlish – yes! As she had told Joan, who had the room next door to hers in Willow Lodge, he was a good-looking chap, make no mistake. So what was a woman supposed to do in this situation? *You go for it, doll*, Joan had advised, putting down three queens with an air of triumph. They were playing poker, a game that sharp-eyed Joan always seemed to win. (Rita suspected she'd been a hustler back in the day, and had already vowed never to start betting with anything other than cocktail sticks.) *Bloody well go for it*, Joan repeated, collecting her winnings with a shaky hand. *A second chance, at our age? Make sure you do it for us girls!*

Do you know what, Joan? she thought, as she saw Michael's figure looming towards them through the bobbly glass. I think I jolly well will, too.

It was just as lovely to see Michael second time round as the first. He had baked some scones for the occasion – rather undercooked, doughy scones, admittedly (bless him for trying though, Rita thought, determinedly chomping her way through and hoping the gluey texture wasn't about to do for her dentures) – and he had bought a few plants from the garden centre, on which she was all too happy to advise. Rita had always prided herself on her sharpness, her observation skills – in another life, she'd have been a detective; nothing got past her – but even so, with all this going on, it took her a little while to realize that something was odd about Becca that day. She had this goofy, dreamy expression on her face the whole time and kept staring into space, smiling to herself, as if Michael's flower beds were the most delightful visions she'd ever laid eyes on. (Take it from Rita: they weren't. The man's gardening skills were almost as abysmal as his scone-making attempts, and that was saying something. Not that she had the heart to tell him as much, of course.)

Michael noticed it too. 'Hello, hello,' he said, narrowing his eyes and considering her. 'Away with the fairies today, are we, Becca, love? Lost in a dream, hey?'

Becca blushed and went all coy, looking down at her lap, her eyelashes fluttering demurely on her pale cheeks. That was when the penny dropped for Rita. 'If I didn't know better, I would think this one was in love,' she guessed aloud, which caused the girl to turn even pinker. Aha. Right first time, she thought with a sideways smile at Michael.

'In love? New boyfriend, is this?' Michael wanted to know. 'Who's the lucky fella, then?' He began to hum 'Some Enchanted Evening', and Rita joined in.

Becca burst out laughing. She was such a pretty thing anyway, but today she had an especially lovely light shining in those green eyes, and looked so happy. 'Oh, he's just this guy I went out with last night. Stop it, you teasers,' she said, as their humming got louder.

'Well,' said Rita, arching an eyebrow. 'Looks like I'm going to need a new hat at this rate. I do love a summer wedding, don't you, Michael?'

'Absolutely,' he said.

'You two!' Becca scolded. 'It was only one date. Come on!'

'Ahh, but when you know, you just *know*,' Michael said. 'Isn't that right, Rita?'

He was smiling at her, his eyes soulful and lingering, and she felt her stomach turn a slow somersault, her breath suddenly catching in her throat. *Goodness, Rita, old girl,* she thought to herself, her knees feeling deliciously wobbly. *You must have had too much sun.* 'Yes,' she heard herself saying, in a voice so far-away-sounding, she wasn't sure for a minute if she had actually spoken. 'Yes, I think sometimes you just do.'

Chapter Forty-Six

Just one date, Becca had told Rita and Michael, laughing off their teasing expressions. Just this guy. But – oh! *What* a date it had been, and – oh, what a guy!

She'd been hit by a flurry of nerves beforehand, unable to help thinking back to the last disastrous date who'd got her name wrong, and the smelly football bore before that. But as it turned out, there was actually something quite relaxing about going on a date with a man who had already seen you at your absolute worst – red-faced, shouting, throwing balled-up paper at his face. Somehow it took the pressure off, somehow there seemed no need to bother with the usual desperate *like-me! Like-me!* attempts of pretending she was cool or sophisticated or ladylike – because they both knew she wasn't. And so she got stuck in to the patatas bravas and the breaded whitebait with gusto, the albondigas and chorizo and Spanish beer, licking her fingers with each salty olive. They swapped funny childhood stories and bad-date experiences, and she found herself laughing so loudly at one point that a man on the next table turned round in surprise. It didn't matter, though; Adam laughed too. And her heart, which had seemed so fossilized until now, mossed over from under-use since her dad had died, gave a joyful *I'm back!* kind of flutter inside.

Adam, in fact, was none of the names she'd called him back when they'd first met. She liked him. He was funny and clever, good company. Sexy, too, in his dark jeans and grey marl T-shirt, laughing at her with those chocolate-brown eyes. She liked that he was competitive, ambitious, driven; made that way by being the youngest of four brothers, he reckoned. She liked too that he'd been so sweet to her nieces and nephew over the cake and had taken their (awful, excruciating) comments so sportingly (thank goodness; she, on the other hand, could easily have throttled Scarlet for putting her clodhopping great foot in it like that). And talking to him was easy. She didn't have to check herself, or try to be someone she wasn't. She was herself, and that was okay.

Best of all, at the end of the evening, when somehow four whole hours had passed in what felt like a single heartbeat and the sky was black around them, they were just stumbling tipsily back towards Rachel's when he stopped in the street, slipped an arm around her waist, and said, 'I think you're pretty fucking extraordinary, Becca Farnham.' And then before she knew it, his lips were on hers, cool and soft, and they were kissing like a couple of teenagers right outside Peacocks. He tasted of red wine, and she could smell his aftershave, clean like the rain, and feel the muscles in his back as her hands slid around him.

It was the sort of kiss that made you feel light-headed, that caused star-bursting sensations to erupt around your body, that made you glad, so glad, to be alive and present. 'Happy birthday,' he said in her ear.

'Well, it is now,' she said back in his.

He was out of her league, she kept thinking, once they had parted ways and she was lying in Scarlet's little-girl bed, smiling stupidly up at the glow-in-the-dark constellations glued onto the ceiling. Way out of her league. He was successful and dynamic; surely too good for the likes of her, dreamy, drifting Becca who liked making things and pottering about in her own world. But he'd said he liked her, she remembered, feeling tingly. He'd said she was *pretty fucking extraordinary*; he'd kissed her with raw passion in a crushing, swoonsome embrace.

Listen to her. Swoonsome, indeed. In a single kiss she had become fifteen again and besotted with a crush. Well – okay, not a *single* kiss, exactly. There had been quite a few, all in all. Enough kissing to intoxicate a woman.

Consider me intoxicated, she had thought ever since. Through her appointment with Rita that next morning, through a trawl around the supermarket, through a dreamy session mopping the kitchen floor and not even caring when

Harvey bounded in after a walk with Rachel and proceeded to leave a trail of footprints right through it. Intoxicated with romance . . . Mmm. That felt good.

'So you know I'm going to have to report back to your mum, in my official role as Hereford spy,' Rachel teased on Friday evening. 'Hot new man, burgeoning tiara and knicker business empire . . . it's all happening for you this summer, Bec.'

They were sitting out in the back garden, a jug of Pimm's on the patio table nearby, a trio of pink-tipped evening clouds up in the sky like giant candy-floss. Becca grinned, fishing an alcoholic piece of strawberry out of her glass and popping it on her tongue, where it fizzed deliciously. 'God help us, she's going to melt the phone by screaming when she hears the news. Brace yourself for imminent deafness, neighbours.'

Rachel laughed. 'Obviously I am going to take at least ninety per cent of the credit for introducing you to Adam in the first place . . .'

'Do, you must. Mum will probably be your willing slave for life when she realizes the significant part you've played in it all.' Becca smiled as she thought back to the first time she'd spoken to Adam on the phone, how strong a dislike she had taken to him. It seemed a long time ago. Since then, she'd travelled so far out of her comfort zone – looking after children, becoming a stand-in (and sit-down) fitness instructor, playing Cupid with Rita and Michael, cooking, cycling, gardening, tiara-making – she could hardly remember what her old safe life back in Birmingham looked like.

'What freaks me out a bit is that I could probably have drifted along forever in my tiny boring world if I hadn't come here this summer, you know,' she went on, thinking aloud. 'It was only really when I was forced to do all these scary new things in your absence that I started wondering if my own life was enough for me – the flat, scrimping along from crap job to crap job, a sad little Sunday Dad dinner with Mum the highlight of my week.'

'And now you think you want something more?'

'Yeah, I think I do. It wound me up at first, Adam, constantly questioning me about work – what's the career plan? Where are you going with this? What happens now?' She pulled a face. 'I felt really defensive. Like, *I* don't know! What are you asking *me* for? But it forced me to think, at least. To get my thoughts in order. What *do* I want to do?'

'And . . .?' Rachel prompted. 'Come up with any answers yet?'

'Well, he gave me a few pointers, of course. Couldn't resist telling me how I should draw up a business plan, identify possible clients, get off my arse and just *do* something, rather than waiting for the perfect job to fall in my lap. Blah blah blah.'

'What kind of business plan, though?'

Becca felt suddenly self-conscious. A high-flier she would

never be. Her idea of a business was very much the home-spun cottage-industry style, rather than anything with legions of staff and huge turnover and management schemes. 'I want to carry on with the sort of work I've always loved doing,' she said hesitantly. 'Making things with other people: jewellery, sewing, crafts – I've realized that this is what really does it for me, makes me happy. Now I just need to be more targeted about putting myself out there and start pitching for jobs. Hen parties, private tuition, after-school craft clubs . . . whoever wants me.' She wrinkled her nose. 'I've even thought of a name for my business.' Now she felt *really* on the spot. 'Make Yourself Happy,' she said with a nervous little laugh. 'What do you think?'

'Make Yourself Happy,' Rachel repeated. 'I love it! That's perfect – because you do make people happy, Bec. You do!' They grinned at each other shyly. Then Rachel's voice became more studiedly casual. 'And this would be back in Birmingham, would it?'

'Er . . .' The six-million-dollar question. 'That was the other thing. I mean, I'll travel anywhere, within reason, at first,' Becca replied. 'But . . . Well, I've come to really like this area. I like being near you and the kids. And – God! I mean, me and Adam, we've only had one drink, one snog, it's not like I'm pinning all my hopes on the two of us living happily ever after or anything but . . .' She shrugged, feeling her cheeks pinken. 'But I'd like to see what happens. I'd like to give us a chance. And seeing as I'm a bit of a free agent right now, I thought I might as well give Meredith notice on the flat and look for somewhere to rent nearby.'

'Oh, Becca!' Rachel's voice was suddenly thick with emotion. 'That would be brilliant. I'd love that. The children would love it too. Oh!' And then Rachel, the most undemonstrative person in the world, had plonked her drink on the table and was launching herself at her sister for a hug, her plastered wrist clonking Becca's spine quite painfully as a matter of fact, but Becca didn't care at all.

Make Yourself Happy, she was thinking, the logo suddenly bright in her head. Rachel and her children made Becca happy. Being here made her happy. This whole summer so far had been an exercise in remembering how it felt to be happy. She hugged her sister back, a huge grin on her face, her mind cartwheeling with excitement about what might lie ahead.

On Monday morning, Becca saw Hayley for her weekly session which proved to be as enjoyably energetic as ever. It was only as they were saying goodbye at the end that Hayley asked smilingly if she'd had any interesting emails recently.

'Me? I don't think so,' Becca replied, feeling confused. Her phone had run out of battery the day before and she'd left it charging. With all the usual Monday mayhem that morning, she'd not had a minute to check for messages. 'Why?'

'Oh, just wondering,' Hayley said, maddeningly. 'Thanks for today, anyway. See you next week!'

Becca cycled home wondering what all that was about. Back at Rachel's, she dumped the bike and ran straight to switch on her phone. Maybe Hayley had sent her a wedding invitation, she thought in excitement. Or some official bridal booking document for the knicker party. Or . . .

Her email icon flashed as the phone came to life, and then the number 220 appeared in one corner of it. Two hundred and twenty new emails? They couldn't all be from Hayley. She stared at it, taken aback, wondering if her account had been hacked and these were two hundred and twenty spambots trying to sell her Viagra or a penis extension. Probably.

Clicking on the icon brought up her inbox on screen – and in the next second her hand flew to her mouth, a faint squeak emitting from her throat, as she saw email after email, a great long list of them, almost all with the subject line 'Tiara'.

No. What? How . . .?

Feeling dazed, she clicked on one at random and scanned the message. Then she clicked another and another, not quite able to believe her eyes. Phrases leapt out at her, tangling themselves in her boggled mind.

I'm a big fan of Hayley George's 'Here Comes the Bride' column and blog
I saw the article in the Sunday Telegraph

> *I'm interested in your bespoke jewellery service*
> *I'm a* Sunday Telegraph *reader and getting married*
> *myself next year, so always make straight for Hayley's*
> *articles . . .*

Wait just a cotton-picking minute, she thought, bewildered. Stop right there. Hayley – *her* Hayley – was in fact an actual proper journalist? Her blog, that she'd mentioned in such an offhand manner, was something to do with the *Sunday* freaking *Telegraph*?

No. She would have said, surely. She would have mentioned that she wrote for a national newspaper. Wouldn't she? Becca racked her brain, trying to think back to what, if anything, Hayley had said about work, but her thoughts kept returning to all the emails she'd received. Those two hundred and something emails! Because of Hayley!

Fingers shaking, she opened her browser and found the newspaper's website, then typed in Hayley's name. This had to be a mistake, she kept thinking. Someone was winding her up.

But then her jaw dropped as a new page opened with Hayley's face at the top, and a list of all the articles she'd written. The most recent one was entitled 'Here Comes the Bride 42: Try a Tiara'.

Becca's heart seemed to have thumped its way up into her throat. Her hands were clammy. Clicking the link to the article opened another page, this one with an artistic soft-focus photograph of the tiara Hayley had made right there at Rachel's kitchen table, and another, more professional shot of Hayley wearing the tiara and beaming into the camera. *Oh my God*, thought Becca, hardly able to believe her eyes. Had this really just happened? To her?

'All hail Princess Hayley!', the piece began.

No need to curtsey, I haven't secretly joined the royal family – but when I'm wearing this little beauty, I feel as if I might as well have. Here's the astonishing thing, though: I made it myself. Seriously! And if you like the sound of some customized handmade jewellery for your own wedding or a special occasion, then you'd better read on, because I have stumbled upon the perfect person to help.

'No,' Becca muttered under her breath. The perfect person – Hayley meant her. Ha! 'No,' she said again in disbelief. 'No *way*.' But as she finished reading the article and then flicked back to all those emails from interested readers, she began to feel the bubbling of an almighty *hell, yes* inside her. Yes, Becca. These appear to be genuine customers. Yes, Becca. This is really happening, right now, to you. Yes, Becca. It looks like your business is well and truly up and running.

A laugh burst from her throat as she wondered dazedly who she should phone first, Hayley or Adam. Then Rachel walked into the room. 'Are you all right in here? What?' she asked, as Becca turned to her, practically gibbering.

'I'm fine,' Becca stammered, pointing at the screen and feeling slightly hysterical. 'Look: orders. Customers,' she gabbled. 'The *Sunday* bloody *Telegraph*. This is it, Rach. This is it!'

Chapter Forty-Seven

Two and a half weeks later

'HURRY UP, AUNTY BEC!'

'WE NEED TO GO!'

'WE'RE GOING TO BE LATE!'

Small fists were beating against the bathroom door and Becca gave her hair one last pat, pulling a face in the mirror. 'Coming! All right! I'm *coming!*'

All eyes were upon her as she descended into the hall, wearing her sexiest midnight-blue bodycon dress, red siren lipstick and heels. She had straightened her hair and spritzed on perfume and had her best pulling knickers on too, just in case.

'Is that really my daughter?' Wendy asked, doing a double-take.

'Blimey,' Rachel commented. 'I know the Poplar Primary School talent show is *the* social event of the year, but you're really going for it tonight, Bec.'

'You look pretty,' Luke said, lifting up his pirate eyepatch to make a closer inspection. 'Can we go now?'

Becca stuck out her tongue at her sister. Not only were they heading to the school talent show (event of the year), but she had a date lined up afterwards, as well Rachel knew. Date number five with Adam, in fact, for drinks and pasta at a rustic Tuscan place that had just opened in town. Mamma Mia. She could hardly wait. 'Let's go,' she agreed.

They made a strange parade walking to school together: one pirate, one violin player, one texting teenager, plus her, Rachel and Wendy bringing up the rear. Rachel was much more confident about going out in public again these days, especially as she was almost completely healed now. That morning they had been back to the fracture clinic for the last time and the plaster had been cut away from Rachel's wrist, revealing shiny pink skin beneath and a fully working joint once more. Next Monday she was due to have the wiring in her mouth removed, and would be free to eat, drink, kiss, laugh, yawn and scream to her heart's content. She had joked about having a ceremonial bonfire on which to destroy the liquidizer and every last soup recipe in the house – or at least Becca thought she was joking, anyway. (Her soup wasn't that bad, was it?)

Over the last fortnight Rachel had been building up her fitness levels: walking in the mountains, some gentle jogging around the park and all sorts of torturous core exercises on a mat on the living-room floor, which didn't half make you feel lazy if you were trying to watch trash television and power through a carton of ice cream at the same time. You could tell it made her feel happy, though – her eyes had started to sparkle again, she joked more with the children, and there seemed a new lightness about her. 'You're actually quite a nice person when you're not mooching about, feeling sorry for yourself,' Becca had told her, only half-kidding, and promptly had a cushion thrown at her head for her honesty.

That was the lovely thing, though – that they had the sort of relationship now that could cope with a home truth here or there, as well as a hurled cushion. Having a sister you got on with was not necessarily all about spa days, being one another's bridesmaids and going on villa holidays together. In Becca's experience, it was shared jokes and knowing looks and taking the mick out of each other. Thrown cushions, too. Nobody said that on the Hallmark cards.

'So am I going to meet him tonight then, this Adam?' Wendy asked. 'Is he coming to the show as well?'

'No,' Becca said. 'Are you mad? Of course he's not.'

'*We* met him, though,' boasted Scarlet, who was of course eavesdropping in front.

'He's going to pay us fifty pounds to make him a cake,' Luke added happily. 'He said so!'

'He isn't,' Becca told Wendy, 'and I'm keeping him away

from you too, for at least the first five hundred dates, so just give up now, all right, because it's not going to happen.'

Wendy pouted. 'There's no need to be so melodramatic about it, Becky,' she said. 'I was only asking.'

Right. And she could ask away until she was blue in the face, but Becca was going to keep Adam to herself for a while. Partly because she couldn't resist winding her mum up by doing so, but also because . . . well, she was basically enjoying just having him to herself right now. He was lovely. Funny. Handsome. *Can I have a plus-one to your weddings?* she had texted all her engaged friends. *Am dating total hottie. Get in!!!*

So far, the two of them had been out for three more dates since that initial evening at Leo's. Dinner at Castle House (fabulous). A bike ride together along the river, until they'd found a meadow full of long grass and wildflowers where they had picnicked on deli-bought quiche and salads, clinking together cold beer bottles as they watched a pair of shimmering dragonflies draw iridescent patterns in the air. And then, most recently, he'd cooked dinner at his place, a splendid stone Victorian house up on Broomy Hill, which had a sun terrace out the back and a view right over the Wye Valley. Steak and chips and a bottle of wine. (Yes, she *had* stayed over. Yes, it *had* been amazing. Yes, she *had* woken up the next morning with the most gigantic grin on her face.)

There must have been some kind of romance chemical in

the Hereford water that summer because Rita and Michael had been spending a lot of time together recently too, by all accounts. Apparently Rita was teaching Michael how to make rock cakes and a really good bubble and squeak, and he in turn picked her up from the home and took her out for day trips – to Berrington Hall and Croft Castle one day, to Telford another. There was even talk of them taking a little walking holiday in his beloved Wales, so it had to be serious.

Rita's course of so-called exercise sessions had come to an end now, and she had apologetically told Becca that Michael had offered to take her to the allotment whenever she wanted, so she had no real need of them any more. Nonetheless, she had recommended Rachel's services to a few of the other residents, and suggested to the manager of the home that Rachel come in and do some gentle 'pensioner-aerobics' (Rita's words) with 'the inmates' (also her words), which sounded promising. And even though Becca no longer had any official reason for seeing the two of them now, she was definitely planning to stay in touch with both Rita and Michael, having become very fond of them during her time in Hereford. She'd popped in just the other week to present Michael with the lampshade she'd finally finished – a simple drum shape with a smart striped fabric – and she'd hung it in his hallway with great ceremony.

A few days later she and Rachel's family had gone to see Michael's band play in a nearby park as part of a mini festival, and it had been a really lovely, jolly afternoon. Scarlet and Luke had got up to dance, while Rita came and joined them on their picnic blanket. Afterwards Scarlet and Michael had had a long chat about music and writing songs, and then Michael had let Luke have a go on the trombone and offered him lessons over the summer if he wanted, and everyone had left feeling happy.

'So tell me again about this place you found the other day,' Wendy said, admitting defeat on the subject of Adam as they turned the corner and approached the school gates. 'Did you take any photos? I'm dying to see it.'

'Oh yes! Here, let me show you on my phone,' Becca replied, getting it out of her bag and flipping through to find the pictures. She still couldn't quite believe she had done it, taking the plunge two days earlier and signing a six-month agreement on a small, light flat on the west side of town. *SAD FACE*, Meredith had texted when Becca told her the news. They were going to get very drunk together that coming Saturday night and reminisce before Becca packed up her belongings and moved out for good. Her tummy churned whenever she imagined herself handing the keys back to Meredith and hugging her goodbye. The end of an era! She would miss her flatmate. But as the saying went, as one door closed, another one was about to open. The door to her very own place, no less. Besides, Meredith had already persuaded her friend Alianor to move into Becca's vacated room, and no doubt the place would soon be humming with lute-playing and the swish of medieval cloaks. It was all good, really.

Her new home was a first-floor flat above an antique-clock shop on a quiet, sleepy sort of road. 'We won't disturb you,' the man running the shop downstairs had assured her when she went to view the flat. 'We only open three days a week now, and I'm actually hoping to retire at the end of the year, so will probably be leaving the premises then anyway.'

Rachel had come with her and as they tramped up the stairs behind the letting agent, she was nudging Becca and raising her eyebrows at what the clock-shop man had said. 'Interesting,' she said in a low voice, 'don't you think?'

'What, that he mends antique clocks?' Becca had replied, confused. 'I guess so.'

'No, that he's likely to leave the shop at the end of the year,' Rachel hissed with a meaningful look. 'Because then it'll be empty . . .?'

Becca had frowned at her sister in the dingy stairwell. 'I don't get you,' she replied, but then the letting agent was opening the front door – her new front door, as it now turned out – and as she stepped over the threshold, she forgot all about the conversation, too distracted was she by what lay beyond.

'Here,' she said now, passing the phone to Wendy to show her. 'What do you think?'

The front door of the flat opened into a tiny hallway and straight through to a lovely airy living room, whose Victorian bay windows let in great shafts of golden afternoon light spangling the slow-twirling motes of dust. It was, admittedly, filthy in there, with a single raggedy curtain hanging drunkenly off its last few hooks at the window, and barely a stick of furniture in the room, but Becca had gazed around at the high ceiling with its froth of grubby cornicing around the edges, the black marble fireplace with its original rose-patterned tiles, the generous dimensions of the room, and was sold, in a heartbeat. 'This could be amazing,' she said under her breath.

The rest of the flat was equally fantastic. Well, it would be anyway, once she'd scrubbed and scoured it free of all the grime, and sluiced gallons of disinfectant and mould killer and damp-proofer around the place, followed by several coats of paint. 'Potential', that was the term used by estate agents – which everyone interpreted to mean 'festering shit-tip'. This place had potential by the bucketload, though. The kitchen was small and rather dated, but functional nonetheless, and the bathroom had an antique claw-foot bath that she could imagine herself wallowing in for many an hour. Best of all, the large double bedroom had French windows that opened out onto – *yes!* – her own tiny balcony, which had just enough space for some pot plants and a folding chair or two.

'Needs a bit of a clean,' Wendy said now, inspecting the photos. 'But it's going to be lovely. Your new home!'

Becca smiled back at her. Her new home – she'd have to

practise saying that. It sounded really good, though. Kind of momentous, too.

And that wasn't all. It was Rachel who had seen the full potential of the place, her sharp business brain noticing what Becca hadn't. 'What I meant earlier,' she'd said as she re-joined Becca in the living room, having busied herself checking out the boiler and other useful practical things, 'about the shop below was, obviously you can see how it goes with your business for the time being –' (*The business!* She had an actual business! That was another concept Becca had to get used to) – 'but if things take off and keep expanding, then you might want your own premises downstairs. A workshop, or a place to hold your hen sessions, or children's parties, or a sewing club, or . . .'

Oh my goodness, yes. *Premises*, she thought, her eyes widening, as she let herself dare to imagine. The clock shop had been rather dark and dingy, a forest of polished grand-father clocks and swinging pendulums, chiming and ticking, all those time-tellers jumbled together. But strip them away and there would be two decent-sized rooms down there, she reckoned: a proper dedicated workspace, if she needed such a thing. She could paint the walls white and hang all the loveliest things she'd made from hooks, like a miniature gallery. The back room could be used as her studio, whereas the big front room could hold a few large tables for people to sit around as well as shelves for her art supplies; she could put a kettle in one corner with pretty teacups, make colourful bunting to string across the ceiling . . .

There went that runaway imagination of hers again. Becca knew that she was getting ahead of herself, letting herself become swept up in a daydream. All the same, she could already picture the outside of the clock shop over-hauled and cleared out, with *Make Yourself Happy* painted in bright letters across the shop front – and it looked amazing.

'What do you think?' Rachel had prompted, when Becca didn't immediately reply. 'I mean, it's a genuine possibility, what with the business starting so well and all. Worth bearing in mind, don't you think?'

'Definitely,' Becca said. 'It would be fab. But yeah, let's see how it goes. I don't want to start counting any premature chickens.'

Rachel smiled at her. 'Look at you, all wise and sensible. You'll be a businesswoman yet, Rebecca Farnham.'

'God, I know,' Becca laughed. 'What's wrong with me?'

In truth, the business had taken off beyond her wildest dreams in the fortnight or so since Hayley's article had prompted that initial deluge of enquiries. She, Rachel and Adam had sat down together and planned out a proper strategy: no more here-and-there accidental bits of work, but instead a proper list of who to target in the first six weeks, with a more ambitious long-term plan for the first year. It had all been rather head-spinning for shambling, let's-see-what-happens Becca. They had written a spread-sheet, and everything. And then she had taken a big, brave breath and thrown herself in right at the deep end.

So far, it was going brilliantly. The water in the deep end was perfect, as it turned out, and she had been swimming furiously ever since, barely pausing for breath. She had over one hundred tiara commissions confirmed already, and two knicker-making hen parties in the diary, as well as a meeting next week with a local youth group about providing some children's arts and crafts days over the school holidays. Just two days earlier, she had gone to see the manager of Rita's care home and had pitched the idea of a weekly craft club – knitting or crochet, whatever the residents preferred – and had been offered a trial run for the following week in return. She was also planning to put an ad in the local free parenting magazine, offering to run children's arts and crafts parties . . . All sorts of things, really. She was busy, anyway, in the best kind of way – and quite literally making herself happy, as her business card suggested.

And so, when the letting agent returned to the room, an enquiring look on his face, Becca had bestowed a beaming smile upon him. 'I'll take the flat,' she'd said impulsively, and squeezed Rachel's hand in a sudden burst of excitement. 'Where do I sign?'

Chapter Forty-Eight

'Good evening, everyone, and thanks very much for coming along to the Poplar Primary School talent show. I'm sure we're all in for a wonderful night, watching some real star performances from our children.'

Mabel sniggered rather rudely, and Rachel elbowed her. They were squashed into tightly packed rows of chairs in the school hall, with the headteacher in full gush on the stage. Somewhere in the audience were Lawrence and Janice; somewhere backstage were both Scarlet and Luke, waiting to come on. It was a real family affair, one that would have been unthinkable six short weeks ago.

Was it really only six weeks since she'd been knocked out in Manchester? It seemed much longer somehow. So much had happened. At last her body was all but mended, though. She had gone for her first run that afternoon and it felt fantastic, like she was back; the proper, real Rachel who loved to push herself and sweat and ache, the Rachel who didn't just lie on the sofa feeling sorry for herself but got out there, under the big open sky, trainers on, ready for anything.

Welcome back, she thought to herself, as her feet pounded the familiar trails, as her heart pumped joyfully, as her limbs felt the much-missed ache of hard work. Oh, it was so good to throw off the misery and feel alive again. The best!

Gradually the pieces were slotting back together to create a new picture: the new Rachel, the new shape of the family. She had braved it out one night with her friends – only round to Jo's house, where nobody could stare at her, for fizzy wine and chat with three other women, but it was a start. A real start. She had missed those women. She loved those women! It seemed ridiculous now that she'd ever pushed them away while she was battling to come to terms with everything going on. Well, not any more. She'd already invited them all to her place one night next week for a rematch, and by then she'd have the wires off her jaws and would be able to crunch through Doritos and pieces of crusty white baguette with the rest of them. (Bring it on. She just could not WAIT to eat properly again. The meals she was already planning! The delights she'd been denied for so long! She would be the size of a house by August, you wait, but every mouthful would be worth it.)

The dog was home; and Lawrence had pulled himself together and started being more hands-on with the children again, and (according to Mabel) even got a job interview in a week's time, which sounded hopeful. Ever since the showdown in Builth Wells he had been civil to her, and a bit more gracious too. What was more, Janice had actually talked him into going to see an anger management counsellor, as he had admitted, rather shamefaced, the last time they spoke. This was major progress. Seismic, in fact. Lawrence's own worst enemy had always been himself, but Rachel had never been able to persuade him to seek professional help or do anything to change that. She knew better than to start tempting fate, but she couldn't help feeling that the Jackson family might finally be over the worst. Full steam ahead to happiness, she thought, crossing her fingers.

On stage, the reception children had finished singing a sweet little song about cats, and then Luke's class were on, yo-ho-ho-ing their way through a pirate dance routine. He had been quite nervous beforehand – it had taken a full five minutes of karate-chopping to feel better (and, Rachel suspected, several jelly babies from his Aunty Becca) – but there he was now, beaming away, flailing his cardboard cutlass above his head as if he was loving every minute.

They all clapped and cheered when it came to an end, even too-cool-for-school Mabel, who gave her brother a double thumbs up as he left the stage. Rachel put an arm around her daughter and gave her a sudden kiss, much to Mabel's surprise. The two of them were getting on so much better lately, the dust having settled from the divorce, boundaries set down but with a restoration of humour to their relationship. The shed had been a real turning point, providing

Mabel with her own space again, as well as a new freedom: a place to take friends that was an adult-free zone. You could hear screeches of laughter floating down the garden from the shed most evenings now, and it was a good sound.

Following the pirates came a gymnastics display, and then they were into some individual performances from the juniors. Rachel tried to pay attention, knowing that Scarlet would want to discuss the entire show in great detail later on with her and would pounce on any hint of parental distractedness as a personal insult.

'And now we have a very special act, which I'm sure you're all going to enjoy,' said Mrs Jenkins, the headteacher. Was it Rachel's imagination, or was there something verging on mischievous about that smile? Was there even a sideways glance to where some of the teachers were sitting? No. She must be seeing things. Everyone knew that headteachers were far too sensible to indulge in mischief. 'It's Henry Fortescue with his lovely poem, called "My Mum".'

There was a polite smattering of applause – led by Sara and her cronies, no doubt. *Oh, spare me*, thought Rachel, trying not to roll her eyes. Here came a gigantic suck-up. You'd have thought the staff would have had enough of Sara Fortescue for one school year, but obviously not.

Henry came on stage, his straw-coloured hair tufting up very sweetly at the crown of his head, one grey sock visibly higher than the other, and despite her dislike of his mother,

Rachel felt herself soften. She'd always rather liked impish, freckled Henry.

'My Mum,' said Henry, clearing his throat. He held out a piece of paper in front of him and silence fell in somewhat weary anticipation.

'My mum likes wine,' he began, whereupon a frisson immediately went through the room. *What?* Had he really just said that? There was a rustle as every adult who'd ever despaired of Sara Fortescue leaned forward to listen more closely.

> *'She thinks it's fine.*
> *She likes to drink it all the time.'*

Somebody snorted with laughter. Another person tittered, and tried to hide it within a cough. Becca had her hand up to her mouth as if worried she might burst out in one of her explosive guffaws.

'How many bottles? Ninety-nine,' Henry went on, oblivious to the ripples of giggles now spreading compulsively through the audience.

> *'Sometimes her face goes really red.*
> *Sometimes she—'*

'That's enough!' Sara shot up in the audience, her face – as in the poem – an unattractive brick-red, her hands clenched unmistakably in fists. 'Henry! That's quite enough!' The giggles were no longer suppressed, but were breaking out rebelliously all around the room by now.

Henry looked down at his paper and then up at his mum, his mouth buckling with uncertainty as he broke off mid-sentence.

'Let the lad read his poem!' someone shouted from the back of the audience.

'Yeah! We want to hear the poem!' came another voice. Rachel and Becca exchanged a glance. Clearly they weren't the only people in the audience to be guiltily enjoying Sara's discomfort.

'Henry Fortescue, get off that stage this minute, do you hear me? Don't you dare read another word,' Sara barked.

'But—' His face crumpled, and tears spurted in his eyes.

'Aww. Poor little thing. He only wanted to read his poem,' a woman tutted behind Rachel.

'Shame,' another woman nearby said, clicking her tongue in disapproval.

Sara was taking no chances, though. She was making her way down the line of parents – 'Oi!' 'Watch it!' 'Hey!' – and clambering onto the stage, where she grabbed hold of her son. But Mrs Jenkins was there, too.

'Excuse me,' she said in an icy tone to Sara. 'Do you mind? Henry is proud of that poem. He spent a long time writing it.'

'But he's making a show of me,' Sara hissed, daggers in her eyes. 'And I'm sorry, but if this is your sad little attempt at making a fool of me, then—'

'Booooo,' someone jeered from the third row. 'Get off.'

'We want Henry. We want Henry.' A chant started up, just a few voices at first, but then growing in volume. 'We want Henry. We want Henry. We want Henry!'

Her face twisted in annoyance, Sara had no choice but to let go of her son. She marched to the side of the stage, where she stood with her arms crossed, visibly bristling.

Rachel found herself remembering the mean-spirited petition regarding Miss Ellis that Sara had been urging everyone to sign, and couldn't help feeling that Sara had had this coming. No wonder Mrs Jenkins had shot that look at her team of staff.

'She is *fuming*,' Mabel said happily.

'Serves her right,' Becca said. 'If she'd just laughed it off, it would have been over by now. Silly moo.'

Mrs Jenkins had a motherly arm around Henry, and was talking to him in a low voice. He glanced across at Sara, wiped the tears from his eyes with his bare arm, and then nodded.

'Henry wants to try reading the poem again,' Mrs Jenkins said gently. 'And this time there'll be no interruptions. Good for you, Henry. Whenever you're ready.'

You could have heard a pin drop as the boy cleared his

throat again and began. The entire audience was willing him on, not least because they were dying to hear how the poem ended.

> *'My mum likes wine.*
> *She thinks it's fine*
> *She likes to drink it all the time.*
> *How many bottles? Ninety-nine.'*

Rachel glanced across at Sara, who looked very much as if she would like to murder someone, preferably by smashing ninety-nine wine bottles across the head. Mrs Jenkins would have to watch her back all summer now.

> *'Sometimes her face goes really red.*
> *Sometimes she giggles when she tucks me in bed.*
> *And in the morning she has a poorly head.*
> *But I love my mum lots and lots*
> *She is pretty and kind and never cross –'*

He shot a nervous glance sideways at Sara. *Wishful thinking, Henry, mate*, Rachel thought to herself.

> *'She is even nicer than blackcurrant squash.*
> *The End.'*

There was a beat of silence, and then the hall erupted in applause. Henry risked another glance over at Sara, and his relief was apparent as he realized that she too was clapping, although her mouth was pressed together in a strange, tight sort of line. Then, looking as if she might burst into tears, she crouched down and opened her arms. 'Awwwww,' said every single person in the room who didn't have a heart of stone, as Henry ran gratefully into them for a gigantic hug.

'Blackcurrant squash all round tonight,' Mabel whispered with a giggle, and Rachel stifled a laugh.

Mothers and children, eh? For something that should be so simple – I gave birth to you, end of – it would never cease to be a complicated relationship for her. (Sara, too, by the looks of things.) After talking it through with Becca and Wendy, Rachel had by now just about come to terms with the shock of finding out that her own mother was less than angelic. She was enjoying a better relationship with her stepmother too, even if this did seem to mean being texted countless photos of slices of cake and cocktails, for some reason.

In an attempt to find a bit of closure in the Emily situation, she was planning to make a second trip up to Manchester over the summer, with the children in tow this time, to lay the ghosts to rest – or at the very least, lay a wreath of flowers at her mother's grave and maybe have a few quiet words. *Don't worry*, she wanted to say. *I turned out okay. And I think I understand.* She was going to explore her parents' city too, possibly with the help of Violet, if she was up for it. Find a few places where her mum and dad had been happy together, walk in their footsteps and hope to feel some peace in her heart.

Don't be put off by what happened in the train station, Violet had written in their most recent correspondence. *It's the most brilliant city of- all. You come from a good place, Rachel – a good place with real heart. Give us a chance, and we'll welcome you back.*

So that was something, perhaps not to look *forward* to, exactly, but which might just provide a little redemption. In the meantime, she had enough to be getting on with, rebuilding her fitness training business and taking back all her old clients, and she couldn't wait to get going. There would be the usual school-holiday juggling affair to manage, of course, but Wendy (good old Wendy!) had offered to come and help out a few days every week, looking after the children while Rachel went to work. If someone had told her about this arrangement at the start of the year, she would not have believed it, and yet here they were. Starting again, a second try at their stepmother–daughter relationship, after all these years. And it was fun, too. Wendy was actually much better company than Rachel had ever given her credit for. Mischievous and unpredictable, but kind too, with her heart worn permanently on her sleeve. A good person to have on your side.

About time, and all. What took you so long? she could almost hear her dad exclaiming from wherever he might be. Well, quite. But they were getting there now, at least.

'Mum! Scarlet,' Mabel hissed just then, nudging her, and Rachel jerked to attention. Here came her middle child walking on stage, that pointy little chin of hers jutting with determination as she positioned the violin against her shoulder and raised her bow with a flourish. Rachel crossed her fingers in her lap, her heart suddenly beating like a sparrow's, fast and fluttery, feeling way more anxious than her daughter looked about the whole thing.

Jingle bell, jingle bell, jingle bell rock . . .

Rachel's eyes swelled with proud tears as Scarlet began to play, cool as a cucumber, despite the fact that there must have been two hundred people crammed into the hall to watch. Look at that girl of hers up there, ten years old, plaits halfway down her back, scabby knees, and with such fierce concentration in every fibre of her body. That girl who'd burned through so much anger this year now stood playing a sweet, bouncy Christmas tune on her violin, as if there hadn't ever been a vengeful thought in her head. *And* they'd had her Grade 2 exam result back that week, and she'd passed with merit. Clearly, composing angry songs about one's terrible parents did wonders for one's technique.

Finishing the song without a single missed note, Scarlet allowed herself a small, brief smile of triumph before making an extravagant bow, and Rachel clapped so hard she found herself fearing for her newly mended wrist. Becca put her little fingers in her mouth and gave an ear-splitting wolf-whistle, shrill enough to have Wendy wincing on the other side of her. 'For goodness' sake, Becky, I might want to use my ears again sometime in my life!' she grumbled, pulling a face.

Rachel laughed, though, especially when Scarlet, hearing the whistle, looked in their direction and waved in delight. Oh, she was going to miss flamboyant Becca when she moved out – they all would. 'Don't be daft, I'll be back all the time,' Becca had assured the children whenever one of them made a wistful comment about her leaving. 'Besides, your mum owes me plenty of dinners, all the cooking and slaving I've done for her. I'll be back to claim them all, don't you worry. Every Sunday lunchtime I'll be knocking on your door, just wait.'

The house would definitely be quieter without Becca's loud laugh, her dreadful singing in the shower, her habit of defusing a potential barney with the children by making them giggle. Rachel was glad for her, though, that she'd found the right place to move on to, with her arts and crafts business taking off and this burgeoning romance with Adam to keep her smiling. She was glad for herself, too, that she now had this new ally and confidante, this person who'd come to know her so well over the last few weeks. Her *sister*. How had she ever managed without her?

Next on stage was a trumpet player, and Rachel found herself thinking about the band they'd gone to see the weekend before, Becca's friend Michael and his pals in the park. Luke had been fascinated by the instrument, begging to have a go, and Michael had been so sweet and patient with him, it had warmed the cockles of Rachel's heart. He was a lovely bloke full stop, as it turned out. Within five minutes of chatting to him, he'd offered to lend them all sorts of camping equipment for their holiday ('You've never been to Rhossili?' he'd exclaimed, looking incredulous. 'Oh, you *must*. It's the loveliest corner of the world, it is') and, on hearing that her car had developed a strange rattle, immediately offered to come over one day and take a look at it. Becca had said before how Michael reminded her a bit of their father, and in that moment, Rachel too could see the resemblance.

'That would be so kind, if you wouldn't mind,' she'd heard herself saying in reply to him. Her, Rachel, who'd always prided herself on never needing any help from anyone. And to think she'd had a go at Becca for her 'interfering' and 'do-gooding', as she'd so meanly termed it! Next time the phone rang and it was someone like Michael, maybe she'd think twice about cutting them off.

'Thank God that's over,' Mabel said in a too-loud whisper as the last act of the evening finished on stage – an amateur magician with an oversized top hat, who had made a pound coin appear from behind Mrs Jenkins' ear.

'We can't go home just yet,' Rachel said, as the audience began getting to their feet. 'You heard what Mrs Jenkins said, they're serving drinks in the foyer. Let's go and grab one while we wait for Scarlet and Luke. Maybe you could say hi to Dad, too.'

Mabel pulled a face. 'You've got very sociable all of a sudden,' she grumbled, but stood up nonetheless and joined the crush of people heading for the exit in a slow-moving trudge.

The foyer was a noisy buzz of people queueing for plastic glasses of lukewarm wine while children raced around, getting underfoot and trying to pinch the biscuits without being spotted. Around them, Rachel could hear several conversations following near-identical loops – *summer holidays*; *hasn't he grown? wasn't it a great show?* as well as a few gleeful mutterings about Henry Fortescue's poem, and how Sara would never live it down.

'I'll get us all a drink,' Wendy said, joining the queue and waving away offers of assistance. Mabel skipped off to speak to her dad and Welsh Grandma, who appeared to be wearing several layers of fleece and walking boots despite the fact that it was a warm summer's evening. Rachel and Becca were left to loiter in a small space by a Sports Day display as hordes of talent-show stars poured past, looking triumphant at their recent stage successes.

'Mum! Mum! Did you see me?' Here came Luke now, barging his way through the crowd, elasticated eyepatch having ridden right up into his hair, giving him the air of a dishevelled young McEnroe.

'I did! We all did! And you were brilliant, Luke, well done,' she replied, hugging him. 'Absolutely terrifyingly brilliant.'

'We *so* got the loudest claps,' he said, with the confident grin of a boy who knew his pirate dancing skills were second to none. 'Scarlet's just coming, she's waiting for Lois,' he went on. 'Can I have a biscuit?'

'Yes, love, you can,' she said, laughing. 'Maybe take one over for Grandma Wendy too, who's nobly waiting to get us all drinks.'

'Hey, there's Scarlet,' Becca said, waving across the throng. 'Ahh, Scarlet and the famous Lois, no less. Daughter of your future husband, if you listen to those two and their plotting.'

Rachel waved too, smiling as she saw her daughter proceed through the mob, arm in arm with a pixie-faced little girl. Despite whatever ridiculous matchmaking the girls had been up to, she was pleased that this friendship had lasted well so far. Scarlet was such a mercurial sort of character, prone to hissy fits and blurting out inappropriate secrets, all of which had resulted in best friends coming and going like buses over the years. Lois, by all accounts, was a keeper – a child who gave as good as she got, an equal in Scarlet's eyes. She really must get on the case and sort out a play date, Rachel thought guiltily, as the girls made their way across the crowded room.

Then they stopped, and she watched as Lois gave a squeal and bent down to hug some dark-haired little sibling with great affection (very sweet, thought Rachel, wishing her children could be quite so nice to one another in public) before then reaching up to hug her father, who . . .

Wait a minute. 'Oh my God,' she said, grabbing hold of Becca's arm. She tried to get a better look at Lois's dad, but he was reaching down to his daughters and was momentarily lost amidst the crowd. Rachel gave a shaky laugh. She was seeing things, almost certainly. 'For a minute I thought Lois's dad was . . .' Then she broke off again, spotting that the girls were now towing Lois's dad towards them, presumably determined to sort out their own sleepover or play session right then and there.

'Shit,' said Rachel, as Lois's dad loomed into view, the younger daughter now perched high on his shoulders. 'I don't believe it.'

'Bloody hell,' said Becca, and gave a low whistle under her breath. 'It's actually him, as well. It bloody well is. Ha! Brilliant. Thank you, the universe. Good one!'

'Who bloody well is? What do you mean, the universe?' Luke said through a mouthful of biscuit, having reappeared beside his mother.

Oh God. Rachel had gone all quivery. She didn't know whether to burst out laughing, or leap behind the Sports Day display to hide. But here came the girls, marching forward with determination in their eyes, and it was too late to escape. *Get a grip, you insane woman*, she told herself fiercely. *Pull yourself together!*

'Mum, this is Lois,' Scarlet said with a beaming smile. 'And this is Lois's dad and little sister. Please can you sort out a time for Lois to come and play in the holidays? PLEEEEEEEASE?'

Lois's dad was looking at her quizzically, as if he recognized her but couldn't quite place her. She, of course, could place him all too well. Seeing as she'd just been placed right in the heart of Awkwardsville. 'Hi,' he said. 'I'm Patrick, good to meet you.'

'Hi,' she said, trying to look normal and not like the blushing idiot she felt inside. 'We've met before, actually. At the fracture clinic?' Oh, cringe. Could she *be* any more embarrassed? It was only the male nurse she and Becca had giggled over, only the man whose bum she'd found herself eyeing up. Well, that was where perving got you, she scolded herself. *Consider this Awkwardsville visitation to be your comeuppance, Rachel Jackson!*

'Of course we have, that's right.' His eyes twinkled as he smiled. (*Stop it, Rachel. Stop noticing his twinkling eyes.*) 'Well, we'd love to have Scarlet round sometime, wouldn't we, girls? We've heard a lot about her.'

'That would be great,' Rachel managed to say. 'And likewise with Lois. Shall we swap numbers and sort out some dates?' She saw Scarlet and Lois high-fiving, and was suddenly worried her words were loaded with completely the wrong sort of meaning. 'I mean, for the girls. Obviously. Play dates.' (*Oh, kill me now. Just put me out of my misery*, she thought, as Becca gave a wicked snort of amusement beside her. Now it looked as if she was flirting really, really badly with him, and she so wasn't. Like she would even dare when her ex-husband – her madly jealous, demented ex-husband, no less – must be prowling around in the background somewhere, probably taking a run-up to rugby-tackle poor innocent Patrick right this very second.)

'Why don't we go and look at these Sports Day pictures?' Becca said to Luke very unsubtly just then, which made the whole thing appear even worse.

But Patrick was smiling and not looking terrified, thank goodness. He must be used to mad women making idiots of themselves. Either that, or he had been a nurse long enough to overlook humans behaving oddly in times of stress. The two of them swapped numbers and promised to be in touch, and then, not wanting to tempt fate with an interruption from Lawrence, Rachel peeled away, claiming she needed to go and help Wendy.

Thump, thump, thump, went her heart. *Thumpity-thump-thump-thump*. Not that she was under any illusions about the chance of such a nice, handsome man remotely fancying her, of course. She wasn't even sure she was ready for any kind of romantic entanglements yet. But a little frisson now and then was good for the soul, right? It made a woman happy. Besides, it didn't hurt to make a new friend once in a while; a new dad friend who was shamelessly good-looking, at that. A new dad friend to whom she might just offer a glass of wine when he came by to pick up his daughter after a play session . . . Well, maybe.

'I *told* you she was nice,' Scarlet said smugly, slipping a hand in hers. 'Didn't I tell you? And she doesn't have a mummy so I told her she could borrow you sometimes, if she needs someone to be extra kind to her, or do her hair or something. Just like you sort of borrow Grandma Wendy as your sort of mum. Is that all right?'

'Oh, Scarlet.' Rachel reached down and squeezed her, feeling a rush of love for her clear-sighted daughter. Sometimes a child's simplistic view of the world was infinitely better than the way adults went about things, complicating life with so many nuances and layers, muddying the waters with past grievances and doubts. 'You are a love, did you know that?'

'Yes,' said Scarlet, snaffling a Bourbon biscuit and shoving it up her sleeve before anyone could stop her. 'Yes, I actually did.'

After a lukewarm glass of pinot cheapo, the six of them walked home. Mabel and Scarlet were in front, hooting with laughter about something or other, Becca and Rachel next (Becca with one eye on her watch – she was meant to be meeting Adam in half an hour, and already looked twitchy at the prospect), followed by Wendy and Luke. Luke was telling Wendy a very long, convoluted story about *Star Wars* characters, and she was listening with great patience and making interested-sounding noises in all the right places, which surely made her a saint.

This evening had gone as well as could be expected, all things considered, Rachel thought. TODAY WE ARE: *HAPPY!* Luke and Scarlet had been thrilled to have both parents *and* both grandmothers in the audience, and had positively revelled in all the resulting praise afterwards. Lawrence had been civil and actually quite jovial, while she in turn had coped with the crowd of parents and not freaked out once. Plus, she had a certain phone number tucked carefully into her handbag, which made her feel just the tiniest bit giddy inside whenever she thought about it.

'Oi! You cow. I hate you!'

Meanwhile, Mabel and Scarlet had come to blows over something – Mabel winding up her younger sister, judging from the way she was laughing uproariously as Scarlet rained punches on her, shrieking the whole time. But then, just as suddenly, Scarlet was laughing too and they were collapsing against each other in the street, shoulders shaking with mirth.

'Girls! For heaven's sake!' Rachel said, but she was only half-scolding and didn't really mind. She pulled an exasperated face at Becca. 'Those two, honestly, I give up. They love each other one minute, and they're at each other's throats the next.'

Becca grinned. 'Well, they're sisters, aren't they?' she replied. 'And it doesn't matter all that much if they hate each other now and then, because deep down, they know they've still got each other's backs.' She slipped an arm through Rachel's. 'Like us, really. Wouldn't you say?'

There was a lump in Rachel's throat all of a sudden. The warm July air felt soft and gauzy around her as she turned to smile at Becca. Her sister, who'd turned everything around this summer; her sister, who'd become her closest friend, whose arm was in the crook of hers right now, warm and friendly and loyal. 'Yes,' she agreed, giving her a squeeze. 'You're right. Just like us.'

THE END

Recipes from the Novel

The Jacksons' birthday cake

Like Becca, my birthday cake of choice would always be a chocolate sponge, preferably filled with whipped cream and raspberries. In fact, I'd quite like one now. To the kitchen!

Ingredients

170g soft unsalted butter
170g golden caster sugar
115g self-raising flour
55g cocoa powder (not drinking chocolate)
Pinch of salt
3 large eggs

For the filling:
125ml whipping cream
175g fresh raspberries

Method

Preheat the oven to 190°C (170°C for fan ovens) or gas mark 5. Grease and line two 20cm sandwich tins.

Cream the butter and sugar until well mixed and lighter in colour.

Sieve the flour, cocoa and salt into a separate bowl and mix together.

Add one egg to the creamed butter and sugar, along with a third of the chocolatey flour mixture and stir well. Repeat for the second and third eggs, adding in further thirds of the flour mixture each time. The batter should be smooth and thick at this point. (If it feels stiff, you can add a splash of milk to loosen it slightly.)

Split the mixture between the two tins and gently spread it to the edges using a knife. Bake in the oven for about 25 minutes until springy to touch.

Remove from the oven and leave the cakes in their tins for 10 minutes before turning out onto a wire rack to cool completely.

When the sponges are cool, whip the cream and spread thickly across the bottom sponge. Add raspberries and carefully sandwich the sponges together. The fresh cream means this cake is best eaten on the day it's baked but should be good for 48 hours afterwards, provided you keep it refrigerated.

Wendy's boozy banana smoothies

I imagined Wendy turning up at Rachel's with her bananas, ice cream and rum and basically chucking them all into the liquidizer with some milk before blitzing the lot. (Then probably sloshing in extra rum for good measure.) If you're looking for a more sophisticated approach, then you could try this recipe using caramelized bananas instead. It's also delicious without the rum!

Serves two.

Ingredients

2 tbsp butter
2 tbsp brown sugar
2 bananas, sliced
25ml light rum
3–4 scoops of good vanilla ice cream
1 glass of milk
Pinch of cinnamon
Grated nutmeg for decoration (optional)

Method

Melt the butter over a medium heat. Stir in the sugar and add the sliced bananas, turning the pieces so that they are covered in the mixture. Cook for 3–5 minutes until the bananas caramelize, then leave to cool.

Put the cooled bananas into a blender along with the rum, ice cream, milk and cinnamon, and whiz them up until well combined. Taste the mixture and adjust to your preference before serving in tall glasses with a sprinkling of grated nutmeg. Enjoy!

Janice's Welsh cakes

I am slightly obsessed with Welsh cakes – there, I said it – and I always used to buy packets of them when in Wales until I discovered that home-made ones are even better and taste AMAZING warm from the pan. This is a really quick and easy recipe.

Makes approximately fifteen.

Ingredients

225g self-raising flour

Pinch of salt

100g cold unsalted butter, cut into small pieces

75g caster sugar (plus extra for sprinkling)

25g sultanas

1 medium egg (only the yolk is used)

3 tbsp milk

You'll also need a 6cm round cutter, a rolling pin and a heavy-based frying pan (preferably non-stick) or a griddle.

Method

Sift the flour and salt together in a bowl, then add the butter and rub into the flour mix using your fingertips until the mixture resembles crumbs. Stir in the sugar and fruit.

Combine the egg yolk with the milk in a jug or small bowl, then add to the dry mixture, stirring together to form a soft dough. You can add a splash more milk if it seems a bit dry.

Flour a work surface and turn the dough out, then roll until about 1cm thick. Use the cutter to cut round shapes, re-rolling to use up all the dough.

If your pan isn't a non-stick one, you might want to lightly grease it with butter (but be sparing; Welsh cakes shouldn't be fried). Heat the frying pan or griddle, then cook the cakes a few at a time on a medium heat, turning them midway through. They should be golden-brown and will puff up as they cook – it should take about two minutes on each side.

Carefully remove from the pan, and dust with sugar. Best eaten warm, with a blob of jam on top if you prefer.

Becca's Cheer-Up Pancakes

In my opinion, pancakes are far too delicious to save for Shrove Tuesday only. These fluffy American-style ones are super-simple to make and great with fruit and crème fraîche, or lashings of maple syrup or even good old chocolate spread. If, like me, you've ever experienced disaster flipping ordinary thin pancakes, you'll be relieved to hear that these smaller, fatter pancakes are thick enough to be turned easily with a spatula. Win–win!

Makes about ten pancakes.

Ingredients

4 large eggs
160g plain flour
1½ tsp baking powder
175ml milk
Pinch of salt

Method

Separate the eggs, with yolks in one bowl and whites in another. Sift the flour and baking powder into the bowl with the yolks, add the milk and then mix until smooth. If the mixture is too thick, add in a splash more milk.

Add the salt to the egg whites, then whisk until stiff and peaking.

Carefully fold the whites into the yolk mixture and gently combine to a foamy batter, trying not to stir out all of the air bubbles.

A non-stick frying pan is best for these pancakes but if you don't have one, melt a little butter in your pan before use. Then dollop a ladleful of the batter into the pan and cook on a low to medium heat for a few minutes. It'll firm up and turn golden underneath quite quickly but don't be tempted to turn it over too soon, otherwise the middle won't cook all the way through. Turn and then cook on the second side for another few minutes, before serving immediately.

extracts reading groups
competitions books new
discounts extracts
extracts extracts discounts
competitions events
books new reading groups
events books
extracts reading groups
new titles reading groups
interviews
events extracts
discounts
new books events
events new interviews books
discounts extracts discounts
www.panmacmillan.com
extracts events reading groups
competitions books extracts new